THE NINTH NIGHTMARE

Recent Titles by Graham Masterton available from Severn House

The Jim Rook Series

ROOK
THE TERROR
TOOTH AND CLAW
SNOWMAN
SWIMMER
DARKROOM
DEMON'S DOOR

The Sissy Sawyer Series

TOUCHY AND FEELY
THE PAINTED MAN

Anthologies

FACES OF FEAR
FEELINGS OF FEAR
FORTNIGHT OF FEAR
FLIGHTS OF FEAR

Novels

BASILISK
BLIND PANIC
CHAOS THEORY
DESCENDANT
DOORKEEPERS
EDGEWISE
FIRE SPIRIT
GENIUS
GHOST MUSIC
HIDDEN WORLD
HOLY TERROR
HOUSE OF BONES
MANITOU BLOOD
THE NINTH NIGHTMARE
UNSPEAKABLE

THE NINTH NIGHTMARE

Graham Masterton

This first world edition published 2011
in Great Britain and the USA by
SEVERN HOUSE PUBLISHERS LTD of
9–15 High Street, Sutton, Surrey, England, SM1 1DF.
Trade paperback edition first published
in Great Britain and the USA 2011 by
SEVERN HOUSE PUBLISHERS LTD.

British Library Cataloguing in Publication Data

Masterton, Graham.
The Ninth Nightmare.
1. Serial murderers–Fiction. 2. Supernatural–Fiction.
3. Horror tales.
I. Title
823.9´14-dc22

ISBN-13: 978-0-7278-6997-5 (cased)
ISBN-13: 978-1-84751-325-0 (trade paper)

Typeset by Palimpsest Book Production Ltd.,
Falkirk, Stirlingshire, Scotland.
Printed and bound in Great Britain by
MPG Books Ltd., Bodmin, Cornwall.

ONE
Room 717

'You will die if you stay here, my lovely,' whispered a harsh voice very close to Katie's ear.

Katie opened her eyes, unsure if she had been dreaming, or if the voice had been real. Her hotel room was completely dark, except for a thin bar of light underneath the door. She lay in the middle of her queen-sized bed with a frown on her face, listening and listening, but all she could hear was the muffled laughter of other guests, returning to their rooms, and the distant thunder of an airplane landing thirteen miles to the south-west at Hopkins International Airport.

She sat up. The red figures on the digital clock beside her bed were distorted by the glass of water she had placed in front of it, but she could see that it was only eleven fifty-eight p.m. She had been exhausted when she arrived in Cleveland this evening, and after picking the bacon and the turkey slices out of a club sandwich from room service and a long hot shower she had gone straight to bed and switched off the lights.

She laid her head back on the pillow and closed her eyes, but she found it almost impossible to go back to sleep. She kept visualizing the faces of all of those elderly people she had met this morning, smiling at her hopefully in case they knew who she was, but couldn't quite place her. Alzheimer's sufferers – every one of them lost to this world for ever, their memories swirling away from them like flotsam on an ebbing tide.

'*You should leave, before it's too late*,' the whispered voice told her. This time it was so close that she was sure she could feel somebody's breath against her ear. She twisted around, her heart thumping, but there was nobody next to her. Nobody that she could see, anyhow. She reached across and switched on her bedside lamp, spilling her glass of water on to the carpet.

The room was empty. Only the couch and the armchair, and the coffee table with the remains of her club sandwich still on it. Only the desk, with her laptop and her red alligator pocketbook.

Only the heavy red brocade drapes, which stirred slightly in the draft from the air-conditioning, like huge lungs, breathing.

She waited and waited for nearly a minute. 'Who's there?' she demanded, although she had a catch in her throat and her voice was much more shrill than she had meant it to be. 'Is there anybody there?'

No answer. Just the drapes, slowly breathing. She swung her legs out of bed and stood up. 'I'm warning you!' she snapped. 'If you don't come out and show yourself, I'm going to call security.'

She crouched down to look under the bed, but there was less than an inch of space between the carpet and the bedstead, and only somebody who was two-dimensional could have hidden under there. All the same, the idea of a two-dimensional man concealing himself under her bed was quite scary.

She went across to the window and pulled the drapes apart. There was nobody in the window bay, and nobody standing on the small balcony outside. She could see the lights of University Circle sparkling behind the trees – and further, to the lights of downtown Cleveland, with the Key Tower and the Terminal Tower and the BP Building dominating the skyline, and the blackness of Lake Erie beyond them.

She left the drapes open while she went across to closet. She took hold of both handles, hesitated for a moment, and then flung the doors open wide. Her coat and her skirt and her orange silk blouse were hanging inside, along with her neatly-folded gray sweater. No man, two-dimensional or otherwise.

'*Shit*,' she said. She was almost certain that she had still been awake, but she must have dropped off to sleep again without realizing it. She went into the bathroom and switched on the light. In the mirror, in her pale green man's shirt, she looked pale and puffy eyed, her short-cropped brunette hair sticking up like a storm-ruffled blackbird. She leaned over the basin and examined herself more closely. She was only thirty-three but she thought she was beginning to look old. Maybe it was meeting so many seniors every day that did it. Maybe their pallor was absorbing her color and her youthfulness, like kitchen paper soaking up cranberry juice.

She had always wanted to be taller than five feet four, but her height hadn't mattered so much when she still had that urchin-like prettiness. Now she thought she was starting to look like a bossy little old lady. She had put on at least six pounds since she had started her charity work (all those fund-raising barbecues and fried chicken dinners) and most of it seemed to have gone to her breasts and her hips. She hated to think that she *bustled* when she walked.

She ran the cold faucet for a few seconds and filled up another glass of water. She swallowed two mouthfuls and then she switched off the bathroom light. As she turned to go back into the bedroom, however, she realized that the reflection in the mirror seemed to have changed. Instead of being tiled from floor to ceiling with white ceramic tiles, the walls appeared to have cream-painted wooden paneling that went halfway up, while the upper part was damp-looking plaster.

Not only that, both the walls and the ceiling were decorated with splatters and exclamation marks and figure-of-eight loops, as if a willful child had been flicking a paintbrush loaded with dark-brown varnish all around the room.

Katie looked down at the floor. She wasn't standing on a thick maroon bath mat any more, but on streaky green linoleum that stuck to the soles of her feet.

She switched on the light again. The bathroom was exactly as it had been before, with shiny white tiles and a shiny white bathtub. She stared at herself in the mirror. She couldn't understand what had just happened, but then her reflection couldn't understand it, either, and looked as bewildered as she did.

She took hold of the light pull but she hesitated for a moment before she tugged it. Supposing the same thing happened again? Supposing she switched off the light and found herself back in that filthy wooden-paneled room, with all those sinister-looking squiggles all over the walls? She couldn't work out if it had been some kind of hallucination, or if she were asleep, and still in bed, and this was a nightmare. But this time she was absolutely sure she wasn't asleep. She was holding a cold glass of water in her hand and she could feel it, the same as she could feel the shaggy bath mat in between her bare toes.

'This is not logical,' she told herself, out loud. 'I am Katie Kercheval and I am standing in the bathroom of Room Seven-One-Seven at the Griffin House Hotel on University Circle, Cleveland, Ohio. I am not standing anyplace else.'

She switched off the light. It took a split second for her eyes to become accustomed to the gloom, but as soon as they did she saw that she was back in the wooden-paneled room. It wasn't a bathroom. It looked more like a laundry room. In the opposite corner stood a large old-fashioned kitchen sink, its sides streaked with dribbles of gray grime. The sink had a single faucet which was wrapped around with a sodden cloth to prevent it from dripping, although the cloth still dripped. Above the sink was a small, high window, with glass so dirty and so green with lichen that it was impossible to see through it. All the same, Katie could tell that it was daylight outside – although it was daylight on a gray, rainy day. She could hear the raindrops pattering against the windowpanes.

She switched the light back on. The laundry room instantly vanished, and she was back in her shiny white bathroom.

'This is *insane*,' she said. She smacked her forehead with the heel of her hand. 'This is totally insane.'

She switched the light off. She was back in the laundry room. The faucet was still dripping and the rain was still pattering against the window. She breathed in and she could *smell* something, too. Something bleachy and faintly fishy. She breathed in again, and this time the smell was even stronger, so that she could almost taste it. American Value Bleach and rancid tuna.

She switched the light back on, and this time she left it on. Maybe she was suffering from exhaustion, or jet lag. After all, she had visited seven cities in as many days – from Atlanta to Houston and then to Albuquerque and Phoenix and Los Angeles and Sacramento. Maybe she had picked up a flu virus, or maybe she was experiencing some kind of weird reaction to her new birth-control pill. But whatever was causing the laundry room to appear when she switched off the light, she didn't want to see it again.

She closed the bathroom door behind her and climbed back into bed, dragging the covers up to her chin. She looked across at the bathroom, but the door remained shut. She was tempted to go back and try turning the light off one more time, to see if the laundry room reappeared, but she decided against it. If she was hallucinating, or pining for some sickness, she was better off staying in bed and getting some sleep.

She reached across and switched off the bedside lamp. The digital clock read 12:09. The room was not as dark as it had been before, because light was shining from both the bathroom and the corridor outside. She turned over, with her back to the bathroom, and closed her eyes.

Ten minutes passed. A woman came along the corridor singing *I Will Always Love You*. A man said, 'Shut the fuck up, Lena, will you, for Christ's sake? You're drunk.'

Another ten minutes passed. Katie sat up in bed again. Maybe she should check the bathroom just once more. Then, if it turned into the laundry room, maybe she should call David and tell him what was happening. After all, David was a qualified shrink. If anybody knew what had led her to believe that her hotel bathroom had turned into another room altogether, it was him.

She stared at the bathroom door. Maybe she should call the management. Maybe there was some kind of noxious gas coming out of the bathroom drains that made you see things that weren't really there.

She switched on her bedside lamp. Instantly, the whole bedroom was different. It was no longer a comfortable four-star hotel room. It wasn't even on the seventh floor any more; it was down at ground level. The walls were blotchy and discolored and the plaster looked diseased with damp. All the way around the room there was the same wooden paneling as the laundry room, with chipped cream paint. The floorboards were bare, except for a frayed, rucked-up rug, and it looked as if the floor hadn't been swept in years.

At the single window hung a shredded net curtain, gray with dirt. Through the grimy window-panes, Katie could make out the back of a row of houses, with roofs that were shining wet in the rain, and fire escapes, and sodden washing hanging hopelessly from one balcony to another.

She looked down at the bedcover she was holding in her hand. It was olive-green, thin and greasy, and it was covered in brownish stains. Her pillows were stained, too, and deeply indented, as if the same person had been sleeping on them every night and never changed them or even turned them over.

The bed stank, too, of dried sweat and dirty hair and other people's sex.

Katie switched off the lamp. Her hotel bedroom returned, Room 717, comfortable and warm and quiet now, and smelling of nothing but her own Chanel Premiere perfume and freshly-laundered sheets. In spite of that, she was shaking with fear and disgust, and she felt as if the floor were tilting underneath her like an ocean liner in a swell. She tried to stand up, but she lost her balance and had to sit back down on the bed again.

She stayed there for a moment, breathing deeply, trying to steady herself, and then she picked up her cellphone and called David's number. It rang and rang but he didn't pick up. Eventually she was put through to his message service.

'David, darling, it's me. Can you call me back as soon as you get this? It's really hard to explain but there's something wrong.' Her voice started to waver, so she took a deep breath. Then she said, 'It's probably just *me*, being hysterical. But I'm so frightened. I daren't switch off the light because when I switch off the light everything's different and horrible. Please, please call me.'

She sat and waited about a minute longer. Then she thought: *this is ridiculous. I know I'm not going crazy, so there must be something wrong with the room*. She picked up the house phone and pressed zero for reception. She didn't care if it was almost twelve thirty in the morning. She just wanted to change rooms.

Again, the phone rang and rang but nobody picked up. She hung up and tried again, but still nobody answered. She tried room service, and then housekeeping. No reply from either of them.

There had to be somebody on duty. A night porter, or a security guard. She put down the phone, went over to her suitcase and took out a mustard-colored roll-neck sweater and a pair of jeans. She dressed herself quickly and tugged a brush through her hair. She stared at herself in the mirror on the back of the closet door and tried to look determined. *I want another room, and I want it now, and I don't have to tell you why.*

Katie opened the door and stepped outside. The door closed itself behind her, with a soft, complicated click. The corridor was in darkness. Maybe the lights were on a time switch, or maybe a breaker had tripped. She put her right hand out to feel the wall beside her, but instead of the silky fabric which she had expected, she felt scabby paint and rough, damp plaster.

'Oh God,' she said. 'Not out here, too.'

She began to see shapes in the gloom, and she realized that she wasn't standing in a hotel corridor at all, but in the hallway of somebody's house, with coats and hats hanging on pegs like a row of witches hanging from a gallows. She could dimly see a hall stand, with umbrellas and walking sticks in it, and the stained-glass panels in a front door, in amber and sickly yellow. She could see that it was daylight outside, and she could hear that it was raining.

There was a *smell*, too. Not bleach and fish, like the laundry room, but dust and dry rot and stale flower-water. It felt to Katie as if the occupants had left the house in the expectation that they would soon be returning, but never had.

She closed her eyes for a few seconds. When she opened them again, she was still standing in the hallway. She listened, and she was sure that she could faintly hear a radio playing, and the laughter of a studio audience.

'Hallo?' she called out. She took three steps along the hallway, until she was standing next to the witch coats. 'Hallo?' she repeated, louder this time.

She took another two steps forward, and now she could see that the living-room door was ajar, and she could hear the radio much more distinctly. A woman's voice was saying, '*It's my birthday tomorrow, George, and I'm expecting you to buy me a present.*'

'*So . . .*' replied a man's voice. He sounded like an African-American. '*You finally hit the roaring forties.*'

'*I'll have you know that I didn't see the light of day until nineteen-thirteen*,' the woman retorted.

'*Holy mackerel!*' said the man. '*You must have been walking around for the first ten years of your life with your eyes closed!*'

There was a surge of laughter from the audience. Katie took a step backward, and then another. She had never heard the show before, but she knew where the catchphrase '*holy mackerel!*' came from. Kingfish, one of the characters from *Amos'n'Andy,* which hadn't been aired on the radio since the mid-1950s.

There was more laughter, louder and longer, and Katie began to panic, as if the studio audience were laughing at *her*. She hurried back down the hallway and fumbled in her back jeans pocket for her room key. When she reached out for the door handle, however, she found that she didn't need it. The door was an ordinary six-paneled house door, and the handle was a simple plastic knob.

She pushed the door open and stepped back into her bedroom, gasping with fright. For a split second, the bedroom was just as it had been before, Room 717 at the Griffin House Hotel.

But then, with a sharp pop, the bulb in the bedside lamp went off, and the room was drowned in darkness again.

Katie stayed where she was, still panting, with her back against the door. She could see the gray light that strained in through the window, and hear the rain pattering. She could smell that bleachy-fishy smell, too, and that greasy odor from the bed linen, except that there were some fresh smells that were even stronger than both of them. A metallic smell, like blood, and another appalling smell that made Katie's gorge rise.

She could still faintly hear the *Amos'n'Andy* show behind the door. But then a voice much nearer, a woman's voice, said, '*Help me.*'

Katie pressed her hand over her nose and her mouth. She stepped toward the bed and as she came closer she could see that there was a red-haired woman lying in it, a red-haired woman with a very white face, almost as if she had made herself up to look like a Venetian carnival mask.

'*Help me*,' she repeated, and held out one hand.

Katie came around the end of the bed and stood beside her, but not too close. The woman looked about twenty-seven or twenty-eight, although her white pancake make-up was cracked and fissured, and her eyes were smudged black with mascara, so it was difficult to tell for sure.

'Who are you?' Katie asked her. 'What is this place? Where are we?'

'*Please*,' the woman begged her, and suddenly a dark runnel of blood slid out of the side of her mouth and on to the pillow.

'What's wrong with you?' asked Katie. She was afraid to approach any nearer in case the woman was suffering from some kind of infectious disease.

The woman took hold of the corner of the quilt with one hand and tried to pull it off her, but she obviously didn't have the strength. Katie hesitated for a moment and then she reached across and drew it back herself.

'Oh God,' she said. 'What happened to you?'

Beneath the quilt, the woman was covered with a sheet, but the sheet was sodden and shiny and dark. That was the metallic smell that had overwhelmed Katie when she first came back into the room – the smell of blood.

'I couldn't stop him,' said the woman, so quietly now that

Katie could hardly hear her. 'I tried, but he was much too strong for me.'

She tried to raise her head from the pillow, but she couldn't. Katie said, 'Don't try to move. I'll call nine-one-one.'

She looked around. There was no nightstand beside the bed, no lamp, and no phone. She dug in the front pocket of her jeans and took out her cellphone, but when she flipped it open the screen was blank. Wherever this bedroom was, it was a dead area, out of range of any cellphone signals.

'Look,' she said, trying to keep herself calm, 'I've had a little training in first aid. Let me try to stop the bleeding. Then I can go find somebody to help you.'

'It's no use,' the woman told her. More blood welled out of the side of her mouth and the stain on the pillow grew wider.

'I can try,' Katie insisted. 'Look – I can tear up this other sheet and use it as a bandage.'

'It's no use,' the woman repeated.

'Just let me take a look,' said Katie. 'I promise I'll try not to hurt you.'

The woman shook her head as if she couldn't understand what language she was speaking in. Katie pinched the blood-soaked sheet between finger and thumb and tugged at it. It felt cold, and wet, and sticky.

'No,' the woman whispered.

'I'm so sorry, but I have to. If I can't stop the bleeding, you may not make it.'

The woman didn't argue any more. She just lay on the pillow, staring unblinkingly at Katie with her green filmy eyes, like somebody who wants to remember a friend they are never likely to see again.

Katie pulled the sheet right off her, and folded it back. At first she couldn't understand what she was looking at. But even when she realized what the red-haired woman's assailant had done to her, she could still barely believe it, and she stood by the side of the bed, utterly stunned, unable to think what she could possibly do next.

'I tried to stop him,' the woman murmured. Her eyes closed and for a moment Katie thought that she might have died, but when she leaned over her, she could see that she was still breathing, with a sticky catch in her throat. Katie couldn't imagine how she had survived at all, let alone managed to speak.

She waited for almost five minutes, biting the joint of her left thumb as if to reassure herself that she was still real, and that she hadn't lost her mind, and occasionally letting out a breathy little *unh*, like a sob. After a while she couldn't hear the woman breathing any longer, but she couldn't summon up the nerve to feel her pulse to make sure that she was dead.

She turned around and walked stiffly across to the laundry-room door. The light was still shining inside it, and she prayed that it was still her hotel bathroom. She looked back at the woman lying on the bed. She didn't know who she was or what she had suffered, but she felt as if she had let her down, even though she had been powerless to save her. Her only consolation was that nobody could have saved her.

She opened the door. Inside, the bathroom was so bright and shiny that she raised her hand to shield her eyes. She closed the door behind her and locked it. She washed her hands in the basin and rinsed the swirl of blood down the drain. She kept her eyes lowered so that she wouldn't have to look at her reflection in the mirror, in case her reflection was doing something else. Once she had dried her hands she climbed into the empty bathtub and sat there, hugging her knees, her eyes tight shut, rocking backward and forward and waiting for morning, if it ever came.

TWO

Room 309

It was less than a half mile to the Griffin House Hotel but John and his passenger had now been sitting at the same intersection for nearly ten minutes, next to a scabby plane tree on which somebody had thumb-tacked a flyer for a missing black-and-white cat.

'Maybe you want to walk,' John suggested, looking at the woman in his rear-view mirror. 'I can bring your bags along as soon as this traffic gets moving.'

'In *these* shoes?' the woman retorted.

John hadn't noticed the woman's shoes when he had picked

her up at the airport, but judging by the rest of what she was wearing, he had a pretty good idea what they must be like. Although it was a gloomy October afternoon, with winter just around the corner, her eyes were hidden behind enormous beetle-like sunglasses with sparkly diamanté frames. She wore a short leopard-print jacket with a high furry collar, on top of a tight purple satin dress with a cleavage that probably would have sent back multiple echoes if you had shouted down it. She smelled very strongly of Boss Intense. Since he had started driving taxis, John had become something of a connoisseur of women's perfumes, especially industrial-strength women's perfumes like this one.

'OK, it was only a thought,' John told her. He looked up at his rear-view mirror again. 'First time in Cleveland?' he asked her.

'Oh, no *way*,' she told him. 'I was born and raised in Brunswick. A fully-fledged graduate of B-wick High. My sister still lives in Shaker Heights.'

'Hey, that's a nice district, Shaker Heights.'

'I guess, if you like boredom and trees. Personally I hate being bored and who needs frigging trees?'

John raised his eyebrows and thought: *Who needs frigging trees? That's classy*. Not the usual caliber of guest he would have expected to take to the Griffin House Hotel.

He adjusted his seat belt around his belly. It was way past two thirty and he still hadn't had lunch yet. He had been planning to go to Quizno's on Euclid Avenue when he had dropped this fare off, to pick up a bourbon grille steak sub. He could almost taste it now: prime rib, mozzarella, Cheddar, mushrooms, sauté onions, all covered with grille steak sauce and served up on rosemary Parmesan bread. His mouth watered so much that he had to swallow.

'Staying here long?' he asked, in a quacky, saliva-filled voice.

'Not if I can help it. I'm only going to my grandma's funeral.'

'Oh, I'm sorry. My condolences.'

'Thanks, but I don't need condoling. I never liked her and neither would you, if you'd ever known her. What a witch. She had a face like somebody looking at themselves in the back of a spoon.'

The traffic began to inch forward. The woman said, 'At last. Thank you, Lord Jesus.'

As they neared the Griffin House Hotel, John could see three black-and-white police cars lined up outside, their lights flashing, and two uniformed officers directing the traffic. The hotel itself was an imposing brown-brick building with Gothic windows and elaborate spires and a gray slate roof. It was surrounded by tall ivy-wrapped oaks, their leaves already turned rusty and yellow. A crowd of people were milling around the wide stone porch – police officers and TV cameramen and hotel staff, as well as rubbernecking bystanders.

'Looks like we've got ourselves a little excitement,' said John. He signaled to turn into the curving driveway in front of the hotel and a police officer flagged him down and made a winding gesture for him to lower his window.

'Just dropping off a hotel guest, officer. What's all the flap-doodle for?'

'Nothing serious, sir. If you want to pull over to the left side there.'

John parked his yellow Crown Victoria close to the left-hand verge, and heaved himself out of the driver's seat. He opened the door for his passenger to step out, and this time he made a point of looking at her shoes. They were purple suede, the same color as her dress, with gold studs all around them, and very high heels. Her dress was so short that he couldn't help noticing that she was wearing purple nylon panties, too. He gallantly turned his head away and looked up at the sky.

It seemed as if all of the hotel's front-of-house staff were busy talking to the police, so John popped the taxicab's trunk and lifted out the woman's pigskin suitcase. It wasn't Louis Vuitton, but it wasn't cheap. She may have started life in Brunswick (or 'Brunstucky' as some disparaging Clevelanders called it, an elision of 'Brunswick' and 'Kentucky') but she appeared to have money – either made it or married it.

For the first time she took off her sunglasses and she was unexpectedly pretty, even if she did have the slightly battered look of a woman who has struggled to make her way in life and had her fair share of fights. She had bright blonde hair, expensively cut in a feathery bell-shape, wide-apart eyes and a short straight nose, and lips that looked as if they were just about to pout. She had a faint scar on the left side of her chin, as if somebody had punched her, a long time ago, somebody wearing a signet ring.

As John began to walk across the driveway, carrying the woman's case, a skinny young black bellhop in a green uniform came loping up to them. 'It's OK, junior,' John told him. 'I got it.'

'Please, sir, let me help you,' the bellhop begged him, trying to take hold of the handle.

John yanked the case away from him. 'Oho, so that's your game! You're trying to stiff me out of my tip, is that it?'

'Of course not, sir. It's my job.'

'I know, junior. I *know* it's your job. But exactly what part of "I got it" do you find so incomprehensible?'

'Excuse me?'

'That's OK, junior. You're excused.'

John carried the suitcase into the reception area, changing hands every three or four steps because the goddamned thing was so heavy. How come women who wore practically nothing always had suitcases that weighed so much? He followed the woman up to the front desk and pinged the bell for her, because there was nobody there.

'Pretty plushy joint, on the whole,' he said, looking around. The reception area had high vaulted ceilings with decorative plasterwork, thick red floral-patterned carpeting, and leather wing chairs gathered around a crackling log fire. On the wall above the fireplace hung a large oil portrait of a severe-looking man in a formal black suit with black silk facings. His face was so pallid that it was almost white, and his eyes were as dead as stones. The only touches of color were his hair, which was gingery-red, and the ring on his right hand, which had a dark red stone set in it.

Close to this portrait hung another smaller portrait, in an oval frame, of a pretty young woman with wild blonde curls. She had her head tilted to one side, as if she were flirting with the artist who was painting her picture.

John pinged the bell again and this time a receptionist came in from the porch, where she had been talking to a police officer.

'So sorry to have kept you waiting, sir. Are you checking in today?'

'Not me – her,' said John, jerking his thumb toward the woman.

'Ms Rhodajane Berry,' said the woman, resting one elbow on the marble-topped counter. 'I booked a queen-sized room for tonight and tomorrow night.'

'Hey,' John put in, 'you're not related to that *Halle* Berry, are you, by any chance?'

The woman turned and stared at him. 'Do I *look* like I'm related to Halle Berry? I mean, I'm not being racist here.'

'Well, you never can tell. It's a funny thing, genetics. And Halle Berry, she's from Cleveland, too, did you know that?'

Rhodajane Berry was still filling in her name and address and credit card details when a bulky man in a flappy gray suit came puffing and panting into the reception area. He was just about the same height as John, about five feet eight, and he probably weighed about the same, too, somewhere in excess of three hundred pounds. He was purple faced, with protuberant blue eyes, and a small curved nose that looked as if it had been stuck on as an afterthought. His eyebrows seemed to be raised in permanent surprise, like two arched-up caterpillars.

He was sporting a wide silk necktie with scarlet and yellow diagonal stripes, and his shirt must have been at least a twenty-two-inch collar, but it still curled upward because it was too tight around his neck.

'Pardon me, people,' he asked, in a hoarse, strangulated voice. 'Did you talk to any of my officers yet?' He reached into his pocket and tugged out a notebook, licking his thumb and turning over the pages. 'What room are you in?'

'I'm not in any room,' said John. 'I'm a cabbie and this lady is my fare.'

The detective peered at Rhodajane Berry with his pencil raised in his hand as if he half recognized her. 'OK . . . what cab company?'

'Alphabet Cabs. My vehicle's parked right outside. You can call them and check if you want to. You want their number? John Dauphin's the name. John Benjamin Franklin Dauphin. The third. From Baton Rouge, Louisiana. Still trying to get back there, one way or the other.'

The detective gave a quick shake of his jowls to indicate that it wouldn't be necessary to check John's credentials. But then he turned to Rhodajane Berry and said, 'How about you, ma'am, what room will you be staying in?'

'She's three-oh-nine,' said the receptionist.

'Three-oh-nine. OK.' He wrote down 309 and sniffed. Then he said, 'Have a good stay, won't you? But if you do hear anything or see anything, here's my card. Give me a call anytime.'

Rhodajane Berry looked taken aback. 'What do you mean, if I hear anything or see anything? What kind of things do you mean?'

The detective hesitated. 'You know, anything out of the ordinary.'

'Anything out of the ordinary like *what,* for instance?'

John had to give it to her, Rhodajane Berry had a voice like a braided-wire whip. It could cut through anything.

The detective shrugged. 'Anything out of the ordinary like the room maybe changing in appearance.'

'*Excah-use* me? The room changing in appearance? I don't get it. How does a room change in appearance? You mean like I'm going to be lying in bed and somebody's going to come in and start to strip off the wallpaper?'

'Well, to be honest, ma'am. I don't know any more than you do. But if it *does* change, in any way at all, call me, please. Likewise if you hear shouting or crying or if you find anybody in your room who isn't supposed to be there.'

Rhodajane Berry said, 'Wait up a second. I seriously do not like the sound of this. Shouting or crying? People in my room who aren't supposed to be there? I'm supposed to be staying here tonight. I'm paying one hundred sixty dollars per night. What the hell kind of crap is this?'

'There's no need for that language, ma'am. I'm just asking you to be vigilant tonight which isn't a whole lot to ask, is it?'

'What happened here?' John demanded, 'What's this all about?'

The detective said, 'You don't have anything to worry about, sir. You won't be staying here. I suggest you get right back in your taxicab now and leave.'

'I won't be staying here but this lady will and right now she's still my fare and that makes her my personal responsibility. So what went down here?'

The detective took a deep breath. Then he said, 'There's nothing for you to get yourself worried about. One of the guests suffered an episode, that's all.'

'An episode? An episode of what? *Days Of Our Lives*?'

'No, sir. She had what you might call a hallucination. She thought her room had altered in some way and she thought she saw a strange person in her bed. When the housekeeping staff found her she was in a state of some distress, but there was nothing in her room to indicate that what she had experienced was real.

'All the same, we've been taking the precaution of asking all of the hotel's guests to call me personally at any time of the night if they think they see or hear anything unusual.'

John dragged out his handkerchief and blew his nose. 'Sounds to me like for no good reason at all you're causing this good lady here a whole lot of unnecessary anxiety for nothing.'

'You're entitled to your opinion, Mr Dolphin,' the detective snapped back at him. 'I'm simply erring on the side of caution. Now, please, if you don't mind, I have to go talk to some sane people.'

'Hey, wait up! Some *sane* people? You're trying to suggest that I'm some kind of nut job?'

'No, sir. Not at all. I didn't say that.'

'Excuse me. You clearly said you have to go talk to some *sane* people, which would suggest to me that you think I'm not one of them. What's your name, detective?'

The detective reached into his breast pocket and took out another card. 'There. If you have any complaints to make, just contact the UCPD. Now I have to get on.'

John held up the card and squinted at it. *Detective Walter B. Wisocky, University Circle Police Department, 12100 Euclid Avenue, Cleveland Heights*.

'OK,' he said. 'Thanks. You can bet that I'll be calling your Chief of Detectives directly after lunch. *Sane* people indeed. The nerve!'

Before he left, however, Detective Wisocky turned back and laid a firm hand on John's shoulder pad.

'Don't think I'm trying to influence you or nothing,' he breathed, very close to John's ear, and his breath smelled of scallions. 'But before I leave here I'll be sure to make a note of your medallion number, and believe me, if you make a complaint against me to the Chief of D's, you'd better drive your cab real meticulous in future. And I mean *real* meticulous. Everywhere, and for ever, amen.'

John looked him in the eye, trying to be challenging, but all the same he was thinking about the number of times he had driven to pick up a fare holding a cheesesteak in one hand and a can of

Dr Pepper in the other, steering with nothing but his fingertips and his right thigh. He thought of all the illegal U-turns which cut minutes off call-out times, and all of the convenient short-cuts which took him the wrong way down one-way streets. He thought of all the times he had driven to the airport on I-71 at more than eighty-five miles an hour, because he was running late for a pickup.

He said nothing, but Detective Wisocky kept his hand pressed down on his shoulder pad and kept staring at him without blinking for a full five seconds to show that he meant business.

'Ma'am,' said the receptionist. 'Here's your key card. I'll have somebody bring your luggage up to your room.'

Detective Wisocky turned and walked off. John watched him for a moment, and then said, 'No, it's OK, ma'am. I'll carry your case up for you.'

He followed Rhodajane Berry to the elevators, which had highly-polished brass doors. He could see himself standing beside her in his crumpled linen suit, his belly bulging over the waistband. He always thought that he could have been handsome if he hadn't loved food so much. When he was a teenager he had looked a lot like Tab Hunter. Well, more snub-nosed, like Tab Hunter pressing his face against a Burger King window. Now he thought he looked like every fat guy who ever was. Fat.

He wasn't sure why he felt so protective of Rhodajane Berry. She must be reasonably wealthy, but she was trashy, too, and he had always been attracted to trashy women. His first serious girlfriend Charlene had been trashy, with the dirtiest laugh and the biggest breasts and the shortest conceivable skirts, but when he had returned from his stint in the Army she had taken one look at him and he had known before a word was spoken that their relationship was over. He might have been the only three-time winner of the Fort Polk prize for culinary excellence, but he had more than trebled in weight. After a long silence, Charlene had said, 'Jesus. It's the Pillsbury Dough Boy.'

'Meeting the rest of your family today?' he asked Rhodajane, as they went up in the elevator.

'Not if I can help it.'

'Oh. Not too close, then?'

'You could say that. They're a collection of mean-minded sons-of-bitches, all of them. I only came here to make sure I got what's coming to me in grandma's will.'

'Oh. So what are you going to be doing tonight?'

'Not going out with you if that's what this is leading up to.'

'Hey, of course not,' John protested. 'I'm just making small talk, that's all. You know, like persiflage.'

The elevator chimed and the doors slid open. Before she stepped out, Rhodajane prodded John with her long purple fingernail and said, 'If there's one thing I'm a real good judge of, Mr John Dolphin, it's men. And I've been watching you watching me in your rear-view mirror ever since we left the airport. And I saw you looking up my dress when I got out of your cab.'

John said, 'All right. I think you're very attractive. Is that a crime? And besides, it's "Dauphin", like the eldest son of the King of France, not "Dolphin" like in Flipper.'

'Pity. "Dolphin" kind of suits you.'

They reached Room 309. John put down Rhodajane's suitcase and opened the door for her. Then he switched on the lights and hefted her suitcase on to the linen chest in the corner. 'Nice room,' he said, looking around. It was decorated in turquoise and gold with brocade drapes and a bedspread to match. He went to the window and peered out. 'You got a great view of the university, too.'

'Really?'

'Don't knock it. I hear they have a first-rate department of anthropology.'

'That's a relief. Switch on the TV for me, would you?'

John switched on the television while Rhodajane sat on the bed and took off her shoes. 'God, my feet. I mean, I really love these shoes, but . . .'

John handed her the remote control. 'You'll have to work this out for yourself. I'm not too good when it comes to technology.'

Rhodajane flapped one hand. 'Anything will do, so long as they're speaking English. I really have to go to the little girls' room.'

When she stood up without her shoes on, she was at least three inches shorter than she had been before. She padded off to the bathroom and closed the door while John flicked through the TV channels. As far as he could he see it was the usual daytime diet: *As The World Turns* and *The Electric Company* for kids, followed by *General Hospital, American Justice* and *The Tyra Show*.

Tyra was talking to a plump young woman who wanted to swallow a tapeworm so that she could lose weight. John wondered if he ought to do the same, but apart from the very idea of it making his mouth feel all greasy and his throat close up, he doubted if any tapeworm could keep up with him. He could finish a whole muffuletta sandwich in less than a minute, complete with extra provolone.

'Hey, you want to come see this!' he called out. An entrepreneur who sold tapeworms on the Internet had joined Tyra and her guest, and was lifting one of them out of a jar, all four feet of it, pale and slippery, with four suckers around its head.

John turned around. Rhodajane was still in the bathroom with the door closed, but he could see himself in the mirror over the dressing table. He could see the reflection of the TV screen, too, but inexplicably the reflected TV screen wasn't showing Tyra Banks and her two guests. Instead, it was showing an indistinct image of a darkened room, as if it was being filmed by a closed-circuit camera. A woman in a stained white nightgown was lying on a bed, and a man was repeatedly walking backward and forward in front of the camera, although John couldn't see who he was, because his head was cut off by the top of the screen.

Baffled, John looked back at the real TV. The tapeworm entrepreneur was lowering the worm back into the jar, along with several other coiled-up companions, and Tyra was screaming and laughing in disgust. John looked back at the TV in the mirror. The man was bending over the woman on the bed and although John couldn't hear what she was saying, it looked from the expression on her face as if she were crying and begging.

'*Ma'am*!' John called out. He heard the toilet flush, and the faucets in the bathroom basin splashing. The man who was bending over the woman on the bed moved slightly to his right, so that he obscured the woman's face. He appeared to be jerking his left elbow backward and forward, in a strange repetitive way. John could only see the woman's bare legs, but they were covered in huge maroon bruises and they were twitching and convulsing as the man continued to jerk his elbow.

'*Ma'am*!' John repeated. He wanted Rhodajane to see this – partly because he couldn't believe what he was seeing with his own eyes, and partly because he was worried that this might be an example of what Detective Wisocky had called 'anything out of the ordinary.'

'OK, OK! Keep your toupee on!' The bathroom door opened, and Rhodajane stepped out, still brushing her hair. 'Sorry if I kept you waiting but I was busting.' She walked across the room and opened her pocketbook. 'How much do I owe you?'

John said, 'The TV, ma'am. Take a look at the TV.'

'Hold up. Let me get my glasses. I can't see a goddamned thing without my glasses.'

As she was rummaging in her pocketbook for her purse and her spectacles, John saw a dark red stain spreading quickly across the sheet on which the woman was lying. The man stood up straight, and for a split second John could see the woman's face again. She seemed to be staring directly at him, her eyes bulging in pain, her mouth dragged downward in a silent howl. Then the TV screen flickered and jumped, and the image of the darkened room vanished, and was instantly replaced by a commercial for HeadOn headache cure, (or nOdaeH as it appeared in the mirror.)

Rhodajane came up behind him wearing her glasses and laid a surprisingly familiar hand on his shoulder. 'So what did you want me to see? Not this goddamned HeadOn commercial? It must be the worst commercial ever! "HeadOn – apply directly to the forehead! HeadOn – apply directly to the forehead!" Jesus, I can hear it in my sleep!'

'No, no, not that,' John told her. 'There was something on *The Tyra Show*, that's all. It doesn't matter.'

'*The Tyra Show*? That crap? You have very strange tastes, Mr Eldest-Son-Of-The-King-Of-France. How much do I owe you?'

'Forty-four bucks, but let's call it forty. The traffic wasn't your fault.'

Rhodajane gave him a fifty-dollar bill and said, 'Keep the change my good man. But don't spend it all on bacon fries.'

John headed for the door and opened it. Before he left, though, he turned around and said, 'Here – let me give you my cell-phone number.'

'What for? I'm still not going out with you.'

'I know that. I'm not asking you to. But just in case.'

'Just in case of *what*, for instance?'

'Just in case something weird happens. Weird things *do*

happen. I've had some pretty weird things happen to me, in my time.'

'You and that detective, you're both as screwy as each other if you ask me. Tweedle-de-dum and Tweedle-de-dee.'

John took a catsup-spotted business card out of his breast pocket and offered it to her. 'More than likely, ma'am, everything's going to be fine. But if you get spooked or anything, and you feel too reticent to phone the cops, give me a call and I can be round here in five minutes flat. I only live in Glenville.'

Rhodajane hesitated for a moment, but then she took his card and tucked it into her cleavage. 'OK, big boy, whatever you say. But I don't believe for one single second that my room is going to change into the chamber of horrors or that I'm going to hear screaming in the middle of the night. And nobody else is getting in here once I've locked this door behind you, and you can be one hundred and eleven percent sure of that.'

'Sure,' said John. He could have tried to explain to her what he had seen on the reflected TV screen, but she would probably think that he was deliberately trying to frighten her so that she would ask him to come around and protect her. Either that, or she would think that he was mentally challenged, or that he had been smoking something more exotic than Marlboro Lights.

'Goodbye, then, Mr Dauphin,' she told him. 'And thank you. You're a gentleman.'

'Well, I was the last time I looked. But don't forget, will you? Anything *outré* occurs, anything at all, anything eldritch, you pick up your phone and it'll be John Dauphin to the rescue. I mean that.'

Rhodajane looked at him and gave him a very slight shake of her head. 'Do you know something, Mr Dauphin? Half the time I don't understand a word you're saying. But I like you. I really dooski. I give you permission to have a dream about me tonight if you want to.'

'Well, I'd be careful about saying that if I were you, ma'am. Some dreams are good, but other dreams are not so good. And *some* dreams you can never really wake up from, even if you want to. Some dreams stay with you for the rest of your life, and you wish you'd never had them.'

Rhodajane looked at him narrowly. 'What are you, some kind of dream expert?'

'In a manner of speaking, yes, I guess you could say that I am.'

They were both silent. It was only for two or three seconds, but in those two or three seconds something passed between them, one of those indefinable feelings that they were more than just cab driver and fare, more than just passing acquaintances who would never see each other again, except by coincidence. Ostensibly they had nothing at all in common, but John pointed at Rhodajane with a pistol-like gesture as if to say 'see you later, OK?' and Rhodajane closed her eyes as if to acknowledge that he would.

John turned and waddled off toward the elevators and Rhodajane stood in the doorway of her hotel room watching him go. Behind her, Tyra was talking to a twenty-two-year-old woman who wanted to auction her virginity on the Internet.

The woman was saying, '*I always dreamed of having a lover . . . but somehow it never happened. Every man I ever met turned out to be a nightmare.*'

THREE
Room 104

Lincoln was sitting alone in a corner booth of the Boa Vinda Restaurant, wishing that he hadn't ordered such a messy dish as *caldeirada*, when his cellphone played *Tracks Of My Tears*. He shook open his white linen napkin and hastily started to wipe the thick tomato-and-saffron sauce from his fingers.

'*Lincoln*?' said a woman's voice, very small and far away.

'Grace?' he laughed. 'Wait up a second, honey, I'm in kind of a pickle here.'

He put down his cell and finished wiping his hands and his mouth. Then he picked it up again and said, 'Sorry. The waiter recommended this Portuguese fish stew and it's absolutely outstanding but you pretty much have to take a bath in it to eat it.'

'*Lincoln*?' the woman's voice repeated, as if she hadn't heard him.

'Grace? Are you still there? You're very faint.'

'*Lincoln*?'

'Listen, honey,' he said, 'why don't I call you back? I'm sitting in the hotel restaurant here and maybe the signal's too weak.'

'*Lincoln*?'

'Hang up, and I'll call you right back, OK?'

He listened for a few seconds more, in case Grace answered him, but as he took his cell away from his ear, he heard a man say, '*Lincoln*?'

Lincoln frowned and lifted up the cell again. 'Hallo? Hallo? Who is this?'

The man sounded hoarse, like a heavy smoker. '*No need for you to know that, Lincoln.*'

'What do you mean, "no need for me to know that"? Who the hell *is* this?'

'*You know what they say, Lincoln. Curiosity killed the cat.*'

'I'm trying to get through to my wife here, so if you don't mind—'

'*You need to listen to me, Lincoln. I'm your friend.*'

'What friend?'

'A *concerned friend. A very concerned friend. So long as you do what I tell you, that is.*'

Lincoln suddenly slapped the table. 'Bennie? Is this you, man? Quit horsing around, OK? I'm trying to finish my goddamned dinner here.'

'*Eat your goddamned dinner then, Lincoln. Enjoy it. But do not return to your room.*'

'If this is your idea of a joke, man—'

'*No joke, Lincoln. Do not return to your room. Not if you know what's good for you.*'

'That's enough, Bennie. It's been a long day, OK? I have two more meetings in the morning and then I'll get back to you. It looks like we can get top billing for Millie D and maybe second spot for The Jive Machine.'

'*You need to listen to me, Lincoln. You'll regret it if you don't. Tonight, I need my privacy, you got that? I don't want any witnesses. Not you, not anybody.*'

Lincoln took a deep breath, and held it for a moment. Then he said, 'If this is you, Bennie, this isn't funny any more. If this *isn't* Bennie, then all I can say is go screw yourself.'

There was a sudden blurt of white noise, and then a thick, persistent crackle, but that was all. Lincoln tried to see who had called him, but the only number that showed up was his own home number, in Ann Arbor. He tried calling Grace again, but he couldn't get a ring tone. He edged his way out of the booth, stood up and started to walk toward the restaurant door.

One of the waiters intercepted him. 'Sir? You finish up already, sir? The *caldeirada* – it was not to your like?'

'The *caldeirada's* terrific. I have to make a phone call, that's all.'

'You don't go back to your room?'

'Excuse me?'

'I said, "Do you want me to keep it warm?"'

Lincoln stared at him. The waiter looked back at him, unblinking. Lincoln was sure that he had said, "*You don't go back to your room?*" but maybe he had genuinely misheard him. The restaurant was noisy, after all, with talking and laughter and clattering cutlery and piped salsa music in the background.

'No . . . you're OK,' he said slowly, and walked toward the restaurant entrance. The maître d' was standing behind his lectern by the doorway, with polished black hair and a little black moustache and a maroon tuxedo. As Lincoln approached he bowed his head and said, 'Good evening, sir. I hope you enjoyed your meal.'

'I'm only stepping out to use my cell. I'm coming back in a minute.'

'You are not returning to your room?'

'Why? What's it to you?'

'Excuse me, sir, I don't follow you.'

'Why should you care whether I'm returning to my room or not?'

'I'm sorry, sir. I still don't understand.' The maître d' looked totally baffled. 'I made no mention of your room.'

Lincoln opened his mouth. He was about to tell the maître d' that he was either a deuce hole or an idiot, but he decided that it was pointless. Instead he gave him a dismissive flap of his hand and walked off.

He was still unable to get a cellphone signal out in the hotel lobby, so he went outside and stood on the front steps of the hotel. A strong gusty wind was blowing from the north-west, off the lake, and dead leaves were skipping across the hotel driveway with a clatter like dancing skeletons. He tried calling Grace again, but all he could hear was the same thick crackling that he had heard before. Maybe his phone was on the fritz. The best thing he could do was go back to his room and call her from there.

No joke, Lincoln. Do not return to your room. Not if you know what's good for you.

He went back into the hotel lobby and took a left at the reception desk. There was a gilt-framed mirror at the end of the corridor and he could see himself walking toward it – a tall, lithe African-American in a black suit and a black silk shirt. His head was shaved which emphasized the Nubian looks that he had inherited from his mother – a thin face with high cheekbones and a straight narrow nose. In fact his features were so sharp that his friends at school had nicknamed him Icepick.

He reached Room 104. As he took out his key card, a hotel chambermaid in a frilly white apron came out of Room 106 next door with clean green towels over her arm. She stopped and stared at him as if she couldn't believe what she was seeing.

'Good evening,' he said, giving her a smile.

'Yes, sir,' she replied, still staring at him. She walked off, turning her head around twice as she made her way along the corridor, as if she were afraid that he was going to come after her. Lincoln watched her until she reached the lobby and disappeared out of sight. He thought: *what the hell was* that *all about*? But then he shrugged and inserted his key card into the lock. She could have mistaken him for somebody famous. Grace maintained that he bore a strong resemblance to the murdered rapper Tupac Shakur, so maybe it was no surprise that the housekeeper had looked at him with such anxiety. He guessed that *he* would be anxious, too, if he met a man who had been shot dead in 1996.

He entered his room and switched on the light. Everything appeared to be normal. The chambermaid had closed the drapes and switched on the bedside lamps, as well as turning down the bed and leaving two chocolate mints in the pillows. Lincoln went across to the desk, picked up the phone and dialed nine for an outside line. While he waited, he rotated his head to ease his neck muscles. It had been a long, punishing day and he couldn't wait to finish his dinner, take a shower and climb into bed.

Instead of an outside line, however, he heard that sharp blurt of white noise again, followed by the soft crackling of static.

Shit, he thought. Maybe there was something wrong with his home phone line. But he hadn't even dialed his number yet, so how could that be? And how come he couldn't get a line either on his cellphone or this regular landline? It didn't make any technical sense.

He dialed zero for the hotel operator. This time, he got a response.

'Operator, how can I help you?'

'I'm trying to get an outside line from Room One-Oh-Four, but all I'm getting is this crackling sound.'

'Hold on, Mr Walker. I'll see what I can do.'

There was a moment's pause, and then he heard the crackling noise again. He dialed the operator again and said, 'I'm still getting it.'

'I'm sorry, sir, you're still getting *what*, exactly?'

'The crackling sound, just like before.'

'I'm sorry, sir. I don't hear it. All I can hear is a regular dialing tone.'

'There's no dialing tone. There's only this crackling sound.'

There was another pause, and then he heard the crackling again. He tried the operator's number again, and it rang, but this time nobody answered.

'This is fucking unbelievable,' he said to his reflection in the mirror. He would have to go to the front desk and see if they could dial his home number for him. He was growing increasingly annoyed now. His dinner was getting cold, he couldn't get through to Grace, and everybody in this five-star hotel was talking five-star bullshit. He was beginning to agree with his late lookalike Tupac, who had once said, '*Reality is wrong. Only dreams are for real.*'

He thought it would be a good idea to take a leak before he went to reception, so he made his way around the bed and headed for the bathroom door. His hand was already on the doorknob when there was a thunderous crash from inside the bathroom and the whole door shook as if somebody had thrown themselves against it. He jumped back, startled, and he almost lost his balance and fell over backward on to the bed.

There was another crash, and then another, and then a tumbling, squeaking noise like somebody falling into the bathtub.

'Who's there?' he shouted. 'What the hell are you doing?'

He took hold of the doorknob again and twisted it, but the door was either locked or jammed. He heard more squeaking and more knocking, and then, suddenly, a woman moaning. Her moan started off quite shivery and low, *ohhhhhhhhhh*, as if she were calling out in dread; but then it grew increasingly shrill and panicky, and then she started screaming at the top of her voice, and begging '*No! No! Please don't do that*! *No! Please don't do that!*'

Lincoln rattled the doorknob and beat on the door panel with his fist.

'Who's in there? Open up! What the hell are you doing? If you don't open up I'm going to call for security!'

The woman's screaming went on for four or five more seconds, accompanied by what sounded like bare heels drumming against an empty bathtub. Then, just as suddenly as the noise had begun, it stopped, and there was silence.

Lincoln waited, his ear close to the door. He tried the doorknob again, and this time the door unlatched, and opened. Inside the bathroom it was completely dark.

'Who's in there?' he repeated.

There was no reply, so he pushed the door open a little further. He could make out the edge of the bathtub now, but it wasn't the shiny white-tiled bathtub that he had been expecting to see. It was an old-fashioned high-sided tub, on four lion's-claw feet, with two large old-fashioned faucets, both of them dripping. By the light that was shining into the bathroom from the bedroom, he saw that the tub was filthy. The sides were streaked with runnels of black and gray dirt, and the enamel inside was decorated with dark brown spatters and diagonal runs and dozens of handprints, as well as a thick greasy tidemark.

There was nobody lying in the tub, however. He must have imagined all that screaming and thumping. Nobody could have jumped out of the tub that quick – and where would they have hidden themselves, even if they had?

In the far corner of the bathroom, high up on the wall, there was a small grimy window, but even though the window was so dirty Lincoln could see that it was daylight outside, even though it was almost quarter of eight in the evening. He could hear a very faint pattering, too, which sounded like rain. He frowned. It had been very windy when he went outside to try and talk to Grace, but it had been totally dry.

He pushed the door open all the way. It met with some resistance; there was a sodden stained bath-towel lying twisted on the floor, as if somebody had been unsuccessfully trying to clean the tiles with it. The tiles themselves were mottled green, with brown splashes across them, and a complicated pattern of bare footprints, pointing every which way, as if somebody had been dancing around the bathroom without their shoes on. They were small and narrow, like a woman's feet, or maybe a child's.

Lincoln took a cautious step forward, and as he did so he saw that there was a shower stall on the opposite side of the room – a shower stall whose glass door was so filthy and fogged up that it was impossible to tell if there was anybody in there. He strained his eyes in the gloom, however, and he thought he could make out a dark hunched shape inside it, but he guessed it was probably nothing but a shadow. There was a toilet beside it, with its mahogany seat raised.

The smell in the bathroom was sickening – like drains clogged up with slimy gray human hair and unflushed urine that had turned dark amber, and something else, too – a horrible thick sweetness that filled up his nose and his throat and made him feel like gagging. It reminded him of the bathroom in his boyhood home in the Brightmoor ghetto – the bathroom in which his older brother Nelson had died on the toilet of a heroin overdose.

The question was: how had his pristine white-tiled hotel bathroom turned into *this*? There was only one door to the bathroom, so he couldn't have chosen the wrong door by mistake. And even if he had, he couldn't imagine the Griffin House Hotel leaving *any* bathroom in such a disgusting condition.

He pulled the light-switch cord. As he did so, and the fluorescent lights popped on, he saw that he must have been suffering from some kind of an optical illusion. The bathroom *was* pristine. The bathtub was shiny and white, with gold-plated faucets. The hand basin was sunk into black streaky marble, and next to it there was a guest amenity tray with complimentary bottles of shampoo and body lotion and aftershave. The shower stall was sparkling clean, with an engraving of seagulls on its frosted glass door. There were towels, but they were all fluffy and dark green and neatly arranged on a heated towel-rail.

Lincoln stared at himself in the mirror. He was surprised by his own lack of expression. He placed his left hand on the marble surround of the hand basin and it was cool and polished and indisputably real. With his right hand he turned on one of the faucets, and that was real, too. The filthy, old-fashioned bathroom had completely disappeared – if it had ever existed at all. This bathroom even smelled good, like green tea bath oil.

'You're losing it, Linc,' he told himself. He went over to the toilet, lifted the seat and relieved himself. He kept on staring at himself as he washed his hands. 'You're really losing it. You're working too hard, that's what's wrong with you. You're always living on the edge. You got to chill, bro.'

He left the bathroom and closed the door behind him, although he didn't turn the light off. He stood for a while at the end of his bed, his head bowed, trying to untangle his thoughts. Then he went over to the phone and pressed nine again. It could be that when he had tried to get an outside line before, he had been suffering from the same delusion that had made him believe that his bathroom was so slummy.

This time, he managed to get a dial tone. He punched out his home number and waited while it rang. It rang and it rang and he had almost given up hope that Grace was going to answer when the phone was picked up.

He said, 'Grace honey, it's me! Sorry I took so long to call you back.'

There was a long silence, and then he heard the same man's voice that he had heard before. '*What did I tell you, Lincoln? What did I specifically tell you? Were you not listening to me, or what?*'

'Who the hell are you?' Lincoln demanded. 'What the hell are you doing in my house? Where's my wife?'

'*I'm not in your house, Lincoln. I'm much closer than that. But I specifically told you not to go back to your room, didn't I?*'

'You listen to me, if you think you can bump my dome you got yourself another think coming. I'm going to track you down, dog, and I'm going to come looking for you and believe me you're going to wish you never got on to my phone line ever.'

There was another sharp hiss of white noise, and then the line returned to its monotonous crackling. Lincoln said, 'Damn,' and then, '*damn*,' and hung up. He thought maybe he should try his cellphone just once more. If he couldn't manage to talk to Grace then at least he should be able to send her a text message.

He looked around the room. Where the hell had he left his cell? Then he remembered. He had put it down beside the hand basin in the bathroom, and forgotten to pick it up.

He went back to the bathroom and opened the door. He had opened it only two or three inches, however, before he stopped himself. He had made a point of leaving the light on, but now the bathroom was dark again. Not only that, he could smell that appalling stench of blocked drains and ageing urine and whatever that terrible sweetness was.

He hesitated for a very long time. Then he reached his hand inside the door and groped around for the light cord. He found it and tugged it but it didn't work. The fluorescent tube must have burned out.

Come on, Linc. Just go in and pick up your cell. You've seen for yourself that there's nobody in there.

He opened the door wider and stepped inside. But there was no cellphone lying beside the hand basin because there was no hand basin, only that old-fashioned bathtub with all of its splashes and drips and its dozens of handprints. He hunkered down to see if his cell might have dropped on the floor, but there was no sign of it. *It must be here in this bathroom in* some *reality, he thought, but it sure isn't here in* this *reality.*

He stood up. He didn't have any choice now. He would have go to the reception desk, not only to see if he could get through to Grace, but to ask them if he could change rooms. There was no way he was going to sleep next to *this* bathroom, not in a million years. It was not only filthy, it was scary, too. How could it be daylight in here when it was dark outside? How could it be raining when he knew for sure that it wasn't?

He turned back toward his bedroom, but now this had changed, too. The bedside lamps had disappeared, and the room was lit only by a single bare bulb hanging by a frayed cord from the ceiling. The queen-sized bed with its green tapestry throw had been replaced by an iron-framed bed with only a soiled striped mattress on it. The thick green carpet had vanished, and now there was only dirty beige linoleum covering the floor. The walls no longer had pictures on them, and there were no drapes hanging at the window. There was a strong musty smell of rats' urine.

Outside the window, he could see gleaming wet rooftops, with gray clouds hurrying over them, and iron fire escapes. This was Room 104, on the first floor, and yet it looked as if it were three stories up, at the very least. It could even be higher. He could hear the soft patter of rain, and police sirens wailing in the distance.

Lincoln thought: *You got to get out of here,* now. *You're going crazy*. He crossed over to the door and tried to open it, but it was locked. He jiggled the handle up and down, and pulled at it, but still the door refused to open. He hammered on it with both fists and shouted out, '*Help! Let me out of here! Help!*'

He paused, and listened, and he was sure that he could hear telephones ringing and people laughing. He banged on the door even harder and screamed, '*Help! I'm trapped in here!*' until his throat felt raw, but still nobody came to let him out.

He stepped away from the door, panting. He gave it a hard kick, and then another. He cracked one of the lower panels but the door was much too solid for him to break down. He knew better than to take his shoulder to it. He had done that, years ago, after an argument with Grace, and he had dislocated his left arm.

Agitated, breathing hard, he paced backward and forward up and down the room. He couldn't understand how or why it could have altered like this. It was not as if he recognized it. The apartment in Brightmoor in which he had been brought up as a boy had been damp and scabby, too, but nothing like as derelict as this. He had hung out with his friends in abandoned houses in Hamtramck and Highland Park, but he had never seen a room that resembled this one in any way, so he doubted if he was reliving some kind of childhood trauma.

He went to the window and looked out, his forehead pressed against the chilly glass. He didn't recognize the neighborhood at all, but wherever it was, it certainly wasn't University Circle, Cleveland, where the Griffin House Hotel was located. It didn't look like any part of Cleveland that he had ever seen; nor any part of downtown Detroit, either.

He had lost his cellphone, and there was no phone beside the bed, so there was no way that he could call the reception desk for help. He thought of climbing out of the window on to the fire escape, and then down to the ground, but what would happen if he did that? In reality, this room was on the first floor. If he accepted an alternative reality, maybe he would become trapped in that alternative reality forever, and never be able to come back.

He was still staring out of the window when he heard a woman's voice calling out. It was so weak that it was barely audible, and it sounded bubbly, as if she had a mouthful of water. '*Please. Please don't leave me here. Please.*'

Lincoln felt a crawling sensation all the way down his back. He turned around and saw that a woman was lying diagonally on the bed, half covered by a stained pink satin quilt. She was dark-skinned, with a plump heart-shaped face and thick wavy black hair – Hispanic, or mixed race. There were plum-colored circles under her eyes, or they could have been bruises. On her left cheek she had a large black beauty-spot, or maybe a mole. Her lips were scarlet and shiny, as if she had thickly applied too bright a shade of lipstick.

'Please don't leave me,' the woman whispered. She had a strong Spanish accent.

'OK, lady,' said Lincoln, trying to sound reassuring. 'I'll try to get you some help.'

'No use doing that,' the woman told him.

'What happened? How did you get in here?'

'*He* brought me here. *El prestidigitator*. He caught me, and he brought me here.'

'Who did?'

'I don't know his name. Don't leave me, please. I'm dying.'

'Are you sick? Did this guy beat up on you? What?'

The woman closed her eyes and didn't answer him. Lincoln hesitated, not knowing if he should try to shake her awake. Probably best not to touch her, he thought. She might have a neck or a spinal injury, and shaking could prove fatal.

He went back over to the door and gave it another kick. 'Open this door!' he screamed. 'Open this fucking door! There's a woman dying in here! Help me!'

There was no response. Lincoln looked back at the bed and the woman still had her eyes closed. What the hell was he going to do now? He could go on kicking at the door but if nobody could hear him what was the point? He could wait until morning, for the hotel housekeepers to do their rounds, but quite apart from the fact that the woman on the bed was close to dying, it was already daylight outside, so when *would* it be morning? And how would the housekeepers get in here, if this was a different reality?

He was still standing by the door when his decision was made for him. He saw nobody and heard nothing, but suddenly he caught the strong raw smell of gasoline, as if somebody had splashed it all around the room. He sniffed, and sniffed again. The smell was so strong that it burned his throat and made his eyes water.

Then – without any warning at all, the woman on the bed exploded into flames. A wave of heat seared Lincoln's face and he stumbled backward, lifting up his hand to shield his eyes. Within seconds, the whole mattress was blazing like a bonfire. Lincoln tried to edge closer, but the heat was so intense that he couldn't get anywhere near enough to drag the woman off the bed. Lurid orange flames licked right up to the ceiling and the bedroom rapidly began to fill up with whirling sparks and billowing brown smoke.

Although she was burning from head to foot, the woman didn't move, or cry out, so Lincoln guessed that she must have died a few minutes before when she had closed her eyes. But in any case there was no time to think of trying to save her. The linoleum flooring was ablaze, spitting and shriveling as it burned, and he knew that he had to get out of the bedroom somehow or *he* was going to die, too – and in only a few seconds. Fifteen years ago, his uncle and his aunt and his four cousins had all died in a house fire in Brightmoor. They had been overwhelmed by toxic smoke in less than two minutes, huddled together behind a front door that they hadn't had the strength to open.

Lincoln pulled out his handkerchief, folded it into a pad, and pressed it against his nose and his mouth. Then – keeping as low as he could – he crouched his way toward the bathroom. In spite of the fire, he was still reluctant to climb out of the window, in case he could never climb back. He reasoned that he could break open the bathroom window if he needed ventilation, and there was plenty of water there, too.

He pushed his way through the bathroom door and quickly slammed it shut behind him. Then he dragged the soggy towel across the floor and wedged it underneath the door to keep the smoke out. He stood for a while with both hands pressed against the wall, coughing and wheezing. He was still shocked and bewildered by the way in which the Hispanic-looking woman had appeared as if from nowhere, and the way in which she had abruptly caught fire. He had smelled gasoline in the seconds before the bed had exploded, for sure, but where had it come from?

He turned around, with his back to the wall, trying to suppress his coughing. If smoke started to seep into the bathroom, he guessed that he could balance on the edge of the bath, break open the window and squeeze his way out. The window frame was just about wide enough. But for all he knew it was a sheer three-story drop out there, and even if he managed to escape uninjured, would he ever be able to climb back in again?

Maybe this is nothing but a nightmare, he thought. *Maybe I was overtired and I went to bed and I'm simply dreaming all this. It can't be happening. It's impossible.*

He reached out cautiously and touched the brass door-handle. It was already too hot for him to hold, and the door panels were growing warmer, as well. He began to think that he had made the wrong decision, shutting himself in the bathroom. At least there had been a fire escape outside the bedroom window, no matter what reality it might have led him into.

He was sweating now, and he wiped his forehead with his shirtsleeve. As he did so, he heard a shuffling noise inside the shower stall. He had seen a dark shape inside it before, but he had assumed that it was nothing but a combination of dirt and shadows. Now he could see that it was moving. Something inside the shower stall was alive.

'Who's that?' he called out. 'Come out here where I can see you!'

There was no answer, and he felt too foolish to call out a second time, in case it was nothing but an optical illusion, or maybe an animal that had gotten itself trapped – a dog or a cat or a raccoon. But then the shower stall door was pushed open with a reverberating shudder, and a man stepped out of it.

Lincoln opened and closed his mouth, and coughed, but he couldn't find the breath inside him to speak.

The man was tall – at least as tall as Lincoln, and maybe an inch or two more – but he was also very thin, with arms and legs that were disproportionately long. He was wearing a black tuxedo with a black silk vest underneath it, and a black shirt with a black bow-tie. His hair was white and ragged and almost shoulder length. What alarmed Lincoln about him the most, however, was his face. It was very pale gray, like a face in a black-and-white photograph, and it was *blurred*, as if he had moved when he was having his photograph taken. Lincoln could make out the dark smudges of his eyes, and the upward-sloping curve of his lips, but that was all. The rest of his features seemed to be permanently out of focus.

'I warned you not to come, now, didn't I?' the man told him, hoarsely. 'You would not listen to me, though, would you? You out-and-out refused to listen.'

'Who are you?' Lincoln demanded. 'What the hell is going on here?'

'Things that are no concern of yours, Lincoln. Things that you would have been wiser to stay ignorant of. But of course it is much too late now, isn't it? You have come here, in spite of the fact that I specifically asked you not to, and you have witnessed what you have witnessed. And I cannot risk *anybody* interfering in what I am doing here. Not you. Nobody.'

'But there's a woman dead out there!' Lincoln protested. 'There's a woman dead out there and the whole goddamned bedroom is on fire! It isn't even my bedroom! And this sure as hell isn't my bathroom, either!'

The gray-faced man tapped his forehead. 'It is the power of the mind, Lincoln, that is what it is. It is the power of the human imagination, unbridled by consciousness. The power of dreams.'

'I don't understand one goddamned word of what you're talking about,' Lincoln told him. 'I don't *want* to know, either. All's I know is, I want to be back in my real hotel room, back in my real reality.'

The gray-faced man shook his head so that his ratty white hair swung from side to side. 'Not possible, Lincoln. You would speak to people and those people would not necessarily understand what I am doing here, but *they* could well speak to other people who *do* understand, and then it would be mayhem.' He paused, and then he said, '"*Mayhem*," from the Anglo-Saxon word meaning to *maim*, or to seriously injure.'

Behind Lincoln, the bathroom door cracked loudly as the heat from the bedroom split the wood. Without any further hesitation, the gray-faced man reached into the shower stall and took out a long cross-cut saw. He lifted it up in front of Lincoln's face and took hold of the end of the blade, so that he could flex it one way and then the other.

'See this, Lincoln? The tool of my trade. Fine Pennsylvania steel with champion-pattern teeth. Cuts through anything, this beauty, faster than any chainsaw.'

Lincoln said nothing, but backed away as far as he could. The gray-faced man came after him, still flexing the saw blade so that it went *whoop – whoop – whoop*.

'You cannot say that I did not give you fair warning, Lincoln,' said the gray-faced man. He was much closer now, and Lincoln found it even more disconcerting than ever that his features were so blurred. It was just as if his face were shaped out of nothing but fog.

'You stay away from me,' said Lincoln. 'If you take even one step closer—'

'You will do *what*, exactly? Scream like a girl, like they all do? They *all* scream, you know, every one of them! They howl like bitches, men and women both! I have never known a single one of them suffer in silence. It is against human nature.'

He stopped flexing the saw, and then without any hesitation at all he slashed it diagonally across Lincoln's right shoulder. It cut through Lincoln's shirt and into his deltoid muscle, almost a half inch deep, and Lincoln could actually hear his flesh rip. Blood sprayed down his arm, all the way to his elbow, and spattered across his cuff.

He crashed backward against the bathroom door and tried to grab the gray-faced man's wrist, but the gray-faced man yanked the saw vertically downward and its irregular teeth tore into Lincoln's knuckles. Lincoln pushed him, hard, with both hands, and the gray-faced man staggered backward, but at the same time the edge of the saw almost took Lincoln's right thumb off. Suddenly there was blood flying everywhere, like a scarlet blizzard.

Neither of them spoke as the gray-faced man came for Lincoln again, swishing the saw blade from side to side as if it were a saber. Lincoln thought: *he's going to kill me. He's going to cut off my fingers and cut my face apart and then he's going to cut my fucking head off.*

There was only one way to escape. As the gray-faced man came closer, he reached across and took hold of the bathroom door-handle. The handle was so hot that it blistered his fingers instantly, and he shouted out '*Aahhhh*! *Shit*!' The wet towel was tangled underneath it but he pulled the door open as wide as he could, keeping himself shielded behind it as he did so.

With a roar like a ravenous lion, a huge orange fireball rolled into the bathroom, hungry for all the oxygen that it could devour. The gray-faced man lost his balance and stumbled backward, colliding with the shower stall and cracking the glass. He didn't lose his grip on his saw, however, and the instant the fireball had dissipated he came for Lincoln again, slashing the saw blade even more violently so that it whistled and sang as it cut its way through the air.

'They *all* scream, Lincoln!' he repeated, in that thick, hoarse voice. 'They *all* scream, every one of them! They howl like bitches! And *you*, Lincoln – you will be no exception!'

Lincoln wrenched the bathroom door even wider. The bedroom was filled with dense brown smoke now, and through the smoke he could see flames dancing like demons dancing in hell. The heat was overwhelming but he knew that he had no choice. He took a deep breath and plunged right into the inferno, keeping his hands held high to protect his face.

'*Fool*!' screamed the gray-faced man. 'You really think you can get away?'

The gray-faced man started to come after him, slashing at the smoke, but Lincoln had managed to find his way to the window. He twisted the catch, burning his fingers again, and heaved the window upward.

Immediately, a huge rush of cold air blew into the bedroom, sprinkled with raindrops. With a deep *whoomph*! the flames jumped up like a fiery Mexican wave, and the gray-faced man temporarily disappeared behind them. Lincoln felt the heat on the side of his face and he could smell his own hair burning, but he climbed out of the window on to the fire escape and dragged down the window behind him. As he did so, he could see the gray-faced man through the flames, with his cross-cut saw still lifted, as if to warn him that this wasn't over yet.

Lincoln looked over the railing. Three stories below him, a narrow alley ran between this building and a derelict warehouse next door, crowded with broken crates and empty window-frames and overflowing trash cans. He grasped the wet handrail and started to make his way down. It was too late now to worry what reality this might be, and if he would ever be able to return. As far as he was concerned he was lucky just to be alive.

He had only just started going down the second storey when one of the metal treads gave way beneath him. His left foot plunged through the gap, right up to the ankle, and the broken tread fell all the way down to the alley, bouncing and clanging when it reached the ground. He lurched forward, grabbing both handrails to stop himself from falling, but then the next tread gave way, and the next, and then the entire section of fire escape on which he was standing came tearing away from the wall.

He didn't know why he continued to grip the handrails, because the whole structure was plummeting into the alley, but there was nothing else for him to hold on to. He wasn't aware of any sound, no banging or clattering, although the noise of the collapsing fire escape must have been a deafening cacophony of falling metal.

All he heard was the rush of air in his ears as he dropped toward the alley below him, as if he were an angel dropping from a great height. He didn't even hear himself hitting the ground.

FOUR

Rooms 237 and 239

Kieran was sitting up in bed watching *Paranormal Activity* and eating handfuls of chili peanuts when Kiera came in through the connecting door in her bright pink knee-length pajamas.

She climbed on to the bed next to him and said, 'What are

you watching this crap for? You have enough trouble sleeping without watching scary movies.'

Kieran clapped another handful of peanuts against his mouth. 'It's good. It's all about this girl who thinks she's being stalked by this demon and she can't get away from it.'

'The same way that *I* am, you mean, by Mickey Veralnik?'

'Mickey Veralnik isn't a demon. He's just a crappy two-bit pain-in-the-ass promoter. You shouldn't pay him any mind.'

'But he's always *there*, right in my face, isn't he? When has he ever missed one single concert? Or one single promotion? Or one single TV special? Don't tell me he won't be sitting in the front row tomorrow night. I'm sick of the sight of him grinning at me and giving me those winks and those little finger-waves. And those endless text messages. "Kiera I know you're a twin but you're the true star! You could shine so much more brightly if you only dumped your brother and let me handle your meteoric rise to fame and fortune!"'

Kieran shrugged. 'Maybe you *should* go solo. You always sang a hundred times better than me.'

Kiera scruffed up his thick blond hair and gave his shoulder a shove. 'We're the Kaiser Twins, stupid! And even if I *did* split up with you, I wouldn't let Mickey Veralnik handle me. I mean, like, *yuck*! That comb-over! And bad breath or what?'

Kieran continued to chew for a while. Then he said, 'What if *I* was to split up with *you*?'

'What do you mean? You don't seriously want to split up with me, do you?'

'I don't know. Yes. No. I guess I'm just bushed, that's all. All this fricking traveling. I don't even know which city we're supposed to be in.'

'Cleveland, Ohio. Tomorrow we open at the State Theater at Playhouse Square for three alternate nights and then we're off to not-so-sunny Cincinnati.'

'Cleveland. Jesus. To think we got famous to wind up in Cleveland – the Mistake on the Lake. If that's not a fricking paradox, I don't know what is.'

The twins sat on the bed in silence for a while. They were seventeen-and-a-half years old, although Kiera was actually older than Kieran by thirty-one minutes. They had blond hair and faces that were almost ethereally good-looking, with wide green eyes and straight Grecian noses and sensual lips. Their manager Lois Schulz often said that they reminded her of the very young Elvis Presley and his twin Jessie – 'Well, they would if Jessie had been a girl instead of a boy, and if he hadn't been stillborn.' Lois often came out with remarks like that.

In actual fact they looked like their mother Jenyfer Kaiser, who had died of an apparent stroke only two hours after giving birth to them. Their father Jim had raised them as if they were the most precious children on earth – and to him, of course, they had been. They were the living reminder of the woman he had loved so much and lost.

Kieran and Kiera had always sung songs together, ever since they were very small. They used to swing on their swing set at the end of their yard in Brentwood, harmonizing *Puff, The Magic Dragon.* To them, singing together was as natural as talking. When they were sixteen Lois had heard them singing in their high school musical *Grease* and had persuaded their father to let her take them on. Within two months they had appeared on *America's Got Talent* and won rapturous applause from the audience, and the day after their sixteenth birthday they had been signed by Sony. Their first album *Kaiser Twins* had reached number nine on the Billboard Top 100.

'I don't know why you think this movie is so scary,' said Kiera, frowning at the TV. 'Ghosts never hurt people, do they? Not real ghosts.'

'That old bum was scary,' Kieran reminded her. 'That one we saw on Santa Monica Boulevard.'

'Well, kind of. But he didn't actually do anybody any real harm, did he? Just stepping right out in front of cars like that.'

'He could have caused a serious accident.'

'Only in somebody's pants.'

Kieran gave his sister a wry smile and shook his head. 'What time do they want us for the run-through tomorrow?'

'Early. Seven at the latest. Lois wants us to make some changes. She wants us to finish up with *Magic Mirror* instead of *I Love The World And The World Loves Me.* She thinks it's much more upbeat and the audience always sing along so we can make it into a really grand finale. She's even hired a twelve-piece horn section.'

'Jesus. I don't know why she doesn't go the whole hog and bring in the Mormon Tabernacle Choir.'

'Oh, come on, Kieran, it's going to be amazing. There's

going to be *hundreds* more mirrors, too, so the whole stage is going to be sparkling.'

Kieran smacked the chili powder from his hands. 'You love all of this, don't you?'

'What, and you don't?'

'Sure I do. I just don't want to spend the rest of my life singing *I Love The World And The World Loves Me,* over and over and over, until I'm about a hundred-and-eleven years old. At some time in my life I want to do something important – something that really makes a difference.'

'Our *singing* makes a difference. We make millions of people happy, don't we?'

'Pizza makes millions of people happy, but that doesn't mean it's important. If you woke up tomorrow and nobody had ever heard of pizza, what difference would it make? Same with us.'

'So what do you want to do? Run for the White House?'

'I don't know. I can't describe it exactly, but I feel like I have this destiny waiting for me.'

'Oka–a–ay,' said Kiera, uncertainly. 'Maybe you'll go to med school after all, and be like some really famous surgeon. I know plenty of people who could do with a head transplant – Mickey Veralnik, for one.'

'You should forget about Mickey Veralnik. I keep telling you, he's not worth it.'

'And you should stop watching this stupid movie and get some sleep. It's half after one already.'

She reached over to grab the remote but Kieran snatched it away from her. 'Just because you're a half hour older than me, that doesn't mean you can tell me what to do. I want to watch the end of this, OK?'

'Have it your way. But if you have one of your nightmares again and you feel like crap tomorrow morning, don't blame me.'

'Do I ever blame you for anything?'

'Yes. Always.'

Kieran flicked a peanut at her and it bounced off her nose. In retaliation, Kiera picked up one of the pillows and whacked him over the head, so that he spilled his peanuts all over the bedcover. '*Shit*!' said Kieran, and hit her with his own pillow. Kiera hit him back and then the two of them clambered to their feet and stood on the bed, bouncing up and down and bashing each other with their pillows.

Eventually – panting and laughing – they both lost their balance and fell over sideways. They lay on the bed, breathless, looking into each other's green eyes. Even after all of these years of growing up together, they still found it a source of fascination that they should look so much alike, and think so much alike. For each of them, it was like owning a mirror which could talk back.

Kiera reached out and stroked Kieran's hair. 'You need a haircut. Your hair is almost as long as mine.'

Kieran said, 'The last time I had a haircut we saw that dead guy, remember?'

'Oh, so you're not going to get a haircut because you're scared you might see him again?'

Kieran said nothing but shook his head. It had been over two months ago but they could both visualize him as clearly as if he were sitting in the bedroom with them now. Kieran had been having his hair cut in the old-fashioned barbershop in the Handlery Hotel in San Francisco. It was a long, mirrored room with a dozen red-leather chairs in a row, and a row of white basins. Kieran had been sitting two chairs away from a bulky, balding man who appeared to be asleep. Nobody was cutting his hair or shaving him, even though there were two barbers at the far end of the room, talking to each other and laughing. Kiera had come into the barbershop, carrying a whole bunch of shopping bags, and said, 'You should see the dress I've just bought! Prada, seventeen hundred dollars!'

The barber who was cutting Kieran's hair had gone to fetch more towels. Kiera had said to Kieran, 'What's the matter with *that* guy? He looks like he's asleep.'

It was then that they had both noticed that the towel around the man's neck was stained bright red, and that the stain was rapidly spreading. Kiera had gone over to him and said, 'Sir? Sir? Are you OK? You look like you're bleeding.'

She had turned his chair around and it was then that the man's head had suddenly dropped to one side, revealing that his neck had been cut open all the way back to his spine. Kiera had looked at Kieran in horror, but they had both realized that what they were seeing was a memory of a dead man, an after-image, like all the ghosts they saw. None of the barbers were cutting his hair or paying him any attention because in reality he simply wasn't there.

Later they had Googled the history of the Handlery Hotel and discovered that Tony Sciarro, a San Francisco gangster, had been murdered in the barbershop in September of nineteen thirty-seven by a man who was dressed as a barber. One diagonal cut with a straight razor had almost taken his head off. His murderer was never identified or caught.

Kiera climbed off the bed and rearranged the pillows. 'Seriously, Kieran, you need to get some sleep. I'll wake you up at six.'

'Make that six fifty-nine. It won't take me more than a minute to get dressed.'

She came up to him and hugged him and gave him a kiss. 'Sweet dreams,' she said. 'And I *mean* it. None of your nightmares.'

A few minutes after three in the morning, Kiera was woken by a soft sighing noise. At first she thought it was a woman crying, but it went on and on for over five minutes, low and persistent, and she realized then that it couldn't be a woman because a woman would have had to pause for breath.

She sat up in bed and listened. After a while she heard a light pattering sound, too, and she thought: *rain*. That's what it sounded like, rain. And the sighing was the wind, blowing underneath the connecting door to Kieran's bedroom.

She could *smell* rain, too, and wet soil; and when she drew back the bedcovers and put her feet on the carpet, she could feel the wind blowing cold against her legs.

She switched on her bedside lamp. Then she crossed over to the door and pressed her ear against it. Before she opened the door she wanted to make sure that she wasn't hearing things. Kieran would inevitably wake up if she entered his room, and he had always found it very difficult to get to sleep. When he was little she had often woken up in the middle of the night to find him standing beside her bed, staring at her, like the girl in *Paranormal Activity*.

Not only could she hear rain pattering against the other side of the door, however, and feel the wind blowing, she could hear thunder, or what sounded like thunder – a deep rumbling sound punctuated by an intermittent *slap*! *slap*! *slap*!

She opened the door, and was immediately met with a strong, blustery wind and freezing cold rain. Kieran's bedroom was no longer a bedroom, it was a steeply-sloping field, and it was no longer night-time, either, although the sky was dark. Low gray clouds hurtled above Kiera's head like an endless pack of hungry wolves, and the long wet grass lashed at her ankles.

On the horizon she could see a stand of oak trees silhouetted against the sky, their branches thrashing and waving in the storm. Not far away, there was an assortment of geometric shapes – triangles and rhomboids and rectangles – that looked like tents. They could have been a military encampment, or a traveling circus. The rumbling and the snapping was the sound of the wind blowing through their flysheets.

Kiera stood in the doorway in disbelief. She turned around, and there behind her was her hotel bedroom, with the bedside lamp shining and the bedcover turned back. She could clearly see her pink robe hanging over the back of the chair. Yet here in front of her was a wild, blustery hillside, and it had to be just as real as her bedroom because she could feel the rain on her face and hear the wind whistling. Where was Kieran's bedroom? And more urgently, where was Kieran?

'Kieran!' she shouted. 'Kieran – where are you?'

Reluctantly, she walked a few yards further into the field. The storm was roaring so loudly that she could hardly hear her own voice, and it began to rain even harder, so that her pajamas were soaked through and clung to her skin and raindrops dripped from the end of her nose. '*Kieran*!' she screamed. '*Kieran*!'

She looked back at her bedroom. She was frightened that the door might close, or disappear altogether, so that she would have to stay here, wherever this was. But so far her bedroom was still there, warm and tranquil, with the bedside lamp still shining.

She smeared the rain from her face with the back of her hand. She was so cold now that she was shivering. She wondered if there was any point in continuing to look for Kieran. If this wasn't his hotel bedroom then maybe he wasn't here at all. Maybe this was nothing but a nightmare and she was still in bed. But it felt far too real to be a nightmare.

She was still trying to make up her mind what to do when – all around the darkened tents – she saw strings of colored lights winking on. There were dozens of them, every one of them blood-red. She could also see an illuminated wrought-iron archway, with illuminated letters on top of it, although from where she was standing she couldn't make out what the letters said. She could hear music, too, carried on the wind. Odd, discordant and eerie, like a barrel organ that was badly out of key.

She turned around and started to high-step her way back through the long wet grass to her bedroom. She had gone only a short distance, however, when she saw Kieran standing about fifty yards away, off to her left. He was bare-chested and his pajama pants were as wet as hers. He had his face lifted toward the wind and the rain but his eyes were closed as if he were praying.

'*Kieran*!' she called him, and hurried over.

He opened his eyes and stared at her. For a split second he looked as if he didn't recognize her.

'Kieran, it's me! Are you all right?'

She took hold of both of his hands. He felt as cold as she did.

'We have to go find her,' he said.

'What do you mean? Who?'

'She's up there. She's been up there all the time.'

'I don't know what you're talking about. Who's been up there all the time?'

Kieran pulled his hands away and started to walk uphill, toward the trees and the tents. Kiera ran after him and caught hold of his arm. 'Kieran – where are you going? We don't even know where this place is! This is supposed to be your hotel room, not a field!'

'It's a dream,' said Kieran.

'How can it be a dream? I can *feel* it! Look at me – I'm soaked to the skin!'

'It's not my dream. It's not yours, either. It's somebody else's. That's why it feels so real.'

'What do you mean? How can we both be in somebody else's dream?'

'I don't know, but we are. And I know that she's up there and we have to go find her.'

'Who's up there?'

Kieran lifted his hand and touched Kiera's forehead with his fingertips. 'Can't you feel her? *I* can feel her.'

Kiera looked at him in bewilderment. But she began to feel a rising sense of excitement, too. She thought she knew who he was talking about. It was impossible, but so was this sloping field, and so was this wind and so was this rain.

'You mean *Mom*?' she said.

Kieran lowered his hand and nodded. 'She's up there someplace. She's been there all the time, ever since the day that you and me were born.'

'How can that be? She didn't go away or anything. She *died*, Kieran.'

'How many times have you and I seen dead people? Dozens.'

'Yes, but none of them was anybody we knew, were they? And we've never seen mom.'

Kieran took hold of Kiera's hand. 'Come on,' he said. 'She's up there and she needs us.'

Kiera looked up at the dark, billowing tents, and the strings of red lights that flickered in the wind like blood cells pouring through human arteries. 'I don't know,' she said. 'I don't like the look of those tents at all. And even if we do find Mom, what then? She's dead. She won't be able to come back with us.'

'Let's just see if she's there first.'

'I don't know, Kieran. It's really scary.'

'Yes, but I'm sure mom knows that we're here. What is she going to think of us if we turn our backs on her and leave her, just because we're chickenshit?'

Kiera took a deep, shivery breath. 'OK, then. But if we can't find her we go back through my bedroom door and we close it and we keep it closed.'

Still holding hands, they struggled up the hill. In some places the grass was waist high, and Kiera felt as if she were wading through a stormy sea. In other places the ground underfoot was rocky and loose, like shale, and they found it difficult to keep their footing.

Several times Kiera turned back to make sure that her bedroom doorway was still there. It was standing in the middle of the wildly-waving grass, softly lit, an unearthly vision of the real world that they had left behind them. She felt like telling Kieran that they ought to go back. Their mother had been dead for seventeen-and-a-half years, and even if they found her, what could they do to help her? But Kieran kept on pulling her up the hill, and his urgency seemed to increase with every step.

At last they reached the encampment. More than a dozen tents and small canvas pavilions were clustered around a huge black marquee, as well as seven or eight trailers and old-style horse-drawn caravans, all of them painted in shiny black varnish and beaded with raindrops. The blood-red lights were strung up everywhere, from one tent to the next, and all around the top of the marquee.

The barrel-organ music was still playing but Kiera found it difficult to tell where it was coming from, because it faded and swelled in the wind. It was a discordant version of *In The Good Old Summertime*, which she and Kieran used to sing together when they were very little, and she couldn't help herself from silently singing the words in her head.

'*In the good old summertime – in the good old summertime—*'

Several of the tents or trailers were lit up inside, but all of the tent flaps were tightly secured and the trailers had black blinds drawn down at every window. It was raining even harder now and the rumble-*slap*! of wet canvas was almost deafening.

Kieran and Kiera made their way around to the front of the marquee. From this angle they could read the red illuminated letters on top of the archway, even though they were trembling in the wind. They said *Albrecht's Traveling Circus & Freak Show*.

Kiera tugged anxiously at Kieran's hand. 'Kieran – she can't be here. I think we're making a mistake. Let's go back.'

'*—strolling through the shady lanes with your baby mine—*'

Kieran said, 'No – I'm sure she's here! It's almost like I can hear her calling to us! Come on – let's just take a quick scout around.'

He went through the archway but Kiera stayed where she was. She had such a bad feeling about this. 'Kieran,' she said. 'Please don't. I'm really frightened.'

Kieran went up to the front of the marquee and took hold of the flap. 'Come on, sis . . . it's only some old circus.'

'Yes, but *freak show*? Who has freak shows these days?'

'I don't know. But there's only one way to find out.'

'*—you hold her hand, and she holds yours, and that's a very good sign—*'

He drew back the flap and pushed his way inside. Kiera hesitated for a moment and then she followed him. The flap was heavy and wet and smelled of soil and diesel oil, and something else, too – something that brought back a strong childhood memory. Popcorn.

Once through the flap, the twins found themselves in a small, stuffy vestibule, not much larger than the inside of a wardrobe, and when the flap fell back it was totally dark inside. Kiera nearly panicked, because she hated confined spaces. But then Kieran pulled back the second flap, and they stepped into the main marquee.

The marquee appeared much larger on the inside than it had from the outside, with at least a dozen gasoliers suspended from the roof, and dark red drapes all around the walls, arranged in swags. Tiers of wooden seats were arranged around a low boarded stage. It was more like an old-time vaudeville theater than a circus tent.

'*—that she's your tootsie-wootsie – in the good old summer-time—*'

Kieran walked out on to the stage and circled around. 'Anybody here?' he called out. 'Hallo there! Anybody here?'

Kiera said, 'For God's sake, Kieran. Supposing there *is* somebody here? We're trespassing!'

'I know – but they're not going to be mad at us, are they? Circus folk, they're always real friendly.'

'Oh, yes? And how do you know? You've never been to a circus in your life.'

'I saw *Toby Tyler*.'

'Oh, sure. And I saw *Something Wicked This Way Comes*.'

Kieran called out again. 'Halloo! Anybody here?' But again there was no reply.

'Come on, let's go,' Kiera urged him. 'This place really creeps me out. And don't forget that we have a rehearsal first thing tomorrow. We have to get at least a couple hours' sleep.'

'OK, OK. But I want to take a quick look around outside.'

They were about to leave the marquee when they heard a sudden clattering of feet behind the tiers of seats. They turned around – just in time to see a diminutive figure in a yellow coat running across the other side of the marquee, a figure no taller than a six-year-old boy. It disappeared almost immediately behind a fold in the canvas.

Kieran seized Kiera's hand and pulled her across the stage and up the aisle between the seats.

'*No*!' Kiera protested.

But Kieran said, 'Think about it! He must know where Mom is!'

'Kieran, Mom's *dead*! This is crazy!'

'Don't tell me that you don't feel her!'

They reached the far side of the marquee and Kieran ran along the canvas wall, pulling it and thumping at it with the flat of his hand, trying to find the fold into which the figure in the yellow coat had disappeared. Kiera stood watching him, exhausted and afraid, but she knew better than to try and persuade him to give it up and come back to her hotel room. Once Kieran had his mind set on doing something, he always pursued it to the bitter end.

'Here!' he called out, lifting up the canvas to reveal an opening.

'*Kieran—*'

'Come on! Hurry!'

He pushed his way into the opening and Kiera followed him. They had a brief moment of battling with the canvas, and then they were out in the open again, amongst the trailers and the caravans, with the wind and the rain in their faces.

'Can you see him?' Kieran shouted. 'I can't see him anywhere!'

They walked quickly between the lines of trailers, looking left and right – even ducking down now and again to see if the figure in the yellow coat was crouching underneath. They reached the last trailer, and they were about to turn back when a dazzling flash of lightning lit up the whole encampment, and in that bleached-out flash they saw the figure in the yellow coat running toward one of the caravans and scaling the ladder at the back of it. The figure knocked frantically at the stable door, and the lower half of the door was immediately opened up. Before the figure scuttled inside, however, it turned its head toward them for a split second so that Kieran and Kiera caught a glimpse of it.

'*Jesus*,' said Kieran, and Kiera felt a terrible thrill of shock.

Although he was dressed as a boy, in his yellow tweed coat, the figure looked more like a giant rodent. His face was covered in brindled hair, even his cheeks and his forehead, and he had a long pointed snout rather than a nose, and protruding brown teeth. His eyes glittered as black as buttons.

He vanished into the stable door, and slammed it shut behind him, and as he did so there was a shattering burst of thunder, as if the whole sky above their heads were collapsing.

'What the hell was *that* thing?' asked Kieran.

'I guess he must be one of the freaks. Rat Man, or something like that. My God. We should really get out of here, Kieran. I mean it.'

'But Mom's here, Kiera. I *know* she is. What if we go back to your bedroom and this place disappears and we can never find it again?'

'You said it was somebody's dream.'

'I know, and I'm pretty sure that it is. But sooner or later they're going to wake up and it's all going to vanish. And what are the chances that they will never have the same dream again – like, *ever*? What's going to happen to Mom then? How will we ever find her then?'

Kiera squeezed her eyes tight shut and covered her face with her hands. This was all madness. How could the two of them be in somebody else's dream? How could their dead mother be in somebody else's dream?

Kieran laid his hands on her shoulders and said, 'Let's give it one last try, OK? Let's go over to that caravan and knock on the door and ask them if they know where mom is. If they don't know what the hell we're talking about, we'll go right back to your room and close the door and try to forget this ever happened. Is that a deal?'

Kiera lowered her hands and opened her eyes. Kieran looked so much like her that she almost felt as if she were appealing to herself.

'All right,' she said. 'But be really careful, won't you? That Rat Man might bite you.'

'Oh, come on. The way he skedaddled off like that, he's probably a whole lot scareder of us than we are of him.'

They crossed over to the caravan into which the figure in the yellow coat had just disappeared. It reminded Kiera of Professor Marvel's caravan in *The Wizard of Oz*, except that it was varnished black and it had a frieze of carved wooden faces all the way around the overhanging roof – some of them leering, some of them scowling, some of them screaming. The rain dripped from every face as if they were all weeping, either with rage or disappointment or fear.

Kieran climbed the three steps up to the stable door. He glanced back at Kiera and then he knocked.

He waited, but there was no answer, and so he knocked again, harder this time. 'Is there anybody in there? We only want to ask you something, that's all! We're not going to hurt you or nothing!'

He waited again. He was just about to try knocking a third time when the shuttered windows in the stable door were both opened up. A bald, white-faced man appeared, wearing tiny wire-rimmed spectacles with mirror lenses. He had a silver ring through his nose and silver hoop earrings in each ear. He was wearing what looked like a silver satin cloak.

'What do you want?' he demanded, in a tired, impatient tone. He had an accent that sounded Eastern European. Czech, maybe.

Kieran said, 'We don't want to disturb you, sir, but we think our mom may be here someplace. In fact, we're sure that she is.'

The bald man looked Kieran up and down, and then looked at Kiera.

'What if she is?' he asked them.

'What do you think? We'd like to see her, of course.'

'And you think that this would do either of you any good?'

'Well, sure. We thought that she died when we were born, but if she didn't – I mean, we have seventeen years to catch up on.'

'You thought that she died?'

'That's what we've always been told.'

The bald man pursed his lips for a moment, as if he were sucking a very sour candy, or thinking. Then he said, 'I suppose it depends on your definition of dying.'

'What do you mean? Either she's dead or she isn't.'

'You think so? You don't know too much about dying then.'

Kiera was shivering and wetter than ever. 'Is our mom here or not?' she called out.

The bald man nodded. 'Yes, she's here OK. But I don't know if you'll be very glad to see her.'

'Just tell us where she is,' said Kieran. 'We'll decide if we're glad to see her when we see her.'

'Very well,' the bald man agreed, with a sigh. He turned back toward the interior of the caravan and said, sharply, 'Stay here, will you? I'm taking these young people to see Demi.'

Kiera couldn't hear the reply clearly, but it sounded harsh and guttural. She looked at Kieran as he climbed down from the back of the caravan but Kieran could only shrug and pull a face to show that he didn't understand what the Rat Man was saying, either.

The bald man closed the two windows in the stable door but reappeared a few moments later wearing a black ankle-length raincoat and a wide-brimmed waterproof hat. He came down the steps and approached them. He wasn't tall, but there was a strongman solidity about him which Kiera found quite intimidating. She felt that you would need to hit him very hard, over and over again, with something like a ball-peen hammer, before he would even blink.

'You're certain you want to do this?' he asked them. He pronounced it 'vont'.

'Yes, we do vont,' said Kieran, trying to sound challenging.

Without another word, the bald man turned and started to walk away, beckoning them to follow him. He led them between the trailers and the caravans, past a fenced-off corral in which twenty or thirty miserable-looking horses were standing in the rain, their heads down and their manes dripping, and a line of massive black Diamond-T trucks, pre-World War Two vintage by the look of them.

They came at last to a small black pavilion, with an awning in front of it which had filled up with so much rainwater that it was sagging between its poles. The bald man drew back the entrance flap and Kieran and Kiera could see that the interior was illuminated by an oil-lamp with a dim green glass shade.

'Demi!' the bald man called out. 'Demi, it's Zachary!'

Kiera looked at Kieran and said, under her breath, 'Mom's name was Jenyfer. Why is he calling her "Demi"?'

Kieran shook his head. 'Maybe it's like a stage name.'

'Demi, you're not sleeping are you? I brung two young people to see you. I think you might recognize them.'

Kiera heard a faint, sibilant voice saying 'What time is it?'

'It's ten minutes of two. You weren't sleeping, were you?'

'No. You know me. I haven't slept in days.'

'You want to see these young people or not? It's up to you, my darling. You don't have to if you don't want to.'

'No . . . all right. I'll see them.'

The bald man pulled back the flap and said to Kieran and Kiera, 'Go on. You can go inside. But remember that she is very delicate. I don't want you to upset her, no matter what you think.'

Kiera ducked her head and went inside the pavilion, with Kieran right behind her. They found themselves in an airless living area lined with moth-eaten velvet drapes in faded maroon. On the right-hand side of the pavilion there was a gilded couch with maroon velvet cushions to match the drapes, and a gilded table with a bowl of black grapes on it. A ghostly-looking gray cat was sleeping on the couch, but as they came into the pavilion it opened its eyes and stared at them with suspicion.

But it was the tall gilded chair on the left-hand side of the pavilion that riveted their attention. It was more like a royal throne than a chair, and the woman who was sitting in it was wearing a coronet of dried flowers. She was startlingly pale, and very thin, and her hair was dead white instead of blonde, but there was no mistaking her resemblance to Kieran and Kiera. She had the same sea-green eyes and the same straight nose and the same sensual curve to her lips.

She was wearing a tight black velvet dress with a high collar and a row of small jet buttons all the way down the front. Her thin, bony hands were resting on the arms of the chair, with long black-varnished fingernails and silver rings on every finger.

The bald man joined them inside the pavilion and took off his hat, deliberately shaking the raindrops over the cat so that it flinched and hissed at him.

'Here is Demi,' he announced. 'Demi, here is your twins.'

'My *twins*?' asked the woman. Her voice was weak but it was very clear. 'How could I have children?'

Kiera could hardly breathe. The interior of the pavilion was very stuffy and here she was, face-to-face with the mother she had always believed to be dead.

'Mom?' she said. 'It's Kiera – Kiera and Kieran.'

The woman frowned at her. 'My *twins*?' she repeated.

'That's right, Mom. You had twins but they said you had a stroke and died.'

'How could I have children?'

'Because you had a husband who loved you, Mom. You had a husband who loved you and he's been grieving for you all of this time.'

'But, my dear,' the woman insisted. 'I *can't* have children.'

With that, she started to unbutton the front of her dress, from the hem upward. As she did so, Kiera suddenly realized with a deep, cold feeling of dread that the woman had no legs. The lower half of her dress which was hanging over the seat of the chair was empty and flat.

She stared at the woman in alarm and said, 'What are you doing? Mom – what's happened to you? What are you doing?'

Kieran said, 'Stop, Mom! Stop! We don't need to see!' But the woman carried on unbuttoning her dress, higher and higher, one small button after another.

Kiera turned to the bald man and said, 'Stop her, please!'

The bald man remained impassive. 'She is a sideshow. She is doing what sideshows always do. They show you what you paid to see.'

'But we didn't pay to see this, for Christ's sake! We're her children! Stop her!'

'I cannot. I would not. She is explaining what she is. She needs to. And you need to understand.'

Now the woman had unfastened her dress all the way up to her breastbone. She was still staring at Kieran and Kiera – not defiantly, not truculently, but with a terrible look of pride in her eyes that almost made Kiera faint with horror.

She parted her dress with both hands to reveal a bony white midriff, and that was all. She had no pelvis, no hips and no legs. Her abdomen ended as a lumpy bag, with the criss-cross scars of sutures all the way around it.

'You see, my dears?' she said. 'I could not possibly have children. I am Demi, the Demi-Goddess, the Half-Woman. I am surprised that you have not heard of me before. I am famous from coast to coast, isn't that true, Zachary?'

The bald man nodded. 'Coast to coast, Demi, my darling. Coast to coast.'

Kiera turned around and collided with Kieran. He grabbed hold of her sleeve, but she twisted herself away from him and pushed her way out of the pavilion. Once she was outside, she began to run back between the trailers and the caravans, past the trucks, past the horses, in between the tents.

She could hear herself panting and see the red lights jiggling in front of her eyes. She ran out of the carnival encampment and bounded down the sloping field, toward the lighted doorway of her bedroom.

'Don't close,' she gasped. 'Please don't close.'

She turned her head around only once, to make sure that Kieran was following her, which she knew that he would, and of course he was. In fact he was less than twenty yards behind her, and gaining on her.

Soon the two of them were running side by side with the thunder rumbling all around them like heavy artillery and the long wet grass whipping at their ankles. They reached the bedroom doorway and Kiera ran straight into it without even breaking her stride. Kieran came hurtling after her and slammed the door behind him.

Kiera fell backward on the bed, whining for breath. Kieran stood beside her, bent forward, his hands on his knees. They stared at each other for a long time, not knowing what to say, not knowing what to think, hardly even daring to understand what they had just experienced.

'That wasn't a dream,' said Kiera, at last. 'Even if it was somebody else's dream. That was a nightmare.'

Kieran pulled up his pajama pants. 'Whatever it was, it really happened. I'm totally soaked through, and look at you – you are, too.'

Kiera looked toward the bedroom door. 'Do you think it's gone?' she asked Kieran.

They both listened. The room was silent, except for the sound of somebody talking in the corridor outside. No rain, pattering against the other side of the door. No wind, blowing underneath it.

Eventually Kieran went across and turned the doorknob. He opened the door about a half inch and peered through it. Then he opened it wide. The sloping field had disappeared. The rain and the thunder and the rumbling tents had all disappeared, too. There was nothing but his hotel bedroom, with the bedside lamp tipped over on to the floor and all of his bedcovers dragged off the end of the bed.

'That *was* mom, wasn't it?' said Kiera.

Kieran said, 'Yes. I could feel it.'

'So what do you think happened to her? And how did she

get into that freak show? And where *is* that freak show? Do you think it really exists?'

Kieran shook his head. 'I don't know. But there's one thing I do know. I'm not going back into the fricking bedroom tonight. You don't mind if I sleep with you, do you?'

At about four a.m., Kieran was woken up by somebody singing, high and breathy. It was only when he had sat up in bed that he realized that it was Kiera, and that she was singing in her sleep.

'*In the good old summertime – in the good old summertime—*'

FIVE

A Disturbing Visitor

David said, 'You're bushed. You need to take it easy. Why don't you cancel this afternoon's visit?'

'Because I promised,' Katie told him. 'It's Mrs Copeland's birthday. And it's only in Coral Gables. I'll be fine.'

'Seriously, Katie, I don't think you're fine at all. That hallucination you had in Cleveland – sure, OK, maybe it was caused by nothing more than exhaustion. But I really wish you'd let Aaron run some tests on you. I just want to make absolutely sure that you don't have peduncular hallucinosis.'

'David – what happened in Cleveland was an aberration. A one-off. Next time I have to go away, I'll make sure that my schedule is much less punishing. You can count on it. And what the hell is "peduncular hallucinosis" when it's at home?'

David pursed his lips to show her that he was far from happy, but he didn't try to dissuade her any further. She would go to the Coral Gables retirement home today no matter what he said, and both of them knew it. He could hardly lock her in her room.

Katie had never loved any man as much as she loved David, but he was controlling by nature and she constantly had to make sure that she protected her own individuality. He was handsome and athletic and he had a buoyant sense of humor, but his psychiatric training always led him to observe closely everybody's behavior, especially hers. Sometimes she caught him watching the way she performed the simplest of everyday tasks like spreading jelly on her toast and she had to challenge him and say 'What? What am I doing wrong *now*? I'm spreading it, like, *compulsively*?'

He finished his coffee and stood up. He was thirty-five, only two years older than she was, but his hair was already steel gray. He had a squarish face and dark blue eyes which he had inherited from his Swedish mother. He wore rimless spectacles which accentuated his very analytical manner.

'I'll be home around seven,' he told her, coming around the table and giving her a kiss on the top of the head. 'Maybe we can go to Shula's tonight and treat ourselves to a steak.'

'I love you,' she said, turning around in her chair. 'And I won't allow myself to get too tired today, I promise you.'

'OK,' he said, kissing her again. 'Just remember that you're the most precious person in the whole of my life. And – since you asked – peduncular hallucinosis is a condition when a patient experiences highly-realistic hallucinations. The most common ones are scary or deformed faces, or strange landscapes, or people walking in a line, or people appearing to be unusually small. It's usually caused by a variety of serious problems in the midbrain, including tumors and subarachnoid hemorrhage. So please understand why I'm concerned for you.'

'*You're* concerned? If that's what I've got, I'm ten times more concerned than you are.'

David left, and she waved to him through the living-room window as he backed out of the driveway in his ruby-red Audi convertible. She cleared up the breakfast plates and stacked them into the dishwasher. Then she went through to the bedroom to get dressed. It was a warm, sunny morning, as it almost always was in Nautilus, and the French windows in the bedroom were open. Outside she could see their small red-brick yard, with its terracotta flowerpots and its sundial.

She had taken two sleeping pills last night and this morning she felt much calmer and more rested. All the same, as she sat in front of her dressing table, putting on her eye make-up, she couldn't help thinking about the woman she had seen in that bloodied bed in the Griffin House Hotel. The woman must have been a hallucination, there was no other rational explanation for it, but she had seemed utterly real. And Katie couldn't imagine why she should have hallucinated about anybody who had been so horribly mutilated.

She took out her coral pink lipstick and was about to apply it when the door chimes rang. She frowned at herself in the mirror. She wasn't expecting any visitors, nor any special mail deliveries. She got up and went to the front door, peering through the peephole to see who was there. It was a young man in a light green linen coat, with a white rose in his buttonhole.

'Yes?' she called out. 'What do you want?'

'Katie? Mrs Kercheval? I need to talk to you. It's important.'

She peered through the peephole again. As far as she knew, she had never seen this young man before, ever, although he strongly reminded her of her music teacher from junior high school. He had short reddish hair and a few freckles across the bridge of his nose, and pale blue eyes. He looked respectable enough, but maybe he was a door-to-door Bible salesman, or a Mormon, or a Jehovah's Witness. But how did he know her name?

'What's it about?' she asked him.

'Something happened to you, Katie. Something bad. I really need to discuss it with you.'

'Who are you?'

'I'm somebody who knows what happened to you, and why.'

'All right, then – what happened to me, exactly?'

'Katie, I can't discuss this on the doorstep. I need to talk to you face-to-face.'

'I'm sorry, I don't think it's a good idea for me to let you in. Not without some kind of ID.'

The young man turned away from the front door, with the his right hand cupped over his ear as if he were thinking, or listening. Then he turned back and said, 'Your grandmother used to sing you a song whenever you came to visit. Do you remember it?'

'My *grandmother*? What the hell do you know about my grandmother?'

But, very softly – so softly that Katie could barely hear him – the young man sang, '*Fly, little falcon, fly high in the sky! So sharp are your claws, so sharp are your eyes! No one can escape you, because you will see, wherever they run to, wherever they flee!*'

Katie stood behind the door for almost half a minute. Despite herself, despite her strong sense of self-control, she had tears in her eyes. She hadn't heard that song for more than twenty-five years, when her grandmother had sung it to her in the living room of her house in Sarasota, overlooking the ocean. She could see her grandmother now, her white hair fraying in the warm Gulf wind, her blue eyes faded, her neck withered, but still beautiful, one hand resting on Katie's head as if she were blessing her, a priestess passing on a benediction.

'*You will turn – yes, you'll spin, and you'll drop from on high! No one can escape you, however they try!*'

She drew back the security chain and opened the door. The young man in the light green linen coat was standing on the porch, both arms held out wide, as if he were trying to show her that he was neither armed nor dangerous. He was grinning at her like a long-lost friend who had found her address on Facebook and turned up without warning to surprise her.

'Katie!' he said.

'I don't know you,' said Katie. '*Should* I know you? How do you know my grandma's bird song?'

The young man kept on grinning. 'Is it OK if I come in? Then I can tell you all about it.'

Katie looked left and right, up and down the street. Only two doors away, Mr Tomlinson was outside in his front yard, trimming his hedges, so she guessed that she could always call out for help if this young man gave her any trouble. Besides, he didn't give her the impression that he would. He was standing well back from her, giving her plenty of personal space, with his arms still spread wide.

'All right,' she agreed, 'but any funny business—'

'Katie, this is very far from being funny business. This is deadly, *deadly* serious.'

She stood back and allowed him to walk into the hallway. She noticed as he passed her that he was wearing a light but distinctive cologne, slightly lemony, with a hint of vetiver grass. He went through to the living room, crossed over to the white leather couch and said, 'May I?'

'Sure, sit down. Do you want coffee? I think it's still hot.'

'No, thank you,' said the young man, raising his hand. 'I never eat or drink during the hours of daylight.'

'Oh, really? You're not some kind of a vampire, by any chance?'

The young man smiled, but when he spoke he sounded completely serious. 'There are no such beings as vampires, Katie. Vampires exist only in folk stories, and in nightmares.'

'Well that's good to know.'

'Yes. But there are beings which are far more frightening than vampires, and they exist not only in nightmares, but in reality, too.'

'Oh, really?'

'Yes, really. We call them Dreads, because we dread them.'

Katie looked at him narrowly. '*Dreads*? Is this a joke?'

'Do I look as if I'm joking?'

'So what, then? Are you trying to scare me?'

'Quite the opposite. In fact: I'm trying to reassure you. But after your experience at the Griffin House Hotel, I think you already know that nightmares can be much more than your sleeping imagination gone wild. Nightmares are another world. Of course we can only visit them when we're unconscious, but then we can only visit the real world when we're awake.'

'You *know* about my nightmare? How?'

The young man hesitated for a moment, as if he were trying to think how to phrase what he was going to say next. 'It's what I do, Katie. You could almost say that it's my job.'

'Are you a cop?'

'No.'

'A private detective, then? No? Not that either? You've been talking to the Cleveland police, though, haven't you? What did they tell you? That I was just some hysterical woman who must have eaten too much cheese before she went to bed?'

The young man shook his head. 'I haven't talked to anybody. There wouldn't be any point. Besides, the police can't deal with this. Only *you* can. Well – you and several others like you.'

'You're talking in riddles. If you're not a cop or a private detective then what's your interest in this?'

'I told you, I know what happened to you, and why. I also know who you are, and what you can do about it. And – most importantly – *how* you can do it.'

'All right,' said Katie. 'You tell me what happened to me, and then I might believe you.'

The young man patted the couch. 'Sit down, why don't you? Take the weight off.'

'I'll stand, thanks, if it's all the same to you. Just tell me what you know.'

'You thought you had a nightmare. In fact you *did* have a nightmare. You imagined that you were in some shabby apartment in Cleveland Flats, although you probably didn't know that it was Cleveland Flats. You found a woman lying in your bed. She was begging you for help. She told you that she tried to stop her killer but he was too strong for her. She was seriously mutilated. In fact she was sawn in half, and I'm sure that you were very frightened.'

'Frightened?' said Katie. 'I was absolutely terrified, if you want to know the truth. But if it was only a nightmare, how come it was all so totally real? I saw it, I *felt* it. I talked to the woman on the bed. I could even *smell* it, for Christ's sake. How often can you smell something you're only dreaming about?'

'Not often, I'll admit,' the young man told her. 'But it was closer to being a memory than a nightmare – somebody else's memory. You happened to stay in Room Seven-One-Seven and the very walls of that room are a witness to what happened, even though it didn't actually happen there.'

'You've completely lost me. I'm sorry.'

'It's not too difficult to understand. Sometime in the mid-nineteen-thirties, a man called Gordon Veitch broke into this woman's apartment in Cleveland Flats. He raped her and butchered her, as you saw for yourself. Shortly afterward, he checked in at the Griffin House Hotel, and dreamed about what he had done to her, in every little detail. His dream was absorbed by the walls of his hotel room, not unlike movie footage being developed on to celluloid.

'When the police eventually went to the woman's apartment to find out what had happened to her, they could find no sign of her, and no evidence at all of how she died. No body, no blood, no fingerprints, no hair, no fibers, no semen, nothing. Every trace of what he did there had been taken away in Gordon Veitch's dream, or nightmare if you prefer to call it that, as if it never happened.

'Besides, Cleveland Flats was a really rundown area, and the police were not going to devote hours of valuable time trying to find some drug-addicted whore. The whole investigation was filed away under missing persons and Gordon Veitch went free. But his *dream* of what he did remains, right until today, imprinted on the walls of Room Seven-One-Seven.'

'I still don't get it,' said Katie. 'How can you take physical evidence away from one place and move it someplace else? Just by *dreaming* about it?'

She was still suspicious that this young man was playing an elaborate practical joke on her. But how did he know everything that she had seen in her nightmare? She hadn't even told Detective Wisocky what the woman had said to her – about her attacker being too strong.

The young man said, 'It's like a magician's trick, in a way. You know how a magician can make you believe that somebody disappears from one cabinet and reappears in another cabinet on the other side of the stage? Some Dreads can do that with dreams. *This* Dread, in particular.'

'But how come *I* had a nightmare about this woman? If she was murdered as long ago as nineteen-thirty-something, surely everybody else who's ever slept in that room would have had the same experience? Or some of them, at least.'

'No, they wouldn't. They *couldn't*, not like you. Maybe one or two of them might have heard whispers, or seen shadowy outlines, or simply had the feeling that there was somebody else in the room with them when there patently wasn't. But *you*, Katie, you're uniquely sensitive, and that's why you saw it.'

'Go on,' said Katie, although she still felt highly suspicious.

'You don't know how special you are,' the young man told her. 'You're descended from a long line of people who have the ability to enter the dreams and nightmares of other people, and to use that ability for the greater good of all humanity.'

'*What*?'

'I know, Katie. I know it's very difficult for you to grasp, because I've never had to call on you before. Many people have a similar ability but they live out their entire lives and I never have to recruit them, ever, because their talents are simply not suitable. But I need you now, and that's why I came here today to talk to you.'

'Who are you?' Katie asked him. 'And what do you mean by "recruit"? You're nothing to do with the military, are you?'

'My name is Springer. I am the earthly representative of what you might loosely describe as the forces of good.'

'Terrific. I was right, then. You're selling Bibles.'

'Katie—'

Katie raised both hands. 'I don't know how you knew my grandma's bird song, or what I dreamed about in Cleveland. Excellent sales pitch, I grant you. But I don't need a Bible, thank you. I really don't. And I think it's time for you to leave.'

Springer said, in a flat, expressionless tone, 'Remember all those nightmares your sister Daisy used to have? Those really scary nightmares about that circus.'

Katie stared at him, breathless with surprise. 'Daisy *died* when she was nine years old,' she said. 'How the *hell* do you know what nightmares she had?'

'I told you, Katie. I'm not selling Bibles. I'm the earthly representative of the forces of good.'

'Daisy never told a soul about those circus nightmares. She never told *anybody*! Only me.'

'I realize that. But like I told you – knowing about nightmares, that's my job. And Daisy's nightmare about the circus is the reason why I'm here today. Your nightmare – the nightmare you had at the Griffin House Hotel – that was part of the *same* nightmare, believe it or not.'

'How could that be?'

'Because the circus doesn't vanish when you wake up. It exists in its own reality. It's going on right now – even during the day, when there's nobody asleep and dreaming about it. Do you understand that? The barrel-organ music is still playing. The clowns are still tumbling. The circus has a terrible unstoppable life of its own, in the world of dreams.'

'You said that my nightmare was part of it, too,' said Katie. She felt badly shaken, and she had to sit down on the opposite end of the couch.

Springer nodded. 'That's because Daisy was the same as you, descended from the same line. If the meningitis hadn't taken her when she was so young, I would have been talking to *her* today, too, and asking her to help us.'

'What *line*? I don't understand any of this.'

Springer said, 'I know you're not very religious, Katie, but the forces of good are embodied in a spirit which is known in the waking world by many different names, and in dream world by the name of Ashapola.

'Ashapola is light. Ashapola is purity. Ashapola protects us from the forces of darkness and destruction, and everything which would jeopardize our civilization and our sanity. Over the millennia, Ashapola has constantly battled to defend our world from being torn apart at the seams.'

'But what does any of this have to do with my nightmare?'

'*Everything* – because the woman you encountered in your nightmare had deliberately been mutilated so that she could be presented as an attraction at the circus. The selfsame circus which your sister Daisy used to dream about.'

'Go on.'

'This circus has survived in the world of dreams for nearly nine centuries, believe it or not. Circus and freak show, I should say, because it has always had giants and dwarves and monkey women and babies with two heads. Until nineteen-thirty-six, it was in hibernation, its freaks and its clowns and its animals all deeply asleep, as if they were dead.

'In nineteen-thirty-six, however, Gordon Veitch found out how to rouse it, although we don't know how, and more to the point we don't really know *why*. He was stopped before he could revive it completely, but he woke it up, and now it seems as if either he or somebody else is trying to finish what he began. For the past seventy-five years the circus has been making itself felt in the consciousness of thousands upon thousands of people, in their dreams. Maybe *millions*. So far, when we dream about it, the music is still very faint and far away, thank Ashapola. But if this latest attempt to bring it back to life is successful, there is a very real risk that the entire world is going to be plunged into darkness and brutality and chaos like nothing that you could ever imagine.'

Katie said nothing, but waited for Springer to carry on. She felt a complete sense of unreality, as if she were dreaming this, too; but however outlandish his story was, Springer had to be telling her the truth. Daisy had told her all about the freaks that had frightened her so much in her nightmares; especially the woman with one eye in the middle of her forehead, and a small creature that was half human and half rat, which used to gibber and curse in all kinds of different languages.

'The story goes that the circus was originally created in the middle of the twelfth century by a Cistercian monk from the Maulbronn monastery in Germany. His name was Brother Albrecht, and he was supposed to have been so handsome that some of the villagers in the Salzbach Valley believed that he was a saint. Maybe he *was* a saint, but if he was, he was a tainted saint, because he had a passionate affair with one of the prettiest girls in the village.

'Unfortunately for Brother Albrecht, she was already married, and her husband came home one day and found them in bed together. After he had beaten Brother Albrecht almost senseless, her husband tied him up and sawed off his arms at the elbows, so that he would never be able to touch another woman. Then he sawed off his legs at the knees, so that he would permanently have to be kneeling on the floor to pray for forgiveness. He daubed the stumps of Brother Albrecht's arms and legs with scalding pitch to prevent him from bleeding to death. I won't tell you what he forced his wife to do, as punishment for her infidelity.'

'That's a horrible story,' said Katie. 'That's absolutely *horrible*.'

'Yes, it is. But I wish it were only a story.'

SIX

Avenging Claw

Katie didn't know what to say. She felt as if she ought to tell Springer to get out of her house, right now, and never come back. But she also felt that he had arrived here this morning with the key to the rest of her life. She had to hear him out, no matter what he was going to say to her. If she didn't, she would never discover what she really was, or what Daisy could have been, and why she had dreamed or hallucinated about that mutilated woman in the Griffin House Hotel. For some reason that she couldn't understand, she also felt a sense of obligation, as if it was her *duty* to listen to him. Maybe 'recruitment' *was* the right word.

Springer said, 'I know that none of this is easy, Katie. It's sickening, most of it, and very scary. But you and all of the others who are like you have no real choice. It is what you were born to do, if you were ever called.'

'Just tell me about the circus.'

Springer stood up and walked across to the window. Outside, over the rooftops of the houses opposite, Katie could see a thick bank of orange cumulus clouds rising up, like the clouds of dust raised by a vast approaching army – still many miles away, but approaching them relentlessly. There would be a thunderstorm by the middle of the afternoon.

'The Cistercian monks came to the village and took Brother Albrecht back to the monastery. He spent months recovering from his mutilation, but according to monastery records he never prayed again. Not for forgiveness, not for the glory of God, not for anything. In fact he swore and blasphemed so much that after less than a year the monks forced him to leave the monastery, and he had to survive by begging in the village square and showing himself off as a freak.

'He had his entire body tattooed with illustrations of demons having sex with women, and he advertised himself as *der Ursprüngliche Sohn des Teufels* – the Original Son of the Devil. He persuaded a local carpenter to construct him a small mechanical cart in which he could push himself around, using the stumps of his elbows to propel himself. There are woodcuts of him in several medieval books about German mythology.'

Springer turned away from the window. 'It wasn't long before he became well known throughout the southern part of Germany, and he was joined by other freaks who wanted to profit from his notoriety. By the spring of the year eleven-fifty-two, he had established a traveling sideshow with more than twenty-five VSPs.'

'VSPs?'

'Very Special People. That's what we're supposed to call them these days. And it's right that we do. They *are* very special. As if it isn't hard enough surviving in this world without suffering from some hideous deformity. But of course Brother Albrecht wasn't *born* without arms and legs. He couldn't rail against his parents, or against God. All he wanted was revenge for its own sake – especially against those who had once admired him so much for his angelic looks and now crowded around him to stare at him in horror.

'His avowed aim was to drag down the whole world to the level of a freak show. He wanted to turn it all into a circus – a world in which art and beauty were either derided or ignored, and the ugliest and the loudest and the most obscene were applauded by all.'

Katie said, 'Seems like he's nearly succeeded, doesn't it? You only have to watch daytime TV.'

Springer looked at her steadily and said, 'Yes. You're right. That's where it all comes from. The reality shows, the hideous art, the raucous music, the worship of trashy celebrities. It all comes from Brother Albrecht and his traveling freak show.'

'But that was – what? – nine hundred years ago. How could the circus have survived all of that time?'

'That was the mistake of the Pope at the time, Eugene III. He was horrified by the way in which Brother Albrecht was glorifying Satan and mocking great art and music, which, in the High Middle Ages, was almost all religious. But Eugene III was also the first ever Cistercian Pope, and he was gravely concerned that Brother Albrecht's circus was bringing the Cistercian Order into serious disrepute.

'Eugene III heard that Brother Albrecht's circus was settled for the winter in a small town called Kempten-im-Allgaü, in Swabia, and he asked his friend the Duke of Swabia to kill Brother Albrecht and scatter the rest of his freaks and burn down all of their tents.

'When the duke's soldiers arrived at the circus encampment, however, they found only nine shivering freaks hiding in a nearby wood. The rest of the circus had vanished. There was no trace of it anywhere. No tents, no wagons, no horses, no caravans, no Brother Albrecht and none of the other VSPs. Not only that, none of the townspeople had seen them leave and there were no tracks in the snow. Only a few hoof prints, and some scattered ashes.'

'So where had the circus gone?' asked Katie.

'The duke's men tortured three of the VSPs they had found in the wood, and eventually they told him what had happened. The circus had been taken away in the same way that the woman in your hallucination was taken away. Brother Albrecht had been tipped off that the Pope was out to destroy his circus so he had taken a sleeping draft and *dreamed* about it – all of its tents and all of its trappings, all of its lions and its tigers and its dancing bears and its scores of assorted freaks – except those nine VSPs who hadn't wanted to go with him. He had dreamed about it so that it disappeared from the real world.'

'An entire circus? How was that possible?'

'Because of the strength of Brother Albrecht's hatred for what the real world had done to him. Because, Katie, the laws of nature are very different in the world of dreams.'

Springer paused, and then he said, 'There was nothing that Pope Eugene could do but place a holy sanction on the circus, so that Brother Albrecht would never be able to wake up and bring it back to the world of reality. A kind of exile, if you like.

'As of now, the circus still hasn't been restored to its full terrible ingloriousness, but *somebody* is trying to bring it back to life, so that very soon we will *all* be dreaming about it, every one of us, every night. That hallucination you experienced at the Griffin House Hotel makes me sure of it.'

'But what can I do about it?' Katie asked him. 'You said that you needed me, but how can I possibly help you?'

Springer came across and sat down on the couch next to her. No man had ever looked at her like this before. He seemed to be trying to show her that he was proud of her, but at the same time his expression was one of sympathy, even of pity.

'Your grandmother, who used to sing that you that bird song, was a Night Warrior.'

'A *what*?'

'A Night Warrior. She could rise out of her physical body when she was asleep, and enter other people's dreams.'

'Now I know you're pulling my chain. Come on, you've upset me. I think it's time you left.'

'But you, too, are a Night Warrior. You can enter other people's dreams.'

'Oh, yes? To do *what*, exactly?'

'To hunt down Brother Albrecht and his circus, and to destroy it for ever. Also, to hunt down whoever is aiding and abetting him. Why do you think you had that hallucination? Why do you think you went to the Griffin House Hotel at all?'

Katie frowned at him. 'I went there – I went there because the Renaissance Hotel called me when I was still in Sacramento and told me they had accidentally overbooked. They said I could stay at the Griffin House for the same price. They even arranged for a limo to pick me up at the airport and take me there.'

'The Renaissance was overbooked?' asked Springer, in mock surprise. 'The Renaissance has more than four hundred forty rooms, as well as fifty suites.'

'I don't understand.'

Springer said, 'It was *I* who called you, Katie, and I who arranged for you to stay at the Griffin House Hotel. Me.'

Katie stared at him in disbelief. 'You *wanted* me to have that nightmare? You actually fixed it so that I would stay in that room and see that poor woman?'

'I'm sorry. I admit it. But how else could I have convinced you that what happens in dreams is just as real as what happens when we're awake?'

'You frightened the living crap out of me! I have never been so scared in my entire life! *And* I called the police! You not only scared me half to death, you made me look like an idiot, too!'

Springer raised his hand. 'Please, Katie, just hear me out. Do you know why your grandmother used to sing you that bird song?'

'What do you mean?'

'Your grandmother sang you that bird song because her name as a Night Warrior was Gryferai – the Avenging Claw.'

'What?'

'As a Night Warrior she could fly like a falcon, so that she could hunt down her enemies from hundreds of feet up, and swoop down on them from high in the air. Let me tell you this: it was your grandmother who found one of the most destructive Dreads ever, the Black Shatterer, who could literally shatter everything that he touched – doors, walls, chairs, animals, even living people. The Black Shatterer could even smash the very air in front of him, which threatened the lives of thousands of people.

'Gryferai found the Black Shatterer, and caught him in her claws, and she lifted him up to such an altitude that he didn't dare to shatter her, in case he fell. He begged for his life and Gryferai said that she would consider sparing him if he shattered his evil companion the Screw-Worm. He agreed, but it was then that Gryferai deliberately dropped him over eight thousand feet. He landed on a small rocky island on the west side of Sarasota Bay and the impact caused him to smash into crystalline glass.'

'My God,' said Katie. She stared at Springer in astonishment. 'Grandma actually took me out to see that island, in her little boat. Black Shatter Island, she called it, although she never told me why. We went out there two or three times – always very early in the morning, so that the rising sun used to catch it. It would glitter so bright that it would dazzle you, as if it were sprinkled all over with thousands and thousands of diamonds.'

'So – do you believe me now?' asked Springer.

Katie was silent for a long time. Then she said, 'I don't know. It all seems so totally far-fetched.'

'You are Gryferai's granddaughter. The Night Warrior genes tend to skip a generation, so your mother didn't have them. But you do. You are An-Gryferai, which means the daughter of Gryferai's daughter.'

'And what does that mean? I can fly? I can catch evil villains and drop them into Sarasota Bay?'

'Yes,' said Springer. 'You can.'

'By the way, why *did* she drop him? I thought he promised to shatter his evil companion for her. What was his name? The Screw-Worm?'

Springer smiled. 'She dropped him because she was sure that he wouldn't really do it. And she dropped him because she knew that she would probably never get a chance like that again. Gryferai's motto was *grijp het ogenblik*, which means "seize the moment."'

Katie said, 'I want to believe you. I really do. But this is all so incredible. It's like finding out that your parents aren't your real parents. No, it isn't – it's much more disturbing, even than that. It's like having your whole life turned upside down.'

'I can appreciate how you feel,' Springer told her. 'Let me see if I can convince you.'

He held out his hand. Katie hesitated and then she took it, and stood up. Springer led her across to the large pine-framed mirror which hung on the wall beside the front door. He positioned her directly in front of it, and stood close behind her like a fashion stylist.

'You're awake now, so I can only use my powers of suggestion to show you what An-Gryferai looks like. But when you go to sleep, and rise up out of your body, this is what you will become, for real.'

Katie stared at her reflection. At first she could see nothing unusual, only herself, still looking tired, with her hair sticking out. But then she became aware that a shadowy outline was forming around her, swimming in the air like ghostly blood-clots. Springer closed his eyes and gradually the outline became clearer and clearer. Soon she appeared to be wearing a helmet – a helmet shaped like the head of a giant falcon, with amber lenses for eyes and a long curved beak. Her entire body was gradually covered in soft brown feathers, except for a blaze of white feathers on her breasts. Behind her, she could make out two huge wings, both of them spread wide, with a span of more than twenty feet.

Springer opened his eyes. 'Lift up your hands,' he told her.

Slowly, she raised her hands, and saw that attached to both of her forearms was an intricate arrangement of metal rods and pulleys, and that each of these mechanisms operated a huge metal claw.

'Try them,' Springer urged her, and she found that when she squeezed her hands, the rods and the pulleys opened and closed the claws, and rotated them, and locked them. Every movement was accompanied by a complicated clicking sound.

'The power of each of An-Gryferai's claws is over seventy-five thousand pounds, which is more than the jaws of life the fire department uses for rescuing people from wrecked automobiles. An-Gryferai can use her claws to cut through the roof of a car, or cut off a man's head, even if he's wearing armor. At the same time her claws are so finely controllable that she can pick a flower with them, or pluck out a single eyelash.'

Katie turned her head from side to side. The falcon helmet was handsome and streamlined and fierce, and it gave her an extraordinary feeling of strength and confidence. This is me, she thought. It's unbelievable, but this is *me.* I am An-Gryferai. I am a Night Warrior.

'Well?' said Singer, with that faint, beguiling smile.

'I don't know what to say,' Katie told him. 'I'm totally overwhelmed.'

Springer laid one hand on her shoulder. 'Look out of the window,' he said. 'No – don't turn around, because you'll lose the illusion that you're An-Gryferai. Look out of the window that you can see reflected in the mirror.'

Through the window, Katie could see the red-flowering bushes in her front yard, and the tall yucca trees outside Mr Tomlinson's house opposite. She could see Mr Tomlinson in his baggy khaki shorts, trimming the edges of his lawn; and in the distance, at the intersection of North Bay Road and West Forty-fifth, a woman in a short yellow dress pushing a baby stroller.

'Now focus on that woman,' said Springer.

Katie narrowed her eyes and peered at the woman intently. As she did so, the woman appeared to come nearer and nearer, as if Katie were looking at her through a zoom lens.

'Keep focusing,' Springer coaxed her. 'An-Gryferai can see for miles and miles, in the sharpest detail.'

Katie kept her eyes fixed on the woman, and after only a few seconds she could clearly make out that she was young and Hispanic, with a plump oval face and heavy unplucked eyebrows, and that she was wearing a yellow headscarf to match her dress and a necklace of large orange-and-green beads. She could also see the baby in the stroller, a chubby little girl in a pink gingham romper suit, waving a pink plastic rattle and furiously kicking her legs. She could hear the rattle quite distinctly.

She turned to Springer and said, 'That's amazing. It's like she's standing right outside the window.'

'An-Gryferai's eyes have an effective range of more than ten miles,' said Springer. 'She also has highly acute hearing. She is the eyes and ears of the Night Warriors, as well as a fearsome fighter in her own right. When the Night Warriors go looking for Brother Albrecht and his freak show, her natural abilities will be essential.'

'What do I have to do?' Katie asked him. 'And *when*?'

'Tonight,' said Springer. 'Before one a.m.'

'*Tonight*? But I have absolutely no idea what to do.'

Springer handed her a slip of paper. 'Before you go to bed, read these words out loud. Once you've recited them, you won't have any trouble dropping off. Then – once you start sleeping – your dream self will rise out of your waking self. I will be waiting for you, to guide you.'

'But these claws . . . I don't know how they work yet.'

'You will, when you become An-Gryferai. You will have all of her knowledge and all of her skills.'

Katie kept on staring at their reflection in the mirror. She had never felt like this in her life. Excited, scared, so pumped up that she could hardly breathe.

'Just tell me this,' she said. 'Is it going to be really dangerous? I mean, what if something happens to me when I'm An-Gryferai? What if I meet somebody like the Black Shatterer and he hurts me?'

'It depends on how badly,' said Springer. 'I won't lie to you, Katie, some Night Warriors do get seriously injured, and it can have an effect on their waking bodies. Some Night Warriors have been killed. Not many, but some.'

'What happens then?'

'Then, their real-life bodies never wake up.'

'Ever?'

'Never. It's like they're in a coma for the rest of their life.'

They sat and talked together for another half hour, until it was time for Katie to go to the retirement home in Coral Gables. She had to make a progress report on several of the residents, especially Mrs Gladys Sweetman, whose senile dementia had been worsening in the past three months, until she no longer recognized her own daughter.

Springer said, 'Whenever he wanted new attractions for his freak show, Brother Albrecht used to send out his agents into the towns and villages of Swabia, looking for people to deform, especially women. Deformed women were always very popular with the crowds who came to his circus, particularly if they performed degrading sexual acts.

'His agents would creep into people's houses at night and commit the most atrocious acts of mutilation. Those women who didn't die from shock or loss of blood would be carried away to join the freak show. There was no point in them trying to escape. Where else could a woman go if she had no arms and no legs, or if her face had been cut off and replaced with that of a dog, or if she and another woman had been inextricably sewn together?'

'My God,' said Katie. 'How did Brother Albrecht get away with it?'

'Because this was the Middle Ages and there was no law

enforcement in the way we understand it now. Apart from that, Brother Albrecht's circus was hugely popular, even if the Pope wanted to close it down. Before the Duke of Swabia came to break it up, it had traveled all over Europe, and as far as Russia, and it made Brother Albrecht a very wealthy man. Thousands of people flocked to see the Centaur who had the upper body of a woman and the lower body of a horse. She would be covered by a stallion several times a day for the entertainment of the crowds. Then there was the Human Cockroach, a young boy with six arms instead of legs, who would publicly eat handfuls of excrement. And so many more, each one more disgusting than the last.

'When Brother Albrecht dreamed it away, the whole circus went into a kind of suspended animation, but I can only guess that his intention was to bring it all back to life one day – and sooner, rather than later. I doubt if he realized that it wouldn't be revived for so many hundreds of years.'

'But if the circus was so disgusting, why would anyone *want* to revive it?'

'I don't know, to be frank. Why does anyone stub out cigarettes on children's arms, or beat women within an inch of their life? Why does anyone commit rape, torture, or homicide? Why do people spray graffiti on beautiful buildings, or throw acid at famous works of art? There's a very dark side to human nature and whoever is trying to bring Brother Albrecht's circus back to life has darkness in spades.'

'How is he going to do it? Do you have any idea?'

'Not entirely. But we're pretty sure that the Griffin House Hotel has always been central to this revival. In seven of its bedrooms – yours included – nightmares of mutilations and murders are imprinted in the walls. Between nineteen thirty-six and nineteen thirty-eight, Gordon Veitch stayed in each of those rooms. What we don't yet understand is what he was trying to do.'

'But Gordon Veitch isn't likely to be alive today, is he?'

'It's possible, if he's become a Dread. A Dread is a kind of a ghost which exists partly in dreams and partly in the waking world, as I do. On the other hand, it might be somebody else altogether, trying to carry on where Gordon Veitch left off. It will be up to the Night Warriors to find out, and track him down, and stop him.'

At a quarter of nine, Springer said that it was time for him to go. Katie opened the front door for him. The cumulus clouds were closer now, and a warm, fretful wind was blowing. In the far distance, over the Gulf, she could hear the rumbling of thunder.

'I'm sorry,' said Springer, taking hold of both of Katie's hands.

'Sorry for what? If it's my destiny to be a Night Warrior, then it's my destiny.'

'You haven't yet entered anybody else's dreams. You may not feel quite so sanguine about it when you do.'

'Well, we'll see. I'm off to visit my dementia patients now. I think I prefer your kind of madness to theirs.'

Springer said, 'I *do* look like Mr Flight, don't I?'

'What?'

'Your music teacher, from Nautilus Junior High. You liked him a whole lot, didn't you? Which is why I came here looking like this.'

He raised his hand in a little salute and walked away down the path. Katie was about to call him back and ask him how he had known about Mr Flight, and more to the point, how he had managed to look almost exactly like him. But then she thought: leave it, maybe you don't really need to know.

SEVEN

Locked Room Mystery

Detective Wisocky closed the file he was working on, tossed down his pen, and said, 'That's it, Charlie. Time for nourishment. Rally's, for a triple cheeseburger. And you're buying.'

Detective Hudson looked up from his desk and said, 'Come on, Walter – I picked up the check for yesterday's lunch.'

'Sure you did, Charlie. But yesterday's lunch was chow fun noodles, right, and chow fun noodles is Chinese, right, which is a totally different ethnic cuisine from cheeseburgers, which is domestic. The last time we ate cheeseburgers *I* paid, and the next time we eat Chinese I'll pay for that. But you can't go confusing your different ethnic cuisines on a financial basis, otherwise we won't know where the hell we are.'

'Well, to tell you the truth, I feel like Mongolian.'

'You goddamned *look* Mongolian, too. What does that have to do with lunch?'

They had almost reached the door when the phone rang on Walter's desk.

'You going to answer that?' asked Charlie.

'What? No. Absolutely not. It's trouble.'

'How do you know it's trouble?'

'It's trouble because it's going to postpone the moment when I can open my mouth and take my first bite of a Rally's triple cheeseburger.'

'You should answer it, Walter. Really. I got a hunch, that's all.'

'You and your goddamned hunches. You got more hunches than Quasimodo.'

Charlie raised one eyebrow, and when the phone went on ringing, and ringing, Walter eventually went back to his desk and scooped it up. 'Wisocky,' he snapped. 'What?'

'Officer John Skrolnik here, detective. We got called out to a house on Corydon Road, reports of a young woman screaming.'

'Screaming? What was she screaming about?'

'Nobody knows, because she disappeared.'

'What do you mean, disappeared?'

'She's not here. The owners of the property heard her screaming upstairs in her apartment but when they went up to find out what was wrong she wasn't there, even though they never saw her leave the house.'

'Who was she?'

'A student. Her name was – hold on – Maria Fortales, just twenty years old. She was studying law at CRWU.'

'I thought all the Crew students had to live on campus, in a dormitory or a sorority house or something.'

'Only for the first two years.'

Walter took a deep breath. 'Maybe she went out for lunch. That's what I'm trying to do, believe it or not. Go out for lunch. Why don't *you* go out for lunch, too? What's the matter with you? You never hungry?'

'Her landlord said that she was screaming like somebody was killing her. He said he never heard nobody scream like that before, never.'

'But there's no sign of her?'

'None. That's why I called you. Don't you remember, the last time we had a missing persons case, you said I could always call you?'

'OK,' Walter admitted. 'So I did. How sweet of me. Corydon Road, what number?'

'Twenty-four eight hundred.'

'Roger that,' said Walter. 'Give us ten minutes.'

He hung up the phone. Charlie was standing right next to him with an expectant look on his face. 'You and your goddamned hunches,' said Walter.

'What is it? What's happened?'

'Apparently some young girl was yelling her tits off like she was being murdered and then she took a powder and nobody knows where she went. And for that I have to forego my lunch.'

'I don't know, Walter,' said Charlie. 'As soon as that phone rang – for some reason it gave me this incredibly strong feeling that something seriously bad is going to happen.'

'You bet your ass it is. My stomach's going to start rumbling, and you're going to have to listen to it.'

They parked behind Officer Skrolnik's white squad car, and climbed out. It was starting to rain, quite hard, and the rain came rustling down through the rusty-colored trees like an expectant audience waiting for the arrival of a great concert pianist.

'Had to fucking rain, didn't it?' Walter complained, and by way of punctuation there was a loud bang of thunder from the direction of Cleveland Heights.

Corydon Road was a quiet suburban avenue less than a half mile from the university campus, and many of its residents let out rooms to students during term-time. Number 24800 was a small green-painted house with a gray-shingled roof and a veranda, with a sagging 1969 Buick Riviera parked in the driveway.

Officer Skrolnik was waiting by the front door. Inside the hallway, his partner was talking to an elderly man with white hair and a baggy gray cardigan. Officer Skrolnik was very tall, with a prominent larynx that bobbed up and down like a Halloween apple whenever he spoke.

'Thanks for coming so quick, detectives. The landlord and his wife are really spooked.'

'What's the landlord's name?' asked Walter.

Officer Skrolnik flipped open his notebook. 'Richard Yarber. His wife's name is Maude. They said that Ms Fortales came back very early this morning, around five thirty, after spending the night with some of her college friends. Around eleven forty-five they heard her screaming but the door to her room was locked and they couldn't get in to find out what was wrong. Mrs Yarber went across the street and asked one of their neighbors to help them – Mr Herman Eisner, he's a retired fire marshal. He managed to kick the door open but the room was empty. No sign of Ms Fortales or anybody else.'

Walter sniffed. 'Couldn't she have climbed out of the window?'

Officer Skrolnik shook his head. 'It used to be their grandson's room and the windows all have childproof bars. Apart from which, it's a sheer twenty-foot drop down to the side of the house.'

'Well, *très* mysterious. Let me talk to them.'

He entered the hallway and Charlie followed him. He showed Mr Yarber his badge and said, 'Detective Wisocky, sir, and this is Detective Hudson. Sounds like you've had a kind of a weird experience this morning.'

'I'll shay,' said Mr Yarber, with his false teeth clicking. 'Shcared the living Jeshush out of ush.'

'You heard Ms Fortales screaming?'

'Never in my life heard nothing sho terrible. More like a pig being shlaughtered than a human being. And shomething elsh, too. Both of ush heard it. Like a *shaw*, if you know what I mean. A rashping noish, like a shaw.'

'A rasping noise like a saw? But when your neighbor broke into Ms Fortales' room, you didn't see a saw?'

The young officer who had been talking to Mr Yarber had to cover his mouth with his hand to hide his grin.

'No,' said Mr Yarber. 'No shign of a shaw anywhere.'

'OK,' Walter told him, laying a reassuring hand on his steeply-sloping shoulder. 'Do you mind if my partner and me took a look at Ms Fortales' room?'

'Shure. Go ahead. Be my guesht. It's upshtairs, shecond on the left.'

Walter and Charlie climbed the narrow, beige-carpeted stairs. The staircase was wallpapered with faded brown roses, and twenty or thirty photographs of the Yarber's sons and daughters and grandchildren were hung higgledy-piggledy on either side, not one of them straight. The house smelled sweetish and musty, as if the windows hadn't been opened in years, and there were dead blowflies lying on the window sills.

Walter carefully pushed open the door to Maria Fortales' bedroom. The Yarbers' neighbor Herman Eisner had kicked the door so hard that he had split the side of the frame and the tarnished brass knob was hanging at an angle. Walter eased himself inside.

On the left, against the wall, there was a single bed covered by a rumpled pink candlewick bedspread. It had three purple cushions on it and a small collection of soft toys – a floppy-eared rabbit, a bright green frog, and a pale green hand-knitted gnome.

Under the window stood a pine desk, with an Apple laptop on it, a half-empty coffee mug, and a thick red notebook bound with five or six elastic bands. A white home-knitted cardigan was drooping over the back of the chair. As Officer Skrolnik had told them, the windows were fitted with horizontal metal bars, so it would have been impossible for Maria Fortales to have climbed out.

On the right-hand side of the room there was a cheap plywood clothes-closet, painted cream. One side of the closet was plastered with dozens of cut-out pictures of circuses and clowns. Almost in the center was a large photograph of a gray-faced clown. He had wild staring eyes and tangled gray shoulder-length hair and dark green lipstick which was curved upward into a maniacal grin, even though his real lips were curved downward.

'Somebody sure likes the circus,' said Charlie, crossing over to take a closer look. 'This fellow here is Mago Verde, the Green Magician.'

Walter sniffed again, took out a crumpled handkerchief and loudly blew his nose. 'How the hell do you know that?'

'I did a study of clowns at the Police Academy.'

'That couldn't have been too difficult. The whole place is run by clowns.'

'No, there's a distinct deviant psychology based around clowns. A lot of killers and criminals are inspired to dress up as circus performers, like John Wayne Gacy, for instance.'

'Oh, you mean Pogo the Clown.'

'That's right. Gacy made himself up as a white-faced harlequin, didn't he, a family entertainer. But he ended up raping and murdering at least thirty-three young men and boys around the Cleveland area and over half of their bodies were never found.'

Walter came up behind him and peered at Mago Verde over his shoulder. 'I never liked clowns, when I was a kid. They always scared the crap out of me.'

'An irrational fear of clowns – that's called coulrophobia,' said Charlie. 'But this particular clown you'd be well advised to be very afraid of. He's what the Venetians call a *pagliaccio diabolico* – an evil clown.'

'Oh, yeah? What's so evil about him, apart from the fact that he looks like Jack Nicholson in drag?'

'Mago Verde always plays cruel and sadistic tricks on his audience. For instance he might produce a small guillotine and show a volunteer that when he sticks his finger in it, and trips the switch, it looks like this really sharp blade is coming down but he's completely unhurt. So the volunteer willingly copies him, and *crunch*! he gets his pinkie chopped off.'

'Hilarious,' said Walter.

'You know what Lon Chaney Junior once said about clowns? "There is nothing funny about a clown in the moonlight."'

'There is nothing funny about clowns in any kind of light, period, and especially in the dark. But what I would dearly like to know is, why did this Maria Fortales have a picture of this freak stuck up on her closet?'

Charlie was scrutinizing the pictures even more intently. 'Mago Verde isn't the only freak here. Look – here's a picture of Prince Randian the Human Caterpillar and Johnny Eck the Half-Boy. They were both in that Tod Browning movie, *Freaks*.'

'Yeah, I saw it,' said Walter. 'That guy didn't have no arms or legs, did he? But he still managed to roll a cigarette, put it into his mouth and light it.'

They both frowned at each other, baffled. Then Walter abruptly opened the closet doors, as if he were trying to surprise whoever was hiding inside it. All that it contained, however, was a row of wire hangers, with dresses and skirts and two short coats, one tartan and the other brown suede.

Walter yanked out the three drawers underneath, but one of them was only a snakes'-nest of thongs and bras and pantyhose, while the other two were crammed with sweaters, purple and crimson and marigold yellow.

'Smell that?' he said, lifting up one of the sweaters. 'She sure liked her vanilla musk.'

Charlie bent over and lifted the side of the bedspread so that he could check under the bed. There was nothing there but a large gray suitcase and a grubby red backpack. He dragged out the suitcase and opened it up but it was empty except for some travel brochures for Mexico and a sewing kit from the Hacienda San Miguel Hotel in Cozumel.

Walter meanwhile went over to the desk. He opened the laptop and switched it on, and when the screen saver appeared it was a picture of the same clown, Mago Verde, standing in a grassy field wearing an ankle-length green coat. In spite of his dark green painted-on smile, his expression was one of unmitigated rage, as if he were furious at having his photograph taken. The sky above him was gray and swollen with rain, and behind him there was a sinister collection of black circus tents and assorted marquees.

Beside one of the tents, half hidden behind its entrance flap, stood a small boy with a washed-out face, almost as gray as Mago Verde in his make-up. He looked both frightened and sad.

The rain sprinkled against the window. Walter picked up the notebook and rolled off the elastic bands. When he opened it he saw that it was Maria Fortales' diary. It was written in purple ink, in rounded handwriting, which was so diminutive that he could barely read it. Every page was full to the last line, and some extra sentences had even been written vertically up the margins.

He turned to the last page, which Maria Fortales had written yesterday.

'What's that?' asked Charlie.

'Diary,' said Walter. 'Listen to this: "*Last night the show was all packed up and ready to leave for Waterloo, Idaho. It rained and rained and it never stopped, and all of the meadow was churned up into thick black mud. I was cold and shivering and even the bears looked miserable. I went to BJ's caravan for warmth even though BJ scares me so much. BJ never stopped ranting and raving although I could hardly understand a word he was saying. Then Natasha came and found me and warned me that The GF was growing impatient and that I should be very careful and have eyes in the back of my head especially where MV is concerned. I don't know what to do. I am so frightened but I don't know how to escape.*"'

Walter turned back a few pages. 'Here we are again. "*Tonight only seventeen people turned up for the show and MV said that The GF was very angry. He wants to move on but two of the trucks are still out of commission and we have to wait for them to be fixed before we can leave here.*"'

He flipped back again, and read some more, and then flipped back again. 'Jesus. She has dreams about this circus every single night. Every single goddamned night. No wonder she's obsessed.'

Charlie said, 'I guess "MV" is Mago Verde. But who's "The GF", I wonder? And "BJ"?'

Walter closed the book, snapped the elastic bands back around it, and handed it over. 'There. Take it home and read it from page one. Maybe you can work out who they are, and why she's so scared of them. You're the clown expert.'

Charlie took the diary and looked around the room again, as if he were half expecting to find her hiding under the candlewick bedspread, or standing completely motionless in one corner so that he hadn't noticed her. 'OK. But it still doesn't tell us what's happened to her, does it?'

'Well, take her laptop, too. Have Morrie go through it, in the lab. My guess is that she's simply gone wandering off someplace without telling her landlord about it.'

Walter lifted the home-knit cardigan off the back of the chair and rummaged in the pockets. The cardigan smelled of vanilla musk, too. 'Hey,' he said. 'Look at this.'

Out of the right-hand pocket he produced a brown leather purse, with Mayan decorations on it, a souvenir from Mexico. He opened it up, and there was Maria Ynez Fortales, frowning at him from her driver's license. A pretty round-faced girl with wavy black hair and pouting lips and a beauty spot on her left lip.

'Well, at least we know what she looks like.'

He went through the rest of the contents. Twenty-seven dollars in cash, a library card, a Visa card, and a business card from

Alphabet Cabs. Also, a student identification card from Case Western Reserve University which carried another photograph of her, this time smiling and wearing a green silk headscarf.

'She wouldn't go out without her purse, would she?' said Charlie. 'So where the hell is she?'

'She's not here, for sure, but I don't see any evidence of abduction, can you? If she went, she went without kicking over the furniture or pulling down the drapes.'

'What about the screaming?'

'Who knows? Maybe she was screaming at her boyfriend or something, on her cell.'

'And the sawing noise?'

'*Pff,*' said Walter, dismissively. 'If you ask me, the old man's hearing-aid is on the fritz. My mom's hearing-aid used to make a noise like a flock of Canada geese.'

'But the door was locked from the inside. The key's still in it.'

'There are ways of doing that.'

'Like what?'

'I don't know. Don't make complications. Think Occam's Razor. The simplest solution is always the most likely.'

They looked around the room one last time. 'Maybe we should get a sniffer dog up here,' said Charlie.

'Yeah, maybe you're right. But let's give it twenty-four hours before we start treating Ms Fortales as a missing person. Like I say, she probably went out without the Yarbers seeing her. The best place for us to go now is CWRU, to see if she's there, or if any of her friends know where she is.'

They went back downstairs. Mr Yarber was still standing in the hallway, with Mrs Yarber close behind him. 'Well?' said Mr Yarber. 'She well and truly vanished into thin air, didn't she?'

Walter gave him what he hoped was a reassuring smile as he headed out the door for the car. 'Don't you fret, Mr Yarber. She'll turn up. There was no foul play carried out in that room, I can assure you.'

'Now, are we going to Rally's or not? My triple cheeseburger is getting cold.'

Charlie didn't start up the engine. 'How did Maria Fortales get out of the room, Walter? Just explain that to me.'

'It's obvious. She wasn't in the room in the first place.'

'So how did she lock the door from the inside? And how come her purse was still on her desk? She wouldn't have gone out without her purse, would she?'

Walter slumped his head forward in defeat, so that his double chins bulged out. 'She evaporated, OK? That's how she did it. She just fucking evaporated.'

'Did you ever see that happen before? Somebody just vanish like that?'

'No, but this business is all about the inexplicable, isn't it? We're not here to explain anything. We're here to find Maria Fortales and/or anybody who did her any harm. That's all.'

EIGHT

Helpless

Lincoln became aware that somebody was saying his name, over and over – not as if they were trying to wake him, but as if they enjoyed repeating it simply for the way it sounded.

It was a young woman's voice, soft and modulated. At first he thought she sounded like Grace, his wife, but then he realized that she had a slight accent. She reminded him of a pretty Creole girl who used to work on the reception desk at K-C Records in New Orleans.

He opened his eyes. At first, everything was foggy. He was lying in an unfamiliar room, lit by bright fluorescent strip-lights. Above him there was a polystyrene-tiled ceiling and when he lifted his head a little he saw that three sides of his bed were surrounded by a pale yellow curtain with an interlocking pattern of seabirds on it.

'*Lincoln*!' cooed the young woman's voice. 'Lincoln, you're back with us! I'm so glad!'

He tried to sit up, but for some reason he found that he couldn't. He felt no pain, but his muscles wouldn't work. He lifted his head a little more and he could see his feet at the end of the bed, in white surgical socks, but he couldn't waggle them. This was more than numbness. He felt as if he were completely absent from the chest down, leaving only his head and his arms.

The girl stood up and leaned over him and to his bewilderment it *was* the Creole girl from K-C records. She was dusky-skinned, with high cheekbones and feline eyes, and her mass of black dreadlocks made her look like Medusa, who could turn men to solid stone. She was wearing a clinging dress in purple jersey with a large amethyst pendant dangling between her breasts and at least a dozen silver bracelets on each wrist.

Lincoln could smell her and she smelled like jasmine flowers on a warm summer evening, in some enclosed courtyard in the French Quarter.

'Can't remember your name,' Lincoln whispered. He gave a dry, abrasive cough, and then he said, 'What was it? I know . . . always reminded me of "ukulele".'

'Eulalie,' the girl smiled. 'Eulalie Passebon.'

'That's it, Eulalie. What the hell are *you* doing here, Eulalie? And come to that, where the hell *is* here?'

'You're in the emergency room at the Case Medical Center, in Cleveland.'

'*What*?'

'You've had a very serious accident, Lincoln.'

Again, Lincoln tried to sit up. He could move his arms, and press down against the mattress with his hands, but he could only raise his head a few inches.

'I can't move! What happened to me? I don't remember.'

'They found you lying on the patio outside of your room at the Griffin House Hotel. You fell, and broke your spine. You're paralysed – temporarily, at least.'

Lincoln stared at her. '*Paralysed*?'

Eulalie took hold of his right hand and lifted it to her lips and kissed it. 'I'm so sorry, Lincoln. This was the very last thing I wanted to happen.'

'Where's a doctor? I need to see a doctor! What are *you* doing here? Has anybody called my wife?'

'Shh,' said Eulalie. 'I'll call for the doctor in just a minute, I promise you. The hospital staff have contacted Grace to tell her what happened to you. She's flying in from Detroit and she should be here in less than an hour. But first of all it's very important that you understand what's happened to you. You need to understand who you are.'

Lincoln began to panic. 'I don't know what in hell you're talking about! I need to see a doctor!'

'Lincoln—'

'I'm *paralysed*, for Christ's sake! I don't know how it happened and I'm lying here in this goddamned hospital bed and you're a goddamned receptionist for a record company in New Orleans. What's going on? Have I gone crazy, or what?'

'Lincoln, listen to me. We don't have much time. Do you remember the man with the gray face and the green lipstick and the long gray hair?'

Lincoln blinked at her. 'What? I still don't know what you're talking about!'

'It was back at the Griffin House Hotel, room one-oh-four. A woman was lying on your bed. She was badly hurt, wasn't she? Then the bed caught fire and you tried to hide in the bathroom but the man with the gray face and the green lipstick was there, hiding in the shower stall.'

Lincoln said nothing, but continued to stare at her wide eyed. As he did so, a flickering image began to move inside his mind, as if he were remembering a grainy old movie that he had seen a long time ago, in some unfamiliar movie theater.

The gray-faced man stepped out of the shower stall, all spindly and dressed in black, and his lips were painted with green make-up into a mad, pointed grin, even though his real lips were tightly puckered with anger. His voice when he spoke sounded as if he had a mouthful of dry sand.

'I warned you not to come, now didn't I? You would not listen to me, though, would you? You out-and-out refused to listen.'

Eulalie said, 'He came after you with his handsaw, didn't he? And the room was burning and the door was locked and there was only one way out.'

'The fire escape,' Lincoln whispered. *Now* he remembered.

'That's right. And it collapsed, and you fell three stories to the ground. And that's how you broke your back.'

Eulalie kissed his hand again, and then she said, 'The hotel staff who found you on the patio, they did the right thing and didn't try to move you. So the chances of your recovering look pretty good.'

'That man who came after me, who was he?'

'We don't know for sure. But we think he could have been a murderer called Gordon Veitch.'

'Who?'

'Gordon Veitch. He raped and killed at least a dozen women in the nineteen-thirties. Maybe it wasn't the *real* Gordon Veitch, because Gordon Veitch is probably dead by now, but a nightmare of Gordon Veitch.'

'A *nightmare*? That doesn't make any sense at all. You're tryin' to tell me that he was only a dream?'

'Maybe he was, maybe wasn't. Another possibility is that he was somebody who was made up to look like Gordon Veitch. A copycat.'

Lincoln said, 'What happened in that hotel room, believe me, that *felt* real. I don't know how it could have been, but I'm lyin' here right now with my back broke, and nothin' comes much realer than that, does it?'

'Whoever that man was, Lincoln, and whether he was real or not, we need your help to track him down and put a stop to what he's doing.'

'You're kiddin' me, right? Look at me, I can't even get out of bed.'

Eulalie leaned forward so that her face was very close to his, almost as if she were going to kiss him on the lips. He could even see his own face reflected in her eyes. 'I'm not Eulalie, Lincoln, even though I look like her. The reason I took on Eulalie's appearance was because you know her and like her, and I needed to gain your trust as quickly as possible.'

'You're *not* Eulalie? Then who the hell are you?'

'My name is Springer. I'm kind of a messenger, an envoy.'

'Who for? DHL?'

Springer shook her dreadlocks. 'I come from Ashapola, who is the spirit of faultless light and absolute purity.'

There was a very long pause. Lincoln didn't know if he ought to snort or laugh or burst into tears. 'You're talkin' about, like, *God*?'

'Ashapola is known to many different people by many different names. But Ashapola is our guardian and our protector. Ashapola is all that stands between the human race and ultimate chaos.'

'You're not some hospital visitor, are you? Where you from, the Baptists or somethin'? You tryin' to convert me?'

Springer smiled. 'I don't need to convert you, Lincoln. You are what you are. You're descended from a long line of people who have the capability of entering the world of dreams and nightmares and fighting on the side of good. We call them Night Warriors. If you like, you're one of Ashapola's army.'

'Say what? I wasn't descended from no Night Warriors. My father was a jazz musician and my grandfather was a cook at The Whitney and my great-grandfather before him worked as a sweeper-upper in the Polish match factory.'

'I know. But apart from being a cook, your grandfather Joseph was Zebenjo the Arrow-Storm. He was a Night Warrior who was capable of firing over two hundred arrows so fast that you couldn't see them coming.'

'Oh, *right*.'

Springer squeezed his left knee through the blankets.

'Feel anything? Anything at all?'

Lincoln shook his head.

'That's because of your spinal injury. But that won't affect your ability to become Zebenjo'Yyx, the grandson of the great Zebenjo, and fire arrows at the same devastating rate as Zebenjo did.'

'Of course I will. Forget about the fact that I can't sit up and I've never thrown anythin' in my life more lethal than a frisbee. Lady – whoever you are – all of this sounds totally insane. It's obvious that I've been hurt real bad. Maybe it happened for real or maybe I was havin' some kind of trip. Maybe I was havin' a nightmare. Maybe I'm *still* havin' a nightmare, right now, and I'm beginnin' to think that maybe I am. But, come on, what's this arrow-shootin' shit?'

Springer stayed where she was, leaning over him, so that he could feel her steady breathing on his cheek. In spite of himself, his testiness began to subside. There was something so attractive about her that he wished he had the strength to raise up his head just two or three inches more, and kiss her. Yet the attraction wasn't so much sexual as spiritual. He suddenly felt that here was a woman who really understood him, all of his ambitions, all of his frustrations, all of his impatience, right down to the very core of his soul. She gave him a feeling of deep relief, as if he had been waiting for this moment of revelation all of his life. As if she had said to him, this is *you*, Lincoln. This is who you really are. No need for posturing. No need for swagger. This is *you*.

Springer reached across and picked up a hand mirror from the nightstand. She held it up so that Lincoln could see his own face in it.

'You can't stand up yet, so I can't show you the way you're going to look when you're a Night Warrior. Not your whole armor, anyhow, head-to-toe, and all of your weapons. But this will be the face that you wear, when you enter other people's dreams. This is the face that the enemies of Ashapola will see, and learn to fear.'

Lincoln looked up into the mirror, but all he could see was his usual face, with a crimson bruise over his left eyebrow, and a split in his upper lip.

'So?' he asked Springer. 'What am I supposed to be lookin' at?'

'Zebenjo'Yyx, grandson of the great Zebenjo, the Arrow-Storm.'

'Oh, of course. I can distinctly see the resemblance.'

'Wait,' Springer chided him. 'Have patience.'

'I need to see a doctor, lady. I need to see a doctor right now.'

'You're not hurting, are you?'

'No. I'm not hurtin' at all. I almost wish that I was. At least that would mean I could *feel* somethin'.'

He looked up into the hand mirror again, and when he did so, he said, '*Shit*!' The face looking back at him was no longer his, but a tan leather mask, intricately decorated with scar patterns and diagonal lines of white paint. It was topped with braided knots of dry red hair, and its mouth was fixed in a ferocious scowl, with what looked like a mixed-up collection of human and animal teeth crammed into it.

He could see his eyes staring out of the mask, and he knew they were his, because they blinked whenever *he* blinked. But the mask itself was terrifying, like a ju-ju mask. His grandfather Joseph used to have one hanging on his front door, with bulging eyes and a red protruding tongue. He had told Lincoln that he had nailed it up there to scare away any bad spirits, but it had scared Lincoln, too, when he was little, and he had always run past it with his hands covering his eyes.

'This is a trick, right?' Lincoln asked Springer. 'Some kind of optical illusion?'

'No trick,' Springer assured him. 'This is the battle mask that Zebenjo'Yyx wears, whenever he goes to war. And you should see his amazing armor, and the weapons he carries. In fact you will.'

She reached down and picked up a small alligator-skin purse. She opened it up and took out a folded sheet of paper. 'Here,' she said. 'This is the invocation that Night Warriors always have to say before they go to sleep at night. Once you have spoken these words, the spirit of Ashapola will visit you in your dreams and invest you with all of the equipment and protection that you require.'

'Lady—' said Lincoln. 'Do you really expect me to believe any of this?'

'Do you believe what happened to you at the Griffin House Hotel?'

'I believe I saw it, for sure. But I don't necessarily believe that it really happened for real. You can go to the desert, can't you, and see lakes, but there's no lakes there at all, only sand. You wouldn't get your feet wet.'

'So how did you fall out of a ground-level window and break your spine?'

'I don't know. Maybe I just fell awkward. I don't even want to think about it.'

'But you have to think about it, Lincoln, because we need you, desperately, and we need you now.'

Lincoln turned his head away and stared at the yellow seabirds on the curtains. 'I'm goin' crazy,' he said. 'I've lost it. I've gone nuts. Admit it – tell me that this is a nuthouse.'

'You're not crazy, Lincoln, and tonight you'll find that out for yourself. But you have to promise me that you'll repeat the invocation. Look – I'm tucking it under the pillow, right here.'

'What does it say?'

Springer unfolded it. '"Now, when the face of the world is hidden in darkness, let us be conveyed to the place of our meeting, armed and armored; and let us be nourished by the power that is dedicated to the cleaving of darkness, the settling of all black matters, and the dissipation of all evil. So be it."'

'Read it again,' Lincoln asked her.

Springer read the words again. After she had finished, Lincoln said, 'These Night Warriors – what exactly are they?'

'They were created by Ashapola to protect us in our dreams. Their original Sanskrit name means "Army of Dreams", although the Greeks and the Romans called them "The Legions of Sleep".'

'Go on.'

'Ashapola created the first human so that she could dream how the world of humans was eventually going to turn out, and he could copy her dreams and make them come alive. Some of her dreams were beautiful beyond any description, but others were violent and chaotic. So the *second* human that Ashapola created was capable of becoming a Night Warrior, to make sure that the first human came to no harm when she was asleep. And that was how the Night Warriors' bloodline began.'

'Come on . . . you're tellin' me that Adam wasn't Adam at all, but some woman?'

'Eve, that's right. Why do you think she was called "Eve"? In Hebrew, her name means "life" or "breathing". But she was created to imagine the world in her sleep, every night when evening fell.'

'A woman. I can't believe it. No wonder the world is in such a goddamned mess.'

At that moment, the curtain around the bed was sharply drawn back, and a doctor and a nurse appeared. The doctor was Indian, with a long face and huge black-rimmed spectacles and a tiny black moustache, while the nurse was plump and red-haired and kept smiling and raising her eyebrows as if she had just been told a hilarious off-color joke and was bursting to share it with them.

'I am very sorry to be interrupting your visit,' the doctor told Springer. 'Please – if you can come back in maybe ten minutes?'

'I have to go now anyhow,' said Springer. She leaned over again and kissed Lincoln on the cheek. '*Tonight*,' she said. 'You won't forget, will you? We really need you. The others will be waiting for you. So will I.'

'Others?'

'At least six more, maybe seven.'

'I don't know. I don't think I can handle any more nightmares.'

Springer kissed him again. 'Please,' she breathed. 'Just be there. Please.'

When she had left the room, the doctor came up to Lincoln's bedside and leafed through his notes.

'I am Doctor Dhawan and this is Nurse Fairbrother. How do you do, Mr Walker? It was I who first treated you when you were admitted.'

'Hi,' said Lincoln.

'Did I hear you say to your friend that you had been suffering from nightmares?'

'Right now, everythin's a nightmare. Am I going to stay paralysed like this for the rest of my life?'

'Of course that is the very first thing you will be wanting to know, sir. What has happened is that you have fallen with considerable impact, fracturing your T10 thoracic vertebra in the middle of your back. I will be able to show you your injury very clearly on your MRI and CT scans.'

Lincoln waited while Doctor Dhawan frowned at his notes again and tugged at his moustache. Eventually, he said, 'What has happened is that a broken fragment of bone is pressing on your spinal cord. You must remember that the spinal cord is very soft, with a consistency like toothpaste, and so it is very susceptible to pressure of this nature.

'At the moment, although you may not be able to feel it, your back is held immobile by a brace. I have also put you on steroids to prevent as much swelling of the spinal column as possible. I will be doing more tests in the coming days, but from what I have seen of your injury so far, I should be able to perform a surgical operation which we call "decompression" and this will be removing the offending fragment of bone.'

'Then I'll be able to sit up, and walk?'

'Eventually, sir, we are very much hoping so. It will take some time, and much therapy. But I believe the prognosis is good.'

Relieved, Lincoln lowered his head back on to his pillow. Nurse Fairbrother wheeled up a blood pressure monitor, picked up his right arm and wrapped the sleeve around it.

'You're that record promoter, aren't you?' she said. 'The Jive Machine? Skootah and the Gang? I really *love* that music.'

Lincoln gave her half a smile. He was preoccupied by what Doctor Dhawan had told him about his chances of recovery; but also by the feeling that Springer had given him that his life was on the verge of changing for ever.

'Millie D, too,' Nurse Fairbrother was saying, as she checked his heart rate. '"*I'm going to dream about you, lover, even when I'm wide awake*." I really love that song.'

'Yeah, cool,' said Lincoln. 'Next time Millie D's in town, I'll make sure you get some front-row tickets.'

'You know what you are?' said Nurse Fairbrother. 'You're an angel.'

An angel? thought Lincoln. *Not just yet, thanks, if it's all the same to you.*

Twenty minutes after Nurse Fairbrother had set him up with a new steroid drip and left him alone, he began to feel sleepy. Grace hadn't arrived at the hospital yet. According to the local news, severe electric storms over Lake Erie had delayed flights into Hopkins International by up to an hour. He watched *Everybody Hates Chris* for a while but his eyes kept closing.

He was right on the edge of dropping off when his left hand slid under the pillow and he found the piece of paper that Springer had given him. He took it out and unfolded it. He didn't really know why, but he began to read the handwritten words on it out loud.

'"Now, when the face of the world is hidden in darkness, let us be conveyed to the place of our meeting, armed and armored; and let us be nourished by the power that is dedicated to the cleaving of darkness, the settling of all black matters, and the dissipation of all evil. So be it."'

He folded it up again and pushed it back under his pillow. *Night Warriors*, he thought. That Eulalie must have been playing some kind of sick joke on him. She had probably been visiting Cleveland on business or seeing some relatives or some such, and heard that he was here in the hospital. He was a celebrity, after all, and they had probably run a bulletin about it on WBNX. But *Night Warriors*, for Christ's sake. She and her friends were probably wetting themselves with laughter right this minute. The coolest record producer in the country, cooler than Puff Daddy even, and he falls out of a first-story hotel window and winds up with a broken back. Never mind, I fooled him into thinking that he was going to be some kind of superhero. And who was he supposed to be? The Arrow-Storm? You got to believe it.

Lincoln closed his eyes. He wasn't asleep yet, but his mind was crowded with jerky, nightmarish pictures. He kept seeing the gray-faced man with the grinning green lips, stepping out of the shower stall with his handsaw. Then he saw the Hispanic woman with the wavy black hair, pleading with him not to leave her. *El prestidigitator*, she whispered. *You don't know what he's done to me.* Then he saw her bed exploding into flames.

This time, however, she didn't lie there motionless, as she had before, like a dead woman on a funeral pyre. This time she sat bolt upright and stared at him, and her hair was a crown of orange fire. This time she stretched her mouth wide open and let out an ululating howl of agony that went on and on.

'Stop!' Lincoln begged her. 'I can't save you! I can't even move! Please stop screamin'!'

But the woman continued to scream even though flames were licking out of her blankets and her nightdress was curling up into blackened rags.

'*Stop*!' Lincoln shouted at her. '*For Christ's sake*, *stop!*'

Her screaming became fainter and fainter, until all that Lincoln could hear was the crackling of the flames. Gradually the woman herself began to fade, like a sepia photograph that has been exposed to the sun for too many years. He thought he could smell smoke, but then that faded too. He lay with his hand on his chest, panting.

'What's happenin' to you, bro?' he whispered. 'You losin' your sanity, or what?' He thought of his batty old grandmother, always hooking her hand around between her shoulder blades and complaining that cats were jumping on her back. He thought of Old Mister Jeffreys who used to sit on a sack of dog food in the corner of the Clay Market on Clay Street, shouting about the Polacks, and how the Polacks were the enemies of the black folks. 'Never used to be so much goddamned sausage around, not till the Polacks took over!'

Exhausted, bruised, his mind fogged by pain suppressants, Lincoln fell asleep.

NINE

Call to Arms

In his previous life, John Dauphin had been a restaurant inspector down in Baton Rouge, Louisiana, which was a job that probably would have killed him before he was fifty. Unlike many of his fellow inspectors, he judged restaurants not only on their ambience and their standards of hygiene and the quality of their cooking, but on how generously they could pile up his plate.

Of course he always expected his pepper-jack shrimp at Boutin's to be crisp and crunchy and spicy on the outside and firm and white and sweet on the inside, but he also expected to be given more than a measly five shrimp per portion. As far as John was concerned, a chef might cook equally as well as Paul Prudhomme or Emeril Lagasse but that didn't entitle him to be a tight-ass.

John had lost his restaurant-inspecting job after some political jiggery-pokery in the East Baton Rouge catering community, apart from reaching the point where he tipped the bathroom scales at 289 pounds, and his BMI was only two more cheeseburgers away from fifty. Last year, with little else to do, he had driven over two thousand seven hundred miles north-east to attend the funeral of his old Army buddy Dean Brunswick III in Presque Isle, Maine, but on the way back his beloved '71 Mercury Marquis had given up on him, dropping its engine on the highway like a cow giving birth, and ever since then he had been trying to earn enough money to limp home to Baton Rouge.

He had chosen taxi-driving as a means of making a living because it meant that he could sit down all day, and eat and drink whenever he felt like it, and he also got to meet a never-ending variety of people. Most of his passengers were quirky and interesting, although some of them were dull beyond all human endurance, especially the business types he picked up at the airport, who sat in the back texting the whole time, or talking on their cellphones. John always thought, can't you stop *communicating* for twenty minutes out of your life, and just look around and breathe the exhaust fumes? OK, Cleveland is a world-class dump, but it does have some redeeming features, like the Cleveland Grays Armory building, which pre-dates the Civil War, and the West Side Market, and the Lake View cemetery, where John D. Rockefeller was planted, and the Rock and Roll Hall of Fame.

The job he detested the most was cleaning out his cab at the end of his shift. Apart from the usual contributions of chewing gum and used Trojans and folded paper napkins filled with spat-out chicken-skin, he had also found an expensive red alligator purse filled with lumpy beige vomit, an upper set of false teeth, a long-dead turtle in a Burger King box, and a white angora scarf that its owner had obviously used to wipe his rear end.

It never surprised him, how disgusting people could be. Before he had taken up taxi-driving, he had already known that people were disgusting, because he had worked in the restaurant trade. What *did* surprise him, endlessly, was how they never seemed to think straight. Instead of saying, "Pardon me, driver, I really need a leak, would you mind pulling over?" they would rather pee into their open briefcase, and walk into the airport with it dripping behind them.

Another reason he detested cleaning out his cab was because the space was so confined and he was so generously built. He had to force his way in through the rear doors and bend down to look underneath the seats, in case anybody had dropped anything valuable or revolting, and this always made him feel as if he were free diving in ninety fathoms under water and he was just about to run out of oxygen.

Today the back of his taxi was reasonably clean, except for a gristly piece of half-chewed sausage that somebody had forced into the ashtray in the armrest. He switched on his Vac'n'Go and gave the seats a quick once-over, and he was about to do the same for the carpets when he saw something sparkling underneath the front passenger seat. He rolled up his left sleeve and pushed his arm into the space beneath the seat, and after two minutes of grunting and scrabbling he managed to hook out whatever it was.

He gripped the door handle and hauled himself, panting, on to his feet. It was a gloomy morning here on Gooding Avenue, in Glenville – so gloomy that he could hardly make out what the sparkly thing was. He squinted at it more closely, and then he realized it was an earring – one of the hoopy, loopy earrings that Rhodajane Berry had been wearing. It was made up of three overlapping gold crescents, each of them studded with zircons. The long curved wire that went through her pierced ear-lobe had bent askew, and that was probably why it had fallen off.

He turned the earring over and over. It was a sign, he was sure of it. He even sniffed it, and it still smelled of Boss Intense.

John believed in signs. He didn't believe that you could see Jesus in the scorch patterns on a slice of burned toast, or that three knocks on the door meant that somebody had died; but he did believe that some things were meant to be, and that if people couldn't find a way to get together, or didn't realize that they *ought* to be together, the natural world would conspire to make sure that they did, like the rabbits and bluebirds in a Disney picture.

He looked around. Gooding Avenue was a short, flat suburban street with small brick-and-clapboard houses set well back from the road. The clouds hung over it like dark gray quilts. There was no other living being in sight apart from a brindled dog trotting from one house to the next, sniffing at the trash cans. If John hadn't been able to hear the traffic from East 105th Street and Lakeview Road, he would have thought that the world had come to an end.

'If this isn't a sign,' he told himself, 'then I'm due for a hefty tax rebate.'

He went into the pale-green-painted house where he rented an upstairs room at the back. His landlady Mrs Gizmo had gone shopping, or to one of her bridge mornings. Her real name was Ada Weiss, but John had called her Mrs Gizmo right from the start. Ada Weiss = A Device = Gizmo.

His room was small and brown and plain, with a sloping ceiling on the right-hand side. He had only one poster on the wall, a hand-colored picture of the ferry landing at Baton Rouge, sometime in the 1890s. He had carried it around with him for so long that it was falling apart at the folds. His bedcovers were all scrumpled up and his trash basket was crammed with empty take-out boxes. He always had to have a late-night sub from Quizno's, usually honey bourbon chicken, so that he didn't wake up at three in the morning feeling ravenous.

He pulled off his brown leather windbreaker and wrestled his way out of his raspberry-colored polo shirt. In his closet he found a pale blue button-down shirt that didn't look too creased, and his tan linen coat. There was a three-inch split in the back of his coat, but if he made sure that he always kept his face toward whoever he was talking to, then nobody would notice.

He washed his teeth and brushed up his thinning dyed-black pompadour and splashed his cheeks with American Crew after-shave. Then he grimaced at his face in the mirror over the washbasin and said, 'Mister *Eee*-resistible, that's you!'

* * *

He knocked on the door of Room 309 and waited. There was no reply at first but he was sure that he could hear voices inside, and they didn't sound like some daytime television show. He knocked again, and then cleared his throat loudly. Still no reply.

Eventually he pressed his ear against the door. He could hear a woman talking, and he was pretty certain it was Rhodajane; he would recognize the drawn-out vowels of that Brunstucky accent anywhere. The other voice was so soft and growly that it was impossible for John to make out what he was saying, but it was definitely a man.

Oh well, he thought. *Maybe the sign wasn't telling me what I thought it was telling me. Or maybe I just got my timing wrong. I should go eat, and come back later.*

He had just started walking back along the corridor, however, when the door opened and he heard Rhodajane whistle and call out, '*Taxi*!'

He stopped as abruptly as if he had been hit on the back of the head by a flying baseball, and slowly turned around. He hoped that she hadn't seen the split in the back of his coat. She was standing in the open doorway with her arms folded so that her breasts were pressed so tightly together that he couldn't have slipped a credit card between them. She was wearing a purple silk headscarf, a very tight purple velour top, and narrow-leg jeans, and another pair of her impossible shoes – in silver this time, with buckles. Her pose was jaunty, and she was smiling – even if it was one of those smiles that said *here we go, I was expecting this*.

'Dead on time, JD,' she told him.

He waddled back toward her with his arms held up in surrender. 'Hey – it's not what you think, believe me.'

'How do *you* know what I think?'

'Sorry, but it's pretty obvious. You think I'm hitting on you. You think I'm some kind of stalker. Whereas that is absolutely not the case.'

'"That is absolutely not the case," huh?'

'Absolutely one hundred thirteen percent.'

Rhodajane thought for a moment, with her lips pursed. Then she said, 'You want to know what I'm really thinking?'

'OK. What are you really thinking?'

'I'm thinking that you found my earring in the back of your taxi and you came here to return it to me. You're hoping that

I'm going to be *so–o–o* grateful that I'll agree to have dinner with you and maybe one thing will lead to another. Or that at the very least I'll give you a sawski by way of a tip.'

John held out the earring in the palm of his hand. 'Here – look – take it. I'm not looking for a tip and I'm not expecting you to come out to dinner with me and I'm not expecting one thing to lead to another, although I acknowledge that it can sometimes happen, you know – one thing leading to another – especially after the cream-cheese *pierogis* at Sokolowski's. They're almost worth learning Polish for.

He paused, and frowned, and then he said, 'Wait up a goddamned minute. How the hell did you know I came here to return your earring?'

Rhodajane kept smiling. 'Your friend told me. He said that you'd show up in exactly twenty-one minutes, and sure enough here you are.'

John leaned sideways, trying to see over her shoulder into Room 309. 'Excuse me? Who – *what* – which friend is that, exactly?'

'Come on in and meet him,' said Rhodajane. 'He's been telling some real interesting stuff. *Weird*, I'll grant you, but interesting.'

She stepped aside so that John could enter the room, but he didn't want to go in first because of the split in his coat. He took hold of her elbow and gently pushed her ahead of him, and closed the door behind him.

'I could sew that for you,' she said. 'You wouldn't think it, but I'm pretty good with a needle and twist.'

John was about to ask her how the hell she knew about *that*, too, but then he saw the figure standing in the bay window with his back to him. He was silhouetted against the gray, subdued daylight, his hands deep in his pockets, his coat collar turned up, his shoulders slightly hunched, but John recognized him immediately. He felt as if he had forgotten how to breathe.

'*Deano*,' he said. 'Deano, is that you?'

The man turned around. The hotel room was so dark that it was difficult for John to see his face, but there was no question that he was smiling.

'Hallo, John. How's it hanging?'

'Deano! I know you're not Deano, so don't try to give me that "how's it hanging" bullshit.'

Rhodajane went over and switched on the bedside lamps. Now John could see that Deano was very much younger than the last time he had seen him. He had died of chronic alcoholism at the age of forty-two, with blotchy skin and rheumy red eyes and a mass of white tangled curls, like a half-starved Santa Claus. But here today, in Room 309 at the Griffin House Hotel, he looked as young as he was when John first met him at Fort Polk, over twenty-one years ago, when they had joined the Army together. Handsome, in a rakish way, with a broken nose like Owen Wilson and piercing blue eyes and short-cropped blond hair. He held out his hand but John ignored it. This wasn't Deano. Deano had been cremated on a gray day up in Presque Isle, Maine, with only four people to sing *Amazing Grace* and one of them had throat cancer.

'Your friend's been spinning me all kinds of fancy stories,' said Rhodajane. 'Like how I'm descended from some kind of family who can walk around in other folks' nightmares and hunt down demons. Hey, would you care for a drink?'

'Best not,' said John, guardedly, without taking his eyes off 'Deano'. 'The cops have been keeping a pretty close eye on me lately. They even pulled me over for taking a bite of my muffaletta sandwich at a traffic signal. It's that fat guy, what's his name? Detective Windsocky. He really has it in for me.'

'Well, *I'm* going to have a drink,' Rhodajane declared. She went across to the mini bar and bent down in front of it so that her purple thong appeared over the waistband of her jeans. 'Champagne, I think. How about you, Deano?'

'Deano doesn't drink,' said John.

'Oh, really? What, are you in AA or something?'

'Deano doesn't drink because Deano isn't Deano. The real Deano is dead and his ashes scattered at the Fairmount Cemetery in Presque Isle, Maine. This is a messenger from the great Power-That-Is, who recruits poor suckers like us to fight the eternal war against good and evil.'

Rhodajane stood up with a half bottle of Cuvée Napa in one hand and a champagne flute in the other. She blinked her eyelashes furiously, as if she were trying to create two miniature hurricanes. 'You mean what he's been telling me is *true*? It isn't just a line?'

'Deano' kept looking at John and smiling, although he didn't say a word.

John said, 'It's true all right, Rhodajane, and I can prove it to you. I never would have had you down as one of us unlucky few, but there you are. Most of us look pretty unlikely in our everyday bodies. One of the last guys who fought with us, he was kind of a retard in real life but inside of those dreams and nightmares, he was a regular genius. I mean it was like eat your heart out, Stephen Hawking.'

Rhodajane turned to 'Deano' and said, 'So who did you say I was supposed to be?'

'Xyrena, the Passion Warrior. The woman who can inflame the sexual desires of everyone and everything she meets – man or woman, demon or beast.'

'There!' said Rhodajane. 'That's some line, isn't it? "Man or woman, demon or beast!" But you're trying to tell me it's for real? If you're not this guy's old army buddy, then who the hell are you?'

'So far as I know, his name is Springer,' said John. 'Well – I say "his" name but he can pop up in pretty much any kind of guise he wants to, male or female. He gets sent here by the Man Upstairs – God, or Gitche Manitou, or Allah. Springer always calls him Ashapola.

'Ashapola is who or what protects the human race from the forces of evil, and believe me there are plenty of forces of evil out there. That's why he created the Night Warriors, which is *us* – you and me, and hundreds more like us. It's our dubious distinction to save the world from corruption, chaos and ultimate destruction. Let me put it this way, ma'am: if there had never been any Night Warriors, the human race would never have survived so long as it has. We would have gone to hell in a handcart centuries ago.'

'So you're a Night Warrior, too?' said Rhodajane. She handed him the half bottle of sparkling wine and said, 'Here – can you open this for me? I don't mean to be rude or nothing, but how did you get past the physical?'

John gently eased the cork out of the bottle so that the gas came out with faintest *piff*! 'Angel's fart,' he told her. 'That's the correct way to do it.'

Then he said, 'Like I told you, none of us look especially prepossessing, present company excepted. You don't have to be Steven Seagal in your waking life to be a tough guy in your dreams.'

'So who are *you*?' asked Rhodajane. 'You know – like I really believe all of this, not.'

Springer came over and laid a hand on John's shoulder. 'This is Dom Magator, the Armorer. He carries most of the weapons that the Night Warriors need when they do battle in the world of dreams. For instance, he has over two hundred different kinds of knives – like a Retinal Stiletto, which – when you throw it – will exactly follow your line of sight, and unerringly hit who or what you are looking at. Or a Spiral Flensing Knife, which will peel whoever you cut with it like an apple, in one long spiral – skin, subcutaneous fat and all.

'He also carries over a dozen guns, like the Density Rifle, which compresses its target down to its ultimate possible density. A two-hundred-fifty pound man can be instantly reduced to the size of a smoking walnut. Or an Absence Gun, which uses quantum physics to negate the existence of whoever it hits. If you get shot by an Absence Gun, you don't get killed. You were never born in the first place. There never was any you. I have to tell you that it makes a most thrilling sound when it hits its victims, like a thunderclap, echoing back for years.'

Rhodajane poured herself a glass of sparkling wine and drank almost all of it in three gulps. She burped and said, 'Excusez-*moi*! I have to tell you two mooks that I am finding it very difficult to get my head around all of this. Either this is some kind of ridiculous set-up for *Candid Camera*, or it's a joke in very bad taste, or you're both out to lunch.'

'It's none of the above,' said John. 'It's for real.'

She prodded her finger into John's chest. 'OK, if it's for real, prove it. You said that you could. So go ahead.'

John looked at Springer and said, 'What are you doing here, man? Is something going down?'

Springer nodded. 'Yes, there is, and it's serious, and it's happening right here, in this hotel. But before I tell you what it is, I think it would be a good idea if we convinced Xyrena here that we're not spinning her a line.'

John took a deep breath. 'When you say *serious*—?'

'I mean serious to the point of the whole world falling victim to the same nightmare, all night, every night. I mean serious to the point of the human race losing all of its morals, all of its scruples, all of its kindness, all of its humanity. I mean what John Milton meant in *Paradise Lost* when he wrote about

"Chaos and Old Night". A hell on earth, John, where nobody respects anybody else's authority, or their dignity, or their freedom, or even their right to life. A mirror image of the US Constitution, if you like, in which it is almost mandatory to do harm to others.'

'That *does* sound serious,' Rhodajane agreed. 'I think that sounds very, very, *very* serious,' and she nodded her head emphatically with every 'very'.

'Then let us prove it to you,' said Springer. He went across to the closet and opened it up, adjusting the door so that John could see himself in the mirror on the back of the door. Springer beckoned to him, and John slowly walked over to join him.

'This is how Dom Magator appears in the world of dreams,' Springer announced.

John stared at his reflection in the mirror. He thought his face was looking baggy and lived-in, and he hadn't realized that his pompadour was now so thin that his scalp was gleaming through. However, Springer rested his hand on his shoulder again, and after a few seconds he began to see the ghostly image of a helmet materializing around his head – big and black and cube-like, with only the narrowest visor for him to see through, and even that was tinted dark green like the vizier in a welder's face-mask. The helmet was encrusted with knobs and switches and locking springs and other small metal attachments.

'Jesus,' said Rhodajane. 'Talk about Transformers.'

Now Dom Magator's battledress began to appear – a heavy cloak made of some soft, gray, metallic material, and underneath it a suit of black, leathery armor, jointed like the thorax of a stag beetle. He wore a wide metal belt, from which seven or eight handguns were suspended, all with decorative handles and elaborate cocking mechanisms and illuminated sights – some laser, some infrared, some ultraviolet. Across his back was fastened a curved chrome-plated frame, in which all of his various knives were fitted, as well as his armory of rifles and bazookas.

His outfit was finished off by heavy-duty knee-boots, to which even more knives were clipped. There was scarcely an inch on his body which had no weapon attached to it.

Rhodajane came up to Dom Magator and cautiously touched his helmet with her fingertips.

'There's nothing there,' she said, in bewilderment. 'I can only feel your hair.' She paused, and then she added, 'What there is of it.'

'Get out of here,' John snapped at her.

Springer said, 'You cannot feel his helmet because this is nothing more than a holographic vision of Dom Magator's battledress. This is the waking world, Rhodajane, and your Night Warriors' uniforms only take on physical reality in the dream world. Likewise, Dom Magator's weapons. We couldn't have anybody running around the waking world with an Absence Gun, or a Successive Detonation Carbine. Think what a terrorist could do with a weapon like that.'

Rhodajane stepped back, and Dom Magator's armor gradually began to fade, until he was back in his crumpled blue button-down shirt and his tan sport coat with the split in the back.

'Now do you believe us?' John asked her, primping up his hair. 'It isn't easy, I'll admit. I didn't believe it myself at first – not until our first mission.'

Rhodajane looked at her champagne glass. 'OK, I guess I have to believe you. That's unless you've slipped me a roofie.'

'So what's happening?' asked John, with a sniff. '"Chaos and Old Night" – that sounds like Satan's involved.'

'A child of Satan, if you like,' said Springer. 'At least, that's what he likes to call himself. His name is Brother Albrecht and he used to be a Cistercian monk. For a very long time, though, he has called himself *der Ursprüngliche Sohn des Teufels* – the Original Son of the Devil.'

'When you say "a very long time",' said John, easing his backside down on the corner of the bed with his feet planted wide apart. 'How long a very long time would that actually be, roughly?'

Springer looked at him with a faraway expression. It was unnerving enough, seeing Deano recreated exactly as he had looked on that humid morning in 1991, when he and John had both showed up at Fort Polk, Texas, as gangling young recruits, but it was even more unnerving to think that Springer might be able to remember what he and Deano had done together.

'I'm sorry,' said Springer. 'Brother Albrecht has described himself as the son of the Devil ever since he was dismissed from his monastery in Southern Germany for blasphemy and other transgressions against God. That was more than eight hundred years ago.'

'*Eight hundred years*?' asked Rhodajane.

'He exists in the world of dreams,' Springer explained. 'Nobody grows old in the world of dreams – not unless they want to, or unless some malevolent spirit makes them wither away. Brother Albrecht runs a carnival, a traveling freak show, a circus of pain and torture and human atrocities. It's already infecting the night-time consciousness of thousands of people, this circus. You only have to look at what's happening in our society. But now we're beginning to suspect that Brother Albrecht is trying to bring it back to life in the waking world, too.

'Can he *do* that? I mean, like, it's only a *dream*. Or a nightmare, by the sound of it.'

'We don't yet know, but we're doing everything we can to find out. We strongly suspect, though, that this hotel is a critical part of whatever Brother Albrecht is planning; and we think that he's being helped out by a one-time mass murderer called Gordon Veitch. If not Veitch himself, then a copycat.

'Veitch used to mutilate or murder his victims in some of the poorest parts of Cleveland, like Kingsbury Run and the Roaring Third. He used to paint his face like a clown, so that nobody would recognize him.

'He was never caught, even though some of the finest law enforcement officers in the country were hunting for him for months. One of them was Eliot Ness, who was Cleveland's Safety Director in those days. The main reason Veitch eluded capture was because he dreamed about every attack that he committed, and then he came here to this hotel, and dreamed it into the walls. All of the evidence that could have convicted him is right here, in the plaster. He left none of it behind, at any of the actual crime scenes.'

'I think I might have seen him here, in this room,' John told him.

'You're kidding me!' said Rhodajane. 'You mean I've been sleeping all night in a bedroom with somebody's murder inside of the walls?'

'I don't know,' said John. 'But when I fetched your bags up

yesterday, and switched on the TV, I saw the TV reflected in the mirror and in the mirror it was showing a different picture altogether.'

'Hey . . . you're giving me the creeps now, JD.'

'I'm sorry, I don't mean to. But it was what I saw. There was a woman lying on a bed and a guy was standing over her with his back to me.'

'Could you see what he was doing?' Springer asked him.

'Not too clearly. But his elbow was going back and forward, like he was sawing. I'll tell you what it reminded me of . . . one of those stage magic acts where the magician saws the woman in half.'

'Oh, my God,' said Rhodajane.

Springer said, 'That was him, I'd lay money on it. That was Gordon Veitch, or his copycat. You didn't have any nightmares last night, did you, Rhodajane?'

'If I did, I can't remember them. I was so bushed I slept like ten babies. Two bottles of Chardonnay didn't exactly help to keep me awake, either.'

Springer said, 'Maybe the dream image in *this* room isn't as powerful as some of the others. Maybe Gordon Veitch didn't actually *kill* the woman you saw in the mirror – only mutilated her. Pain, of course, is a very efficient conductor of spiritual images, but nothing like as graphic as the passing of a human spirit. It could very well be that the woman he attacked here could still be alive, someplace – either in the waking world or the world of dreams.'

'What, like, sawn in half?'

'It's amazing what the human body can withstand. You remember when we went to Fort Hood, John, and saw that young corporal crushed under a tank track? He was talking and laughing like nothing had happened. He even smoked a cigarette while he was lying there.'

'Oh, sure,' said John. 'He was fit as a fiddle until they moved the tank off of him.'

Springer said, 'Anyhow, we need to go looking for Gordon Veitch as a matter of extreme urgency. The music from Brother Albrecht's circus is growing louder and nearer every night. The chaos is coming closer, and you have no idea what this world is going to be like when it arrives.'

'Yeah, the January sales at Dillard's.'

'You will be ready to go tonight, won't you, Dom Magator?' Springer asked him.

'*Tonight*? Hey – I'm not so sure about that. I have a late shift tonight, finishing at one.'

'In the case you'll have to cancel it. Xyrena?'

Rhodajane swiveled around to see who he was talking to before she realized that *she* was Xyrena.

'*Me*? Tonight? You're kidding. I have my grandma's funeral this afternoon, and then a reception afterward.'

'Xyrena, it's critical. You *have* to join us.'

Rhodajane pulled a face. 'Well . . . they're holding the reception right here, in the Griffin Room. I guess I could find an excuse to sneak off a little early. To tell you the truth, it would be a relief. My family make the Munsters look normal.'

Springer said, 'I need you asleep by one a.m. at the latest. And – please – try to keep your drinking within reasonable limits. Too much alcohol can affect your dream body as well as your waking perceptions, and the chances are that you're going to have to make plenty of split-second judgments.'

'Talking of my dream body, Mister Old-Army-Buddy-Who-Ain't-Really, I still have no idea what my dream body is going to look like. If I can turn on "man or woman, demon or beast", I must look pretty damned hot.'

Springer raised his eyebrows. 'You do. You will. I promise you.'

'Then show me. You showed me what *he's* going to look like – Dom Magator. Let me see *me*.'

Springer hesitated, and looked across at John, but John pulled a face that meant, *why not*? *She's going to find out anyhow, and sooner rather than later*.

'Very well, then,' said Springer. 'Step over here and face the mirror. Try to empty your mind as much as you can. Think of nothing at all, but the surface of a lake.'

Rhodajane stood in front of the mirror, still with her arms folded. Springer said, 'Relax, now. Arms by your sides. Breathe very gently, as if you're floating on the water.'

'Old army buddy or not,' Rhodajane said to John, out of the side of her mouth. 'Your friend here is some character, isn't he?'

'Please, Xyrena, relax.'

Rhodajane stared at her reflection, and to begin with it was obvious that she was trying very hard not to laugh. After a few seconds, however, the air around her head began to glitter and sparkle, as if it were filled with scores of tiny fireflies, and a high curved crown began to appear on top of her head, made up of the finest filaments of light. Two curving epaulets appeared on her shoulders, as high as the epaulets of a Japanese gala costume, and then, with a soft rumble, a huge cloak of rich golden fabric billowed out from her shoulders, rising and falling and curling in a dream wind that none of them could feel.

Around Rhodajane's neck seven gleaming gold neck-rings materialized, so that it looked as if her neck were elongated. At the same time the diamond-shaped heads of two golden snakes peeped out from between the toes of each foot. They slid out and formed themselves into an elaborate pair of very high heels – first of all coiling themselves into the shape of shoes and then pouring relentlessly up her calves and around her knees, around and around her thighs, until they finished up as a pair of high golden boots.

But it was the gradual appearance of her breastplate that made Rhodajane's mouth slowly drop open. It was a perfect replica of her naked torso, in highly-polished gold. Her big, full breasts, complete with dimpled nipples. Her slightly rounded stomach; and her navel, like a tiny shining mollusk. Below that shone a golden facsimile of her plump, bare vulva, complete with a peeping clitoris.

'Oh my *Gawwd*,' she said. 'I *cannot* walk around like this, flaunting my pussy! Not even in somebody's dream!'

'I did tell you,' said Springer. 'Xyrena arouses man or woman, demon or beast.'

'But I'm showing everything I've got. Well, I'm not really, but as good as.'

'Xyrena is the ultimate paradox,' Springer told her. 'She attracts, she arouses, she fascinates. Did you know that the word "fascinates" comes from *fascinum*, which was a penis-shaped object worn around the neck in Ancient Rome, and often used in medieval witchcraft? If a woman fascinates a man, she gives him an erection, and that's just what Xyrena does. But even though it looks so revealing, nothing can penetrate Xyrena's armor, and believe me, Xyrena herself is deadly.'

Rhodajane pouted at herself in the mirror. She struck an

exaggerated pose to the left and then to the right, and then she slowly tottered around in a circle. Underneath her voluminous gilded cloak, her back was armored in the same polished gold, with her shoulder blades and her dimpled buttocks as perfectly replicated as her breastplate.

'Well, I don't know . . .' she said, thoughtfully. 'Maybe I could get used to this I do have a pretty good figure, though I say it myself.'

'But what's the point?' John asked Springer. 'OK, fine, she turns people on. As a matter of fact, she's making me feel distinctly twitchy in the BVD department right now. But why does she do it?'

'Hold out your hands, Xyrena,' Springer instructed her. 'That's right. Spread out your hand so that your fingers are totally rigid.'

Rhodajane did as she was told, and almost immediately eight long fine needles slid out, one from the tip of each finger. The needles were at least three inches long, and slightly curved inward.

'Xyrena arouses her intended prey until they're blinded with lust,' Springer explained. 'Then she takes them into her arms and embraces them – whether it's a *he* or a *her* or an *it*. All she has to do then is run these needles into their back. They're forged out of an alloy of titanium and ultrasound, way beyond the range of human hearing, and they can pierce through anything. Skin, leather, chitin, armor. Absolutely nothing can bend them or deflect them.'

'So she gives her prey a few little pricks,' said John. 'Then what?'

Rhodajane turned around to face him and struck another pose, her hands on her hips, her crowned head slightly tilted to one side. 'I'm really turning you on, aren't I, John?'

'Let's just get this over with, shall we?' John protested. 'I have to go eat before I can think about sleeping.'

Springer said, 'The needles enter the victim's veins and his blood literally boils. It usually takes less than twenty seconds for his entire blood supply to evaporate, and that's between five and six liters. Then, of course, he's dead. It's a very effective way of killing somebody at very close quarters.'

'Do you have anybody in particular in mind?' John asked him. 'This clown guy, for instance?'

Springer didn't answer, but closed the closet door so that Rhodajane's Night Warrior costume instantly vanished.

Rhodajane said, 'Oh, no. Not the clown guy. I feel like every guy I ever went to bed with in the whole of my life was some kind of clown.'

TEN

A Night to Dismember

Walter wedged himself into his usual corner booth in Rally's, smacking his hands together in anticipation of his triple cheeseburger. Outside the sky had grown even darker, and raindrops began to patter against the windows as if somebody were throwing handfuls of raisins at them.

Netta their waitress came over to take their order. She was four feet ten and as squat as a Munchkin, with fraying gingery hair and a swiveling cast in her right eye which always made Walter feel seasick. 'Hi, big feller,' she greeted him, taking her notepad out of her red checkered apron. 'Guess you want your usual?'

'You got it, sweet cheeks. But maybe today I'll go for the *loaded* fries.'

'The loaded fries? With the Cheddar cheese sauce and the ranch dressin' and the bacon bits?'

'Those are the very babies I had in mind.'

'You do know that a single regular-sized serving of loaded fries contains nine hundred eight calories, which is almost half your recommended daily intake?'

Netta's right eye was fixed on the clock on the wall, as if she were timing how much longer he had to live.

'Is *that* all? Sheesh! In that case, you'd better fetch me the jumbo-sized serving.'

Charlie ordered a plain hot dog, no bun, mustard only, no ketchup, and a Diet Coke.

'I don't know how the fuck you can live on that, Charlie,' said Walter. 'You need calories. Calories are very much maligned. They make your brain work, among other parts of your body. And do you know what they put in hot dogs? Chicken's feet.'

Charlie looked across at him with total seriousness. 'Believe me, Walter, if I thought that eating a triple cheeseburger would help me to understand how Maria Fortales got out of her bedroom, I'd order one, same as you. *And* the loaded fries.'

'We need to ask Mossad,' said Walter.

'Mossad?'

'You know, the Israeli secret service people. They whacked that Hamas dude in his hotel bedroom in Dubai, didn't they, but they left his door locked from the inside, with the chain fastened, even. Now, how did they do that? I don't have a clue. But it must be possible because they did it.'

Netta brought their drinks over. As she set down Walter's Gatorade, she accidentally knocked his glass and spilled it. Walter grabbed two handfuls of napkins from the dispenser and frantically dabbed at the spreading soda to stop it from pouring across the table top and on to his pants. He didn't want to spend the rest of the day looking like he'd peed himself.

'Netta, for Christ's sake!' he blurted out, but he managed to bite his tongue before he said, '*Why don't you watch what you're doing?*' He didn't want to hurt her feelings.

'I'm real sorry, Walt,' said Netta. 'I've been as clumsy as a ox all mornin'. I haven't been sleepin' good.'

Walter wiped up the last of the Gatorade. 'You need a man to share that lonely bed of yours, Netta. That's what you need.'

'A man? What good would a man do me? I need to stop havin' them nightmares more like.'

'What nightmares?'

'Them circus nightmares. I've been havin' them every single night for weeks and weeks and they always wake me up and I'm shakin' and sweatin' like nobody's business.'

'*Circus* nightmares?' asked Walter. He felt a crawling sensation down his back, as if a cockroach had dropped into his shirt collar. 'What kind of circus nightmares?'

'Oh shoot, you don't want to know about them. Probably some psycho-mological thing from out of my childhood. I'll go bring you another soda.'

'No, wait up,' said Charlie. 'Tell us what they're like, these nightmares.'

Netta shrugged. 'I always have them round about the same

time of night, about two a.m. I'm walkin' up this grassy hill and it's rainin' cats'n'dogs and I can hear this music playin' like all off-key. Kind of music you used to hear when a carnival came to town, only all the notes are wrong.'

'Go on,' Charlie encouraged her.

'Right at the top of the hill I see all of these tents, and they're all black, with red lights hangin' off of them like shinin' drops of blood. And I walk between the tents and there's trailers and animal cages all covered over with black tarps and the music's still playin' but I can't work out who's playin' it or where it's comin' from.

'*In The Good Old Summertime*, that's what it sounds like, only like I say it's all off-key and none of the notes are right.'

'Is there anybody else there, in your nightmare, apart from you?'

Netta shook her head so that her jowls wobbled. 'Not to begin with, but when I carry on walkin' between the tents I see shadows runnin' hither and thither and I can hear people mutterin' and coughin' and some people whinin', too. Then I always turn this corner and there's a row of trailers and I see this small critter go scuttlin' across the grass from one trailer to another and he goes scamperin' up the steps more like a rat or a groundhog than a person, but he's wearing a coat like a person and this weird kind of hat.

'I try to call out, *hey, where am I? I'm lost!* But somehow the words won't come out, like somebody's got their hand pressed over my mouth. And this small critter stops at the back of the trailer and starts jabberin' at me like five different languages all at once.'

'Can you remember what he says?' asked Charlie.

Netta frowned. 'Only a couple of words. Somethin' that I guess sounds Frenchish, like "prennay guard". Then some stuff that's all mixed up and don't make no sense at all. "Coop sign pianos." And "may go wordy". And "gang up you start". That's what it sounds like, anyhow, but he says it over and over and over, that's how I remember it so good. He says it over and over and over.'

'OK, so he spouts all this gibberish,' Walter prompted her. 'Then what?'

'He opens the door and disappears inside the trailer, and I'm left out there all on my ownsome, and it's still rainin' cats'n'dogs and the music's still playin'. I'm about to turn around and go back the way I come but then I hear a woman sobbin' her heart out. I follow the sound of her sobbin' and it's comin' from inside of this little black tent.

'I push my way into the tent but there's no woman inside it, only a man in a black suit and he's standin' with his back to me. I say *excuse me, sir,* but at first he don't answer. I say *excuse me* again and then he turns around and he has this clown face and he's grinnin' this greasepaint smile at me even though his *real* mouth ain't grinnin' at all.

'He says somethin' to me but I don't understand what it is and I'm so darn scared that I fight my way back out of that tent and I run and I run in between the tents and the trailers and down the hill and that's when I usually wake up.'

Charlie said, 'That's some nightmare, Netta.'

'Every night, too. Every night the same. For weeks and weeks and I don't know how to stop havin' it. And I don't know *why* I'm havin' it, or what it's supposed to mean. Like, dreams are supposed to have meanin's, aren't they? Like you dream about a pigeon poopin' on your head and that means you're goin' to win the lotto.'

'This clown you see, what color is his make-up?'

'His face is like gray but his lips are shiny green.'

'And he has long gray hair?'

Netta fixed him with her good left eye. 'How do you know that?'

'Because I know a whole lot about clowns and I think that this particular clown is called Mago Verde, the Green Magician. Part clown, part conjuror. And you heard that rat-person say "may go wordy", right? "May go wordy" – that could be "Mago Verde".'

'Hey,' said Netta. She was impressed. 'That's exactly what it sounded like, Mago Verde.'

Charlie said, '"Prennay guard", you're right, that's French – "*prenez garde*" – and that means "beware". Sounds like this rat-creature was telling you to watch out for Mago Verde.'

'How about "coop sign pianos"? What does that mean? And "gang up you start"?'

'I don't have a clue,' Charlie admitted. 'But give me some time, and I'll work on it.'

Netta said, 'Guess you think I'm losin' my reason. It's the

stress, probably. My brother Kyle lost his job at the Brook Park engine factory last September and he and me have been strugglin' to make ends meet ever since.'

Walter took hold of Netta's piggy little hand and gave it a reassuring squeeze. 'You're probably right. Maybe you should talk to your pharmacist – ask him for something to help you sleep more heavy.'

When Netta went off to refill Walter's soda glass, Walter leaned across the table and said, 'How about that? Netta's been having the same goddamned nightmares as Maria Fortales. The same – in every detail. How in hell's name can *that* happen?'

Charlie pulled a face. 'It's not totally unknown for strangers to share the same dream. Some psychologists think that dreams are like an alternate state of reality, rather than an alternate state of consciousness.'

'Meaning exactly what, exactly?'

'You know, like that Second Life thing you can do on the Internet – turning yourself into a sexy-looking avatar and leading a double life in some tropical fantasy world. And Carl Jung believed that the entire human race shares a collective unconscious.'

'Oh, yeah? Carl Jung must have gone to see that last Mel Gibson movie. The whole audience was collectively unconscious, including me.'

Netta brought them their food. Walter immediately picked up his triple cheeseburger in both hands and took a large bite; but Charlie said, 'Were you ever scared of clowns, Netta, when you were a kid?'

Netta shook her head. 'Clowns? No, never. I *loved* clowns. They used to make me laugh.'

'You never had a scary experience at a circus, or a carnival?'

'I was sick as a dog once on the Tivoli Spin-out Ride at the Ohio State Fair. But then so was most everybody else. But I don't know. Maybe somethin' bad happened to me when I was a kid and I got some kind of horrible memory that's just comin' out only now.'

Walter flapped his hand at Charlie and said, with his mouth full, 'Eat.' At that moment, however, his cellphone rang. He picked it up and said, 'What? I'm on my lunch break.'

But he listened, and then he said, 'Where?' and at the same

time he slowly lowered his triple cheeseburger back on to his plate.

'Something wrong?' asked Charlie.

Walter nodded. 'That was Skrolnik. He had a call from the School of Law where Maria Fortales was studying. There was blood dripping out from the bottom of her locker.'

'Jesus. Did they open it?'

'Of course. They thought that she might be locked up inside of it, and still alive.'

'But she's not?'

Walter turned to Netta and said, 'Hey, sweet cheeks, the call of duty calls. Could you put this burger into a box for me, so that I can take it out?'

He waited until she had taken his plate back to the kitchen before he turned to Charlie and said, 'They found her arms, that's all.'

'Only her arms?' Charlie looked down at his hotdog and pushed his plate away.

'Maybe that was the sawing noise that old man Yarber said he could hear.'

'But there was no blood. How do you saw off a girl's arms without spraying a whole lot of blood around?'

'Search me, Charlie. Let's go take a look for ourselves.'

It was raining even harder by the time they turned into the parking lot outside the George Gund Building, where the School of Law was housed. An ambulance was parked there already, its red lights flashing, as well as two squad cars and a black Grand Voyager from the Cuyahoga County coroner's office.

Officer Skrolnik was waiting for them underneath the slabby concrete entrance.

'Sorry about your lunch, detectives,' he said, although he didn't look sorry at all, only tired.

'When did you get the call?' asked Walter.

'Only about forty-five minutes ago. One of Maria's friends was trying to slip a note into her locker when she noticed that there was blood seeping out of the bottom of the door. She went to find the co-director. The co-director called nine-one-one and then she had the janitor cut off the padlock.'

'OK. Lead on, MacSkrolnik.'

Officer Skrolnik ushered them into the shiny marble lobby

area, which was arranged with pale turned-oak sculptures that looked like gigantic doorknobs and chess pieces. Then he led them along the corridor where the students' gray steel lockers were lined up.

One of the locker doors was wide open, and bent almost double, and three police officers and two CSIs were gathered around it, as well as a paramedic and a bored-looking deputy coroner. Walter and Charlie joined them, with a few desultory 'hi's' and 'how's it going's?' One of the CSIs was taking pictures, so that whenever his camera flashed, everybody appeared to jump two inches in the air.

Walter went up to the locker and looked inside. 'Ah, shit,' he said. 'I had a feeling this was going to turn out bad.'

In the locker's top compartment, two human arms were folded over each other, almost as if they had been patiently waiting for somebody to open the locker door and find them. Above the elbows, both arms were heavily smeared and spattered with congealing blood. Below the elbows, they were dusky-skinned, with sprinkles of tiny moles on them.

'Would you look at that?' said Charlie. 'He didn't even bother to take off her jewelry.'

Twisted around the left wrist was a silver Mexican bracelet with red-and-green flowers enameled on it; and on the third finger of the left hand there was a latticework silver ring. On the third finger of the right hand there was a ring with a single topaz in it. The nails of the right index finger and the right middle finger were both bitten right down, almost to the quick.

'Look here,' Walter told him. 'More clowns.'

Scotch-taped to the back of the bent locker door there were dozens of photographs of Pierrots and augustes and saltimbanques, including three nearly-identical pictures of Mago Verde. There were a few other pictures, too – Emilio Zapata and Carlos Santana and Our Lady of Guadalupe, the patron saint of Mexico – but most of the pictures were of clowns.

One of the CSIs came rustling up to them in her blue Tyvek suit, a fortyish woman with a sallow face and unplucked eyebrows and very pale blue eyes, as if all the death and mutilation that she had seen during the course of her career had leached most of the color out of them.

'Both arms were sawn off approximately eight centimeters below the shoulder,' she told them. 'We'll have to take them back to the lab, of course, but I'd say that the perpetrator used a regular garden-variety handsaw.'

'Any way of telling if she was still alive when he took her arms off?'

'From the copious bloodstains on the upper part of the arms, I'd say yes. But with any luck she may have been sedated.'

Walter looked around. 'Find any blood trails?'

'Unh-hunh. Not a drop outside of this locker.'

'Are we sure that this is Maria Fortales?'

'We'll be taking prints, of course, and DNA. But Ms Lipschitz ID'd her jewelry.'

'Ms Lipschitz?'

The CSI nodded her head toward the opposite side of the corridor. Officer Skrolnik was talking to a stocky woman with cropped gray hair and circular spectacles and a thick plaid skirt. When he saw Walter and Charlie looking their way, he beckoned them over.

'This is the co-director, Naomi Lipschitz,' he said. 'Ms Lipschitz – this is Detective Wisocky and this is Detective Hudson.'

'We're very sorry about what happened here, ma'am,' said Walter. 'It must have come as one heck of a shock.'

'Who could have *done* such a thing?' asked Ms Lipschitz. Tears were crowding her eyes and dribbling down her cheeks like the rain that was dribbling down the window. 'Maria – she was such a vivacious young girl. And *such* a hard-working student. Everybody liked her.'

'You're absolutely sure that it's her?'

Ms Lipschitz nodded. 'The bracelet, and the rings, I don't have any doubt. And I was always scolding her about biting her nails.'

'You say that everybody liked her. Maybe you can think of somebody who didn't like her quite as much as all the rest?'

'No – nobody that I can think of. Our students are all *very* competitive, believe you me, but they're *far* too busy to waste their time on personal feuds and petty animosities. All of the ground floor here – this is the Milton A. Kramer Law Clinic Center. The students here get involved in real-life court cases, so that they can gain practical experience, and their workload is highly demanding.'

'Was Maria Fortales involved in any real-life court cases?'

'Of course. Every student is given a caseload of several court actions at once. Maria Fortales was currently involved in three, so far as I know. One was an action for disability benefit; the second was a DUI; and the third was a case of domestic violence.'

'OK,' said Walter, 'we're going to need details of all of those. And every other case she's ever been involved in, going right back to when she first enrolled. You never know – one of her clients may bear a grudge against her for some reason.'

'I can't imagine why any of them should. But, very well, detective, yes, I'll make sure you get them.'

She started to turn her head to look behind her, but Walter laid a hand on her shoulder and restrained her. 'Give it a couple of minutes, OK? You don't want to see this.' The CSIs had wrapped up Maria Fortales' arms in clear polyethylene and were stowing them into a black zip-up body-parts bag, the type they usually used for torsos and severed heads. The arms looked to Walter as if they had been detached from a storefront mannequin.

'Do you think she's dead?' Ms Lipschitz asked him.

Walter shrugged. 'We can't tell for sure, ma'am, but I think I hope so.'

'How could anybody do anything so cruel? How *could* they?'

'I don't know the answer to that. I wish I did. Or then again, maybe I'm glad that I don't.'

He turned to Charlie and said, 'OK . . . what we need to do now is talk to all of Maria's fellow students, and all of her professors, and most of all we need to find out who was the last person or persons to see her alive. We also need to discover if she had any boyfriends that nobody knew about.'

'I think I should be running some background checks on Mago Verde,' said Charlie.

'Huh? What the hell for?'

'I still have this very strong intuition that Mago Verde is the key to all of this.'

Walter tried his best to sound patient. 'Charlie,' he said, 'listen to me. You're not supposed to have intuitions.'

'But *you* do. You have them all the time.'

'I know I do. But that's because I have a very short span of attention. You – you're not supposed to have intuitions. You're supposed to be *procedural,* get it? You're supposed to collect all of the available evidence, and carefully analyze it, and then come to logical conclusions that will stand up in court. It's not your style, jumping to conclusions and then screaming at people until they're prepared to admit that they're guilty, even if they're not. That's my job.'

'I understand that, Walter. But Maria Fortales disappeared from a locked room, and that was just like some kind of conjuring trick, right? And she's had her arms sawn off, which is just like another kind of conjuring trick. If anybody could pull this off, it's a conjuror, which is exactly what Mago Verde is.'

Walter took a deep breath. 'OK, then, what exactly do you propose to do, o intuitive one?'

'First off, I think I ought to find out if any local clowns have been making themselves up as Mago Verde recently. I should check out any circuses or carnivals within a fifty-mile radius at least, and any children's entertainment agencies. The yellow pages, too. If none of that gives me anything, I'll need to check if Mago Verde appeared in any circuses or carnivals in Cleveland in the past thirty years at least; and if anybody ever got arrested for any kind of felony while wearing Mago Verde greasepaint, and what that felony was.'

Walter stared at him for a long time with heavy-lidded eyes. He looked like a lizard basking on a rock. Eventually, however, he tugged at the end of his nose and said, 'OK, you win. I guess what you're saying makes some kind of sense, although I don't exactly know what. I'll call the captain and have Burrows and Gysin come out to do the routine questioning.'

Charlie said, 'Trust me, Walter. I know it sounds wacky but I genuinely think I'm on to something here. After I've checked out Mago Verde I'm going to do like you said and read all the way through Maria Fortales' diary. I don't believe that it was any kind of coincidence, Netta having the same nightmare that she did. I'm also going to try and work out what that rat-character was supposed to be saying.

He took out his notebook and flipped it open. '"Coop sign pianos" and "gang up you start". I'm sure it means something.'

'Sure it does,' said Walter. '"A bird in the hand makes it really difficult to blow your nose."'

Walter returned to his apartment well after eleven p.m. that evening, and he was exhausted. He hung up his trench coat in the narrow hallway and then went through to the kitchen. This morning's half-empty coffee mug stood on the draining board by the sink, next to a plate that was covered in yellow semi-circles of solidified egg-yolk.

He went directly to the fridge and took out a Miller, which he popped and swallowed straight out of the can, loosening his necktie with one finger. Then he went through to the living room and collapsed backward on to his sagging brown corduroy couch. He switched on the television and it was *Shatner's Raw Nerve*, William Shatner interviewing Rush Limbaugh, a repeat, so he switched it over to *Nightline*, although he kept the sound muted.

He lay there for a while, trying to relax, but grisly images of Maria Fortales' severed arms kept jumping into mind's eye, like pictures from a flicker book, with that Mexican bracelet and those silver rings.

He was deeply troubled by the Maria Fortales case. It was like a jigsaw puzzle in which the pieces seemed to belong to two different pictures, or even more, and he had the feeling that even if they managed to complete it, they wouldn't understand what he was looking at, like *Washington Crossing The Delaware* all mixed up with *American Gothic*, with maybe a bit of wallpaper from *Whistler's Mother* thrown in. The perpetrators he usually collared fell into one of four predictable categories. They were either creepy psychotic stalkers with halitosis who tortured and killed people to compensate for their own personal inadequacies; or moronic blue-collar bullies with tattooed necks and the temperament of pit-bull terriers; or equally moronic members of the Folks or the Latin Kings or the Waste Five gang who felt it was a matter of honor to stab or shoot anybody who disrespected them; or gray-suited office-workers who had simply cracked under the strain of everyday life – losing their jobs, or losing their children in some heartbreaking custody settlement.

But whoever had taken and dismembered Maria Fortales had much more obscure motives than any of these. He and Charlie hadn't been able to get any kind of handle on *how* he had abducted her, let alone *why*. To begin with, he had been skeptical about Charlie's intuition that Mago Verde was somehow involved, but in truth he had a nagging suspicion that Charlie maybe on to something. This was no ordinary missing persons case. This was all about nightmares and circuses and conjurors and clowns. And what about Netta? Netta had experienced nightmares that were almost identical, but of course there was no apparent connection between Netta and Maria Fortales. One was a trainee lawyer and the other was a hamburger waitress with screwy eyes, and so far as he knew they had never met. All the same, Walter felt that he had been deliberately given a very forceful nudge. How, or by whom, he couldn't begin to understand. But just like Charlie, he was beginning to feel that the circus was coming.

He jolted, and opened his eyes. He had been dropping off to sleep.

Walter heaved himself upright. As he did so his cellphone rang. He rummaged in his pocket until he found it, and then he snapped, '*What*?'

'Sorry, Walter, didn't mean to disturb you. It's Charlie.'

'What's up, Charlie?' he asked him. 'Don't you ever fucking sleep?'

'I was lucky . . . I think I got a rough translation of what that rat-thing was saying to Netta.'

'You're kidding me.'

'No. I was talking to some of the guys at the station and one of them speaks Spanish. He said that "pianos" sounded like "*piernas*" which is Spanish for "legs". So "coop" could be French for "cut" and "sign" could be German for "*sein*" meaning "yours". So the whole phrase could be a multilingual mish-mash that actually means "cut off your legs".'

'Come on, Charlie, that's stretching it a bit, don't you think?'

'Maybe so, if the context was different. But what we have so far is "beware Mago Verde, he will cut off your legs". And that makes sense, doesn't it, considering what happened to Maria Fortales—'

'OK, OK, I'll go along with it just so far as it goes. What about the other bit? "Gang up your start" or whatever it was.'

'I was lucky there, too. Detective Smit overheard us, and he still speaks pretty good Dutch. He said that "gang up your start" sounded like "*gang op uw staart*", which means "walk on your tail".'

'So what this rat-thing was saying to Netta was: "*Watch out for Mago Verde because he's going to cut off your legs, and you'll be walking on your tail.*"'

'Exactly.'

'You realize this could be total bullshit, and it doesn't mean anything like that at all?'

'It makes sense, Walter. What else could it mean?'

'You need to remember who said it, Charlie. A creature that looked like a rat, from out of some waitress' nightmare. It's not real. It's Alice In Fucking Wonderland.'

'A *recurring* nightmare, Walter. A nightmare she's been having so often she can actually remember what the rat-creature was saying to her.'

Walter suddenly thought of the popcorn that he had smelled, as he dozed off on the couch, and the off-key music, and the thumping of the circus tents in the wind that blew across the meadow.

'OK,' he said, grudgingly. 'Let's talk about it in the morning. Maybe you're right. Maybe we need to go on a clown hunt.'

ELEVEN

Heavenly Twins

Springer said, 'Two more Night Warriors will be joining you tonight. That will make six in all.

He counted them off on his fingers. 'Dom Magator, the Armorer; An-Gryferai, the Avenging Claw; Zebenjo'Yyx, the Arrow Storm; you, Xyrena, the Passion Warrior; as well as Jekkalon and Jemexxa, the Lightning Dancers. We'll be going to see Jekkalon and Jemexxa right now.'

'Do they already *know* they're Night Warriors?' asked Rhodajane.

Springer shook his head. 'Not yet. But they very soon will. They're staying here, in this hotel, on the second floor.'

'Do you want us to come with you?' John asked him. He didn't feel too enthusiastic about it, but at the same time he *was* Dom Magator, the senior ranking Night Warrior, and he was the only one amongst them who had yet had any experience of combat in the world of dreams. Because of that, he thought that he had some responsibility to give Springer his support –

and besides, the more backup you had when you were fighting in somebody else's nightmare, the better. He didn't yet know what a Lightning Dancer actually did, but it sounded as if a whole lot of lethal voltage was involved, and that could only be to the Night Warriors' advantage.

'Yes, please come along,' said Springer. 'I think it would help a great deal if they met you face to face. You know yourself that it isn't exactly easy, accepting that you're a Night Warrior.'

'OK. What are their names?'

'Jekkalon and Jemexxa. "Jekkalon" means "acrobat" and "Jemexxa" means "twin".'

'I meant their *real* names. Their waking names.'

'You probably know them. Or you've heard of them, anyhow. Kiera and Kieran Kaiser.'

Rhodajane let out a high-pitched squeal. 'The *Kaiser* Twins? You're kidding me! The Kaiser Twins are Night Warriors? I don't believe it! I *love* the Kaiser Twins!'

'Their late mother was Azurina, the Sky Dancer. It was a very great loss to us when she was abducted.'

'She was *abducted*?' said Rhodajane.

'Kidnapped, yes. Taken away. Not her waking body, but her dream personality, so she never woke up. In the end they turned off her life support.'

'I thought she died of a stroke, just after giving birth. That's what it said in *OK!* magazine, anyhow.'

'That was what everybody thought, Xyrena, including her doctors. But she was abducted in her sleep by a Dread called the Gray Memory. The Gray Memory took her out of revenge, because she had seriously injured the Gray Memory's sister, the Pale Confusion, during a battle in the dreaming world. The Pale Confusion could never walk or speak, ever again, either in the dreaming world or the waking world.'

'The Gray Memory and the Pale Confusion,' said Rhodajane. 'Jesus! *They* sound spooky.'

'Well, they were, yes – although I don't think "spooky" quite sums up how dangerous they were, and how scary. We're pretty sure that the Gray Memory is still hiding in somebody's nightmare someplace, although we haven't sensed her presence in more than seven years. It's possible that she was injured at the same time as her sister was hurt. She could be dead, but I don't think so. My feeling is that she's biding her time, so that she can get her revenge on the rest of the Night Warriors who were fighting with Azurina.'

'When she abducted the Kaiser Twin's mother – what did she do with her?'

'She gave her to Brother Albrecht, by way of a gift. Evil people are always doing favors for other evil people; just like good people do favors for good people.

Springer paused for a moment, as if he was thinking about times gone by and all of those people whom time had carried away.

Then he said, 'The Gray Memory and the Pale Confusion were part of a nightmare army of over a hundred Dreads. They were trying to destroy the human race by erasing our memories – rubbing them out and blurring them. If they had won, none of us would be able clearly to remember our childhood, or one single word of what we were taught when we were growing up. We wouldn't recognize our own parents, or even remember where we lived. We wouldn't know what we had done an hour ago, or even five minutes ago. We would have been like orphans, who can never find their way home.'

'That sounds too much like me to be funny,' said John. 'Like, ask me what I ate for breakfast, and I couldn't tell you.'

'I wouldn't want to know,' Rhodajane retorted. 'Besides, it would probably take too long for you to recite the entire order. Let me guess, though: you had pancakes.'

'I *always* have pancakes. How can you seriously call it "breakfast" unless you have pancakes? That's like having a funeral service without a stiff.'

'Come on, you two,' said Springer. 'Let's introduce ourselves to Jekkalon and Jemexxa.'

They left Rhodajane's room and walked along the corridor together with all the grim-faced determination of a posse in a cowboy movie. Two passing guests turned around to stare at the three of them in bemusement – a fat man with a pompadour in a bursting sport coat, a big-breasted woman in very tight jeans, and a curly-headed young man in a billowing raincoat.

They went down in the elevator to the floor below. Rooms 237 and 239 were on the north-east side of the Griffin House Hotel, the only two rooms at the end of a short private corridor, which was cordoned off with a thick night-club-style rope. It was guarded by two huge black men with shaved heads and mirror sunglasses and black suits that rivaled the size of Brother Albrecht's circus tents.

John and Rhodajane approached them cautiously, expecting to be stopped. But as they came nearer, the security guards unhooked the rope, and pressed themselves back against the walls on either side, so that their double-chins bulged out. 'Afternoon, Ms Schulz. How's it going?'

'Fine, thanks, Sherwin. How are you, Lamar? I think we're all set for tonight.'

John turned around and accidentally stumbled over one of the security guard's feet. That voice wasn't Deano's. That wasn't even a man's voice. He and Rhodajane were being closely followed by a small Jewish-looking woman with a haircut like a jet-black skullcap and a large complicated nose and pouting crimson lips. She was wearing an electric-bronze suit with padded shoulders and a flared waistline and a skirt that was much too short and tight for her age.

'Come on, John!' she said, pushing him forward. 'Always such a *klutz*!' She looked up at the security guard and said, 'Sorry, Lamar.'

'No problem, Ms Schulz.'

The Jewish-looking woman took hold of John's sleeve and Rhodajane's sleeve, too, and pulled both of them along the corridor together until they reached Room 237.

'What in *hell* is going on here?' Rhodajane protested. 'Who are you? What the hell happened to what's-his-face?'

The woman stared up at her and her eyes were glittering intently. 'I *am* what's-his-face, Xyrena. How do you think I can gain access to any place I need to? How do you think I can win people's confidence? Whoever people trust, whoever they confide in, that's who I am.'

'And right now?' John asked her.

'Right now, John-boy, I'm a dead ringer for Lois Schulz, the Kaiser Twins' manager. It's an illusion, that's all. I can look like anybody. I could look like *you*, if I wanted to.'

'What if the real Lois Schulz is here right now?' asked Rhodajane. 'You're going to walk in and there's going to be *two* Lois Schulzes?'

'No chance of that. Right now the real Lois Schulz is at the State Theater, making last-minute adjustments to the lighting sequences for tonight's show. And she's not very happy, so she's going to be gone for some time.'

'OK. I believe you. I don't know *why* I believe you. I shouldn't believe you. But I believe you.'

Springer gave a quick knock at Room 237 and called out, 'Hi, there, kids! It's only me!'

She opened the door and walked right in. Rhodajane grabbed John's sleeve and let out a squeaky, hysterical whisper right into his left ear. 'The Kaiser Twins! It's really them! I can't believe it!'

'Come on,' said John. 'They're only human, just like us.'

'But they're so *famous*! And I *love* them!'

Kieran and Kiera were both in Room 237. Kieran was sprawled out on the bed in a torn red T-shirt and gray jogging pants, playing *Killer Zombies*; while Kiera was perched on the rococo stool in front of her dressing table, wearing nothing but a Rams football shirt, polishing her toenails with purple glitter.

'You're back quick, Lois,' said Kieran, without taking his eyes off the TV screen. 'Are you happy with all of those lights now?'

'Actually, I brought a couple of old friends of mine to see you,' said Springer. John was still fascinated by Springer's transformation into 'Lois Schulz.' Enormous gold hoops as big as parrot perches swung from her ear lobes and she wore knobbly semi-precious rings on every finger, as well as an ostentatious sapphire brooch in the shape of a death's-head moth. 'This is Rhodajane and this is John. Say hi, twins.'

Kiera looked up from her toenails and said, 'Hi.' Kieran simply lifted his left hand and twiddled his fingers in a wave.

Springer said, 'The reason I brought my friends here is because there's been a change of plan.'

'Change of plan?' frowned Kiera. 'What does that mean?'

'It means you won't be singing tonight. You'll be doing something more important instead.'

Kiera looked up from her toenail-polishing. 'We're not singing? Why?'

Springer patted her shoulder in a motherly way. 'You won't be singing, my darling, because you can't sing when you're asleep, and when you're awake you can't fight. And tonight I need you to sleep, and to fight.'

'*Lois* . . . what *are* you talking about?'

'I know, I know. I sound like a *meshuggenah*. But how crazy did you feel when you opened up that door right over there and found yourself out in a field, and it was raining cats and dogs?'

Kiera lifted her head and stared at Springer wide-eyed. 'Lois? How did you *know* about that? Kieran – did *you* tell her?'

'I never said a word. I swear to God.'

Springer patted her shoulder again. 'Kieran didn't tell me, my darling. I knew what was going to happen even before it happened. In fact I *arranged* for it to happen. Why do you think I chose this particular hotel for you to stay in?'

'You *knew* what was going to happen? How could you have known?'

'You opened the door, Kiera, and there you were. You and Kieran climbed the hill to the carnival. It was raining and thundering and the tents were black and the lights were red and you met some very strange people there, didn't you? A little man who looked more like a rat, and a bald man called Zachary.'

'I don't believe this,' said Kieran. 'I just don't fricking believe this. It was only a *dream*!'

But Springer carried on. 'Most important of all, you saw your mother. Your poor mother, who you believed was long dead, mutilated and put on show for everybody to stare at. Demi – the Demi-Goddess, the Half-Woman.'

Kieran swung his legs off the bed and stood up. His hair was sticking out sideways, as if he had just stepped inside from a hurricane. 'How do *you* know about our mom, Lois? Come on, Lois, how the hell do *you* know? We thought it was only a nightmare, but we believed that we were sharing it because we're twins. I mean, we share all kinds of feelings, all the time. But how do *you* know all about it?'

Springer sat down on the side of the bed. 'I look very much like Lois, Kieran, but I'm not Lois.'

'I don't get it. Is this a joke? If it is, it's in pretty shitty taste.'

'Lois is still at Playhouse Square – the real Lois, that is. My name is Springer. I can take on the physical appearance of anybody I want to. Watch me. Who was your best friend at school? Kenny Ballantine? You remember Kenny Ballantine?'

Kieran looked confused. 'Of course I remember Kenny Ballantine. He broke my goddamn iPod.'

Right in front of them, Lois Schulz began to alter. She grew taller, and her shoulders grew wider. Her black skullcap hairstyle gradually grew lighter, until it was medium-brown, and scruffy. Her face grew broader, and her eyes changed color from brown to hazel. Within less than thirty seconds, she was no longer a musical agent with dangling earrings and bright red lip gloss, but a sprawling young man of seventeen or eighteen, with holes in the knees of his Levis and a T-shirt with a black-and-white print of Kurt Cobain on the front of it.

Kieran stared at him, stunned. 'Kenny?' he said. '*Kenny* – is that really you?'

'No,' said Springer. 'It's not really me. But you asked me what I was capable of, didn't you, and that's one of the many things that I'm capable of. I needed to convince you that your mother is still alive, and that you can rescue her, if you want to.'

'But she was cut in half!' Kiera interrupted. 'Not only that, she doesn't even know that she's our mother! Even if we rescue her, what are we going to do with her? Her mind's gone, her legs have gone.'

Kieran said, 'She's still our mother. We can't *leave* her like that, in that carnival? By the way, where the hell *is* that carnival?'

'You were right about it the first time,' said Springer. 'It exists only in the world of dreams. For now, anyhow. But that doesn't mean that it's any less real than anything that exists only in the world of reality. You can bring your mother back, if you want to. You would obviously have to arrange for her to receive intensive physical care and psychological rehabilitation. But you're not poor, are you? And who knows, you might even get your original mother back – or a little part of her, anyhow.'

'Oh my God,' said Kiera. 'You're really frightening me now.'

'Well, just sit and listen,' said Springer. 'When I'm through, you can either tell me to get the hell out of here and never come back, or you can agree to help us save your mother, and scores of other people, too.'

'What other people?'

'Your mother isn't the only one who has been taken away by that carnival. Over the years, over the centuries, there may have been hundreds of them. Men, women, children, even babies. Some of them were born freaks, but many of them were deliberately mutilated and deformed so that they were turned into freaks.'

'That's so terrible. But *why*?'

'Because the man who started the carnival is determined to bring out the worst in human nature. He wants to see an end to love, kindness and charity. He wants to see nothing but cruelty and depravity and wholesale, meaningless war. In other words, he wants his personal revenge on God.

'If he can bring his carnival back from the world of dreams into the world of reality, it will spread around the world like the worst contagion you can ever imagine. A moral sickness like the Black Death, only a thousand times worse.

'This is why I've come here today. This is the time when we need to act, and fight back, or the whole planet is going to turn into a slaughterhouse.'

Kieran said, 'I don't know whether to believe you or not, dude. But you sure look like Kenny Ballantine. You're the spit of him. Even got that warty thing by the side of your nose.'

Carefully and quietly, Springer explained who he was and where he had come from. He told them about Ashapola, and how the purity of Ashapola could protect every person on earth, regardless of their religion or their core beliefs. He told them about the Night Warriors, and how their mother had been Azurina, the Sky Dancer, and how, as twins, they had both inherited her powers.

He also told them about Brother Albrecht, and how his arms and legs had been amputated, and how that had led him to set up his carnival and freak show.

When Springer had finished, he sat back to let his words sink in. Kieran and Kiera stared at each other in complete silence, but it was obvious that they were sharing their thoughts about everything that he had told them.

Eventually, Kiera said, 'How could we have been these Night Warriors all of our lives and never known that we were?'

'Because you weren't needed, until now. Some Night Warriors go through their whole lives without finding out, simply because their special abilities were never called for.'

'I never knew I was, not until last year,' John told her.

'And *I* never knew until about an hour ago,' said Rhodajane.

'So who are you supposed to be?' Kieran asked John.

'Me? I'm Dom Magator the Armorer. I carry every kind of

handgun and rifle and bladed weapon that you can possibly think of, and most of which you can't. You want a pistol that can make somebody half a mile away go stone deaf? You want a knife that you can throw through solid concrete? How about an Amnesiac Rifle, that can make your enemy forget who he is and what the hell he's supposed to be doing there?'

'This has *got* to be a joke,' said Kieran. 'Amnesiac Rifle? Who are you trying to kid?'

'It's no joke,' Rhodajane assured him. 'I'm Xyrena, the Passion Warrior. I can turn on anything that has a pulse, and a few things that don't, I wouldn't be surprised.'

Springer said, 'The best way for me to convince you that I'm telling you the truth is to show you what Jekkalon and Jemexxa actually look like.'

'Jekkalon?' Kieran protested. 'What kind of a stupid name is that?'

'Actually, Jekkalon is a highly-respected name amongst the Night Warriors,' said Springer. 'The very first Jekkalon was a servant at the court of the Egyptian pharaoh Seti the First in the year twelve ninety-one BC.'

'Now I'm *sure* you're kidding me.'

'Not at all. The demon goddess Nepththys ambushed Seti in his dreams and took him to her palace in the dry desert. She tried to mummify him in his sleep, so that he would be powerless to act out his dreams. We all have to act out our dreams in order to stay fit and sane, but Nepththys was hoping that she would drive Seti mad and that she could turn the entire kingdom of Egypt into a barren wasteland.

'But Jekkalon and Jemexxa followed her, and Jekkalon vaulted over the walls of Nepththys' palace, which had always been believed to be impregnable. He blinded Nepththys and her priests with lightning, which Jemexxa had reflected from a distant electric storm. Seti escaped, and rewarded Jekkalon and Jemexxa with great riches.'

'Well, it's a cool story,' said Kieran. 'Sounds like something out of *X-Men*.'

'Do you want to see yourself as Jekkalon?' asked Springer. 'All you have to do is stand in front of that mirror.'

'Go on, Kieran,' Kiera urged him. 'You know you love looking at yourself more than anything else in the world.'

Kieran walked across to the large oval cheval mirror in the

corner of the bedroom. Springer stood up and joined him, laying a hand on his shoulder.

'Be patient,' said Springer. 'It doesn't take long.'

Kieran shook his head. 'Jesus, man. You look so much like Kenny, I can't believe it. Remember that time you swung on that rope over Mill Creek Falls, pretending to be Tarzan so that Susan Ladenes would be all impressed, and the rope broke and you fell in head first and broke your arm?'

'It was my collar bone, as a matter of fact,' Springer corrected him.

'This is totally crazy,' said Kieran.

He turned away from the mirror for a moment, grinning at Kiera in disbelief, but Kiera suddenly said, '*Look*! Just look at yourself!'

Kieran turned back, and there, in the mirror, he saw a reflection of an athletic young man wearing a skintight suit made of some glittery black fabric that looked as if it had been cut out of a starry night sky. On his head he had a sleek black helmet with slanted black lenses covering his eyes and two long antennae.

'Is that me?' said Kieran. He leaned forward to look at himself more closely, and his reflection leaned toward him. 'Shit! It really *is* me!'

'To be more accurate, it's Jekkalon,' Springer corrected him. 'But, yes, it really is you.'

'And I'm some kind of an acrobat? Is that it?'

'The best. You can jump, you can roll, you can run on stilts as fast as most athletes can run on their feet. You can walk on a high wire without using a balancing pole and you're one of the greatest trapeze artists that ever was. Double flips, triple flips, easy.'

Keiran stood back, and spread his arms wide. 'This is unbelievable. This is absolutely un-fricking-believable. I *am* Jekkalon. I can *feel* it. I know that I can really do all of that stuff.'

'Well – you can't quite do it yet,' said Springer. 'You'll have to wait until you're asleep, and dreaming. You don't want to risk hurting yourself, like your old friend Kenny.'

'So how do I go about making people go blind?' Kieran asked him. 'I don't seem to be carrying any guns or nothing.'

'Take a look at your hands.'

Kieran raised both hands and turned them over. The palms of each hand were so highly reflective that he could see his face in them.

'So I got shiny hands, so what?'

'Kiera – stand beside him,' Springer asked her. Kiera put down her bottle of nail polish and came across the room. As she stood beside her twin brother, her reflection in the mirror began to shine, and soon she was wearing a tight silvery suit as sparkling as Kieran's, and a wedge-shaped silver helmet to match. On her back, however, she was carrying a metal grid like a hiker's backpack frame, except that it was covered with layers of complicated copper shapes like fall leaves, each connected by wires and circuit-breakers and switches.

'Jemexxa is acutely sensitive to any static electricity stored in the upper atmosphere,' Springer explained. 'She can almost *smell* it, even if it's twenty miles away and thirty-five thousand feet high. She attracts it in exactly the same way as a lightning rod attracts lightning, and stores it up in the framework that she carries on her back. Then – when Jekkalon needs to zap somebody – like Nepththys and her priests for example – Jemexxa raises her hand and sends him a bolt of lightning. Or *two* bolts, one from each hand, if he needs them. All he has to do is angle his hand so that the lightning ricochets off it and hits whoever or *what*ever he wants it to.'

Kiera looked at the palms of her hands and they were as highly reflective as Kieran's.

Springer said, 'See – it's as simple as shining a sunbeam from one mirror to another.'

Kieran and Kiera looked at each other again. Their helmets gave them the appearance of two giant praying mantises, one black and the other silver.

As they stood there, their Night Warriors uniforms gradually faded. After less than a minute, Kiera was back in her football shirt and Kieran was wearing his T-shirt and his jogging pants.

'So what's it to be?' Springer asked them.

'I just don't know,' said Kiera. 'It's all so much to take in. I can't decide if I'm dreaming all of this, or if it's real, or if you guys are pulling some kind of scam.' She started to sound panicky. 'Like, how can we cancel an entire sold-out concert? That's two thousand five hundred seats. And we're supposed to be on stage in less than three hours, for a final soundcheck.'

John shrugged. 'Like Springer says, sweetheart, it's entirely up to you. But if you don't come with us, the rest of us will have to go anyhow, and from my experience we're going to need all the firepower we can muster.'

Kiera clapped her hands over her ears in frustration. 'Even if we say yes, Lois will be back soon, and there's no *way* that she's going to let us cancel tonight's concert and drop off to sleep, just like that! Think of all the money that the promoters are going to lose if we don't show! Think of all the money that *we're* going to lose. And how can we let so many fans down? They'll *hate* us for it! They'll never forgive us!'

'OK,' John told her. 'If that's the way you feel. But what about your mom, trapped in that freak show? Are you just going to leave her there?'

'She's not real. She's just a dream. You said so yourself.'

'Right now she is, yes. But people suffer, sweetheart, even in the world of dreams. And if we don't stop Brother Albrecht from bringing his carnival back to *this* world, she won't be a dream any more. She'll be real, and suffering for real. Brother Albrecht will put her on show, along with all of his other freaks, so that the paying public can come along and gawp at her.'

Kieran said, 'He's right, Kiera. We can't let that happen.'

Kiera sat down at her dressing table again and stared at three reflections of herself in its mirrors. 'Look at me,' she said. 'Selfish Kiera and mean Kiera and uncaring Kiera.'

But Rhodajane came and stood behind her and laid her hands on her shoulders. 'Honey, all of us are selfish, and all of us are mean, and none of us give a shit. That's the way I've been all of my life – with men, and with money, and with my own dear sisters. But you only have to do one thing for somebody else – just one – for no other reason except that you believe it's your duty as a human being, and God will forgive you for all of your heartlessness, and you might even find that He gives you a heart by way of saying thank you.'

Kiera wiped tears away from her eyes. Springer came up to stand beside Rhodajane and said, 'When you walked into that dream last night, Kiera, that wasn't even your dream. Kieran knew that, didn't you, Kieran? It was being dreamed by a young girl of eight years old who was staying with her parents in Room Six-Two-Five. Your psychic sensitivity enabled you and

Kieran to enter her dream and find out what had happened to your mother.

'You can see the dead, can't you – you and Kieran?'

'You know about that, too?' said Kieran. 'Is there anything you *don't* know about us?'

'To Ashapola, Kieran, all human beings are an open book. All I do is turn the pages and read what's written there.'

'So you know we saw some bum on Santa Monica Boulevard jumping in front of the traffic and never getting hurt; and some gangster with his throat cut in the barbershop at the Handlery Hotel in San Francisco; and some drowned woman in the Japanese Garden in Portland, just lying under the water in the pond smiling up at us like she was happy at last.'

'Yes,' said Springer. 'And that's why you can be so useful to us. We suspect that Gordon Veitch could be one of those dead people who won't lie down. A Dread, we call them. That's why he can move so easily from the real world to the dream world, and back again. He can appear, he can disappear, whenever he feels like it. But he won't be able to hide from you two, in either world.'

Kiera reached out and took hold of Kieran's hand. She briefly closed her eyes and gave him an almost imperceptible nod.

'OK,' said Kieran. 'We'll do it.'

'You're sure about that?'

'We're sure,' Kiera told him. 'Kieran's right. If there's any chance of rescuing our mom – we have to try, at the very least.'

'The point is, how do we get out of here?' asked Kieran. 'Sherwin and Lamar won't let us out of their sight, even if you turned yourself back into "Lois". The promoters pay for them, to protect their investment.'

'Oh, don't worry,' said Springer. 'I've already booked a room on the fourth floor, room Four-Three-Nine, directly above this one. All you have to do is climb two stories up the fire escape. I left the balcony doors unlocked. Meantime, I'll leave here through the front door and tell your bodyguard friends that you're not to be disturbed.'

Kiera said, 'So you have everything arranged already. How did you know we were going to say yes?'

Springer was gradually changing his appearance, from Kenny Ballantine back into Lois Schulz. They all found it fascinating to watch, as "Kenny" dwindled down to five feet four and his hair turned dark and his long gangly legs became skinny and bowed, with shiny black pantyhose and black patent shoes with very high heels.

'How did I know you were going to say yes? You're natural-born Night Warriors, that's why. You're Jekkalon and Jemexxa, the acrobat and the acrobat's twin. That's who you are, even more than Kieran and Kiera Kaiser. It's your destiny.'

TWELVE
Night Flight

By midnight, David was snoring softly with his green mask over his eyes. Katie eased herself out of bed and went through to her dressing room. She opened up her white satin-covered jewelry box and took out the folded slip of paper that Springer had given her. Before she opened it, she looked at herself in her dressing-table mirror.

'You don't have to do this, Katie,' she told herself. 'If you'd rather take a rain check, what can he do to you? He's just a young guy who happens to look a whole lot like Mr Flight, that's all.'

Actually, she wasn't so sure about that. If Springer was capable of showing her what she looked like when she was all dressed up in her Night Warriors suit, maybe he was capable of making sure that she wore it, and that she went out hunting for this Gordon Veitch character, and Brother Albrecht's carnival, whether she wanted to or not.

She held up the piece of paper. To her surprise, the words on it seemed to be written in her own handwriting. Very softly, she read them out.

'"Now, when the face of the world is hidden in darkness, let us be conveyed to the place of our meeting, armed and armored; and let us be nourished by the power that is dedicated to the cleaving of darkness, the settling of all black matters, and the dissipation of all evil. So be it."'

Katie thought that the words sounded rather pompous and medieval, but in spite of that she still found them stirring, and she particularly liked the phrase about 'the place of our meeting, armed and armored', which reassured her that she was not going to be alone, but part of a fighting force with other Night Warriors.

She crept back into the bedroom and slid herself under the covers. David was lying on his right side now, and talking to himself. As far as she could make out, he was giving a lecture, but it all sounded like nonsense. '*Not psychotic, no. Umbrellas. And everybody has to go now.*'

He was talking so loudly that she was afraid that she wouldn't be able to fall asleep, but somehow the words that Springer had given her to read had affected her as if she had taken a strong sedative, and after only a few minutes her eyes began to close. The illuminated clock on the nightstand beside her read twelve twenty-seven.

Darkness flooded into her mind; and at the same time she began to feel lighter and lighter. With the abrupt buoyancy of a helium balloon caught by a gust of wind, she bobbed up from her bed and floated upward, toward the ceiling. Startled, she rolled around in mid air, and as she did so she looked down and there she was, her own sleeping self. Her short brunette hair was already tousled, and she was touching her cheek with one hand as if she were making sure that she was real.

She rolled around again, so that she was facing upward, just as she reached the ceiling. She held up both hands to prevent herself from being pressed up against it, but her hands disappeared right into the plaster as if it were nothing but the softest of fine white sand. The rest of her followed, with a thick *shushing* sound, and she found that she was rising through the attic, where all of their suitcases and their books and their old furniture was stored. She saw the carved pine headboard from Daisy's bed, the bed in which poor little Daisy had died, and somehow that gave her all the more determination to carry on. Even if she hadn't been able to save Daisy, she could save other innocent children.

She kept on rising, and passed through the attic ceiling as easily as she had passed through the bedroom ceiling; and then the roof shingles; and in a few seconds she was high above the house. To the south she could see the glittering lights of Miami Beach, and to the west she could see clear across Biscayne Bay to Morningside Park. To the north, on the far side of the Surprise

Waterway, she could see La Gorce Country Club, and an endless red stream of tail lights on Collins Avenue, like blood corpuscles flowing through the darkness.

Now she hung suspended for a few moments. At first she could feel the breeze from the ocean blowing against her face and ruffling her hair, but then her helmet began to take shape, and her head was soon enclosed in the distinctive falcon-shaped helmet of An-Gryferai. The lenses that protected her eyes were tinted amber, but her night-vision was stunning. She could clearly see all the way to the Golden Glades interchange, which was nearly twelve and a half miles to the north-west. All she had to do was lightly touch the side of her helmet with her fingertips, and she could see even further, with just as much clarity. She could even read the traffic sign on I-95 for Fort Lauderdale Airport, and see a small plane taking off, with the lights on its wing tips flashing.

She looked down and saw that she was now dressed all over in the soft brown-feathered plumage of An-Gryferia, with white feathers across her breasts. On each forearm her powerful mechanical claws had materialized, with all of the rods and ratchets and pulleys that operated them. She squeezed them open and shut, and rotated them, and each movement was accompanied by a satisfying series of whirrs and clicks.

Her wings had developed, too. They were strapped to her back and her upper arms with a soft leather harness, which allowed her to open them by flexing her shoulders. At first they were folded, and very heavy, but An-Gryferai soon discovered that when she opened them up, they were caught at once by the warm updraft from the ground. With a rumble of wind-blown feathers, she was carried even higher up into the air, until she could see the sparkling curve of the Florida Keys, all the way south to Plantation Key, and that was over seventy-five miles away.

She spun slowly around and around, marveling at the way she could fly, and how far she could see. She flapped her wings cautiously, only three or four flaps, and she was lifted over fifty feet higher into the air. Then she stretched them as wide as she could, and angled them into the wind. She swooped down, and then up, and then she dared to plummet head first toward the ground, breaking out of her dive less than twenty feet from the seventh hole at La Gorce Country Club. She flew the length of the lake on the right-hand side of the hole, so that she could see her reflection flashing over the surface of the water. An-Gryferai, in her falcon helmet, the Avenging Claw.

When she reached the far end of the lake, she was about to soar up into the air again when she saw a solitary figure standing beside the trees. Her eyesight was so sharp that she could identify him at once as Springer. She tilted to the left, and then feathered her wings so that she landed only a few yards away from him, although she nearly lost her balance as her feet touched the ground, and finished up her flight with a scurrying little run.

As she stood there panting, Springer circled around her, nodding his head in admiration. An-Gryferai thought he looked different – darker, taller, more intense – less like Mr Flight and more like her first boyfriend Gideon, who had been seventeen years older than her. Very attractive, but domineering.

'You look wonderful,' said Springer. 'Your grandmother would be very proud of you.'

'Thanks, it's amazing. I could see all the way down to the Keys.'

'You'll have to travel far and fast tonight,' Springer told her. 'We've noticed that the president of a meat-packing company in Chicago is dreaming about Brother Albrecht's carnival. He lives in the Drake Tower, on Lake Shore Drive. Dom Magator and the rest of your team will be waiting for you right outside.'

'*Chicago*? But that's over a thousand miles! It's going to take me all night to get there!'

Springer smiled. 'You're forgetting, An-Gryferai. You're dreaming. You're not bound by the laws of the physical world. You're a Night Warrior. Katie's asleep in her bed, but you can go anyplace you want, as fast as you want.'

'But *how*?'

'Use your natural instincts. An-Gryferai has all the natural sense of direction of a migratory bird. She uses the Earth's magnetic field to guide her, just as migrating birds do. The only difference between An-Gryferai and a migratory bird is that a bird has to fly to its destination by flapping its wings – whereas you can fly there just by thinking about it.'

'But—'

Springer laid his hand on her shoulder, and for a moment she felt the same sense of being controlled as she had with

Gideon. But then he said, 'You know where Chicago is. You know where Lake Shore Drive is. Have confidence in yourself, An-Gryferai. Inside your mind you have a map of everywhere, and you have the ability to use it. Compared to your navigational skills, a satnav is a clumsy toy.'

He took his hand away. He was nothing like Gideon, not at all, because Gideon always used to make her feel that she was useless and stupid, whereas Springer made her feel that she could do whatever she put her mind to.

'Close your eyes,' Springer told her. 'Now visualize the coordinates of Lake Shore Drive, Chicago, and *be* there.'

Katie closed her eyes. In her mind's eye, she could see an extraordinary illuminated map of the entire United States, a tracery of fine shining filaments set against a seamless black background, like the sky at night. Instinctively, she steered her mind north-north-westward, and the map began to rotate. Far beneath her, she saw spatterings of light that she recognized as Orlando, Gainesville, Atlanta, Louisville and Indianapolis. She felt no sensation that she was moving. There was no slipstream blowing through her feathers. She felt only that her consciousness was carrying her to the western shore of Lake Michigan, and the glittering conurbation of Chicago and all of its suburbs.

It took her only seconds. She had seen *Stargate SG1* on TV, where squads of soldiers were transported through a wormhole in space from one planet to another, almost instantaneously, in a roller-coaster rush of colored lights. But that was nothing compared to the silent, effortless way in which she had simply *thought* herself from one city to another.

As she approached East Lake Shore Drive, she opened up her eyes and opened up her wings, too, so that she could fly down the last thousand feet. She didn't have far to go. The Drake Tower was directly beneath her, a red-brick apartment block in the beaux-arts style – thirty stories and nearly three hundred fifty feet high.

Suddenly she could hear noise, too – of honking traffic and the wind whipping off the lake, and a helicopter *thump-thump-thumping* over Cicero.

An intense blue light flashed from the roof garden of the Drake Tower, and as she see-sawed downward with her wings outstretched, she saw Dom Magator and Zebenjo'Yyx and Xyrena and the twins Jekkalon and Jemexxa, already gathered together and waiting for her. To her surprise, Springer was there, too, in the same form in which he had appeared to her on the golf course at La Gorce Country Club.

Zebenjo'Yyx was busy marveling at his outfit. Lincoln lifted his right arm, and then his left. Attached by straps to the upper side of each forearm, all the way from his elbows to his wrists, there was an elaborate mechanism which looked like the workings of a crossbow, with tightened cords and a system of cogs and ratchets. Each mechanism was loaded with three arrows, with viciously-barbed heads on them, six arrows altogether. But when he turned his head further and looked at his upper arms, he saw that there were three further arrows on each of those, too. He reached behind him, and realized that he was carrying even more arrows on his back, in a herringbone pattern, and that he had an extraordinary kind of quiver rising out of his back, like a scorpion's tail. In all, he reckoned he must have been carrying more than a hundred arrows, and they were all connected to hooks and pulleys, so that when one arrow was fired, another arrow would immediately tilt over his shoulder and slide along his arm to replace it.

When An-Gryferai touched lightly down on the roof, Springer came over and took hold of her arm. 'Everybody, this is the last member of our team, the Avenging Claw.'

He led her across to the other Night Warriors, and introduced her. Dom Magator said, 'Very pleased to meet you, little bird-lady. I have to say that I ate a chicken bigger than you once, spit-roasted, at Pluckers Restaurant in Baton Rouge.'

'I'll take that as a compliment. I've been trying to lose weight.'

An-Gryferai was slightly taken aback by Xyrena, with her high golden crown and her billowing golden cloak and her naked-look breastplate. It was more than just her appearance – her shiny golden breasts and her shiny golden genitalia. When she took hold of An-Gryferai's hands to welcome her, An-Gryferai felt a strange electrifying sensation, as if Xyrena had slyly drawn her fingertips up the inside of her thighs, and intimately touched her.

Springer noticed her quick, involuntary shiver. 'Xyrena is the Passion Warrior,' he explained. 'She has the same effect on everybody, man or woman. It's her principal weapon.'

'Same as it is for most women, wouldn't you say?' Xyrena put in.

Now Zebenjo'Yyx came forward. His wooden arrow-launchers clattered as he walked. 'Good to have you here, Avengin' Claw. Some fancy-dress party, don't you think? If I hadn't nearly been killed by this Gordon Veitch guy, I would have thought this was some kind of seriously bad joke.'

'I still can't believe any of it,' said An-Gryferai. 'I keep thinking that it's all a dream, but then it *is*.'

Jekkalon and Jemexxa introduced themselves – Jekkalon in his gleaming black suit and Jemexxa in her dazzling silver suit. They both nodded their helmets and said, 'Hi, pleased to meet you,' but An-Gryferai thought that they seemed diffident and edgy and not very happy to be here. She didn't know that earlier that evening, three-and-a-half thousand disgruntled fans had almost caused a full-scale riot at the State Theater in Cleveland when they realized that the Kaiser Twins were not going to be making their promised appearance.

'All right,' said Springer. 'We don't know how much longer this gentleman's dream is going to last, so we have to make this quick. His name is George Roussos and he's the president of ABR Foods, which is one of the major meat-packers in Chicago. He's asleep in his apartment on the twenty-seventh floor, along with his wife Margarita.'

'How do we get in there?' asked Jekkalon. 'This has to be a high-security building, right?'

'You flew here from Cleveland, didn't you?' said Springer. 'You're insubstantial. You're a dream, just like the rest of us. You can pass through the walls as easily as you passed through the ceiling of the Griffin House Hotel.'

'Come on,' said Dom Magator. 'Let's do it, before this meat-packer starts dreaming about something else, like short ribs or navel pastrami pieces.'

Springer arranged the six of them so that they were standing together in a tight circle, almost too close for comfort. 'OK?' he said. 'Now think *sink*.'

They sank through the floor of the roof garden with the same soft *shushing* sound that Katie had felt when she had risen through the attic of her house in Nautilus. Then they descended through the master bedroom of the penthouse apartment on the thirtieth floor, which was unoccupied, stuffy and airless, with its blinds drawn; and then through the master bedroom of the apartment below. Here, a middle-aged couple lay dozing in front of a huge flickering TV which took up most of the opposite wall, their eyes closed and their mouths wide open.

'*Murder, She Wrote*,' said Dom Magator. 'That's enough to send anybody to the land of Nod.'

But without hesitation, the Night Warriors continued to sink through the thick cream carpet, and the ceiling below, down to the twenty-eighth floor. In this bedroom, the king-sized bed was empty, but the sheets had been dragged halfway on to the floor, and a couple were having a shouting match in the brightly-lit en-suite bathroom.

'You were making eyes at that whore *all* evening!' the woman was screaming. 'Don't tell me you weren't!'

'That *whore* as you call her could help us to land a multi-million-dollar contract, you lamebrain!'

But before they could hear any more of their argument, the Night Warriors' descent continued, down through the patterned carpet to the twenty-eighth floor apartment below. With a faint *shush*, they alighted as softly and silently as parachutists in George Roussos' bedroom. Here, they stopped, and looked around.

Xyrena said, 'Jesus! Whore's boudoir, or what?' but Dom Magator held up his finger to indicate that they should stay quiet. All the same, Katie had to agree with her. The bedroom was decorated in a style which she could only have described as Greek Billionaire Bombastic, with a gilded four-poster bed, and purple velvet drapes, and bow-fronted Regency nightstands. On either side of the window stood two life-size statues of Greek muses, Urania the goddess of astronomy and Thalia the goddess of comedy.

Dom Magator beckoned to them, and the Night Warriors gathered around the right-hand side of the bed, where George Roussos was sleeping. He was lying on his back in purple silk pajamas which matched the purple velvet drapes. His comb-over had strayed across the pillow like seaweed, and the bottom two buttons of his pajama jacket were unfastened, revealing a huge furry stomach.

His wife Margarita lay with her back to him, a pink chiffon scarf tied over her head to protect her platinum-blonde pleat.

George Roussos was twitching and muttering in his sleep,

and every now and then his left elbow would jerk up, as if he were trying to push somebody away.

'He's still having the carnival dream,' said Springer. 'Go on, Dom Magator. You know what to do. But let's do it quick.'

Dom Magator said, 'OK. Everybody ready for this? Here goes nothing.'

He raised both arms and pointed his fingers upward. There was a few seconds' pause, and then a sharp crackle. Two narrow streams of sapphire-blue light jumped out of the ends of his fingers and joined together in an apex next to George Roussos' sleeping body. A strong smell of ozone filled the air, and the two streams of light jerked and twitched like electrocuted snakes.

Slowly and evenly, Dom Magator lowered his arms, using the twin streams of light to describe a shimmering octagonal figure in the air, close to the side of the bed.

'This is the portal which will take you into this gentleman's dream,' said Springer. 'All you have to do is to step through it, and you will find yourself right inside his mind.'

Zebenjo'Yyx bent down and tried to peer into the center of the octagon, shielding his eyes against its intense sapphire-blue brightness. 'I can't see *nothing* inside of there, only pitchy-black dark.'

'Our friend here is dreaming about someplace dark, that's why,' said Dom Magator. 'Don't worry, I have plenty of night-vision goggles and gunsights if we need them. Let's just hit the bricks, shall we?'

'We can *really* step through here?' asked Zebenjo'Yyx.

'We really can,' Dom Magator assured him. 'And just to prove it to yourself, you can go first.'

Zebenjo'Yyx shook his head and lifted up both hands in mock surrender. 'That's OK, man, you've done this before. *You* go first. I'll stand back and watch how you do it.'

'Will you please just *go*?' said Dom Magator. 'I need to have somebody on the other side to cover the girls when *they* come through. It's called, like, *chivalry*. It's also called good tactical sense. We don't know what the hell might be waiting for us through there, do we?'

'Yeah, precisely, man. That's what concerns me.'

Xyrena linked arms with him and said, 'Come on, big boy! Don't tell me you're chicken!'

'Who said anything about chicken?' Zebenjo'Yyx protested.

'There's a whole world of difference between "chicken" and "circumspect".'

All the same, he cocked the arrow launchers on each of his forearms, turned to the rest of the Night Warriors, and said, 'This is it, then. Like my grandfather used to say, you can't make no omelets without breakin' no legs.'

'Eggs,' Xyrena corrected him.

'My grandfather wasn't just a cook. I know that now. He was Zebenjo the Arrow-Storm. So when he said "legs" I think he maybe *meant* legs.'

George Roussos let out a loud grunt and shifted his bulk sideways. At the same time, inside the octagonal portal, the Night Warriors saw lightning flicker, and they distinctly heard the rumbling of distant thunder.

Springer said, anxiously, 'Hurry, Zebenjo'Yyx! If our friend here changes his dream, or if he wakes up, we could have wasted this entire night's mission.'

Without any further hesitation, Zebenjo'Yyx ducked his head down and stepped through the portal. He vanished from the bedroom with a sharp snapping sound, like a high-voltage electrical short, as if he had never been there.

'He's *gone*,' said Jemexxa. 'That's incredible.'

Dom Magator said, 'Why don't you and Jekkalon go next? Then An-Gryferai and Xyrena. I'll bring up the rear.'

'Well, nobody can say that you don't have plenty of rear to bring up,' said Xyrena.

Dom Magator said, 'Good joke, Xyrena. But don't let's forget how dangerous this could be, and that some of us might get badly hurt, or even killed. So, you know, let's get serious, shall we? And keep our eyes open. And our ordnance ready. If there's any weapon you need apart from your natural allure – like a gun of any kind – you only have to ask.'

'Oh, I'm serious, mister, believe you me,' Xyrena retaliated. 'Don't let one or two wisecracks fool you. I've spent my whole life fighting and I can assure you that the skin underneath this armor is just as tough as the armor itself.'

Dom Magator looked at her through his green-tinted visor for a moment, and then he said, 'OK. Let's get hustling, shall we?' He could have told her that talking tough wasn't enough when you were fighting in the world of dreams, but he decided it was best if she found out for herself. Fighting in the world of dreams was terrifying, chaotic, and violently disorienting. Nothing and nobody ever stayed the same. The terrain could drastically alter right beneath your feet, from limestone butte into fever-ridden bayou, and the weather could change, too, from a summer heatwave to a midwinter's blizzard, all without a moment's warning.

Jekkalon stepped through the portal, followed closely by Jemexxa. An-Gryferai went next. She had no idea what to expect, and the sharp *snap*! as she passed from the real world into the dream world gave her a jolt. But immediately she felt rain pattering against her helmet, and when she stood up straight, she found herself on a hillside, under a black, lowering sky.

Lightning was stalking across the horizon on crooked stilts, as threatening as the Martian tripods in *The War of the Worlds*. Jekkalon and Jemexxa were standing only a few feet away to her left, while Zebenjo'Yyx had taken up a position on top of a low promontory off to her right, his right arm cocked up like a sentry holding a rifle.

An-Gryferai waded through the grass toward Jekkalon and Jemexxa. 'Some dream for a meat-packer!' she shouted.

Jemexxa tilted her helmeted head toward her and shouted back, 'This is the same place that Kieran and me found ourselves, when we went through the door at the Griffin House Hotel! Except that the carnival was right at the top of the hill there, and now it's not!'

'It must have moved on!' said An-Gryferai.

Behind them, Xyrena appeared, closely followed by Dom Magator, with all of his guns and his swords and his serried racks of knives.

An-Gryferai shouted at Dom Magator, 'Jemexxa said that she and Jekkalon were here before, in this same exact place! She said that the carnival was up on top of the hill, but it's gone now!'

Suddenly, in her ear, as clearly and as warmly as if he had been standing right beside her, Dom Magator said, 'We don't have to yell at each other, An-Gryferai. We all have a close-communications system inside of our helmets, except for Xyrena, who has an induction loop in her crown. This means that we can talk to each other in our natural voices, at any distance. Switch is on the left-hand side, under your ear protectors.'

'Oh,' said An-Gryferai. 'I didn't realize.'

Jekkalon hadn't been listening. 'Are they the same, then?' he screamed. 'Dream time and waking time?'

'I can hear you, for Christ's sake!' said Dom Magator. 'You don't have to bust my goddamned eardrums!'

'Sorry!' said Jekkalon. 'But it was only last night when Kiera and me saw the carnival here. So if dream time is the same as waking time, then they couldn't have traveled too far since then, could they? For starters, they would have had to pack up all of their tents, and all of their equipment, and hitch up all of their trailers, and that would have taken them *hours.*'

'Dream time is different, for sure,' said Dom Magator. 'But this carnival has more than dream people in it. It has *real* people, and you can't mess around with time too much when you have real people involved. Real people have to live out their lives sequentially.'

'So what does that mean?' asked Xyrena.

'It means that the carnival can't travel backward and forward in time, the same way that *we* can, as Night Warriors. So the whole shebang has to carry on like a real carnival, hour by hour and minute by minute and day by day. And that's to our advantage, now that we're hunting for them. They can't dream themselves back to nineteen thirty-six, for example, to get away from us.'

'In that case, let's go huntin' for them,' said Zebenjo'Yyx. 'I'm just itchin' to get my revenge on that freak who broke my frickin' back!'

'They won't be far away,' said Dom Magator. 'This is where our meat-packing pal started his dream, right here, which is why *we* entered it here. Judging by his physical condition, he couldn't have walked too far to catch up with them.'

He turned to Xyrena, as if he were challenging her to make some smart remark about *his* physical condition, but Xyrena simply shrugged. Then he said, 'An-Gryferai, how about taking off and having a look around? Just be careful – it looks like it's pretty damned blowy up there.'

An-Gryferai walked a few paces up the hill, with the wet grass lashing at her knees. Then she flexed her shoulders and spread her wings, and the wind immediately plucked her upward.

Dom Magator had been wrong; this weather was very much more than 'pretty damned blowy'. This wasn't at all like the warm, serene thermals in which she had floated so triumphantly over the Florida coastline. Here, the wind was harsh and cold and ill-tempered, constantly switching direction and velocity. Bursts of rain kept exploding against her helmet, and the lightning seemed to be crackling so close to her that she was afraid of being electrocuted.

She was buffeted by downdrafts again and again, and at one time she was almost beaten back down to the ground, and her boots actually kicked against the grass. But she struggled and dipped and spun, and tilted her wings to catch every rising gust of wind that she could, and at last she managed to fly up to the top of the hill.

She battled upward and looked around, repeatedly angling her wings to steady herself. It was clear that the carnival had been here, and only recently. The ground had been churned into glistening black mud by scores of criss-crossing tire tracks, and there was trash scattered everywhere – broken orange-crates, chicken carcasses, dirty diapers, worn-out tractor tires. Near the center of the site a wide oval area had been covered several inches deep with sawdust, which is where the big top must have been pitched. Over on the right, a large bonfire was still smoldering, filling the night with acrid smoke, and stray sheets of paper were dancing across the muddy furrows as if they were panicking that they had been left behind.

'How's it going?' asked Dom Magator, inside her helmet.

'Jekkalon and Jemexxa were right: the carnival *was* here. I'm just trying to work out which way it went.'

'Maybe you're going to need a little more altitude.'

An-Gryferai flapped her wings even harder. The wind was howling and screaming now, and she felt as if she were swimming the butterfly stroke through a mountainous sea. But gradually she managed to gain height, until she was nearly two hundred feet over the hilltop, and she could see more than ten miles in every direction. She adjusted the lenses in her helmet to improve her night vision and sharpen her focus. Two black crows tumbled past her, even more helpless in the wind than she was.

She could see now that the carnival had processed down the opposite side of the hill, like a vast Civil War army on the move. Its tractors and its wagons had crushed deep parallel tracks in the grass, and there were hundreds of hoof marks and footprints too, so she had no difficulty in working out which way it had headed. She adjusted her lenses yet again, turning her head slowly from side to side to sweep the distant horizon. Eventually, less than five miles away, half hidden by smoke and fog, she made out a cluster of houses and barns and workshops, close to the edge of a leafless birch wood. The carnival had assembled nearby, a collection of twenty or thirty trucks and trailers, as well as horse-drawn caravans and elderly automobiles. She recognized a huge black Packard Phaeton from the mid-nineteen-thirties, because her grandfather used to own one, although he had never driven it.

Refining her vision even more acutely, she saw dozens of carnival folk to-ing and fro-ing from the carnival wagons to the houses and workshops. Some of them looked like riggers and circus hands, because they were wearing plain gray coveralls and heavy-duty gloves, but others were dressed in far more fanciful costumes, with red-and-yellow striped tailcoats and long capes of faded velvet in oranges and greens and grays.

Several of them were hopping on crutches, or walking frames, and An-Gryferai saw at least two of them, legless like beggars from a Breughel painting, pushing themselves across the grass in little wooden boxes with wheels.

She spun around in the air, and gave the rest of the Night Warriors a furious wave.

'It's here!' she told them. 'Brother Albrecht's carnival is here!'

'Great,' said Dom Magator. 'Everybody ready for this? Everybody ready to kick some eight-hundred-year-old ass? Let's go get 'em!'

THIRTEEN

Dogs of War

An-Gryferai dipped and wheeled over the brow of the hill, flapping her wings, waiting for the rest of the Night Warriors to catch up with her. She stayed as close to the ground as she could while still keeping the circus in sight, even though it wasn't easy. At this low altitude, she had to battle against mischievous crosswinds and abrupt drops in air pressure. Her shoulder muscles were aching with the effort, but she didn't want to fly any higher in case any of the carnival folk happened to look back and catch sight of her, Dom Magator had already warned the Night Warriors that it was a priority to surprise Brother Albrecht, if they could, because they had no idea if or how the carnival folk could retaliate.

'Let's just put it this way,' Dom Magator had said, 'this guy has been traveling around with his freak show for eight hundred years, kidnapping women and children and cutting their arms and their legs off, and inflicting all manner of deformities on them, and nobody has been able to stop him yet. Not priests, not princes, not goddamned sorcerers, even. So let's be intelligent, shall we, and assume that he has *some* way of defending himself?'

Now the Night Warriors had all gathered at the top of the hill. An-Gryferai beat her wings strongly so that she gained another twenty feet in altitude. She focused her lenses toward the carnival and transmitted into each of the Night Warriors' helmets a high-definition 3-D image of what she could see. She showed them the wide trail of tire-tracks and footprints that the traveling carnival had left behind it in the long wet grass, and then she showed them the settlement beside the birch trees, and the carnival site itself, half obscured by drifting woodsmoke and mist.

Dom Magator said, 'We need to pinpoint Brother Albrecht's exact location. If we can take *him* out first, I think we'll have much less organized retaliation from the rest of the freaks.'

'My guess is he's goin' to be real well protected,' said Zebenjo'Yyx. 'Like the gang leaders in Brightmoore and Hamtramck. You couldn't get near those brothers for guns and muscle.'

'Why don't *I* go down there and look for him?' Xyrena suggested. 'I mean, *I* don't look threatening, do I?'

'Absolutely the opposite,' Don Magator agreed. 'But are you sure that's a good idea, going down there unarmed? We don't yet know how these people react to strangers. They might blow you away as soon as look at you.'

'They're entertainers, aren't they? Trapeze artists and jugglers and clowns, and very special people. I don't think they'll give me any trouble.'

'OK, but I think Jekkalon and Jemexxa should go with you. They're both acrobats, so if anybody's going to get a warm welcome from carny folk, I guess they will. Besides, they don't look like they're carrying weapons, even though there's plenty of lightning around for Jemexxa to zap them with, if she needs to. Zebenjo'Yyx and An-Gryferai and me, we'll take up tactical positions as close as we can without being seen, and cover you.'

An-Gryferai flapped down to earth again, with a nimble skip, and shook the rain off her wings. 'All ready?' asked Dom Magator. 'Here goes nothing.'

The five Night Warriors fanned out and began to walk toward the carnival. Over their heads, the electric storm became even more dramatic, with lightning crackling from one cloud to another and thunder rolling almost continuously. Chilly rain slashed sideways across the grass.

Dom Magator switched on the heat sensors that displayed infrared body images on his visor. This allowed him to make second by second checks on the movements of the carnival people, in case any of them betrayed signs that they had caught sight of the Night Warriors coming toward them. But they all appeared to be far too preoccupied, swarming backward and forward between the carnival site and the settlement by the birch trees.

Suddenly – right in the center of the carnival trucks and caravans – he saw four tall poles being erected, with black pennants flying from the top of them. Within less than thirty seconds, in a series of huge convulsions, the big top began to rise, like a harpooned whale rising from the depths.

At the same time, all around it, twenty or thirty smaller tents and marquees were mushrooming up; and off to the right, a large gang of circus hands were bolting together a long row of animal cages. They assembled the cages in only a few minutes, and then at least a dozen trucks were noisily backed up to them. The trucks' rear doors were thrown open, and ramps dropped down with a fusillade of banging and clattering. After a few moments, trainers dressed in flamboyant coats and tall hats and wigs appeared, leading out tigers and bears and elephants and zebras.

Once the animals were all safely locked up, the trucks were driven away to the far side of the carnival site. Meanwhile the trailers and horse-drawn caravans were being marshaled into a rough semicircle. It all happened so quickly that it was like watching a speeded-up movie. Electricians climbed up ladders to suspend strings of red lights between the cages and the caravans and the tents, and in front of the big top an archway was hauled up into position. A generator blurted, and all the lights flickered on, while the illuminated lettering over the archway spelled out *Albrecht's Traveling Circus & Freak Show.*

After a few more seconds, the Night Warriors heard music on the wind, occasionally interrupted by thunder. *In The Good Old Summertime*, played on a barrel organ.

'My God,' said Dom Magator. 'If this doesn't make me feel like a kid again.'

They had reached a low ridge about a hundred yards away from the perimeter of the carnival site. Dom Magator sent Zebenjo'Yyx off to the right, so that he could cover Xyrena if and when she entered the big top. He sent An-Gryferai off to the left, close to the settlement of houses and barns, so that if she needed to take off and fly, the birch trees behind her would make it harder for anybody on the ground to see her.

He gave Xyrena a quick embrace, his heavyweight armor clanking against her gold-plated breastplate. Then he shook Jekkalon and Jemexxa by the hand, and said, 'Break a leg, OK?' All of a sudden he felt like Uncle Buck, not only because he was so well built, but because he really cared for these two young twins. They were good-looking, they were hugely successful, and they had nightly faced audiences of thousands. But this was their first time in Night Warrior combat. Dom Magator was confident that they had inherited all of the tactical skills they needed, but they had no experience yet of how harrowing it could be, fighting in nightmares; how bizarre, or how bloody.

Xyrena and the twins started to walk toward the carnival tents. As they did so, from inside the big top, the Night Warriors heard a muffled drum roll, and then a man bellowing through a megaphone. They couldn't make out what the man was saying, but his announcement was immediately followed by a discordant blast of trumpets and a smattering of applause.

'Sounds like show time,' said Zebenjo'Yyx.

'Xyrena, Jekkalon, Jemexxa . . .' said Dom Magator. 'You take it real easy, you hear me? And keep us up to the minute,

OK? You need us, you just yell, and we'll be right there before you can say "catfish po'boy with everything on it".'

Xyrena circled around the back of the caravans and trailers, with Jekkalon and Jemexxa staying close behind her. Just as before, when Kieran and Kiera had explored the carnival site on top of the hill, all of the trailers had black blinds drawn tightly down at the windows, although they could hear voices and music and occasional bursts of shouting from inside some of the trailers, and there was a pungent smell of tobacco smoke on the wind.

From the direction of the big top, they heard another drum roll, longer this time, followed by another fanfare of trumpets, and another round of applause.

'I think we should go see what's going on,' said Xyrena. 'If it's some kind of show, then the chances are that the Big Cheese is going to be there.'

'Can't we find our mom first?' asked Jekkalon.

'Come on, Jakki, you know what our priority is,' Xyrena told him. 'We have to pull the rug out from under this freak show as soon as we possibly can.'

'You *will* help us find her, though?'

'Like I said to my first husband, I promise I'll try to keep my promise, but I can't promise.'

They walked along the line of animal cages. The stench of tiger's urine and elephant's dung was overwhelming, and made Xyrena's eyes water. The tiger snarled at them listlessly, but its eyes were dull and its fur was patchy and even if it managed to escape from its cage, Xyrena doubted if it had the strength even to run after them, let alone eat them. The bear was in much the same condition, sitting in one corner of its cage, endlessly rocking backward and forward like a mental patient in a rundown asylum.

In the last cage a Great Dane bitch was lying on her side on a heap of dirty straw, apparently asleep. Her pale honey-colored coat was caked with black mud and she was so undernourished that her ribcage was showing.

Jemexxa went up to the bars of the cage and said, 'Such a beautiful dog. We used to have one when we were little – Princess, we called her. We used to be able to ride on her back, like a pony. Look at her – how could they treat her so bad?'

'Come on,' Xyrena urged her, 'we have to get going.'

But just then the Great Dane stirred on her straw, and lifted herself up on her front paws, and turned her head around. Jemexxa clamped both hands over her mouth and took two staggering steps backward. Jekkalon said, 'Holy shit! I don't believe it.'

Even Xyrena found it impossible to believe what she was looking at. The Great Dane had the head of a human woman. She was very pallid, with a heart-shaped face and raggedy brown hair and pale green eyes, although the whites of her eyes were bloodshot. Her cheeks were streaked with dirt and there were clusters of dark red sores around her lips.

She stared at Xyrena and Jekkalon and Jemexxa, occasionally blinking. Then she stood up on all fours and came trotting over to the bars of the cage.

'Who are you?' she said, in a reedy voice, as if she were being half strangled. Xyrena could see now that there were crude stitch-marks all the way around her neck, where her head had been sutured to the Great Dane's body. 'Do you live in the *village*? I've never seen you before.'

'No,' said Xyrena. 'We don't live in the village. We're just kind of passing through.'

'You don't belong to the circus?'

Xyrena shook her head. She found the dog-woman both horrifying and fascinating, both at the same time, but more than that she felt desperately sorry for her.

'You're naked but you're not naked,' the woman frowned.

'Well, that's my armor,' Xyrena explained. 'I'm a kind of a freelance warrior. Like a mercenary only I don't get paid for it.'

'A warrior?' the dog-woman asked her.

'Like I say, kind of.'

The dog-woman thought for a moment, and then she said, 'Would you kill me?'

'Excuse me? Would I *kill* you? Of course not.'

'If I *begged* you to kill me, would you kill me?'

Xyrena didn't know what to say. She opened her mouth and then she closed it again.

'Look at me!' the dog-woman insisted. 'I used to be pretty. I used to have a husband, and children. I used to be so happy. Now look at me. I'm not even human any more.'

'What *happened* to you?' asked Jemexxa.

'A clown happened to me. A clown with a gray face and gray hair and a bright green smile.'

'What did he do to you, this clown?'

'I first saw him at the Empire Fair, in Sioux Falls, South Dakota, where I used to live. It was so long ago now that I can't even remember when it was. I saw him smiling at me through the crowd and I smiled back at him, and he gave me this little wave with his fingers. Then I took the children home and he was waiting for me, in my living room. How he got there before me and how he got into my house I shall never know.

The dog-woman's eyes suddenly filled up with tears. 'That was the end of my happiness. That was when hell started.'

'This *clown*—' Xyrena prompted her.

'Most of the freaks call him Mago Verde, or the Green Magician, but Zachary always calls him Gordon. Zachary – he's the Freakmaster – he's in charge of all of the living exhibits, like me.'

'Gordon – that wouldn't be Gordon *Veitch* by any chance?'

'I don't know. I only know Gordon.'

'And he's still here now, with the carnival?'

Elizabeth nodded. 'Yes. But he's always coming and going. Sometimes he disappears for days on end, but then he comes back and shuts himself up in his caravan for weeks and nobody sees him. All of the other clowns hate him. The freaks hate him and the animal trainers hate him. But the Grand Freak thinks he's wonderful. The Grand Freak treats him as if he was Jesus Christ, almost.'

The dog-woman was out of breath now, and panting painfully. Xyrena waited for a few moments, and then she said, 'The Grand Freak? Who the hell is the Grand Freak?'

'Brother Albrecht. He calls himself the Grand Freak because he wants everybody to pity him. He doesn't want anybody to forget that he was beautiful once and how much he's suffered. But he doesn't care how cruel he is to other people. He loves to see them tortured – even little children.

She paused again, to catch her breath. Then she said, 'Please kill me. *Please*. I tried to strangle myself with my collar, and once I tried to bite off one of my paws so that I bled to death, but Brown Jenkin found me, both times.'

'Who's Brown Jenkin?'

The dog-woman gave a shivery shake of her head. 'He's a *what* rather than a *who*. Half a human being and half a rat. But he helps Zachary to keep his eye on all of us freaks, just to make sure we don't harm ourselves. I'm sure that he has some kind of a sixth sense, because when one of us can't take it any more, and wants to end it all, he always sniffs it out, and stops us.'

Xyrena said, gently, 'Tell me your name.'

'My name? You don't need to know my name to kill me. It would be easier for you if you didn't know it.'

'Please, tell me your name.'

'Elizabeth. But my husband always called me Betsy.'

'Well, listen, Elizabeth, I can't kill you.'

'Why not? You said you're a warrior. Don't you have a gun?'

'I couldn't kill you if I wanted to because you're still real.'

'What are you telling me? That this is only a *nightmare*? Then how come I never wake up?'

'Because this carnival is all a dream, but not *your* dream. It's Brother Albrecht's dream. Over the years he's imprisoned dozens of real people inside of it, so that they can't escape. We think that he sends this Gordon character back to the waking world to find victims for him – innocent men and women just like you – and then he brings them back here and turns them into freaks for his carnival.'

'So you can't kill me but I can't ever get away?'

'You *can* get away, Elizabeth, and you will, just as soon as we can deal with the less-than-brotherly Brother Albrecht. And Gordon the Clown, too, while we're at it.'

Tears were streaming down Elizabeth's filthy cheeks and she was shivering with misery. Jemexxa put her hand through the bars of the cage and stroked her tangled hair. 'Please,' she said. 'Trust us. Just let us break up this carnival and then you'll be free. Our mom's here, too – the Demi-Goddess. We want to save her, too.'

Elizabeth was too exhausted to say any more. She crept back to her bed of straw and lay down, her ribcage rising and falling with effort.

Xyrena said to Dom Magator, 'Did you pick up any of that?'

'Yes, most of it, especially that Grand Freak stuff. Good going, Xyrena.'

He said something else, but his voice was drowned out by

another drum roll from the big top, and another fanfare of trumpets, and more applause.

'I think it's time we went in and took a look-see,' said Xyrena.

Jekkalon said, 'There's a flap in the canvas in back, that's how we got out the last time. With any luck we should be able to sneak in without too many people seeing us.'

Jemexxa looked up at the thundery clouds. 'I think I could use some charge first.'

She reached behind her and twisted two L-shaped levers, one on each side of the rack of storage cells on her back. Then she raised both hands, palms outward, as if she were praying to some Native American sky deity. In fact she was dowsing for negative electrical charges building up in the clouds – that type of cloud-to-cloud-to-ground lightning known as an 'anvil crawler.' At first she felt only a slight tingling sensation in the tips of her fingers, but as she slowly moved her hands to the right, the tingling became an uncomfortable prickling, like nettle rash, and then a sharp fizzing sensation that penetrated right under her fingernails. Within less than thirty seconds, however, she had located the point of maximum atmospheric tension – well over a hundred kiloamperes. It was located only about three and a half miles away, in a huge black cloud that was hanging over the summit of a hill. She lifted her hands higher and waited.

'This is not going to take too long, is it, honey?' asked Xyrena. 'We need to get into that big top before one of these freaks catches us and turns us into poodles.'

Jemexxa didn't answer her. She knew that there was no need, because a few seconds later a fan-shaped array of lightning lit up the clouds, spitting and shriveling like burning human hair. Four or five branches jumped directly toward her and struck the open palms of her hands. There was a sharp crack and a superheated blast of air which almost knocked them over and for a few moments they were all blinded. But with a high-pitched jittering noise, like a horde of rats scuttling up a drainpipe, the charges ran up the insulated cables on Jemexxa's arms, and into the capacitors on her back, and she promptly twisted the two L-shaped levers back to their closed position, and snapped them shut.

She glanced up at the head's-up display inside her helmet. It read 270c.

'That should more than do it. Two hundred seventy coulombs.'

Jekkalon said, 'That's incredible. I even know what a coulomb is. How the hell do I know what a coulomb is? I flunked every single science subject when I was in high school.'

'Don't ask me,' said Xyrena. 'I don't understand *any* of this Night Warriors malarkey. But suddenly I know things that I never ever knew I knew. I even know who wrote *In The Good Old Summertime*, would you believe?'

Jekkalon said, 'Dom Magator? We're going to enter the big top now. Not by the front entrance – we're going in back.'

'Don't worry. I'll have An-Gryferai keep you under close surveillance, and Zebenjo'Yyx and me will move in closer and cover you. If it comes to any shooting, though, make sure that you hit the deck real quick. Zebenjo'Yyx isn't called the Arrow Storm for nothing, and I'll be toting my Absence Gun and my Boomerang Knife.'

'Be careful, though,' put in Jemexxa. 'Most of these people are innocent victims, and some of them are real.'

'I'll be careful,' Dom Magator assured her. 'My Army buddy Rick Mantovani was killed in Iraq by friendly fire, but there's nothing even remotely friendly about an Absence Gun, no matter who's firing it.'

Jekkalon led the way between the smaller tents and marquees toward the back of the big top. Above their heads, the thunder and lightning were moving away now, but the rain was drumming down harder then ever. Jemexxa began to have an uneasy feeling that George Roussos might be close to waking up, in which case they would have to exit this dream as quickly as possible. Springer had warned them that if this happened, the dream wouldn't simply collapse around them, leaving them standing by George Roussos' bed, where they had first entered it. This happened with normal dreams and nightmares, but this dream wasn't normal. This was Brother Albrecht's dream, and George Roussos was only dreaming it because for some reason Brother Albrecht wanted him to.

If George Roussos woke up while the Night Warriors were still here, inside this dream, the only way for them to get out of it would be to wake up Brother Albrecht, if that were possible, or kill him.

They reached the back of the big top. Rainwater was spouting off the sloping roof and splattering on to the grass all around them. Inside, they could hear music playing – lewd, discordant blues – and people shouting and cheering. Every now and then there would be another drum roll, and another screech of trumpets.

Jekkalon made his way along the wall of black canvas, punching and tugging at it to find the flap from which they had escaped the last time they had dreamed that they were here. As he was still struggling to locate it, a motley group of clowns and circus hands suddenly appeared through the rain, less than ten yards away, accompanied by a woman with a pair of mechanical wooden legs, like the legs of two artists' easels, all joints and struts and pulleys, which made her at least six inches taller than any of her companions. Her unnatural height was emphasized by a huge black tricorn hat that looked as if it might have been worn by an encephalitic pirate.

The Night Warriors turned their faces to the canvas so that no light would be reflected from the lenses in their helmets, and stood perfectly still. They stayed that way while the group passed them by, talking and tittering. One of the clowns shouted out, 'Who's *this*, then?' and let out a laugh that was almost a series of screams. Xyrena thought for a split second that he must have seen them, but the group continued walking, and so the clown must have been laughing about somebody else altogether. The group disappeared around the next corner of the big top, and the last the Night Warriors heard of them was the arthritic creaking of the woman's wooden legs.

After a furious search along the back of the tent, Jekkalon at last discovered the flap. He held it open while Xyrena and Jemexxa pushed their way through.

Unexpectedly, the big top was crowded with hundreds of people. All the gasoliers were alight, but even so the illumination inside the tent was strangely dim, as if they were looking at it through a fine gauze curtain. The air was humid and stuffy and smelled of wet soil and human sweat. Although there was so much music and drumming and cheering, the sound was muffled by the dark red velvet drapes that hung all around the auditorium. At least a dozen trapezes hung from the roof of the tent, swaying slightly, as if some acrobat had recently swung from one to the other.

This is just like a dream, thought Jemexxa, but of course it was a dream.

The Night Warriors kept themselves hidden behind the last row of seats. Xyrena said, 'Dom Magator? The whole place is packed. Where did all of these people come from? There must be three hundred here, at the very least.'

'They're all of the people who are dreaming this dream,' Dom Magator told her. 'If you look around, you'll probably see George Roussos someplace.'

'Not from here I can't. We're right in back.'

'That doesn't matter. George Roussos isn't important right now. The main thing is, can you see Brother Albrecht?'

'I'll take a look. Don't go away now, will you?'

Xyrena lifted her head with its high gilded crown and looked cautiously toward the stage. At first her sight line was obscured by a bulky woman with frizzy red hair, so she took two or three steps sideways until she was standing at the end of the nearest aisle, and she could see most of the stage quite clearly.

On the left-hand side of the apron, a seven-piece band of black musicians was playing that slow, off-key blues number – one of those down-and-dirty blues numbers that would have had deeply suggestive lyrics if anybody had been singing it, like *I Need A Little Sugar In My Bowl*. The band were all wearing brown-and-yellow-striped satin vests and immaculately-pressed brown pants, and it was only when Xyrena looked at them more intently that she realized what was so freakish about them.

Four of them were two pairs of conjoined twins, the sides of their vests slit open because their abdomens were connected with a thick band of skin. They were so closely connected, in fact, that their faces were pressed together, and the trumpeter and the clarinetist had to share the playing of their instruments – the trumpeter using his left hand to finger the register key of his twin's clarinet, and the clarinetist using his right hand to mute his twin's trumpet.

The other three were conjoined triplets. Two of them were joined at the side of the head, while the second and the third were joined at the shoulder, so that one of them had no left arm and the other had no right arm. Between the three of them they were playing banjo and alto sax.

They were accompanied by a pianist, who was sitting behind them at a shabby red upright piano. He was thin and pale, with a half-starved face and curly white hair, but what was immediately striking about him were the two curved horns which protruded from the top of his head, each of them at least nine inches long. Xyrena guessed that they must have been grafted on to his skull to give him the appearance of a devil or a demon or a faun. He was naked to the waist, with a scarred, emaciated back; but it was only when Xyrena moved a few feet to the right that she could see that he was completely naked. Not that he was exposing himself – he was covered from the waist down in shaggy white fur. He had no feet, only hooves, which he was using to jab at the loud and the soft pedals. He had been literally cut in half, and his hips and his legs replaced with those of a Rocky Mountain goat.

Xyrena was so horrified that she couldn't take her eyes off him. Jekkalon and Jemexxa came up close behind her. 'Holy moly,' Jekkalon breathed. 'I never saw anything like that in my whole goddamned life. Never. That is so *gross*.'

The pianist swept his fingertips all the way up the keyboard, to the plinkiest note at the top, *plink*! Then he sat with his horned head dropped down and his arms hanging limply at his sides and staring at the floor. A few moments later, with a collection of squeaks and honks, the jazz band petered out, too. The audience gave them a smattering of applause, but almost immediately they were drowned out by another ferocious drum roll, and another strident fanfare of trumpets.

Out of the red velvet drapes at the back of the stage burst a hugely fat man in a ringmaster's top hat and a bottle-green tail-coat and shiny black knee-boots. He swaggered up to the footlights, cracking a ringmaster's whip.

'Ladies and gentlemen! And those who are both, or neither! Welcome to Brother Albrecht's Traveling Circus and Freak Show! This evening we have gathered you here to celebrate the penultimate step toward the realization of our dreams! And when I say "realization" I mean "*real*-ization" – our seemingly endless nightmare at last made flesh! A triumphant return to the world of reality from the world of dreams in which we have been so cruelly and unjustly exiled for so long!'

There was a short pause before anybody in the audience applauded, and when they did, the clapping sounded half-hearted and sporadic. One or two of them cheered and whistled, but the Night Warriors noticed that there were just as many who sat with their hands in their laps, although they looked more bewildered than hostile.

'Today I am overjoyed to tell you that the great Mago Verde has brought us back sacrifice number eight! Not only that, he has already dreamed her abduction and her mutilation into one of the bedrooms of the Griffin House. Her pain is now part of that building's fabric, mixed with its very molecules, joining the seven other sacrifices whose suffering is secreted within its walls!'

Again, a few desultory handclaps, accompanied by coughing and the shuffling of feet.

The ringmaster cracked his whip three times. 'Now there remains only one more sacrifice to be made before the gates to the waking world will be flung open to us, and the circus can pass through, with its bells and its trumpets and its clowns! One more nightmare, that is all – just one! And then we can bring chaos and anarchy to the entire planet, and undo the works of God for ever!

'Ladies and gentlemen! And those who purport to be one or the other, or neither! I give you the greatest Dread who ever walked the world of reality and the world of nightmares – Mago Verde, the Green Magician!'

More clapping, more enthusiastic this time, and one or two piercing whistles, and then through the curtains appeared the gray-faced clown with the poisonous green smile. He circled around the stage with a self-satisfied strut, nodding his head to acknowledge the applause – occasionally flicking his long gray hair with his fingertips and blowing kisses, as if he were pretending to be gay.

'Thank you, my friends, thank you,' he said. 'Thank you dreamers all for joining our dream.' His voice was hoarse and barely audible, so that everybody in the audience had to strain to hear him. 'You are all *far* too kind to me – unlike the shits who are under the delusion that they run this circus!

He paused, and gave a real grin underneath his painted grin. 'They all detest me, every one of them! And do you know why? They detest me because I am the only one, *ever,* who has shown himself capable of giving them what they want! I am the only one who can lead them back through to the waking world, and give them back the real life which they have almost forgotten.

'You would think they would show me some *gratitude*,

wouldn't you? But no! They are all so *jealous*! I have the ear and the confidence of the Grand Freak himself, our beloved Brother Albrecht, and they *hate* that! But the Grand Freak knows that nine sacrifices have to be made, and that every one of those nine sacrifices has to be dreamed into the walls of the Griffin House, and that nobody else can do that, except for *moi*! Only then will he be able to wake up out of his dream, and lead his circus back to reality.

'Of course the Grand Freak loves me! How could he *not* love me? He escaped into this dream eight centuries ago, thinking that he could easily return to the waking world whenever he wanted to, and continue to wreak his revenge on God, and all of God's creation. But he reckoned without Pope Eugene. Pope Eugene cast a holy sanction – Sanctus Sanctio – which prevented the Grand Freak from waking up. And so for eight hundred years he continued to dream this dream. This wonderful, terrible, fearful, depraved and disgusting circus, which is everything that Heaven deplores, on wheels!

He stepped backward, toward the curtains, and then he called out, 'Bring on the sacrifice!'

There was some tussling behind the curtains, but after a few moments two clowns staggered out, carrying high between them a bentwood chair. One of the clowns was in traditional white face and dressed entirely in white, while the other was made up like an Auguste, with a wild gingery wig and scowling red lips and baggy check pants.

Sitting in the chair, and tied to it with cords, was a plump young Hispanic girl with wavy black hair. She was wearing a long sleeveless dress of dirty gray linen, heavily bloodstained, and Xyrena could immediately see why. She had no arms, only two stumps at her shoulders which had been covered with thick gauze pads and adhesive tape to prevent them from bleeding, although both pads were now dark brown with congealed blood.

The two clowns carried the girl to the front of the stage and set her down facing the audience. 'Behold!' cried out Mago Verde, performing a little fluttering dance around her. 'The eighth offering! *Número ocho*! Maria Fortales is her name! A Mexican beauty beyond compare!'

It appeared to Jemexxa that the girl was concussed, or drugged, or dreaming. She made no sound at all, and her eyes roamed around as if she couldn't understand where she was, or what was happening to her. But even if she were semi-conscious, her eyes were filled with tears, and tears were glistening on her cheeks.

The audience of assembled dreamers started a slow handclap, as if they approved of this latest victim, but were growing impatient to see what would happen to her. Dom Magator said, 'What the two-toned tonkert is going on in there, Xyrena?'

But he didn't have to wait for long to find out. Mago Verde returned to the curtains at the back of the stage and cried out, 'Now! The spectacle that you have all been waiting to see! The Arch-Dreamer himself! The creator of all of this unholy carnival! The Grand Freak, Brother Albrecht!'

FOURTEEN

The Eighth Sacrifice

This time, with a thunderous drum-roll, all of the curtains were drawn back. Immediately, out poured a crowd of clowns, acrobats, dancers, jugglers, fire breathers and wildly assorted freaks.

Even though the Night Warriors were themselves dressed in bizarre costumes, suitable only for fighting in nightmares, they stared at Brother Albrecht's circus performers in disbelief. A legless man in a scarlet satin costume turned backward flip-flaps all the way across the stage, while a one-legged woman in a ballet tutu spun around and around so fast that it was almost impossible to see her face – until she eventually stopped spinning, and they could see that she had the long narrow snout and the glassy yellow eyes of a timber wolf.

Crawling awkwardly around in the background was a whey-faced boy with a pudding-basin haircut and a black one-piece swimming-costume of the style worn by men in the nineteen-twenties. He had to crawl – or to *lurch*, rather – because both of his legs had been replaced by somebody else's arms, and two more arms had been surgically attached to the sides of his body. He had six arms altogether, so that he looked like a human spider, and that was probably how Brother Albrecht billed him.

Xyrena stared at all of these monstrosities and shook her head. 'Dom Magator, I think you need to get in here with that Absence Gun of yours and de-exist everything in here. I can't believe what I'm looking at. This isn't just revenge on God. This is revenge against everything that ever lived.'

Even as she spoke, a fire breather in a spangled costume tilted his head back and blew a fine haze of lamp oil into the air. The oil drifted back downward, and it was only then that he ignited it, so that for a few seconds his entire head was on fire, his eyes closed but his mouth wide open in a silent scream. He stepped back grinning in a cloud of smoke, his face blackened, with the tips of both ears still alight, so that he looked like a demon freshly arrived from hell. Almost immediately a woman appeared beside him in a bonnet decorated with crimson ostrich plumes, and a crimson crinoline dress. Her face was beautiful but mask-like, as if she were a porcelain doll rather than a human being. Her bodice was unlaced to expose what should have been her breasts, but her breasts had been removed and replaced with two breast-shaped birdcages with blue cockatiels perched inside. The cockatiels fluttered and squawked while the woman smiled serenely at the audience and gave them little Marie Antoinette waves.

Jemexxa gripped Jekkalon's hand and said, 'Look – *look*! It's Mom!'

Sure enough, their mother Demi the Demi-Goddess was being wheeled on to the stage by Zachary. She was balanced on a small gilded cart with a black velvet cushion on it. She was staring unfocused at nothing at all.

'We could snatch her,' breathed Jekkalon. 'We could run down there and snatch her and they wouldn't even know what had hit them.'

'No, you couldn't,' said Dom Magator, close to his ear. 'You'd be caught before you got anywhere near her, and you'd fuck up this whole operation. So don't even think about it, you hear?'

'Yeah, OK. I know. Sorry. It's just seeing her like that. It doesn't matter what they've done to her, she's still our mom.'

'I know that. But *concentrate*, dude. Any sign of the Big Cheese yet?'

'Not so far.'

But he had barely spoken when there was another flourish of trumpets, and out of the darkness at the back of the stage rolled a four-wheeled contraption about the size of a stagecoach, with huge spoked wheels. It was painted glossy black, with a domed canopy of black leather, which completely concealed its occupant.

It was being pushed forward by naked men and women, at least ten of them, every inch of whose bodies was decorated with tattoos, although the Night Warriors were too far away at the back of the big top to see what the designs were. But what they could see was that all of their legs had been amputated below the knee and replaced with much longer prosthetic legs with absurdly high heels, more like designer boots than feet, so that all of them, both men and women, stood well over six-and-a-half feet tall. Their heads had been shaved and fitted with crowns and antlers and bells. They jingled as they walked, and the wheels of the black contraption squeaked in accompaniment.

The black contraption was rolled right up to the chair where Maria Fortales was tied, and then it stopped. The naked men and women remained where they were, standing beside it, motionless. Xyrena could see now that their genitalia had been tied up tightly with elaborate cat's-cradles of very thin twine, so that their flesh bulged in diamond-shaped patterns. Now Mago Verde came prancing forward, bowing and nodding his head.

'Here it is, Brother Albrecht! The eighth offering! How close we are now, to the great day of glory! Only one more sacrifice to bring back to you after this one, and then you can cry out *up stakes*! and *wagons roll*! and return to the world where men can really be tortured and women can really be fondled!'

The ringmaster stepped up now, and took hold of the framework of the black canopy which covered the inside of the black contraption. 'Ladies and gentlemen! And those undecided! I proudly present to you . . . the Grand Freak, Brother Albrecht!'

He was just about to raise the canopy, however, when Xyrena felt something wrench violently at her sleeve – something so strong that she was pulled right around in a semicircle and almost lost her balance. At the same time, she was half deafened by a screech and a chattering noise, and then a nasal voice shouting out, '*Arresto*! *Parada*! *Ne soulevez pas la* canopy! *Wij hebben hier* strangers! *Arresto*! *Parado*!'

Jekkalon and Jemexxa turned around, too. Tearing at Xyrena's sleeve was the rat-creature that they had first encountered when they came looking for their mother. Now that they could see it close up, they realized that it was much more human than rat, and although it was so diminutive, and so hunched-up, it was more man than boy. It was wearing the same yellow tweed coat as before, and a strange pair of brown britches with buttoned-up spats.

'Don't open up the *verrière*!' it screamed. '*Questa gente* – they are spies! *Feinde*! Enemies!'

'Let go of me, you freak!' Xyrena snapped at it, pulling her sleeve free. 'We're not spies! We just came to see the show!'

'Ha! Ha! *Vous* say that?' the rat-creature retorted. 'This show is invitation only, for people who are dreaming Brother Albrecht's dream. Are *you* dreaming Brother Albrecht's dream, or *êtes vous* poking in your nosepipe?'

On all sides, the audience were twisting around in their seats to see what the tussling was all about. From the stage, the ring-master bellowed out, 'Brown Jenkin! Bring them up here! Let's see who they are, shall we, these spies of yours? Come on! Bring them up here!'

Xyrena said to Dom Magator, 'They've caught us out, John.'

'Yes, I get that. Just don't panic.'

'What shall we do? Zap 'em?'

'*No* – not yet!' Dom Magator cautioned her. 'We need to take out this Grand Freak first. Without him, none of this would exist, so try to play along for now. An-Gryferai is airborne already, right above you, and me and Zebenjo'Yyx, we're moving in to give you some close support. We won't let you down, sweetheart, I promise you.'

'I just don't want them to cut my arms off or turn me into a schnauzer, that's all.'

'Trust me, Xyrena, not a chance of that.'

Five burly circus hands in gray coveralls had come around from the rear of the big top, cutting off any chance of escape. Not that they wanted to escape: first of all they wanted to confront Brother Albrecht. Brown Jenkin tugged at Xyrena's cloak and said, 'Come on, then, *ma belle*! Up on the stage, you lovely nudie lady! You make me want to suck your breast buttons! You make me want to stick my fingers into your sticky pussy-pie!'

Jekkalon said, 'Xyrena – want me to fry the little bastard? Just say the word!'

But Xyrena said, '*No*. We want to get your mom out of here, don't we? And like Dom Magator said, we don't know if they have any weapons, or some other way of defending themselves.'

Inside their helmets, they heard Zebenjo'Yyx say, 'Keep cool, OK? Me and the Dom, we're right outside now. We're only seconds away if you need us.'

Xyrena, Jekkalon and Jemexxa followed Brown Jenkin as he bustled down the aisle toward the stage. The noise from the audience and the performers on the stage was deafening – shouting and whistling and clapping and stamping of feet. Jemexxa hesitated as they approached the apron, but the circus hands were right behind them, and one of them gave her backpack a shove.

'Hey!' Jekkalon protested, turning around and raising his fist; but Xyrena took hold of his arm and said, 'Let it be, Jekkalon. You'll have your turn.'

Brown Jenkin led them up three steps on to the stage, and they were immediately surrounded by a mass of clowns and freaks and little people, all pushing at each other so they could touch them and prod them and pull at Xyrena's cloak. In their Night Warriors outfits, they were just as much of a curiosity to the carnival folk as the carnival folk were to them. Jekkalon elbowed his way through them, although one dwarf retaliated by kicking him in the shin.

'You little shit!' Jekkalon shouted at him, but by then the dwarf had scrambled back into the crowd.

'Over here, strangers!' called Mago Verde, and beckoned them over to the black coach-contraption. Its black leather canopy was still tightly closed, so that it looked like a giant woodlouse. Xyrena walked across the stage first, with a seductive sway of her hips. Mago Verde eyed her up and down with his eyes glittering, twisting the ends of his hair between his fingers.

'Well, well! And aren't *you* something? Where have you appeared from, you temptress? What a crown you're wearing! You look like the Queen of Someplace-or-Other.'

Xyrena said nothing, but gave him a provocative smile.

Mago Verde's hand moved down and adjusted the crotch of his pants. Xyrena kept on smiling because she knew what effect she was having on him – the same effect that she had on everybody.

'You're not *from* here, are you?' asked Mago Verde. He leaned closer to her, so that she could see the fine fissures in his green-and-gray greasepaint. She could even *smell* it, as well as stale tobacco, and his vinegary body odor. 'In fact, you *are* the Queen of Someplace-or-Other, aren't you? Here, and there. The Land of Awake and the Land of Fast Asleep.

He paused, and then he said, 'In *fact* – you're not having this dream, are you, like all of these other poor suckers in the audience? You're like *me*, aren't you, honey-dripper? You're just visiting. Except that – unlike me – *you* weren't invited. Not by me, or Zachary, and not by Brother Albrecht, neither. So what in the name of all that's unholy are you *doing* here?'

Xyrena took two steps nearer to him, so that she could lay both of her hands on the dusty shoulders of his black suit.

'You got wood, don't you?' she murmured.

'What?' He leaned his head forward. He hadn't heard her clearly, because of the hubbub from the audience and the freaks who were still crowding around them.

'I said, "You got wood." Your pecker is so hard you could drill a hole in the ground with it, and you're just aching to push it inside me, aren't you? You think you'll go crazy with lust if you don't.'

Mago Verde stared at her, and for the first time she saw uncertainty in his eyes. 'Who the hell *are* you?' he said, his voice even hoarser than ever, so that he had to clear his throat.

'My darling . . .' Xyrena purred at him. 'I am anybody you want me to be, and then some. You feel like you're going to explode, don't you? Can you imagine me sucking you? Can you imagine the tip of my tongue swimming round and around you, like an eel?'

With a grunt of frustration, Mago Verde gripped both of Xyrena's wrists and gradually lifted her hands off his shoulders. He was trembling all over with the sheer effort of resisting her, as if he were lifting two hundred-pound barbells instead of a woman's arms. '*Ringmaster!*' he shouted. '*Open the canopy! Let the Grand Freak see who has come to pay tribute to him!*'

Xyrena kept on smiling at him. 'So *that's* it! You don't dare to give in to those baser instincts, do you? – not in front of your lord and master! But if the Grand Freak hadn't been here, you would have done, wouldn't you? You would have screwed me in front of all of these people, wouldn't you, and reveled in it! You would have danced around the stage crowing like a barnyard cockerel! But oh, no! You don't dare, do you? Not in front of your lord and master!'

In truth, Xyrena's heart was banging inside of her breast-plate and she was terrified about what was going to happen next. But she still felt an enormous power over Mago Verde, and over every man and woman and freak who was clustering around her. She aroused them, she made their blood tingle, in spite of themselves. Mago Verde wanted her. They *all* wanted her. She induced the kind of lustful hysteria that led men to rape the plainest of women and women to submit to men whom they hated. The ringmaster's face was so congested that it was almost purple. His eyes were bulging and she could tell that she had pumped up *his* blood pressure, too.

He cracked his whip, however, and bellowed, '*All hail to the Great Creator of Nightmares, the Arch-Dreamer, the Grand Freak himself, Brother Albrecht!*' – cracking his whip again and again to accentuate each syllable.

At the same time, he turned a handle on the side of the four-wheeled contraption, like the handle of an old-fashioned sewing-machine, and as he did so, the black leather canopy gradually began to fold up, revealing what was hidden underneath it.

Everybody on the stage dropped on to one knee – those who had knees – and everybody who was wearing any kind of hat or headgear removed it, and held it reverently against their chests.

'*Your crown, you bitch!*' Mago Verde hissed at Xyrena. '*Take off your crown!*'

'I don't take off my crown for anyone,' Xyrena retorted. 'You said it yourself, didn't you? Yes? I'm the Queen of Someplace-or-Other.'

'Then tell your friends to take off their helmets!'

'They're not my friends, they're my bodyguards, and they *never* remove their helmets.'

Mago Verde was obviously furious, but it was too late now. The black leather canopy had been folded right back – and there, exposed for everybody to see –was Brother Albrecht, the Grand Freak, *der Ursprüngliche Sohn des Teufel,* the Original Son of the Devil.

'*Shit*,' said Jekkalon, and Jemexxa whispered, 'Oh, my God.' Even Xyrena, who was trying to keep up her sassy streetwalker act, was taken aback. She had to take three quick breaths to steady herself before she said, '*Dom Magator, he's right here! Center stage! Brother Albrecht, in the flesh! Or what's left of him.*'

The four-wheeled contraption contained a shell-shaped seat, upholstered in worn black leather, and inside this shell-shaped seat sat Brother Albrecht. He was dressed in a sleeveless jerkin of brown velvet with a high collar embroidered with gold thread. His arms were nothing but stumps and his legs had been sawn off at the knees, but his shoulders and his chest were muscular and well developed. It was his face, though, that had caused Xyrena to catch her breath. He was devastatingly handsome, with sapphire-blue eyes and chiseled cheekbones and a wide, strong jaw. His lips were sensual and slightly parted, as if he had just finished kissing someone, or saying something deeply suggestive. His hair was long and blond and tangled, but tied up with fraying golden cords, and decorated with dead white flowers. He could have been the model for a Pre-Raphaelite portrait of Jesus.

Brother Albrecht's jerkin was open to the navel, and like the naked men and women who had escorted his contraption on to the stage, his body was decorated up to the neck with a swarming mass of tattoos – scores of intertwined illustrations of devils and monsters and women performing grotesque sexual acts with dogs and goats and slavering demons. It looked, in fact, as if he had turned himself into a living blasphemy – a challenge to everybody who had faith. *Look at me! I dare you to turn your face away! Christians took my arms and my legs and turned me into a freak and banished me for ever! Would you have any faith in the Lord, if He had allowed you to be reduced to this?*

In a deep, blurry voice, he said, '*Mein achtes Geschank*. My eighth gift. Is it here?'

'*Hier, Ihre Anbetung*,' chittered Brown Jenkin. '*Recht vor Inhnen. Allbe bereit geändert zu werden.*'

Brother Albrecht arched his back so that he could peer over the side of his black contraption, where Maria Fortales was sitting tied to her bentwood chair. He stared at her for a long time without saying anything. Maria Fortales was sobbing now, not only from the persistent pain from her double amputation, but in utter despair and disbelief. She repeatedly threw her head from side to side and kept twisting her body in her efforts to get herself free.

'*Sie ist volkommen*,' Brother Albrecht nodded, at last. 'She is perfect. *Sie haben gut getan,* Mago Verde. You have done well.'

Mago Verde bowed in acknowledgement. 'For you, master, anything. I know that you will reward me generously when the time comes.'

'Her new arms?' asked Brother Albrecht. '*Ihre neuen Arme*? Are they ready yet?'

Xyrena was surprised that he spoke English, even if he did speak it with a very thick German accent, and not with any kind of German accent that she had ever heard before. A medieval German accent, she guessed. But then she thought: this is a dream, after all, and it's *his* dream, so I guess he can speak any language that he wants to, in his own dream.

Mago Verde waggled the fingers of both hands at the ring-master. Whatever this signal meant, the ringmaster clearly understood it, because he wheeled around on his heel and let out a piercing two-fingered whistle. From behind the curtains somebody called out, 'Almost ready, *signore*! Almost ready!'

'Then *quick*! At the double! You are keeping the Grand Freak waiting!'

Mago Verde leaned over the side of Brother Albrecht's seat and said, 'Your attention, please, your worship. Before we give this divine young lady her new arms, I have to tell you that we have three unexpected visitors.'

Xyrena tilted her head toward her microphone. 'Are you there, John?' she asked Dom Magator. 'It looks like we're going to be needing some backup in a couple of minutes.'

'We're right outside the big top, sweetheart. Locked and loaded, both of us. An-Gryferai is dead overhead.'

Brother Albrecht focused his sapphire-blue eyes on Xyrena and gave her a penetrating look that made her feel as she had become as transparent as water, and that he could see right through her armor to her naked body, and into her very bones. Into her thoughts, too, and her emotions, and everything that she had ever said or done or cared about.

'How can a visitor be unexpected?' he said. He looked at Jekkalon and Jemmexa, too. 'How can you three people walk into my dream without my dreaming it? *Es ist nicht möglich*.'

Jekkalon stepped forward. 'No disrespect, dude. We heard about your circus and we just wanted to take a look for ourselves. Me and my sister, we're acrobats. Trapeze artists. We have a kind of professional interest, if you know what I mean. We only wanted to size up the competition.'

'Mago Verde?' Brother Albrecht demanded. 'How did these people get here? Are they *real,* or do they come from somebody else's dream?'

'Oh, they're real all right, your worship. As real as I am. But I don't yet know where they come from, or how they got here.'

Brother Albrecht said to Xyrena, 'Come here, *Fraülein.* I want to look at you.'

Under her breath, Xyrena said to Dom Magator, 'He wants me to come closer. With any luck I'll give *him* the twitch, too.'

'Just play it cool, Xyrena,' Dom Magator warned her.

'What's he going to do? Grab ahold of me? Chase me round the stage? The guy doesn't have any legs.'

'Just watch yourself, that's all. He hasn't survived for eight centuries without having some kind of serious power.'

Xyrena approached the black contraption and then stood in front of Brother Albrecht, her chin tilted up defiantly, her coronet shining, her heavy golden cloak rippling behind her in a wind that nobody else could feel.

Brother Albrecht said, 'What is your name, *Fraülein*?'

'Xyrena. Well – among others. My daddy used to call me his little Fruit-Loop.'

'Are you *real,* Xyrena?'

'The last time I looked in the mirror, yes.'

'You come from the waking world, *nicht wahr*? How did you get here? You realize that this is *my* dream, this circus? *Mein Traum, verstehen Sie*?'

'I know that. But you have plenty of real people here already, don't you? We didn't think you'd object to two or three more. And we're only passing through, you know? Like Jekkalon says, we're taking a professional interest, that's all.'

Brother Albrecht's left eyelid twitched, as if he had a nervous tic. As haughty as he was, Xyrena guessed that their appearance in his dream had not only baffled him but troubled him, too. It was even more obvious that he was beginning to feel the effect of her sexuality. He shifted uncomfortably in his seat, and between his thighs his brown velvet jerkin had visibly started to swell, and she knew that she was arousing him.

'Tell me, Xyrena,' said Brother Albrecht. 'Do I *know* you?'

'I very much doubt it, unless you've ever been to The Knick Bar in Milwaukee.'

'Are you a witch?'

'A *witch*? What kind of a compliment is that?'

'You have magic about you. You are fascinating me. But of course you are aware of that, yes? You are doing it deliberately. You think because I am a fallen priest that I do not know how to resist your allure.'

His words sounded very stilted, every syllable perfectly pronounced, as if he were reading them from an English phrase book.

Xyrena shook her head. 'Not a witch, Your Freakness. Only a woman. But then *you* know all about women, don't you? How dangerous they can be. How much you can lose, if you're not very careful. '

Brother Albrecht was about to reply when all of the clowns and the freaks the animal trainers shuffled noisily backward, and the audience filling the big top let out a low moan of apprehension, like the moan of passengers when an aircraft hits an air pocket and drops several hundred feet without warning. Through the crowd of performers on the stage emerged a thin Italian-looking man dressed in a shiny emerald-green suit, pushing in front of him a large wire cage on wheels. He was closely followed by a sallow man with an iron-gray hairpiece and heavy George Burns spectacles. This man was wearing a long white lab coat spattered with brown stains, and thick brown leather gauntlets.

They were greeted and led forward to the front of the stage by the ringmaster, who cracked his whip and shouted out, 'Ladies and gentlemen! Perversions and distortions! I give you Signore Guido Serpente, reptile charmer of unparalleled mesmerity, and Doctor J. Friendly, surgeon of a thousand unimaginable agonies!'

Signor Serpente pushed the cage right up to the edge of the stage, and then stepped away. Jemexxa was closest to the cage, but at first she couldn't understand what was inside it. All she could see were gray dusty-looking coils, like worn-out hosepipes.

'*Voilà!*' Brown Jenkin cried out, prancing around the cage. '*Sind hier die neuen Arme für dieses reizende Mädchen!*'

At first, Brother Albrecht didn't take his eyes away from Xyrena. But then he said, 'Let us talk later, *Fraülein*. For now, this is more important.'

'You're the boss,' Xyrena smiled at him. Mago Verde had noticed the effect that Xyrena was having on his lord and master, and was glaring at her with undisguised venom.

Brown Jenkin unfastened the catch on the door of the cage, and then Doctor Friendly reached inside with both hands. The 'hosepipes' immediately reared up and it was only then that Jemexxa realized what they were: two huge snakes, each at least six feet long, and each as thick as a human arm. They both had flat, anvil-shaped heads, yellow eyes, and forked tongues that flickered out between their fangs.

'Oh my *God*!' she said. 'I'm totally terrified of snakes!'

Jekkalon took hold of her arm and pulled her back, and Xyrena came up and stood close beside her.

'What the hell are they going to do with *those*?' asked Jekkalon.

But suddenly it became horribly clear. Signor Serpente returned to the front of the stage, this time pushing a hospital gurney, with a grubby sheet draped over it. On top of the gurney jingled a tray of surgical instruments, scalpels and forceps and clips, as well as a kidney-shaped steel dish containing needles, sutures and swabs.

Brown Jenkin jumped up next to the gurney like an eager child and snatched one of the scalpels. With a rat-like chattering noise, he scurried around to the back of Maria Fortales' chair and began to slash at the cords that bound her. Maria Fortales was screaming now, but Brown Jenkin ignored her, and Mago Verde was actually smacking his hands together in delight and laughing at her. Brother Albrecht heaved himself up even higher in his shell-shaped seat, using his knees for leverage, so that he had a better view of what was happening.

Once Brown Jenkin had cut through the last of her cords, three of the circus hands came forward and lifted Maria Fortales out of her chair. She kicked and jackknifed her body and carried on screaming until her voice was nothing but a reedy squeak, but the circus hands bundled her on to the gurney and strapped her down with wide canvas belts, one around her chest, one around her pelvis, and another round her knees.

Doctor Friendly had meanwhile lifted one of the snakes out

of the cage. Xyrena didn't know what kind of snake it was, but she guessed that it was venomous, because he was gripping it tight behind its jaws so that it couldn't bite him. It writhed and twisted even more violently than Maria Fortales, so that two of the circus hands had to help him stretch it out on the gurney right next to her, and keep it pinned down.

Brother Albrecht's eyes were blazing blue with excitement, like the flames from two blowtorches, and he repeatedly kicked the side of his seat with his amputated left knee. '*Frau und Schlange*!' he said, in a voice quivering with excitement. 'Woman and snake! *Gerade wie der Garten Eden, noch einmal*! Just like the Garden of Eden, all over again!'

Selecting a scalpel, Doctor Friendly held the snake tightly in his left hand, about eighteen inches from the end of its tail. Then, without any hesitation, he cut off those last eighteen inches, slicing through its muscle with his scalpel and then clipping through its spine with a pair of surgical pliers. The snake was thrashing so furiously from side to side that the two circus hands had to use all of their strength to keep it on the gurney, but Doctor Friendly continued his operation unperturbed, as if he had undertaken this type of surgery dozens of times before.

Mago Verde approached the gurney and bent over Maria Fortales, and underneath his green painted grin he was grinning for real. She had stopped screaming now, out of exhaustion, but she stared up at him in absolute terror, and Jemexxa could see that she was saying something to him. She couldn't hear what it was. The crowd and the circus folk were all making far too much noise, but from the movement of her lips she was sure that it was '*please*.'

Doctor Friendly ripped off the adhesive tapes that were holding the thick gauze pad over Maria Fortales' left shoulder. He pulled off the pad, which was caked with dried blood, exposing raw, half-healed muscle and a sawn-off stump of white humerus.

For the first time he turned around to Brother Albrecht and addressed him directly. He had a warbling, monotonous voice, almost as if he were chanting plainsong in church rather than talking.

'This is now the most interesting part of the operation, your worship. And also, I have to admit, the most difficult. I attach the muscles and nerves of the human shoulder to the muscles and the nervous system of the snake. In this way, our dear young woman here will be able to use the snake as a substitute for her absent arm.

'I will also connect the snake's cloaca to the young woman's internal organs so that it will be able to eat and sustain itself and use her digestive system to dispose of its waste.

He paused, and took off his spectacles. His eyes rolled around as if they were two planets in contra-rotating orbits. 'These snakes are a crossbreed of both reticulated python and krait. Python for strength and size; krait for its venom, which is sixteen times more toxic than cobra venom. When she has both snakes attached in place of her arms, this young lady will be the most dangerous female that any man has ever met. They will not hurt *her*, of course, because they will depend on her for their very existence! But Medusa the Gorgon will be nothing compared to this charmer! Imagine the shows that you can put on, your worship! Challenge the men in your audience to make love to her, and see if they can escape with their lives!'

Mago Verde clapped again, and whooped. Unable to clap, Brother Albrecht closed his eyes and nodded his handsome head in tacit approval. The audience, both men and women, shrieked and whistled with excitement. They might have been dubious about Brother Albrecht's freak show when they first arrived in his dream, but now they were growing ever more aroused. Xyrena could see that Brother Albrecht was aroused, too, judging by the bulge in his jerkin. He mouthed something at her, but it must have been in German, because she couldn't even lip-read it.

Doctor Friendly replaced his spectacles, picked up another scalpel, and started to cut at the muscle of Maria Fortales' shoulder. The pain must have been unbearable, because she found her voice and screamed even louder than before.

Xyrena turned to Jekkalon and Jemexxa and said, 'Enough, already! I'm calling in Dom Magator. I'm not standing here watching this girl being butchered. You with me? As soon as they come busting in, Zebenjo'Yyx can zap that doctor and put him out of action. You go for Mago Verde.'

'What about the Grand Freak?'

'I think we should leave the Grand Freak to Dom Magator.

He's the one with the Absence Gun. One shot from that and that'll be the finish of him. He won't even be history.

'John?' she said. 'Did you hear that? We need you in here like *now*.'

'Busting in already, baby – have no fear!'

FIFTEEN
Skirmish In Hell

Soon after Xyrena and Jekkalon and Jemexxa had disappeared into the big top, every clown and circus hand and freak had crowded in through the illuminated archway to see the show, and within minutes the carnival grounds had been deserted, leaving only the animals and the quasi-animals sitting miserably in their cages.

Dom Magator and Zebenj'Yyx had cautiously climbed to their feet and looked around. 'Clear,' Dom Magator had decided, and behind his fearsome African mask, Zebenjo'Yyx had nodded.

They had scrambled over the ridge where they had first taken cover, and then they had dodged their way through the rain toward the big top. They had run with their shoulders hunched, like a two-man SWAT team – Zebenjo'Yyx keeping his right arm held out straight in front of him in case he needed to shoot off a sudden burst of quarrels, and Dom Magator holding up his Absence Gun, with his finger on the trigger, ready to fire.

The Absence Gun looked like a Gatling machine-gun, with five rotating barrels, except that the barrels were made of pale green ceramic and the gun itself had a stock like a rifle. It worked on the principle of quantum decoherence, producing a wave function which made it a scientific impossibility that its target had ever existed. It was the third stage beyond the paradox of Schrödinger's cat, in which a cat in a sealed box was both alive and dead at the same time. Anybody who was hit by an Absence Gun was neither alive nor dead, and never had been.

Over by the trees, An-Gryferai took a short run and launched herself into the air, her wings softly thundering. She quickly gained altitude, and flew up high over the top of the tent. Then she started to wheel around the four black pennants which were flapping wetly from its flagpoles. She was buffeted by the wind and the rain, and blinded by fitful flashes of lightning, but she managed to keep steadily circling, waiting for Dom Magator to give her the word to attack.

For the past ten minutes, Dom Magator and Zebenjo'Yyx had listened closely to everything that had been happening to Xyrena and Jekkalon and Jemexxa, so that when they pushed their way in through the main entrance and marched side by side into the auditorium, they had a good idea what would confront them. Even so, as they reached the stage, crowded with clowns and freaks and fire breathers, and with Brother Albrecht sitting in his black contraption in the center, Zebenjo'-Yyx said, 'Jesus *Ker*-ist! This ain't no circus! This is hell on wheels!'

All around them the audience were baying with bloodlust, both men and women. They sounded like a pack of hounds, more than three hundred of them, closing in for the kill. Many of them standing on their seats so that they could get a better view of Maria Fortales as Doctor Friendly prepared to suture the snakes on to the stumps of her shoulders. One woman had lifted her nightdress at the front and was gnawing at the hem in excitement.

Trumpets were blaring, drums were rattling, and the clowns and freaks were stamping their feet on the stage, so that the noise was overwhelming.

'Zebenjo'Yyx, sic that bastard in the white coat!' Dom Magator ordered. 'Jekkalon – Jemexxa – hit that fricking clown! The green one!'

Brother Albrecht caught sight of them. 'Who are these?' he shouted, and he was so angry that flecks of spit flew from his lips. '*Wer traut such, meinen Albtraum einzutragen*? Who dares to enter my nightmare?'

But without any hesitation, Zebenjo'Yyx raised his right hand again. Lincoln couldn't consciously understand how he knew how to fire his arrows, but for some reason he did. Not only that, he did it with speed and casual expertise, as if he had let them off hundreds and hundreds of times before. He raised his right arm and pointed it directly at Doctor Friendly. Then he closed his fingers, and squeezed his fist tight, striking Doctor

Friendly with six arrows. There was a sharp rattling sound as the arrows flew out of the release mechanisms on his forearm. Doctor Friendly was thrown backward by the impact and hit his head against the front wheel of Brother Albrecht's contraption. The two circus hands who had been holding the snake down ducked sideways for cover, but Zebenjo'Yyx raised his left arm and shot both of them, two arrows in the chest and one between the eyes for each of them. The snake twisted and rolled off the gurney and dropped with a thump on to the stage. Before it could slither out of sight, Zebenjo'Yyx shot it with seven arrows, all the way along the length of its body. The final arrow nailed its jaws to the floor.

Mago Verde, however, didn't wait. He struggled through the crowd of performers to the far side of the stage, and leaped off, forcing his way between members of the audience up the right-hand aisle. Brown Jenkin whirled around and saw him, and shouted out '*Attente moi*! Mago Verde! Shit-*merde* you bastard! Wait for me!' He immediately jumped after him and struggled up the aisle close behind him, snatching at his coat and screaming at him. '*Attente moi*! *Attente moi*! Wait! They will *schneiden* me if they catch me! You know that!'

But as Mago Verde tried to escape, Jekkalon pushed his way to the rear of the stage, where two vertical ladders ran up to a trapeze platform. He scaled one of the ladders so quickly that he looked like a human spider. He paused for only a split second, balancing on his toes. Then he swung from one trapeze to another, double-flipping and triple-flipping, flying over the audience toward the rear of the auditorium. The audience looked up in amazement, and immediately hushed.

Jekkalon reached the last trapeze platform well before Mago Verde had managed to fight his way up the aisle to the back of the big top. 'OK, Jemexxa!' he called out. 'Give me some of that sweet, sweet voltage!'

Jemexxa, who was still on the stage, lifted her right hand, with its shiny reflective palm. Jekkalon did the same. Mago Verde seemed to guess what was likely to happen, because he started to struggle back down the aisle again, and then he ducked his head down and hunched his way along a row of seats, trying to use members of the audience to shield himself. Brown Jenkin kept close behind him, still screaming and chattering.

Jekkalon swung from one trapeze to another, until he was

dangling right over Mago's Verde head. He held out the palm of his hand and aimed it at Mago Verde, and told Jemexxa, '*Now*!'

An intense flash of lightning jumped out of Jemexxa's hand and struck Jekkalon's with an ear-splitting bang. At the very last second Mago Verde grabbed Brown Jenkin under the arms and heaved him up in front of him. Brown Jenkin didn't even have time to shout out before his head exploded. Brains and bone shrapnel were sprayed all over the audience who were standing around him, and a cloud of brown smoke rolled up into the air, mostly from his scorched tweed coat.

Mago Verde slung Brown Jenkin's body aside and vaulted over the next row of seats, and then the next. Jekkalon swung after him, from one trapeze the next, but Mago Verde managed to keep dragging members of the audience in front of him, one bewildered dreamer after the other, so that Jekkalon didn't dare to take a shot. If he killed any of the real people who had been drawn by Brother Albrecht into this dream, he couldn't be sure what would happen to them in real life.

Mago Verde rolled over the last tier of seats and disappeared. Jekkalon swung after him on his trapeze, spinning in a wide circle, but he couldn't see him anywhere.

'You nailed him yet?' asked Dom Magator. He was panting hard.

'Not yet. I lost him. He probably escaped out back, where we snuck in. Do you want us to go after him?'

But Dom Magator said, 'Forget him for now. We got ourselves a whole lot of trouble on the stage.'

Jekkalon twisted around on his trapeze and saw that the clowns and the freaks and the circus hands were gathering protectively around the black contraption in which Brother Albrecht was sitting. But they were not just shielding their lord and master from Jebenzo'Yyx and Dom Magator. They were tearing open their shirts and their blouses and their silky clown costumes and baring their chests, as if they were inviting the Night Warriors to kill them.

Even Brother Albrecht's entourage of naked tattooed men and women were clustered around him, too, their arms held wide open, making no attempt to protect themselves. Xyrena thought that it looked like a nightmare production of *Hair*.

'*You will leave my dream now!*' Brother Albrecht shouted at the Night Warriors, and he was incandescent with anger. '*You will leave my dream now, all of you, whoever you are, and you will never return!*'

Dom Magator climbed up the steps on to the stage. A white-faced clown came waddling toward him, as if to intercept him, but Dom Magator waved his Absence Gun at him, and said, 'You want to cease to exist? You're going the right way about it,' and the clown gave him a horrified grin and waddled away. Dom Magator approached Brother Albrecht.

'Sorry, pal,' he told him. 'Me and my friends can't leave just yet. We came here to bring this whole disgusting charade to a well-deserved conclusion and we won't be saying our good-byes until we've done it. Now, if this collection of oddities and short asses know what's good for them, they will elect to stand peacefully aside and let us get on with the business in hand.'

He lifted his Absence Gun, double-cocked it, and leveled it at the clowns and the freaks who had gathered themselves between him and Brother Albrecht. He saw a pretty little pale-faced girl standing directly in front of the Grand Freak. She had straggly brown hair and a long floral dress with a lacy collar. She gave him a hesitant smile, but when he looked down at her feet he realized why she probably wasn't afraid to die. She had the black-and-tan paws of a German Shepherd, instead of feet.

He thought that he would probably be doing all of these people a big favor, canceling out their existence as if they had never been born. But he knew that it wasn't his call.

Xyrena stepped up beside Dom Magator, and said to Brother Albrecht, 'Don't you have a *conscience*, Mister Grand Freak? You're responsible for all of these people. You wouldn't want to see them hurt.'

'I *have* seen them hurt!' they heard Brother Albrecht shout back to them, although he was barely visible behind the jostling crowd of freaks. 'I hurt them myself, and often! And mutilated them! It's all part of the show! All human life is pain and suffering and disappointment, no matter what lies God tells you! Pain and suffering and disappointment are the price we have to pay for being born!'

Dom Magator aimed his Absence Gun and tried to get a fix on Brother Albrecht's head, but the freaks kept moving and nodding and leaning at different angles so that he found it impossible.

'What you are trying to do is fruitless!' Brother Albrecht added. 'Now I want all of you to leave my dream and never come back! You will see it again, soon enough, when I bring it to the waking world! You will hear our music and see our black flags waving, and you will know that we have come to preach the truth about God, and the fallacy of human charity, and the pleasures of endless agony!'

'Not a fricking chance,' said Dom Magator. He nearly caught Brother Albrecht in his cross hairs, but the pale little girl moved her head into his line of fire, still smiling at him.

'Man, I think you should go for a shot whatever,' said Zebenjo'Yyx. 'How many of these freaks are goin' to survive, when this circus breaks up? Most of them, they're only *dream* people anyhow. You can't hurt nobody who's only a dream!'

But at that moment Brother Albrecht shouted out, '*Flammen*! *Flammen*! *Geben Sie mir Feuer*!'

'What?' said Zebenjo'Yyx. 'What in hell's name he talkin' about?'

They soon found out. The fire breather came stalking toward them, stiff-legged, his face still smudged with soot from his last display, like a marionette which has just been snatched out of a bonfire. His cheeks were swollen, his eyes were watering, and Dom Magator suddenly realized that he had a mouthful of lamp oil.

'Hit the deck!' he shouted, and at that instant, with a soft roar, a huge ball of orange fire enveloped the Night Warriors, so that their armor and their costumes were set ablaze. Xyrena was the most vulnerable: she wore only a crown instead of a helmet, but Dom Magator spun himself around as the flames rolled toward them and shielded her face with his upraised hand. All the same, Xyrena yelped as the fire singed her hair.

Zebenjo'Yyx blew out the flames on his forearms, and then twisted around and around, furiously trying to see where the fire breather had disappeared to. 'You all right, Xyrena?' he asked. 'You not burned or nothin'? Everybody else OK?'

Jekkalon had swung back from the rear of the big top now, and he landed on the stage next to Jemexxa. Small flames were still flickering on her legs but he quickly smacked them out.

Dom Magator looked back toward Brother Albrecht's contraption, to see if he could manage to get a clear shot this time. For a fleeting second he saw Brother Albrecht's face, in profile, and Brother Albrecht looked angrier than ever. All this tussling was holding up his eighth sacrifice, after all – and not only that, Zebenjo'Yyx had killed his surgeon and one of his snakes. Dom Magator saw him sharply in his sights, and was just about to fire when an elderly woman with blood-red eyes deliberately blocked his line of sight. She had an expression on her face that explicitly challenged him, 'Go ahead, if you dare – *kill* me! There's nothing I'd like better!'

Zebenjo'Yyx came up to join him, still stiffly sticking out his right arm, ready to fire. 'Where's that fire-eatin' mother? He almost choked me.'

Before Dom Magator could answer him, there was another soft roar, from the other direction this time, and for a second time the Night Warriors were enveloped in a huge ball of flame. Zebenjo'Yyx fired off five or six arrows, two of which were blazing, but the fire breather was far too quick for them, and pushed his way back into the crowd. Dom Magator checked his infrared sensors to see where he might have gone, but for the few vital seconds in which he might have located him the ambient heat was far too high, and all he could see was dancing black ghosts, like a Balinese shadow-theater.

'Nobody hurt?' he asked.

In the confusion the clowns and the freaks and the children had all started to drag Brother Albrecht's contraption back toward the rear of the stage.

'I still say *take* the goddamned shot!' shouted Zebenjo'Yyx. 'Back in Hamtramck, you wanted to waste somebody, you just cruised by and you sprayed the whole street, no matter who was standin' there! Sometimes it's the only way, man, believe me!'

But Dom Magator looked up toward the ceiling of the big top and said. 'I got a better idea. An-Gryferai – you hear me?'

'I hear you!'

'Can you cut your way in through the roof?'

'You bet! Be glad to! You don't know how stormy it's getting out here!'

'OK, then – do it! Then fly straight down here to the stage and grab the guy in the orange flame outfit! He's a fire breather, and he's being a royal pain in the ass! Take him outside and drop him as far away as you like, and from as high as you like! Just get rid of him!'

'There's a pretty murky-looking pond in the woods,' An-Gryferai told him. 'I could drop him in there. That would put his fire out.'

Within just a few seconds, Dom Magator heard a rippling, rumbling sound overhead. An-Gryferai was slicing open the thick black canvas with one of her claws, and the wind was making it flap like a sail.

She made a cut over twenty feet long, and then another cut diagonally across it, in a star shape. The howling of the wind and the sudden cold spray of rain on their heads made everybody in the auditorium look up. Without any hesitation, An-Gryferai folded her wings and came plunging through the cut, head first like a skydiver.

Down below her, on the stage, she could see the flame breather in his orange leotard, circling around the back of Brother Albrecht's black contraption. He was obviously trying to reposition himself so that he could spurt out another blast of fire at her fellow Night Warriors. He was filling his mouth with lamp oil from a large glass flask and he was almost the only performer on the stage who wasn't looking up at her.

She came soaring down, and as she did so, with a brisk clicking noise, she extended her mechanical claws. She hit the flame breather in the back, her claws crunching deep into his deltoid muscles, and with three strong beats of her wings she lifted him clear off the stage and high up over the audience. He tried to shout out in shock, but his cheeks were bulging with lamp oil and he breathed most of it into his lungs.

She lifted him higher and higher, while he spluttered and choked and kicked his legs in a vain attempt to wrestle himself free – even though he would have dropped more than seventy feet if he had managed it. An-Gryferai beat her wings harder and harder, until she had almost reached the ceiling of the big top. But as she rose nearer and nearer to the star-shaped cuts she had made in the canvas, she realized that the fire breather was much heavier than she had estimated him to be, and that she would have to spread her wings much wider than the cuts she had made in order to be able to lift him out of the big top and into the open air.

Not only that, the storm outside was howling even more fiercely than before, and she didn't think that she had the strength to battle the downdraft that was blowing in from outside – not when she was carrying a struggling man who must have weighed nearly two hundred pounds.

Maybe she should do what her grandmother Gryferai had done to the Black Shatterer, and simply let go of him. But there was no guarantee that the drop was enough to kill him, and put him out of action for ever.

'Jekkalon!' she gasped. 'Jemexxa!'

'What's wrong, A-G?' asked Jemexxa.

'I can't lift him out through the roof – he's far too heavy and the wind's too strong!'

'What are you going to do?'

The fire breather was close to asphyxiating now, and thrashing his arms and legs even more violently. It was only because An-Gryferai's claws were buried so deep in his muscles that she was able to hold on to him. The wind shrieked in through the cuts in the canvas and made her dip and spin in mid-air.

'I'm going to drop him, but as soon as I let go of him, I want you to zap him!'

'You got it! Jekkalon?'

Jekkalon said, 'Got you!' He pushed his way through to the rear of the stage and mounted the ladder that would take him back up to the trapeze platform. None of the clowns or freaks made any attempt to stop him. They were too busy dragging Brother Albrecht off the stage, and out of Dom Magator's line of fire. They were even shouting out a ragged chorus of, '*Heave*!' and, '*Heave*!' Dom Magator kept trying to get a clear shot, but even though Brother Albrecht no longer had his fire breather to keep the Night Warriors at bay, he still couldn't manage it, not without the risk of hitting an innocent performer.

'I swear to God, man!' Zebenjo'Yyx shouted at him. 'You just need to total the whole frickin' lot of them!'

Dom Magator was almost beginning to believe that he was right, and that firing indiscriminately into the crowd was going to be the only way to ensure that the Grand Freak was eliminated for ever. But at that moment, high above their heads, An-Gryferai released her grip on the fire breather, and Jekkalon launched himself off the trapeze platform and performed a triple backflip to intercept the fire breather as he came down.

It was all over in a fraction of a second, but it seemed as if it took for ever, like a slow-motion ballet. As soon as An-Gryferai released her mechanical claws from his shoulder muscles, the fire breather dropped toward the stage, his arms flailing as if he were trying to swim. Jekkalon was tumbling over and over in mid-air, and as he did so, he extended his right hand, rotating his wrist so that his reflective palm would line up with Jemexxa's.

Jemexxa fired a dazzling lance of lightning out of her right hand. It hit Jekkalon's hand with a deafening crack, and instantly ricocheted upward. The fire breather exploded still thirty feet up in the air, the lamp oil in his lungs detonating in a massive orange fireball bigger than those he had breathed out over the Night Warriors.

Fragments of flesh sprayed all across the audience, as well as bones that whirled over and over as if somebody were juggling with them, and surrealistic loops and skeins of skin. As Jekkalon reached the next trapeze, and deftly caught hold of it, the whole of the big top was already in an uproar, with men roaring in disbelief and women screaming in horror, and performers and circus hands running in all directions.

The clowns and the freaks who were dragging Brother Albrecht's contraption off the stage were momentarily dazed with shock. They stood staring at the fine drizzle of blood which drifted across the auditorium, and the scorched tatters of orange clothing which were the very last to come see-sawing down to the ground.

For the first time, as the girl with the dog's paws and the old woman with the blood-red eyes watched the smoke from the explosion curl away, Dom Magator had an unobstructed line of fire. He aimed his Absence Gun until he saw Brother Albrecht in his sights, tousle-haired, impossibly handsome but still frowning in fury, and he pulled the three-stage trigger. The ceramic barrels whirred around, and the air in front of the gun appeared to ripple, as if he were looking at Brother Albrecht through the hot rising fumes of a coke-fired brazier.

SIXTEEN

Send In The Clowns

Dom Magator had fired an Absence Gun only once before, at an elderly man who had appeared in a small boy's recurrent nightmares about being abused. In reality, the boy had never been abused, and the man in his dreams was long dead, but the only way to rid him of his nightmare was to make sure that the man had never existed at all. The thunderclap when the man had vanished had been the most exhilarating sound that Dom Magator had ever heard, and had left him deafened for several hours afterward – even in the waking world.

He pressed the first of the three sequential triggers, but tonight nothing happened. No hum, no thunderclap. Nothing at all. Brother Albrecht slowly turned around to frown at him, but even when he realized that Dom Magator was aiming his Absence Gun at him, he gave him nothing but a contemptuous shake of his head.

Dom Magator fired another wave, and then another, stopping only when the little girl with the dog's feet stepped into this line. But they had no effect on Brother Albrecht at all.

'What's wrong, bro?' asked Zebenjo'Yyx, in frustration. 'You *had* him, you totally had him! Don't tell me you *missed*?'

Dom Magator looked down at the Absence Gun in bewilderment. 'You can't miss with this baby. It's soul searching. It *knows* who you want to hit, and it always hits them, even if it hits a few other people who happen to be standing in the way.'

'Then what the hell happened?'

Brother Albrecht's black contraption had now been pulled right to the very back of the stage, and the ringmaster was furiously winding the handle that operated its black leather canopy. Just before the canopy folded down over his head, Brother Albrecht gave Dom Magator a sloping, sardonic smile. A few seconds later the heavy velvet curtains were jerked across the stage and the contraption and all of its attendants disappeared.

'What do we do now?' asked Xyrena. 'We've blown it, haven't we?'

'Where's our mom?' said Jekkalon. 'Kiera – did you see what happened to Mom?'

Dom Magator looked up. Up above them, An-Gryferai was slowly circling down to the stage.

'Are we going to try and save this poor girl here?' said Xyrena. Maria Fortales was still lying on the gurney, her left shoulder exposed. She was shuddering slightly, but it looked as if she was unconscious.

Xyrena walked across the stage toward her, but she was immediately surrounded by more clowns and freaks and little people, all of them with threatening scowls on their faces.

'Where's our *mom*, for Chrissakes?' said Jekkalon. 'She was here a few minutes ago.'

The big top was filled with people talking and shouting and milling around. Although the clowns and the freaks looked hostile, and kept crowding around them and barring their way, they didn't seem to be making any attempt to attack them. They had killed Doctor Friendly and two circus hands and the fire breather, but none of the performers seemed to be interested in exacting revenge.

Dom Magator turned around and looked at the audience, and then he suddenly knew why. The rows of seats were emptying fast – not because the dreamers were walking out, but because they were vanishing. They had probably been jolted out of REM sleep by the grisly spectacle of the fire breather being blown apart, and one by one they were waking up.

'*Crap*!' he said. 'Is George Roussos still here? *Quick*!'

An-Gryferai switched on her sensors and scanned the remaining members of the audience, from one side of the big top to the other, and back again. But even as she did so, more of them simply vanished, and the auditorium was beginning to take on the appearance of a checkers board, with counters being taken faster and faster.

'Jesus, An-Gryferai!' Dom Magator shouted at her. 'Is George Roussos still here or not? If he's woken up already, we're screwed! We're going to be stuck here in this goddamned nightmare with no way of getting out of it until he dreams it again! *If* he ever dreams it again – 'cause I sure as hell wouldn't want to, if I were him!'

'I don't see him!' said An-Gryferai. 'I don't see him anywhere!'

'*Sheeit*!' said Zebenjo'Yyx. 'How much worse luck can any one person *get*, man? I'm crippled by day and stuck in some asshole's nightmare by night!'

'No – no, wait a minute!' An-Gryferai interrupted him. 'I see him now! George Roussos! He's sitting right at the end of the sixteenth row, talking to some woman. It looks like the woman's upset, and he's trying to comfort her.'

'Then let's get the hell out of here, right now!' said Dom Magator.

'What about our mom?' Jekkalon begged him. 'We can't just leave her here!'

'We'll be *back*, Jekkalon!' Dom Magator told him. 'We *have* to come back! We still haven't finished off Brother Albrecht yet!'

Dom Magator took hold of Xyrena's arm and helped her to climb down from the stage. The clowns and the freaks nudged them and pushed them, but none of them made any serious effort to stop them, especially when Zebenjo'Yyx pointed his finger at them, and Dom Magator unholstered a large nickel-plated handgun.

'You know what this is?' he demanded, waving it from side to side. 'It's called a Jangle Pistol. You know what they call it that? Because it *jangles*, and when it jangles it shakes your teeth out, that's what it does. *All* of your teeth – incisors, canines and molars, so you end up as gummy as a geriatric. Now, get out of my fricking way, unless you want to be sucking rusks for the next eight hundred years.'

The clowns and the freaks lifted their hands in mocking surrender, and some of them jeered, and pursed their lips to pretend that they had no teeth already, but they stayed well back. The Night Warriors jostled their way out through the main entrance of the big top and emerged into the wild and windy darkness. As An-Gryferai had warned them, it was stormier than ever, and a blizzard of leaves and twigs were flying through the air. A wooden chicken-coop was being blown between the caravans, over and over, with three black chickens squawking inside it.

They started to head back the way they had come, toward the hill. But before they had reached the last of the tents,

An-Gryferai saw what looked at first like a long line of fir bushes waving in the field up ahead of them. She said, 'Hold it, everybody! Wait up just a second!' and focused on the bushes more closely. They had pointed tops but they weren't swaying in the same way that bushes would sway. When she switched on her night-vision clarifier, she realized that they weren't bushes at all, but *clowns* – clowns wearing black and white and blood-red suits, and that all of them were wielding knives or clubs or sickles or catapults. Their faces were painted in a variety of classic clown expressions – dead white and expressionless, or scowling in exaggerated hostility, or madly grinning.

'*Clowns,*' warned An-Gryferai. 'And it looks like they seriously don't want us to escape from this dream.'

Dom Magator reached over his shoulder to the rack on his back and unfastened one of his rifles. 'Acoustic Carbine,' he said, pulling back a chrome lever at the side to arm it. 'It resonates in your enemy's inner ear and throws him off balance.'

'What about your Absence Gun, man?' asked Zebenjo'Yyx. 'That would wipe the smiles off of their faces – and for ever, too.'

'Unh-hunh,' Dom Magator told him. 'You only use an Absence Gun as an absolute last resort. Think about it. If a person never existed, then their children never existed, neither. So their grandchildren never existed, nor their great-grandchildren, all the way down the line. You understand me? Some of these clowns could be hundreds of years old, right, and have literally *thousands* of descendants. It could be a twenty-generation massacre.'

'OK, man. I get it. But if you're going to throw them off balance, then you'd better do it, like, *now*! It looks like they're heading this way!'

He was right. The long ragged line of clowns was marching toward them, all with that bustling, exaggerated walk that clowns use in their circus acts. They were brandishing their clubs and their sickles and their knives were flashing in the darkness, and as they came hurrying nearer, the Night Warriors began to hear them hooting and howling.

Dom Magator lifted his Acoustic Carbine and fired into the thick of them. The shot from the carbine was ultrasound, high above the range of human hearing, so that at first the other Night Warriors thought that nothing had happened until over a dozen of the clowns started to stagger and stumble and bump into each other. The resonance from Dom Magator's rifle was vibrating the vestibular nerves inside their ears beyond all human tolerance, and they simply couldn't keep their balance.

Dom Magator fired again, and again, and more clowns tumbled and fell. But Jemexxa said, 'There are *hundreds* of them! Where are they all coming from?'

She was right. Even as the front ranks of clowns collided with each other and fell to the ground, more of them came surging out of the darkness, with white faces and silvery-green faces and faces fixed in greasepaint grimaces.

'This is a nightmare, don't forget!' Dom Magator reminded her, aiming at a tall clown with a ghostly white face and pouting black lips. 'Just about anything can happen in a nightmare!'

He kept on firing, but it was rapidly becoming obvious that even with his Acoustic Carbine he wasn't going to be able to bring down all of the clowns on his own – not before the clowns managed to get close enough to attack them hand-to-hand.

'*Zebenjo'Yyx!*' he shouted. '*Give 'em a quick burst, will you?*'

Dom Magator was always reluctant to kill the people he encountered in dreams, no matter how aggressive they were, because there was no way of telling if they were a figment of some dreamer's imagination, or real people dreaming about themselves. If they were real, their real selves might not actually die, but so much of their consciousness was involved in creating their dream that there was a high risk that they could suffer severe brain damage. If that happened, they could remain in a comatose state for the rest of their lives, unable to wake up, ever.

But now the clowns were swarming so thick and so fast that even Dom Magator's Absence Gun wouldn't be able to annihilate them all. The clowns rose ceaselessly out of the ground like the army of skeletons in *Jason and the Argonauts*, grown from the Hydra's teeth. Their howlings and their hootings began to develop a terrible rhythm of their own, *ha*! *ha*! *ha*! *ha*! like derisory laughter.

'Let's back off!' shouted Dom Magator. 'If we go back through that settlement maybe we can outflank them – approach the portal from the other side!'

He locked his Acoustic Carbine back into its rack, and selected a squat black handgun from the weapons that were swinging from his belt. It was a Sonic Blinder, which used very low level sound-waves to increase the pressure of the optic fluid in its target's eyeballs until they burst. For dream people, the blinding was permanent – at least until the dream was over, and they vanished into oblivion. Real people suffered nothing worse than temporary blurring of their eyesight, when they woke up.

Dom Magator fired at the nearest group of clowns, and they immediately spun around and dropped to their knees, clamping their hands over their eyes and wailing in distress. As they went down, Zebenjo'Yyx let off another storm of arrows, more than a hundred of them, and scores of clowns behind them fell into the grass.

Dom Magator took Xyrena's hand and started to jog toward the settlement, his weapons and his equipment clanking and jingling with every step. Jekkalon and Jemexxa followed close behind, and Zebenjo'Yyx brought up the rear, turning around every few yards to fire off another volley of arrows.

As Dom Magator had expected the clowns stopped chasing after them directly, and instead turned toward the hilltop. They knew that the Night Warriors would have to return to the portal through which they had entered George Roussos' dream, and they clearly thought that they could cut them off before they could get there. Dom Magator prayed that George Roussos would stay asleep long enough for them to circle around and reach the portal from the opposite side of the hill.

Just before the Night Warriors reached the settlement, he looked around and saw the clowns sweeping up the hillside, hundreds of them, a dark clamorous tide.

The settlement was a rundown collection of shacks and barns and what looked like workshops. Dim lamps were burning in some of the windows, and Dom Magator could hear hammering and sawing, people shouting to each other, and singing. The wind had died down and the thunder had cleared away, but it was still raining, a steady downpour that seemed to have been dreamed up by Brother Albrecht to make them feel hopeless and dejected.

They splashed through the puddles between the shacks and the workshops. A small boy of about nine years old was sitting on the porch of one of the shacks, wearing only a tattered brown shirt and britches, and brown boots without laces that were two sizes too big for him. He looked up at them as they approached, his short hair sticking up on the crown of his head, his eyes wide. His face was smudged with dirt as if he hadn't washed in weeks.

Xyrena went up to him and hunkered down beside him, her golden cloak flapping in the mud.

'Hi, honey. What's your name?'

'Michael.'

'That's a very fine name. What are you doing out here in the rain, Michael? You look so *cold*, and you're soaked right through!'

'I don't have anyplace to go.'

'Isn't this your folks' house?'

The boy shook his head. 'I can't *find* my folks.'

'Don't they live here?'

He shook his head again. 'No. They're awake.'

Dom Magator came up. 'Hey, kid,' he said. 'Don't I know you? I've met you before, haven't I? You're the boy they call Michael-Row-The-Boat-Ashore-Hallelujah. I didn't recognize you with your face so dirty.'

'Are you hungry, little boy?' asked Xyrena. 'You sure *look* hungry.'

'Xyrena,' said Dom Magator, 'we really have to hit the bricks. If George Roussos wakes up we're going to be trapped here just like little Michael.'

'Can't we take him with us? Look at him.'

Dom Magator took off his glove and scruffed Michael's hair. 'I wish we could. But we both know why we can't, don't we, Michael?'

'I liked my other dream better,' said Michael, wiping his nose with the back of his hand. 'In my other dream they gave me Cheerios and milk and cookies and sometimes they gave me ice cream.

He blinked, and Dom Magator could see tears in his eyes. 'In my other dream, my mom came to visit me. But now she doesn't and I don't think she knows where I am.'

'Let's just take him,' urged Xyrena. 'We can do that, can't we?'

Dom Magator helped her to stand up and drew her aside. Jemexxa and Jekkalon went up to Michael and said, 'How are you doing, buddy? Pretty darn miserable out here, on a night like this.'

'I had a puppy but I don't know where it's gone,' said Michael. 'I think the Packers took it.'

'The Packers? Who are they?'

Michael pointed to the nearest ramshackle workshop. 'They're in there. They're always chopping. Chopping and sawing.'

Xyrena said to Dom Magator, 'Why can't we take him with us? It's *technically* possible, isn't it?'

'Of course it is,' Dom Magator told her. 'But in real life Michael has Mobius Syndrome. It's a rare congenital birth defect. In real life, Michael can't walk, or talk, or eat. He can't even suck a bottle of formula. He spends most of his time asleep, and dreaming. I don't know how he got himself into *this* dream. Maybe Brother Albrecht wanted to display him in his freak show, but then realized how serious his disability actually was. I guess there isn't a whole lot of entertainment value in watching some poor kid just lying there, drooling.'

Jekkalon came over. 'Are we going to take him with us or not? We can't very well leave him here.'

Xyrena said, 'We have to. Dom Magator will tell you why.'

Jekkalon frowned at Dom Magator. 'We really can't?'

'No. I'm sorry. And we really have to get moving.'

'Can't we just find his puppy for him? He said that some people called the Packers took it. They're in that workshop. We only have to ask them politely if they'll give it back to him, and tell them that we'll blow their heads off if they don't.'

Dom Magator checked the instruments on his wrist. 'OK. You can try. But you have thirty seconds flat.'

Jekkalon jogged across to the workshop, followed by Jemexxa and Zebenjo'Yyx. The workshop had a sagging roof and windows that were opaque with grime. Its guttering was crowded with clumps of moss so that the rainwater clattered noisily down the outside walls. For the first time, Dom Magator saw a faded sign over the door that said *Roussos Meat Packers*.

'You see that?' he said. 'This has to be the reason why Brother Albrecht wanted George Roussos to share in this nightmare. He needed his expertise in meat-packing.'

'Oh my God,' said Xyrena. 'You're not telling me what I think you're telling me?'

'We should go,' Dom Magator told them. 'If those goddamn clowns reach our portal before us—'

But Jekkalon went up to the workshop door and tried the handle. Inside, they could see dazzling lights shining and they could distinctly hear chopping noises, but the door was locked.

'Leave it!' said Jemexxa. 'Come on, Jekkalon, we need to get out of here like *now*!'

But Jekkalon said, 'What was the point of us visiting this dream at all? We couldn't kill the Grand Freak, we couldn't catch Mago Verde, we couldn't save our mom! The least we can do is save this poor kid's puppy!'

With that, he kicked at the workshop door. It cracked, but stayed shut. He kicked it again, and again, and the third time it juddered open.

'Jekkalon!' said Dom Magator. 'Forget it! We don't have the time! It's a *puppy*, for Christ's sake!'

'It's the principle! We're supposed to be warriors, aren't we? Well, let's do some warrior stuff! Let's be heroes!'

He disappeared in through the door. Dom Magator said, 'Come on,' to Zebenjo'Yyx, and lifted his Sonic Blinder out of its holster. However rashly Jekkalon was behaving, they couldn't let him enter the workshop without backup. If the clowns reached the portal before they did, they would just have to fight their way through, regardless of the consequences – even if Dom Magator had to use his Absence Gun.

The workshop door led them into a narrow corridor. There was a changing room on the right-hand side, in which blood-stained coveralls and red safety helmets were hanging up on pegs. The air was thick with the sweet, cloying smell of dried blood and feces, as well as cigarette smoke and sweat.

The chopping noise was much louder now, as well as persistent sawing. One man was singing *O Sole Mio*, and two other men were whistling two totally different tunes, out of key. Dom Magator and Zebenjo'Yyx came to the end of the corridor and found themselves on a platform of planks and scaffolding overlooking the main body of the workshop. Jekkalon was already halfway down the steps, but it didn't appear as if anybody was paying him any attention. The workshop was crowded with at least twenty-five men, all of them in dirty coveralls, and all of them wearing red safety helmets, and all of them far too busy cutting and chopping to notice two or three strangers.

It looked as if Dom Magator had been right. Brother Albrecht must have drawn George Roussos into his nightmare tonight because he needed the skill of his workforce. These men were nothing more than dream figures, but this was only a dream, and while they were here, they could do whatever Brother Albrecht needed them to; and what they were doing was butchering.

The interior of the workshop had been set up as a meat-packing plant, with rows of stainless-steel hooks suspended from rails, and stainless-steel tables for cutting and trimming and disemboweling. There were two rows of pressure lamps hanging from the ceiling, hissing loudly, which illuminated the workshop with a bleached, unearthly light.

On the tables lay cattle and pigs and other more exotic animals, like llamas and mountain goats. The men were bent over them with boning knives and saws, cutting them in half and removing their legs and their heads. The cutting and trimming tables were running with blood, and the paunch table, where cattle had their bellies slit open to let their bowels drop out, was thickly splattered with manure as well as blood.

Dom Magator looked around the workshop in disgust. When he was a restaurant inspector in Baton Rouge, he had visited more filthy slaughterhouses than he could count, mainly to find out how hamburgers had become contaminated with *E-coli* bacteria. But this place was a hundred times filthier, and the grisliest spectacle that he had ever seen.

'*Shit,*' said Zebenjo'Yyx.

'Exactamundo,' said Dom Magator.

It was then that he realized that none of the slaughtered animals had been skinned – even the shaggiest goat. Not only that, none of their meat had been cut from their carcasses in the usual way – no steaks, no spare ribs, no hocks. He thought of Brother Albrecht's freak show and it dawned on him what was happening here. These animals weren't being butchered for their meat. Strictly speaking, they weren't being butchered at all – they were being *disassembled* so that their heads and their legs and their bodies could be mixed and matched with human beings.

'Jekkalon!' he told him. 'Jekkalon, we need to get out of here!'

But Jekkalon ignored him, and started to walk quickly along the side of the workshop. At the far end, in a shadowy corner, there was a row of cages with various animals in them. Dom

Magator could make out at least three sheep and a German Shepherd.

For a few seconds, Jekkalon was out of sight behind one of the cutting tables. But then he reappeared, and he was carrying a golden Labrador puppy over his arm.

'I got it!' he said.

He reached the steps that led up to the platform where Dom Magator and Zebenjo'Yyx were standing. As he started to clamber up them, however, one of the slaughtermen looked up from the pig that he was cutting apart, and roared out, 'Hey! You! Where the hell do you think you're going with that dog?'

Jekkalon ran up the rest of the stairs so fast that he collided with Dom Magator when he got to the top. By now, all of the slaughtermen had turned around and seen what was happening, and they came rushing toward the bottom of the steps, brandishing axes and boning knives and saws. They were led by a thick-necked giant with a bare, blood-spattered chest, who was bellowing like a bull.

'*Get out of here!*' Dom Magator told Jekkalon. Then, to Zebenjo'Yyx, 'Give me some covering fire, will you?'

Zebenjo'Yyx held up both arms and rattled off two streams of quarrels. The giant slaughterman was already mounting the steps, but he let out one last stentorian bellow and then he toppled backward, bringing down three of his companions with him. His body was unceremoniously heaved aside so that the rest of the slaughtermen could start to climb the steps, screaming and shouting even louder than before.

Dom Magator took two or three steps back, then lifted his Absence Gun, with the focus set in three stages, from narrow to medium to panoramic. That meant that a concentrated wave function would hit the slaughtermen first, and then two further wave functions would hit the killing floor, and then the entire workshop itself.

Two of the slaughtermen reached the top of the steps and came lurching toward him. They were both wearing brown leather skullcaps and floor-length leather aprons, and both were carrying bloodstained axes. They looked solid enough, but their faces were smudged and unfocused, with dark holes for eyes and no distinct features. Dom Magator knew that this was because George Roussos was dreaming about them, and although George Roussos knew how many slaughtermen he had working for him, he had no clear idea of what each of them actually looked like.

'Give us back that dog, you thieving bastard,' growled one of them, in a thick Polish accent.

'Or else what?' said Dom Magator.

'Or else you wind up like one big hambooger.'

The slaughterman came forward, swinging his axe rhythmically from side to side, like *The Pit And The Pendulum*. Although the man's face was so blurred, Dom Magator could tell that he was grinning.

'You don't know how much I'm looking forward to this,' he growled, swinging his axe faster and faster, in a figure of eight, until it whistled.

Dom Magator pulled the first trigger and – instantly – the slaughterman vanished, as did the rest of the slaughtermen scrambling up the steps behind him. Their knives and saws and axes fell to the floor with a clattering, ringing noise, like handbells. Technically, this was a paradox, because the slaughtermen had never existed to pick up their knives and their saws and their axes in the first place. But the paradox was only temporary, because the Absence Gun was set to eliminate their tools, too, and all of the cutting tables where the animals were being dismembered, and then the whole building.

There was a barrage of ear-splitting thunderclaps as the air rushed in to fill the vacancies left by the non-existent slaughtermen. Even inside his heavy protective helmet, Dom Magator was temporarily deafened. But he fired again, and again, and then there were two more catastrophic bangs, so violent that the ground quaked beneath his feet.

When he lowered his Absence Gun, Dom Magator saw that there was no workshop any more, no killing floor, no animals and no slaughtermen. He was standing in a briar thicket, with nothing in front of him but trees. The rain was still dredging steadily down, and when he turned around he saw the shack where Michael-Row-The-Boat-Ashore-Hallelujah was sitting on the porch, and Jekkalon, and Jemexxa, and Xyrena, and Zebnenjo'Yyx, all standing around him.

He looked back to the trees where the workshop had been. But there had never been a workshop, and there had never been any slaughtermen. He felt at least half satisfied with what they had achieved. Even if they had not yet succeeded in putting an end to Brother Albrecht and his hideous traveling carnival, they had at least thwarted his attempt to create even more freaks.

Michael was hugging the golden Labrador puppy in his arms. Dom Magator walked across to him and said, 'We have to go now, Michael. But we'll be back, young feller, I promise you, and we'll get you out of this nightmare, and find you a really happy dream where they give you Cheerios and your mom can come visit you. At least you have your puppy back.'

'Thank you,' said Michael. His mouth was turned down and he was trying very hard not to cry. 'You won't forget about me, will you?'

Jemexxa hunkered down beside him and stroked the puppy's head. 'We won't forget you, Michael. Ever. When me and my twin brother go on to the stage next time, we'll sing *Michael, Row The Boat Ashore*, and we'll dedicate it especially to you.'

'Does your puppy have a name?' asked Xyrena.

Michael nodded. 'He's called Froggy.'

'Froggy? That's a pretty unusual name for a puppy. Most kids would have called their puppies, like, *Doggy*.'

Michael rested his cheek against the top of the puppy's head. 'That's what my mom used to call me when I was a baby. She said I looked like a little froggy.'

Dom Magator saw that one of the needles on his seismic sensor had started to tremble. That meant that George Roussos was now rising through the last phases of REM sleep toward consciousness, and that he would soon be awake.

'Right,' he said. 'Now we really do have to get the hell out of Dodge.'

SEVENTEEN

Flesh Forward

They ran in silence, like six shadows flickering between the tree trunks, their feet making barely any noise at all. They startled a few deer, and as they reached the edge of the trees, half a dozen gray grouse burst out of the undergrowth in alarm, like feathered bombs. But they kept on running.

They had to circle around the right-hand side of the hilltop to stay out of sight of the clowns from Brother Albrecht's circus until the very last moment.

As soon as they were clear of the trees, An-Gryferai started to run even faster, and flap her wings. She lifted off into the drizzle, and rose higher and higher as if she were climbing up one invisible flight of stairs after another. Soon she was almost a hundred feet over their heads, and a hundred yards ahead of them.

Although it was still raining it was gradually beginning to grow lighter, and the mist was shining like a breathed-over mirror. An-Gryferai switched on her green fog-lenses, and, as she beat her wings and rose up to more than two hundred feet, she could see the rabble of clowns and freaks pouring over the hilltop and hurrying down the long grassy slope. The leading clowns were already less than a quarter of a mile away from the Night Warriors' shimmering octagonal portal – the portal that was their only way back into George Roussos' bedroom, and the world of reality.

'Dom Magator—' she panted. 'They've almost reached the portal already. There's no way we have any chance of reaching it before they do.'

'In that case, sweetheart, we'll have to meet them head on. I still have plenty of fancy ordnance left. But if we're forced to use the Absence Gun – well, that's just too bad. I'm worried that I might hit the portal, that's all. If the portal doesn't exist any more – we're Gregged, believe me.'

'In that case, let's hustle,' said Zebenjo'Yxx. 'It's not goin' to do us no good standin' around discussin' nothin', and that's for sure.'

They ran even faster, with An-Gryferai sweeping and swooping overhead. Inside his helmet, Dom Magator could hear them all panting in chorus. He thought at first that they might have a chance of reaching the portal first. But as they came around the hilltop, however, and ran down the slope together, they saw that the clowns were already waiting for them – hundreds of them. They were standing in a long line, their pointed hats drooping, their make-up streaked by the rain. They weren't moving. Most of them had their arms folded, and they were simply staring at the Night Warriors with a combination of real and painted hostility.

The white-faced harlequin with the blackberry lips was standing right in front of the portal. It appeared that he was the leader, since all of the other clowns were standing well back. He was holding a curved scimitar which he kept circling around and around, so that it flashed in the mist like a steel propeller. Directly behind him, framing him, was the crackling blue electric portal, and by the expression on his face it looked as if he was challenging the Night Warriors to try to reach it.

Dom Magator stepped up to face him. 'How about letting us pass, pal?' he shouted out. 'We didn't come here to hurt none of you, believe me.'

'*Oh*!' replied the white-faced harlequin, in a croaky, drawn-out voice. 'What about the fire breather? I think you hurt *him* somewhat. And what about Doctor Friendly? Looked like a pincushion by the time you'd finished with that unfortunate fellow, didn't he?'

'He deserved it. Trying to sew snakes on to that poor girl's arms. How sick is that?'

'Depends on your definition of sick, my friend. Life is sick, from beginning to end. Think how we're born! Our faces squeezed out of our mothers' nether regions like rabbits out of a tight pink hat! Only to grow, and suffer, and then to decline, and our teeth to drop out, and finally our hearts to seize up, and our bodies to become a tumbling mass of maggots! Don't you call *that* sick?'

'Listen, bro – are you goin' to let us through or what?' Zebenjo'Yyx challenged him, raising his right arm and clicking the elaborate wooden levers that prepared his arrows for firing.

The white-faced harlequin shook his head from side to side and made a tick-tocking sound with his tongue as he did so. 'The Grand Freak wants you to stay here. The Grand Freak wants you to join his circus. Think of what wonderful attractions you would be! The fat man and the bird woman and the black archer and the glittering twins, not to mention the naked woman who isn't naked at all!'

Out of the side of his mouth, Jekkalon said to Jemexxa, 'How much lightning do you have left? We could cremate this idiot in two seconds flat!'

But inside their helmets Dom Magator quickly said, '*No*, Jekkalon! This close to the portal, one of your lightning strikes could short it out. Then we could *never* get back.'

High above their heads, An-Gryferai was circling and circling through the clouds, sometimes appearing, sometimes disappearing. 'Hey, D.M. – how about I dive down and grab him?' she said. 'He wouldn't survive a drop of two hundred feet, would he? And then we'd be clear to go.'

But Dom Magator looked at the crowds of clowns assembled on the other side of the portal. If An-Gryferai swooped down and hoisted this white-faced harlequin up into the air, and let him drop, the rest of the clowns would fall on them like a human tsunami, and six Night Warriors wouldn't stand a chance. For all of their arrow storms and wave-function rifles and intuitive throwing-knives, they would be overwhelmed by sheer numbers. Brother Albrecht could dream up as many clowns as he wanted to, and they would never be able to kill them all.

'I'll make you a deal, OK?' Dom Magator suggested to the white-faced harlequin. 'You let us go through that portal, and out of your way, and I won't use my Absence Gun on you.'

'Your *what*?' croaked the clown.

'Oh – you never heard about Absence Guns? You know what an Absence Gun can do? It doesn't kill you. It doesn't even *hurt* you. It simply makes sure that you never existed, ever. You get hit by an Absence Gun and your parents never had you.'

'I'm not making no deals with you, tin man,' the clown retorted. 'The Grand Freak sent us here to bring you back to the circus, and that's exactly what we're going to do.'

Dom Magator hesitated. Zebenjo'Yyx could easily take out the white-faced harlequin with a quick storm of arrows; or Dom Magator could use a weapon against him that posed less of a risk of damaging the portal than the Absence Gun. But it would be suicide. If they brought down the white-faced harlequin, the rest of the clowns would never let them escape. They would either tear them to pieces right here and now, or tote them triumphantly back to Brother Albrecht's circus, where they would be cut apart, and sewn back together again with limbs taken from all kinds of animals and reptiles, and that would be even more unbearable than death.

Inside Dom Magator's helmet the seismic sensor quivered again. George Roussos was stirring, which meant that he had only minutes to make up his mind, if that. But before he could decide what to do, Xyrena came forward and touched his arm.

'Let *me* try, John,' she murmured. 'Maybe this is one situation that can't be solved by firepower alone, if you know what I mean.'

'What the hell can *you* do against all of this rabble?'

'Watch me.'

Without saying anything else, she walked right up to the white-faced harlequin, her crown glittering and her gilded cloak idly flapping. The white-faced harlequin stopped whirling his scimitar around and around and looked her up and down, his eyes restless with prurient interest. Raindrops were quivering on her gleaming metallic breasts and the sensual curve of her stomach, and dripping from between her legs.

'So, my lovely lady . . . who are *you*?' he asked her, in his frog-like voice.

Xyrena reached out and laid her hand on his sloping left shoulder. 'You don't need to know my name, Clown. You *want* me. Isn't that enough?'

He stared at her for a long time with those kohl-blotched eyes. Xyrena was the least heavily-armed of all the Night Warriors, but in her own mesmerizing way she was one of the most lethal. And she was fearless, too. To approach the harlequin so closely, and to start stroking his white-painted cheek, that took ice-cold nerve, especially since he was still gripping his scimitar, and he could have slashed her throat at any moment.

'You want me so bad, don't you, Clown?' said Xyrena. 'So what if it's raining, and so what if hundreds of your fellow pranksters are watching us. What do you care? You want me here and now – right here in the grass.'

'*Jesus*, Xyrena,' said Dom Magator.

But Xyrena murmured, 'Get ready, John. As soon as he's distracted, you guys make a dive for the portal.'

'What about you?'

'I'm a big girl, John. I can take care of myself.'

All of the Night Warriors had heard her. An-Gryferai circled down closer, and said, 'I'm ready, Dom Magator. Just give me the word and I can fly straight through.'

'I'm not sure I like this,' said Dom Magator. 'In fact I don't like this at all.'

'Well, neither do we,' Jekkalon retorted. 'But what choice

do we have? You want to end up with some orang-utan's face, instead of your own?'

Now Xyrena was untying the ruff around the white-faced harlequin's neck. She whirled it teasingly around her finger and dropped it into the grass. Then she started to unbutton his sodden wet clown suit. She tugged it off his shoulders, revealing a narrow white chest with a prominent ribcage. He neither helped her nor resisted her, but his nostrils flared and he began to breathe very deeply, his chest rising and falling, and his eyes never stopped roaming over her gold-plated breasts.

Uneasily, Dom Magator looked around at the crowds of clowns gathered on the slopes. He would have thought that they would have started to become restive by now, especially since their leader seemed to have temporarily forgotten what the Grand Freak had sent them here to do. But they were all staring at Xyrena with as much fascination as the white-faced harlequin, and some of them were clutching their clown suits between their legs and rhythmically squeezing their fingers.

Xyrena knelt down in front of the white-faced harlequin and wrenched his pants all the way down, tearing the thin white cotton as she pulled them over his shoes. Now he was completely naked, except for his white conical hat. His penis was standing up as stiff and white as a bone, with only the faintest tinge of purple on the glans. His scrotum had shrunk so tight that they had almost disappeared inside his body.

'Lie down,' Xyrena ordered him, but she said it very gently and warmly. 'Lie down, Clown, and you can have me.'

The white-faced harlequin lay down in the long wet grass. He looked thin and vulnerable, more like a boy than a man. Xyrena unfastened the buckles that held her armor in place, and opened it up, like a golden seashell. Underneath, she looked exactly the same, except that now she really *was* naked – her breasts were real breasts, that swung when she moved, and her nipples knurled tightly in the rain. She laid her armor on the ground, and then she approached the white-faced harlequin as he lay in the grass in front of her.

'Come on!' she taunted him. 'How much do you want me?'

'I want you more than any woman I ever met,' he croaked back at her.

'Do you want me more than diamonds? Do you want me more than gold?'

'Yes, yes!'

'Would you go blind for me?'

'Anything!'

Xyrena smiled and said, 'That's what I needed to hear.'

She tossed back her cloak and then she knelt astride him, her head held high, with a strangely serene smile on her face. With her left hand, she took hold of his erect penis and guided it up between her thighs, until the glans was nestling between the parted lips of her vagina. She looked down for a moment in satisfaction, but when the white-faced harlequin attempted to force his penis deeper inside her, she gripped him very tight, so that he couldn't.

He struggled for a moment, bumping his hips up and down. 'What are you doing to me?' he demanded. 'I want you! *I want you*!'

'You said you wanted me more than anything?'

'Yes! Yes! Yes, curse you! *Yes*! I have to have you, you whore!'

'Do you want me more than life itself?'

'*Yes*!' he screamed at her, with spit flying out of his mouth. 'Yes-yes-yes-yes! *Yes*!'

When he said that, Xyrena took her hand away from his penis and sank downward on to his hips, slowly allowed the weight of her body to take him deep inside her. He let out a terrible groan like a man having his bowels dragged out of him by a medieval torturer, part agony and part ecstasy, and his head dropped back into the grass.

Dom Magator turned back to the rest of the clowns. Almost all of them had their eyes closed now, and all of them were swaying backward and forward, as if they were anemones on the bottom of the ocean. He looked down at Xyrena, and she was rising and falling in the same rhythm, lifting her hips so high that the tip of the white-faced harlequin's penis almost slipped out of her, hesitating, and then lowering herself slowly down again.

It was then that it began to dawn on Dom Magator what Xyrena must have understood intuitively. Each of these hundreds of clowns, *physically*, was an individual. Each one of them was dressed in a wildly differing outfit, and each one of them wore his own distinctive face-paint. If you killed any one of them, he fell, without affecting any of the others. But inside their heads, they were one and the same person. They all shared a common consciousness. They were all Brother Albrecht.

When Xyrena had aroused the white-faced harlequin, she had aroused all of these hundreds of clowns at the same time, just as she had affected Brother Albrecht when she had confronted him on the stage. Even now, it was possible that Brother Albrecht, back at the circus, was sharing this same sexual excitement.

Xyrena rose up and down two or three more times, and then she said, '*Go, John! All of you! Go now!*'

As if to emphasize the urgency of the situation, the seismic sensor in Dom Magator's helmet started to let out a repeated buzzing noise. George Roussos' eyes were flickering and he was only seconds away from waking up.

Dom Magator hurried Jekkalon and Jemexxa to the portal. They turned, and the portal lit up their faces in intermittent flashes of electric blue. 'We can't go without Xyrena!' Jemexxa insisted.

'Don't worry! *Go*! I'll take care of her! If she doesn't make it, we can always come back for her!'

Jekkalon and Jemexxa hesitated a split second longer, but then Zebenjo'Yyx forcibly pushed them toward the portal. 'Go! You supposed to be warriors! Warriors do what they damn well tol' to!'

The twins disappeared through the portal with a sharp crackle of static. Then An-Gryferai landed nearby, folded her wings, and ducked through the portal after them, with another crackle. Zebenjo'Yyx caught a whiff of scorched feathers.

'*Come on, man! Your turn!*' he shouted. But Dom Magator was still hovering protectively over Xyrena as she continued to bring the white-faced harlequin closer and closer to a climax. The harlequin had started groaning again, and all of the other clowns had started groaning, too, in a hideous chorus, and swaying their hips even more lasciviously backward and forward.

'I'm OK, John,' said Xyrena, in a low, businesslike voice. 'I have this all under control. I'm sliding the needles out of my fingers right now.'

Dom Magator said, 'Zebenjo'Yyx – it's OK – she's just about to give our white-faced friend the needle treatment. *Go*! We'll be right behind you, I swear it!'

Xyrena bent forward over the white-faced harlequin, kissing his blackberry-painted lips and biting his neck. He was almost delirious, and his feet were arched with sexual tension. He was right on the very brink of ejaculating, and his eyes were tight shut.

'Oh, yes!' he shouted. 'Oh, yes! Oh, yes! Oh, my Lord Lucifer and every demon that ever was!'

Suddenly, however, he started to shudder, and to kick, and to toss his head from side to side. He made gagging noises, like somebody trying to be sick on an empty stomach. Gradually, Xyrena sat up straight and it was then that Dom Magator could see that she had spread both hands wide across his chest and run the long needles that protruded from the ends of her fingers into his ribcage.

There was a spitting, sizzling noise. The white-faced harlequin struggled even more furiously, and then smoke began to puff out of his lips. He uttered another extraordinary cry, more like a whoop than a scream, as Xyrena's needles brought the blood in his body to boiling point. His white skin was suffused with blotches of crimson, and he started to blister.

He stared up at Xyrena but he couldn't see her because both of his eyes had been poached white.

'You said you'd go blind for me, didn't you?' Xyrena reminded him.

He tried to speak, but all that came out of his mouth were more puffs of smoke. His head fell back and his bloated white face was mercifully covered by the grass.

'RIP,' added Xyrena, much more quietly. 'You said you wanted me more than life itself. Well, you got what you wanted.' She paused, and then she lifted herself off him. In the rigor of death, his penis was still erect.

On the slopes, the hordes of clowns were milling around, bewildered and shocked. They had shared the white-faced harlequin's passion so they must have shared his pain. Dom Magator picked up Xyrena's armor for her and took hold of her hand. 'Come on, Rhodajane, we need to get out of here prontissimo!'

'I'm not decent!'

'Who cares? Even when you were decent you weren't decent! Now, go!'

He pushed her through the dazzling blue portal – *crackle*! – and followed right behind her – *crackle*! – just as the first of the clowns reached them, howling and waving their knives and their clubs. One of them managed to pull back the elastic of his catapult and fire a pebble into the Roussos' bedroom. Zebenjo'Yyx was kneeling close beside the portal and in retaliation he loosed off three arrows.

Dom Magator said, '*No*! They won't—'

But it was too late. The arrows hit the bedroom wall and stuck there, shivering like wheatstalks in the wind. The instant he had stepped through it, Dom Magator had closed the portal behind him, and the way through to Brother Albrecht's nightmare had been sealed off.

'Sorry, man. Didn't want them comin' through after us, is all.'

'They wouldn't have. They *couldn't*. They can stop us from getting through but they can't get through themselves. They'd be fried.'

Zebenjo'Yyx plucked his arrows out of the bedroom wall and slotted them back into his quiver. Meanwhile Xyrena was fastening the buckles on her gilded armor and tugging her cloak straight. On the bed next to them, George Roussos was still asleep, but he was beginning to stir, and they could see his pupils darting from side to side beneath his eyelids as he came closer and closer to waking up.

'Let's go,' said Dom Magator. 'We didn't manage to knock out Brother Albrecht tonight, but we learned a whole lot, didn't we, and next time we'll make sure we do it right.'

'What I don't understand is why the Absence Gun had no effect on him at all,' said Jekkalon. 'You zapped that meat-packing plant, right, and everybody in it. Why couldn't you zap Brother Albrecht?'

Dom Magator shook his head. 'I have no idea. But right now, it's past six a.m. We need to get back to our beds. Thanks, everybody. For a first outing you all did real good.'

They embraced each other in a circle, and as they did so they rose upward through the ceiling of George Roussos' bedroom, and up through the bedrooms above it, and out on to the rooftop of The Drake Tower. It was light now, and Lake Michigan was sparkling with early-morning sunlight.

An-Gryferai spread her wings and peeled away to the south-east, to Florida. The rest of the Night Warriors flew east toward Cleveland.

Meanwhile, George Roussos swung his legs out of bed, and stretched, and yawned. He hadn't had such a bad night's sleep in years. Nothing but nightmares about cutting up animals – all kinds of animals, not just cattle and pigs and sheep. And *clowns*, and he had always hated clowns, ever since he was a small boy.

He checked the clock on his nightstand. Six seventeen. Time to take a shower and get to work. But then his eye was caught by the framed wedding photograph next to the bedside lamp.

He reached over and picked it up. He said, 'What the *fuck*?'

The glass in the photograph was shattered like a spider-web. He stood up, still frowning at it, and as he did so he trod on a smooth brown pebble.

EIGHTEEN

The Sleepers Awake

Kiera opened her eyes to see Lois Schulz smiling at her.

'At last you're awake, my darling, *Gott zu danken*!'

Kiera blinked and looked around her. She was no longer in the fourth-floor room that Springer had booked for them at the Griffin House Hotel. Instead, she was lying in a hospital bed, in a sunlit room with pale green walls and framed prints of pink orchids all around. When she tried to turn over and sit up she realized that her left arm was connected to a vital signs monitor.

'*Lois*? Where *is* this? What am I doing here?'

'University Hospital, my darling. Kieran is here also.'

'What am I doing in a hospital? I'm not sick!'

'Oh, you're not sick? Hah! You could have fooled me!'

'Why, what happened?'

'Who knows, already? Yesterday evening I came to your hotel room to take you and your brother to the concert and you were gone. I went crazy! My first thought was that you had been kidnapped! You know, for ransom or something like that! It was only by chance that one of the maids said that she had gone into another room on the fourth floor to take in some clean towels, and she had seen you both asleep, and recognized you. Otherwise, we would have had the police searching the whole of Cleveland! The whole of Ohio, even!'

'I'm sorry,' said Kiera. 'We really didn't mean to worry you.'

'*Worry* me? *Worry* me? Even when we *found* you, we couldn't wake you! Believe me, we tried! I shook you! I screamed in your ears, wake up, wake up! But you wouldn't wake up, neither of you, so what did I do? I called nine-one-one of course. I thought maybe you'd both been taking that Georgia Home Boy or that Special K or whatever.'

Kiera said, 'Lois, you know we never take party drugs. You know that.'

'Well, of course. The doctors gave you a blood test and he said you were clean like whistles. He tested for everything and he couldn't understand why you wouldn't wake up. He thought maybe it was some kind of a coma.'

'I don't know. Maybe we were just exhausted.'

'If you were so exhausted, why didn't you tell me? Why did you sneak off and hide like that? Don't you trust me to take care of you? I could have maybe rescheduled.'

'Oh, get real, Lois. You think you really would have?'

'Well, maybe not. But how exhausted do you have to be to sleep through a seven-and-a-half million-dollar concert? Do you know what the *penalties* are going to be? The refunds! Do you have any idea how much our insurance premiums are going to go up? You were *exhausted*? God made the whole world and He took only one day off!

She paused for breath and then she said, 'At least your next concert isn't until Saturday. I should have such luck.'

'I'm sorry, Lois, truly I am. But there are some things which are much more important than money.'

'Name one. Please. I'd love to know what it is.'

At that moment the door opened and Kieran appeared. His hair was sticking up as if he had just woken up and he was wearing yellow hospital pajamas. 'Hi,' he said. 'You're awake!'

'Oh, great,' Lois greeted him. 'The other Comatose Kaiser. So how are *you* feeling?'

'OK, I guess,' Kieran told her. 'Kind of bushed, but that's all.'

'How can you be *bushed*? You two, you've been sleeping all night like dead people!'

'I've been telling Lois how sorry we are,' said Kiera. 'But I *have* tried to explain that money isn't everything.'

'Kiera's right,' said Kieran. 'So we miss one concert. It isn't the end of the world. Unlike the end of the world, which *is* the end of the world.'

'I would just like to know what it is that means more to both of you than your careers.'

Kieran sat down on the end of the bed. 'Our mom, Lois. Our mom is more important. And, like I say, the end of the world. That's more important, too.'

Lois looked from one twin to the other. 'Your mom. Your *mom*? You know how sorry I am, but your mom is long ago passed over.'

'Passed over, yes,' said Kieran. 'But not passed away.'

'I don't know what that means, Kieran. I don't have the faintest idea what you're talking about.'

'If it comes to the end of the world, Lois, then believe me, you will.'

David shook Katie's shoulder and said, 'Wake up, sleepyhead. I have to be gone in an hour. I made you coffee.'

Katie sat up in bed and frowned at him. 'What time is it?'

'A quarter of eight. I thought I'd let you sleep a little longer.'

'*Urrgghh*,' said Katie, falling back and wrapping her head in the pillow. 'I feel like I haven't slept in a week.'

David pried the two sides of the pillow apart. His face was very serious. 'That's what I wanted to talk to you about. You were so restless last night. In fact "restless" is the understatement of the century. It was like you were having a full-scale fight with somebody. Flapping your arms and kicking your feet and twisting around and shouting.'

'Shouting?' said Katie, staring at him suspiciously. 'What was I shouting?'

'All kinds of stuff. Something about how stormy it was, and how you couldn't lift somebody out through the roof. I mean, really weird things like that. You said you could see some circus, but it was too far away and you needed to gain more height. I swear to God you sounded like you thought you were flying.'

Katie reached up and touched his cheek with her fingertips.

'It was only a nightmare, David. That's all. Maybe I've been working too hard.'

'All the same, when I get back from Denver you and I are going to go talk to Aaron. Or Miriam, if you'd prefer.'

'David, I keep trying to tell you. I'm perfectly OK.'

'No, you're not. Something's happened to you. You've changed.'

She looked at him for a long time without saying anything, trying to communicate with her eyes that she *had* changed, yes, but that her feelings for him were as strong as ever, maybe even stronger. How could she possibly tell him that she was An-Gryferai, and that she had flown in a rainstorm over a circus, and snatched a fire breather into the air, so that her fellow Night Warriors could blow him up?

How could she make him believe that she had fought against clowns and freaks and barely escaped from the most terrible nightmare that had ever threatened the human race?

'I love you, David,' she said, very softly.

'I still want us to talk to Aaron. Will you do that for me?'

Katie nodded. 'Of course I will. I *have* changed, I know that. But it's not for the worse, and it doesn't affect you and me. People grow up, that's all. Even when they reach our age, they can discover really important things about themselves that they never knew before.'

'So what have *you* discovered about yourself that's so important?'

'I think I've discovered that I'm much braver than I thought I was; and much more adventurous.'

'*Braver*?' David plainly couldn't understand what she was trying to tell him. But he leaned forward and kissed her forehead and said, 'OK. That's good. We'll talk about it some more when I get back. Just take care of yourself, you hear?'

John was woken up by a furtive tapping on his bedroom door. He opened his eyes and looked up the sloping ceiling above his bed. Then he turned his head to check what time it was. Ten after eight. Jesus. He felt as if he had been drinking tequila slammers all night.

More tapping. He knew who it was – Mrs Gizmo, his landlady. She always knocked like that, as if she was afraid to disturb him. 'John?' she called out, querulously. 'John? Are you awake? I don't hear you snoring!'

'OK, Mrs Gizmo!' he called out, in a clogged-up voice. 'I hear you!'

He heaved himself off the bed and went to the door. Mrs Gizmo was standing outside on the landing, but when she saw that he was wearing only a droopy red sweatshirt she immediately turned her back to present him with her iron-gray braids and her narrow widow's shoulders in her floral-print apron.

'You have a visitor,' she told him.

'A *visitor*? At this time of the morning?'

'He says he's an old Army friend of yours.'

John puffed out his cheeks. He might have known it. Dean Brunswick III – Deano. The *late* Dean Brunswick III, aka Springer.

'Do you think you could tell him to come back in maybe an hour?' John asked Mrs Gizmo. 'I seriously need some sustenance first. Like, some buckwheat pancakes would be good. Do you have any maple syrup left? That Coombs Family Farm stuff, I could pour that over everything. I could pour it over *broccoli*, even.'

But before Mrs Gizmo could reply, a familiar voice called out, '*Hi–i–i*, John! Good to see you again so soon! How's it hanging? Well, I can see for myself!'

Dean Brunswick III came bounding up the stairs. The *young* Dean Brunswick III. He beamed flirtatiously at Mrs Gizmo as he passed her on the landing, and then he came up to John and gave him an affectionate back-slapping hug.

John said, 'You'd better come in. Thanks a million, Mrs Gizmo.'

'Quite all right, John,' said Mrs Gizmo, and went downstairs without turning back.

John led Springer into his bedroom. 'You'll pardon me if I put on some pants.'

'Oh, sure. Wow, it smells like mozzarella in here. That's not your feet, is it?'

John was pulling on a pair of comfort-fit Levis. 'Just because you can make yourself *look* like my old dead Army buddy, that doesn't give you the license to talk to me the way he used to. That's the leftovers from a pepperoni pizza, if you must know.'

Springer sniffed and said, 'Mmm. Appetizing. Not.'

John sat down on the bed and rolled on a pair of bright green Argyle socks. 'What happened last night, that was a fiasco. We could have gotten ourselves permanently trapped in that dream, like forever and ever, amen, and then what?'

'I still can't understand what went wrong,' said Springer. 'You had Brother Albrecht in your sights, didn't you, at point-blank range? I've never known an Absence Gun to misfire before.'

'I don't think it *did* misfire,' John told him. 'Only a short time afterward, I zapped that meat-packing plant, didn't I? And the gun worked perfect.'

Springer went to the window and looked out over Mrs Gizmo's scruffy back yard, with her washing hanging sadly on the line. 'Maybe it wasn't a weapons failure at all,' he suggested. 'Maybe Brother Albrecht has some way of protecting himself.'

'Oh, you mean like a force field, from *Star Trek*?'

'No, nothing like that. Nothing technical. Whenever you Night Warriors enter other people's dreams, you may be trespassing inside their minds, so to speak, but there's nothing they can do to shield themselves against your weapons, any more than you can shield yourselves against *their* weapons, if they happen to have any.'

'All the same, the Absence Gun didn't work on Brother Albrecht, did it?' said John. 'It was *his* dream, right? Maybe he simply dreamed that it wouldn't work.'

'He couldn't have done that,' Springer told him. 'The whole carnival set-up – the clowns and the freaks and the acrobats – yes, those are all Brother Albrecht's creation. But being Dom Magator is *your* dream, and in *your* dream your Absence Gun never misfires, and there is absolutely nothing that Brother Albrecht could have done to jam it or deflect it.

He pressed the palms of his hands together, as if he were praying. 'I'm talking about some other kind of protection. I don't really know what. Maybe something more *spiritual*.'

John dragged a Kleenex out of a battered box, and noisily blew his nose. 'The Absence Gun works on a wave function, right?'

'That's right.'

'OK, then – supposing for the sake of argument Brother Albrecht doesn't exist on the same wavelength as anybody else? Supposing he's visible, but not quite there? Like supposing he exists a nanosecond ahead of us, or a nanosecond behind? Or a micromillimeter off to the left, or micromillimeter off to the right?'

'What are you saying?'

'I'm saying that if you fire an Absence Gun at somebody like that, it wouldn't have any effect, would it? If somebody wasn't actually *there*, you couldn't make them cease to exist, could you?'

Springer turned away from the window. 'It's a theory, I suppose,' he said, doubtfully. 'I don't know what Einstein would make of it.'

'Screw Einstein, it makes sense to me. Kind of, anyhow. Do you have a better idea?'

'I don't know, John. I have the feeling that there's a whole lot more to Brother Albrecht than meets the eye. He's so *bitter,* you know? So angry, and so *cruel*, and he hasn't stopped railing against God for eight hundred years. How can anybody stay so vengeful for so many centuries?'

'Well – that's a question we have to answer asap,' John told him. 'But there's no future in us going back into Brother Albrecht's dream unless we work out a way to effectively bust his ass, is there?'

'I agree with you, John, one hundred and ten percent. But the situation is critical. From what Mago Verde said, it's going to take only one more sacrifice before Brother Albrecht can break the sacred sanction that Pope Eugene placed on him, and then he'll be able to lead his circus back here into the waking world. That poor girl who had her arms cut off, she was the eighth sacrifice. We have to find a way to stop Brother Albrecht before Mago Verde finds him a ninth.'

John blew his nose again and thought about it. It came as no surprise to him that Springer knew every detail of what had happened in Brother Albrecht's nightmare last night. Springer had a cerebral connection to everything that the Night Warriors experienced when they entered other people's dreams. When they returned to their bodies in the morning, all of their impressions flowed into Springer's consciousness as if he were living through them himself – a kind of psychic debriefing, with sights and sounds and smells and conversations and even emotions. He had shared their elation when the fire breather exploded. He had also known how frightened they were when they thought that the clowns had barred their way back through the portal.

John said, 'I think the answer is for us to go looking for Mago Verde, or Gordon Veitch, or whatever the bastard calls himself. If we can stop *him*, we can stop Brother Albrecht getting his final sacrifice, or *delay* it, anyhow. And we know for sure that we can take *him* out, because he skedaddled like a jackrabbit when Jekkalon went after him at the circus. If he was invulnerable, the same as Brother Albrecht, he would have stayed put and given us the finger.'

He sniffed. 'The only trouble is, where the hell do we find him?'

'The Griffin House Hotel,' said Springer. 'To start with, he attacks his victims in all kinds of random locations. Back in the nineteen-thirties, he went for women in the slums like Kingsbury Run. Later, he went for more upscale neighborhoods like Bratenahl. But no matter where he actually kills them, or mutilates them, where does the evidence always finish up? In the Griffin House Hotel, inside the walls.'

'Well, yes,' John agreed. 'But by the time he dreams his ninth sacrifice into the hotel walls, it's going to be a little too late for his victim, isn't it? She'll have been cut in half already, or set on fire, or had her arms or her legs sawn off, or maybe both.'

'I know, John, but I don't see any other way. Ashapola weeps for all of his children, but the most important thing is to stop Mago Verde from taking this ninth sacrifice through to Brother Albrecht's dream. Once that happens it's going to be "Chaos and Old Night". You've seen that circus for yourself, first hand, and you've seen how much it excites people, how it gets them baying for blood. It's frightening.

'We *have* to stop Brother Albrecht from bringing it back to the waking world. If we allow that to happen, it's going to trail pandemonium behind it, wherever it goes.'

'OK,' said John. 'The Griffin House it is.' He went to his bedroom door and opened it.

Springer blinked at him. 'You're not going to put on your shoes?'

John gave him a long, sober look. If the situation hadn't been so desperate, he probably would have laughed.

Rhodajane had just stepped out of the shower when they knocked at Room 309. She opened the door with a pink towel wrapped around her head like a turban and a pink toweling robe with *Griffin House Hotel* embroidered on it. Without her false lashes and her make-up, John thought she looked surprisingly young, although her eyes were a little puffy.

'Well, good morning, boys!' she greeted them. 'I was just about to order some breakfast on room service. Want some?'

'Coffee and pancakes would be good,' said John. 'And tell them not to be tight-assed with the maple syrup.'

Springer said, soberly, 'You did a very brave thing last night, Rhodajane. You saved all of your fellow Night Warriors.'

Rhodajane walked over to her dressing table and sat down in front of the triple mirrors. She pouted at herself and then she said, 'I did what Xyrena is supposed to do. Xyrena's the super slut, right? It wasn't difficult. That poor clown didn't know whether he was coming or going, and in the end he did both.'

'It may not have been difficult, Rhodajane, but it took great nerve. Ashapola is aware how courageous you were, and Ashapola is deeply appreciative.'

'We didn't manage to take out El Grando Freako, though, did we? Are we going to have another crack at him tonight?'

'Actually, we're considering a different approach,' said Springer.

'I sure hope so. I'm still sore from the last approach.'

John shook his head in amusement, but Springer stayed deadly serious. 'For whatever reason, Dom Magator's Absence Gun had no effect on Brother Albrecht, so we're going to go for Mago Verde instead, to see if we can stop him from taking Brother Albrecht his ninth and last sacrifice.'

Three Rhodajanes looked at Springer out of her triple mirrors. 'OK – you take out Mago Verde. But won't Brother Albrecht simply find somebody else to bring him victim number nine? Another one of those – what do you call them – *Dreads*?'

'I don't know,' Springer admitted. 'I can't tell for sure if Mago Verde is Brother Albrecht's *only* contact with the waking world, but so far I haven't sensed the presence of any other Dreads in this vicinity, not for hundreds of miles, and so I'm assuming that he is.

'If Brother Albrecht doesn't receive his ninth sacrifice, he'll have to stay in the world of dreams for ever – or at least until he recruits some other Dread to do his dirty work for him.

Which may be hundreds of years. Or *never*, let us pray to Ashapola.'

John said, 'The thing is, sweetheart, we don't know where Mago Verde is going to find his next victim, which is why we've come here, to the Griffin House. Sooner or later, no matter where he first attacks them, he stays here and dreams them into the walls of this hotel. We don't know why. But from this hotel he passes them on to Brother Albrecht's circus.'

'It's my guess that he mutilates them as a way of preparing them for Brother Albrecht's dream,' said Springer. 'He makes it physically impossible for them to think of returning to their normal life. Then – once they arrive at the circus – Brother Albrecht decides what kind of freaks he wants them to be turned into, and his surgeons get to work on them and finish what you might call the finer details. The dogs' faces, the goats' legs. All of the other abominations.

'Throughout history, in *all* religions, from the Aztecs to the Norsemen, a sacrifice is only considered to be spiritually meaningful if the victim is willing to accept their fate – happy, even. Whenever a Viking chieftain died and was burned on his boat, one of his female slaves would volunteer to die with him. By the time Brother Albrecht has finished with them, I very much doubt if any of *his* victims aren't willing to stay in his circus. They can never return to the waking world, can they, and pick up their lives where they left off? Not if they have no legs, or snakes instead of arms, or a face like a llama.'

Rhodajane was pouting at herself as she applied bright red lip gloss. 'What if *I* tried?'

John frowned at her three reflections. '*What*? What if you tried *what*?'

'What if *I* tried to take out Brother Albrecht, the same way I took out that clown?'

'I don't know,' said Springer. 'Brother Albrecht is no ordinary man, and I don't think he ever was. What goes on inside of his mind, nobody knows.'

'I have no intention of appealing to his *mind*, Springer! I'm going to appeal to his . . . Kercheval. He might not have arms or legs but he's not lacking in that department.'

'Too darn dangerous,' said John, dismissively.

'Then why the hell was I invited along last night?'

'You were chosen for this mission so that you would distract

Brother Albrecht's attention,' Springer explained. 'We know that he has a fatal weakness for women. That's what got him mutilated in the first place.'

'I took out that harlequin, didn't I – and that harlequin was dreamed up by Brother Albrecht. If the harlequin went for me, so will he.'

'But this time, sweetheart, he's going to be ready for us, and he's going to know all about your needles, and how you could make his blood boil.'

'I still think I ought to try.'

'And what happens if he takes *you* out, instead? Where does that leave the rest of us? If the Absence Gun doesn't have any effect on him, I doubt if any of the rest of our weapons are going to be much good.'

Springer said, 'Listen – all of this is academic until we find Mago Verde. Maybe, when we do, we can persuade him to tell us if the good Brother Albrecht has any other weaknesses, apart from women.'

'Oh, you mean we could torture him?'

'No, I don't. There are other ways of extracting information from people without torturing them.'

'Like *bribing* him?'

'In a way, yes. Remember that Mago Verde is a Dread, who can shift at will from the waking world to the dream world, and back again. But in the human sense, Dreads are not alive. They are something between ghosts and zombies. And if there is one thing that all Dreads crave more than anything else, it is to have their humanity back.'

'But how can we offer him that? I don't know about you, but I'm fresh out of humanity.'

Springer closed his eyes for a moment. When he opened them again, his pupils were a very pale agate color, and luminous. 'Ashapola is the greatest power in the universe, John. Ashapola can turn the night into day. Ashapola can heal the sick and make the dead dance.'

'OK,' said John. 'I'll take your word for it. But what we need to do now is set up some kind of surveillance, right? One of us needs to keep an eye on the hotel lobby in case Gordon Veitch tries to register, and the rest of us should patrol the corridors. Whatever happens, we mustn't let him slip into the hotel unnoticed. Otherwise we're screwed.'

NINETEEN
Hunt The Clown

Detective Wisocky was studying the menu outside the entrance to the Boa Vinda restaurant when Detective Hudson came toward him across the hotel lobby, accompanied by a white-haired old man in a brown three-piece suit.

He checked his wristwatch and said, 'It's five after six, Charlie. You're twenty minutes late. I was just about to go in and order the tilapia with peanuts. I never ate tilapia with peanuts before. Come to that, I never ate peanuts with tilapia.'

'Sorry, Walter. We had to stop off on the way and buy a new battery for Henry's hearing aid. By the way, this is Henry Marriott. Henry – this is Detective Wisocky.'

The old man held out his hand. He was small and frail, with a bulbous nose and large hairy ears, and he put Walter in mind of a miniature version of Jimmy Durante. He wore a crisp white shirt with a red silk necktie and a matching red carnation in his buttonhole. His hand felt like a turkey's claw.

'Good to meet you, Henry,' said Walter. 'My partner tells me you used to run the Clown Museum down on Pearl Road. When was that?'

'What's that?' asked Henry, cupping his hand to his left ear. The background music in the hotel lobby didn't help, and neither did a business executive standing right next to them, yelling into his cellphone.

Walter leaned forward and shouted, '*When – did – you – run – the – Clown Museum?*'

'Oh! Got you! I was there for almost forty-eight years, from August nineteen hundred and thirty-five through June nineteen hundred and seventy-nine. I was only eighteen years old when I started. I took over the running of it when I was twenty-seven, which was in nineteen forty-four, because Mr Cascarelli was called up to join the Marines. He was killed at Okinawa, poor fellow. Stepped on a mine and got blown to smithereens. Good way for a clown to go, though.'

Charlie said, 'Henry knew Gordon Veitch. In fact he knew him better than most – didn't you, Henry?'

Walter laid a hand on Henry's angular shoulder. 'Let's go through to the bar, shall we, Henry? It's a whole lot quieter in there, and you'll be able to hear me better. What would you like to drink?'

'A long slow comfortable screw up against a cold hard wall, if that's OK.'

Walter looked across at Charlie and raised one eyebrow, but Charlie simply shrugged. 'That's kind of a circus drink, I guess.'

They walked across the lobby toward the Lantern Bar, passing beneath the portrait of the stern-faced man with the reddish hair and the formal black suit. As they did so, Henry stopped and pointed up at him and said, 'Now *there's* your guilty party. Gilbert T. Griffin.'

'Gilbert Griffin? Gilbert Griffin built this hotel and it's the best hotel in Cleveland. What's *he* guilty of?'

'Meddling with things that shouldn't be meddled with. That's what he's guilty of.'

'OK . . .'

'That's Gilbert Griffin and the girl next to him, that's his child-bride Emily Griffin, God rest her soul, wherever her soul might be.'

'I see. You'll have to tell us about it.'

They found a dark corner booth in the Lantern Bar, with squeaky black leather seats. Walter would have given anything for an ice-cold Coors, but he had to settle for a Diet Coke. Sometimes he wished he had picked a career in which drinking was not only acceptable but obligatory, like politics, or acting, or writing fiction. Charlie ordered a glass of water, with a twist.

'So you knew Gordon Veitch,' said Walter, when Henry's cocktail arrived.

'You bet. We *all* knew him, all of us clowns. Gordon Veitch was Mago Verde, the Green Magician. His father before him, Daniel Veitch, *he* was Mago Verde, too, and he handed it down to Gordon – the make-up, the tricks, but most of all that mean malicious attitude. If there was ever a son-of-a-bitch on this planet it was Daniel Veitch and if there was ever a son-of-a-son-of-a-bitch it was *Gordon* Veitch. But let me tell you one thing. Gordon Veitch may have been mean and malicious to everybody else, but he was never once mean and malicious to me. I guess you could say that he took me under his wing.'

'How did you come to meet him?' asked Walter.

'I met him at Corey's Circus. I used to work there after school, making myself some money by mucking out the animals. You ever smell lion shit? There is no worse smell on this planet than lion shit. Well, tiger shit maybe.

'I got to know some of the clowns and most of them were good to me, considering I was nothing more than a part-time shit-shoveler. Bongo especially. He was Portuguese, believe it or not, and his real name was Remi. He helped me to design my own make-up and he lent me some of his outfits and he showed me how to juggle with knives and how to walk on the low wire and how to fall on my ass without hurting myself.

'But it was Mago Verde who took a real shine to me, especially if I ran errands for him, like placing bets on the horses and bringing him cigarettes and bottles of hooch. All of the other circus folk, though, they stayed well clear of him. He would trip people up when they were carrying boxes of light bulbs; or he would do this trick when he threw an egg up into the air and catch it in a velvet bag, but when he asked some sucker to dip his hand into the bag and pick the egg out for him, the bag was cram-full of razor blades. Like I say, he was a regular son-of-a-bitch. He had the *power*, though, no mistake about that.'

'The *power*?' asked Walter. 'What power was that, exactly?'

Henry sucked noisily at his cocktail. Then he held it up to the light and said, 'Not bad. But too much sloe gin.'

'What *power*, Henry?' Walter pressed him.

Henry blinked at him as if he had never seen him before in his life. But then he lifted one finger and tapped it against the side of his bulbous nose. 'Daniel Veitch had given Gordon a whole lot more than his make-up and his magic tricks and his mean and malicious attitude. He had passed on the family knack of stepping into other people's dreams. That's what he told me, anyhow, and he *proved* it to me.'

'Excuse me? Stepping into other people's dreams? How exactly did he do that?'

'Search me. But he always insisted that he could do it, and once he told me that he had stepped into one of *my* dreams when I was sleeping – a dream I was having about fishing out on Lake Erie and my boat was sinking – and he described that dream to me in every detail – just like he had actually been there, too, standing right behind me.'

'OK,' said Walter, trying not to sound too skeptical. 'Go on.'

'Well, the dream thing, that's where Gilbert Griffin came into it, and Gilbert Griffin was the real instigator of what happened next, although I never told nobody about it because nobody would never have believed me.'

'So what makes you think that *we're* going to believe you?'

'You can believe me if you want to, or not if you don't. I'm ninety-three years old now and I don't give a rat's ass. But I might as well tell somebody before I cash in my chips and it might as well be you. Especially young Charlie here. He understands about clowns, don't you, Charlie?'

'All right,' said Walter. 'What heinous act of heiniosity did Gilbert Griffin commit?'

'It was that child-bride of his, Emily. He was nuts about her – and you can see from the picture in the lobby how cute she was. But in July of nineteen thirty-five, only eighteen months after they were married, she came out of Kroger's Family Store on Noble Road up in Cleveland Heights and she was knocked down by a speeding automobile and she died two days later in hospital.

'Gilbert Griffin, he was inconsolable and it was public knowledge how grief-stricken he was. He placed advertisements in the *Plain Dealer* every day, offering thousand-dollar rewards to any mediums who could contact Emily in the spirit world so that he could talk to her and tell her how much he missed her. That's when Mago Verde got in contact with him and said he could visit Emily in his dreams and bring him back messages from her, and even letters. But that wasn't all. For a price, he said, there was a way that he could bring her back to life.'

'Jesus,' said Walter. 'Did Gilbert Griffin believe him?'

Henry sucked more cocktail and nodded. 'He surely did. Mago Verde told *me* about it, too. According to him, it was some hocus-pocus they devised in the Vatican in the Middle Ages. You know what hocus-pocus is, don't you?'

'Hocus-pocus? What are you talking about? Sure I do.'

'No, you don't. I can tell by your face. Hocus-pocus comes the Latin *hoc est corpus*, which is the words they speak in the Eucharist when the communion wafer is supposed to turn into flesh. If you can turn a biscuit into a person, it can't be too much trouble to turn a *dream* into a person, can it?' He tapped his forehead. 'Don't look so surprised, detective. There's a whole encyclopedia up inside of this head. I wasn't no director of no museum for forty-eight years without learning nothing, even if it was only a clown museum.'

Walter said, 'OK. I'm impressed. So what was this hocus-pocus, exactly?'

'Mago Verde told me that you had to make a trade. To bring one dead person out of the world of dreams and back to the world of reality, you had to take nine innocent people from the world of reality and take them through to the world of dreams, like forever. Nine for one.'

'Why nine?'

Henry rolled up his eyes as if he were talking to a six-year-old child. 'Because nine is the magic number which is the beginning of everything. Nine makes everything tick. Time, space, life, death – everything runs on the number nine. Nine is like the key to the universal clock. So *nine* people had to be taken away before *one* could come back.'

'Oh, yeah?'

'Why do you think we say that cats have nine lives? And "a stitch in time saves nine"?' He held up nine fingers, and counted each of them in turn. 'In the Christian religion, there are nine orders of angels. In Hebrew, God has seventy-two names, and seven and two add up to nine. In Arabic, God has ninety-nine names. The Mayans believed that nine was a sacred number, and in China, on the ninth day of the ninth month, the day of Double Yang, people believe that their dead and faraway friends can appear in front of them.

'Nine is the number that makes dreams work. Next time you have a dream, try to remember how many nines appeared in it. Could be anything – nine doorknobs, nine cakes, nine people, nine trees. But I guarantee you, the number nine will be in there someplace.'

'I don't dream, Henry,' said Walter. 'I don't dream *ever.*'

'You do, detective, even if you can't remember it. Next time, try to remember. Nine bottles of beer hanging on the wall, nine willing women.'

'So what happened?' asked Walter, trying to change the subject. 'Mago Verde conned Gilbert Griffin into thinking that he could bring his beloved Emily back to life, and in return Gilbert Griffin paid him to kidnap nine innocent people and take them off to the land of nod? That sounds suspiciously like conspiracy to me, if not murder for hire.'

Henry shrugged. 'I never had no proof, detective, which is why I never told nobody for all of these years. What would have been the point? They probably would have carted me off to the funny farm. But it was only a few days after Mago Verde went to see Gilbert Griffin that he quit the circus without saying so much as goodbye to nobody, and then all of them killings and all of them disappearances started in the Cleveland Flats.

'There was all manner of suspects. At first Eliot Ness thought it was some doctor from Glenville. Then he thought it was a longshoreman called Cruddick. But there must have been at least one eye witness who said it was somebody dressed up as a clown, because the cops came around two or three times to Corey's Circus, and each time they ransacked the place. They never found Mago Verde, though. Mago Verde had flown the coop, and none of us ever saw him again, which made us all think that he could have been the killer.

'Once Eliot Ness came around to Corey's Circus in person, although he didn't talk to me. I always remember how he had this dark shiny hair parted in the center, and a red necktie.

'They never caught Gordon Veitch though, did they?' asked Walter.

'No, they didn't. Not to bring to trial, anyhow. There was more murders and more rapes, and more disappearances, and in August of nineteen thirty-eight the cops got a tip-off about the whereabouts of Mago Verde and they burned down half of Shantytown. There was a huge public hoo-ha, especially in the press, but after that the killings stopped, so the cops presumed that they had done their job, and that Mago Verde was dead.'

'But you blame Gilbert Griffin for what happened?'

'Who else? I'm ninety-nine percent sure that Gilbert Griffin paid Mago Verde to kill or kidnap those innocent people. And what was more, he gave Mago Verde the wherewithal to take his victims through to the world of dreams.'

'The wherewithal? What do you mean by that?'

'Mago Verde told me that all nine victims had to be dreamed about, and each of the nine dreams had to be arranged in the same building in a special mystical pattern – an *ennead*, which means a figure of nine. It was like a psychic combination-lock, that's how he put it. Once you had dreamed all nine dreams in the same building, in the right pattern, the doors to the world of dreams would be opened up, *click-clickety-click*, and a person could be taken through from one reality to the other, or *vice versa*.'

'I see,' said Walter. 'Or rather, I *don't* see. To be totally honest, I don't understand what the fuck you're talking about.' He was pretty sure that Henry didn't hear him say that, because Henry simply shrugged.

'We never found out if Mago Verde was shooting us a line or not. Eighteen women was murdered or raped in all, but only seven people disappeared for good, five women and two men. So maybe he didn't make the nine before the cops got him.'

'Tell me,' said Walter. 'Have you ever seen Mago Verde since August, nineteen thirty-eight?'

Henry shook his head. 'No, sir. Not once. And let's face it, even if the cops didn't get him, Old Father Time would have done for him by now.'

'Yes. You're right. Although somebody else could be wearing his make-up, couldn't they?'

'Sure. But stealing some other clown's face, that's the worst thing that any clown could do. They *never* do that, ever. Stealing a man's face is like stealing his soul. If somebody is passing themselves off as Mago Verde, then I'd sure like to know who it is.'

'Yes, Henry. Me too.'

Once Henry had gone, Walter drained his Diet Coke and then snapped his fingers at the waitress. 'Get me a beer, would you?'

'What do you think?' asked Charlie.

'About Henry? I think he's wandering, the poor old coot.'

'But how was Maria Fortales taken out of her room?'

'What – you believe that Mago Verde spirited her away in some *dream*? Come on, Charlie. I'll have to send you off on a psych break if you start talking like that.'

'But what Henry said – it all fits, doesn't it? And if there were seven disappearances back in the thirties, that means that Maria Fortales could be the eighth.'

'You can count. Congratulations.'

'If Maria Fortales is the eighth then there's only one left to before Mago Verde opens up the door between the world of dreams and the world of reality.'

'So what? He's going to bring back a child-bride who must be ninety-two years old by now.'

'She wouldn't have grown any older, Walter, any more than Mago Verde would. She's in a dream.'

'Whose dream? Who the hell do you think dreams about *her* any more? Almost everybody who ever knew her must be dead by now.'

'I still think there's some truth in what Henry told us. What about that Mrs Kercheval, who had that hallucination in Room Seven-One-Seven? She thought she saw a mutilated woman in her bed, didn't she? Maybe that was one of Mago Verde's dreams.'

Walter covered his face with his hands and said nothing for a very long time. When he looked up again, he said, 'Charlie . . . dreams are dreams. They're not real. You can't cross from the real world into the world of dreams because there's nothing there to cross into. Dreams are like your brain trying to make sense of your life, that's all, and most of the time they can't make heads nor tails of anything.'

'You said you didn't have any dreams.'

'I don't. Not printable ones, anyhow.'

The waitress brought Walter his beer, and he drank half of it in one gulp, leaving himself with a white foam moustache. 'Jesus, I needed that.'

Charlie was anxiously biting at the edge of his thumbnail. 'Listen, Walter, I know you don't believe a word of what Henry was telling us, but I spent a long time studying clowns. I got to know them, the way they think. The clown code of honor. Clowns play tricks but they don't tell lies. And they have a long history of psychic sensitivity. I still think we ought to follow this line of enquiry a whole lot further.'

'Meaning what?'

'For starters, we ought to check all of the rooms in this hotel and see if we can come up with some kind of pattern. Not just forensic evidence – something more like the pieces of a puzzle. Henry talked about a figure of nine, didn't he? Something's going down here, and it's going down tonight. I can feel it. Something weird.'

Walter finished the rest of his beer and belched into his fist. 'I thought I told you before, Charlie. *Me* Hunch Detective. *You* Deductive Detective. Leave the frissons to me, OK?'

'OK. But don't *you* get any sense that something in this hotel is out of whack?'

'Sure I do. I get a sense that I need another beer, and maybe some giant pretzels.'

'And then we can check out the rooms?'

Walter's head dropped in resignation. 'OK. I give in. *Then* we can check out the rooms – but only so long as the manager allows us to do it without a warrant. If he doesn't object, ask him if we can borrow a floor plan and a couple of pass keys. But I hope you realize that this hotel has one hundred thirty rooms and nine suites. It's going to take us forever.'

Charlie stood up. 'You're not going to regret this, Walter. I really think we're going to have this case cracked.'

'*Cracked* is the word for it.'

Charlie went off to the find the manager, and Walter turned around to wave to the waitress and order another beer. As he did so, he saw John step out of the elevator and walk past the entrance to the Lantern Bar.

He squeezed his way out of the booth and waddled out into the lobby. John had found himself an armchair underneath a potted palm, and was shaking open a day-old copy of the *Baton Rouge Advocate*. Walter approached him and stood right in front of him, with his arms folded.

John lowered his paper. The headline was *Iguana Regulation Bill Killed*. The state senate had decided it was unnecessary to control the sale of pet iguanas, despite the fact that they could grow to ten feet long and pose a lethal threat to children and small animals.

'Not taxi-driving tonight?' asked Walter.

'Taking some time off, detective. Catching up with some homespun gossip from B.R.'

'Right here? In the Griffin House Hotel?'

'Is there a law against it?'

'Not that I know of.'

John looked up at Walter, unblinking. It was obvious that Walter felt that there was something suspicious about him sitting here, but he couldn't think what it was. After a few moments, Walter said, 'OK. But watch the attitude, OK?'

'Oh, you bet,' said John. 'I'm keeping my attitude under constant scrutiny.'

Walter returned to the Lantern Bar, although he stopped and turned around before he went back inside, and gave John a look that almost made the potted palm wither up. John, for his part, shook his newspaper ostentatiously, lifted it up high in front of him, and pretended to read an article about people in Baton Rouge burning trash in their back yards and creating too much toxic smoke.

John was sitting in the lobby to keep a watch for Mago Verde. He didn't expect Gordon Veitch to walk into the hotel wearing his clown make-up, but he reckoned he could pick out a Dread without too much difficulty. There was something about Dreads which he always recognized – a *blurriness*, as if he were seeing them through a fogged-up window.

From his vantage point beside the potted palm, he could clearly see the main entrance, as well as the elevators and the stairs. He could also see the entrance to the Lantern Bar and the Boa Vinda Restaurant and the corridor that led to the hotel parking-lot in back. The only way that anybody could enter or leave the hotel without him noticing them was if they climbed up one of the fire escapes.

He checked the time by the art deco clock standing by the reception desk. Seven-twelve. Kieran had promised to relieve him after two hours and he knew that he was going to need relieving. The smell of pan-fried escalopes of veal was wafting his way from the restaurant and he hadn't eaten since twelve thirty.

Upstairs, meanwhile, Kieran, Kiera and Rhodajane had walked up and down every corridor and looked into every door that was open. When they returned to Rhodajane's room, they found Springer sitting on the balcony, keeping an eye on the fire escapes.

'Nothing,' said Kieran, as he closed the door behind him. 'Maybe he's not coming.'

'Oh, he will, I'm absolutely sure of it,' said Springer. 'After your attack on him last night, Brother Albrecht is going to be very anxious to complete the sacrificial ritual as soon as possible. Think about it: this could be his last and only chance to bring his circus back to reality.'

It was growing dark outside, and street lights were beginning to twinkle all around University Circle.

Kiera said, 'What if we miss him? What if he manages to get into the hotel without us seeing him?'

'Then you'll have to go after him in Brother Albrecht's dream, and hope that you can nail him before he manages to hand over his sacrifice.'

'And if we can't get to him before that?'

'I don't know,' said Springer, gravely. He was still in the guise of Dean Brunswick III, but he was beginning to look older and grayer than he had at first, as if the alcoholic ravages of Deano's later life were catching up with him. 'I guess you'll just have to give it all you've got, and hope for the best.'

'That sounds like a plan,' said Kieran. 'Not.'

'I don't know what else I can say,' Springer told him. 'For some reason, Brother Albrecht appears to be invulnerable to the most powerful existential weapon in Dom Magator's armory. Maybe he's vulnerable to something more rudimentary – like a regular bullet-firing gun, or a crossbow bolt, or an ax.'

'You think we should try chopping his *head* off?' said Kiera, her eyes wide with revulsion.

'It wouldn't hurt,' said Rhodajane. 'Not *us*, anyhow.'

Springer said, 'Anyhow, all we can do is wait. Mago Verde may have abducted and mutilated a ninth victim already, but he still has to come here and dream what he did to them into the hotel walls. Hopefully, that should give us enough time to find him. And even if we *can't* find him, thousands of people all around the Great Lakes will be asleep by then, and dreaming, and at least some of them will be dreaming about Brother Albrecht's circus. We can enter one of their dreams and go after him.'

'I have a real bad feeling that this isn't going turn out too good,' said Kiera.

'And what about our mom?' asked Kieran.

'I can't tell you,' said Springer. 'You'll have to play this as it comes. If you get the chance to rescue her, then take it. But I can't offer you any guarantees. I can't even offer you a plan. The truth is, with Brother Albrecht, I don't even know what we're up against.'

TWENTY
The Ninth Nightmare

By twenty after eight, Walter had checked out seventeen rooms and two de luxe suites. It was police procedure at its most procedural, and to make matters worse he wasn't even sure what he was supposed to be looking for. A pattern? An *ennead* – whatever the hell that was?

Five of the rooms he had thankfully found unoccupied, but when he had knocked at the doors of all of the others the patter had always been the same. 'Good evening, sir, madam. Real sorry to disturb you but my name is Detective Wisocky from the University Circle PD and I'm making a routine security check of all of the rooms in the Griffin House Hotel. Do you mind if I take a quick look around? It will only take a moment.'

Almost every time, the guest had asked him, 'What exactly is it you're looking for, detective?'

'Signs of disturbance.'

'Oh.' Pause. 'So what do they look like, these signs of disturbance?'

'Hard to describe. But – you know – we always recognize them when see them.'

'Oh.'

Maybe Charlie had been talking b.., but in some of the rooms that Walter had walked into – not all of them – he had felt a distinctly unwelcoming atmosphere. Not exactly a tangible chill, but a feeling that there was somebody else's presence here, somebody hostile, apart from the current guests. It had given him the same discomfort that he felt when he walked into an unfamiliar house, when the owners were away, or when they had been killed. Even the family photographs over the fireplace seemed to frown at him disapprovingly.

After he had finished checking every room on the sixth and seventh floors, he sat down on the couch next to the elevators and unfolded his hotel floor-plan. Taking out his pen, he marked a cross against every room where he had felt unsettled. Five on the sixth floor and three on the seventh floor. Only eight altogether. But when he laid one floor-plan over the other, he saw that it would have taken the addition of only one more room to make a nine-cornered star.

He sat back. Now, was this a coincidence or what? He was tempted to call Charlie and tell him what he had discovered. But he had picked those eight rooms only because of some indefinable feeling of unease, and not because of any empirical evidence that Mago Verde or Mago Verde's successor had ever been there. OK, so he was Hunch Detective, but maybe this was one hunch too far. He didn't want to look like an asshole.

He looked at the floor-plans again. The room which would have completed the nine-cornered star was Room 702, which had been unoccupied. Maybe he hadn't experienced that unwelcoming feeling in Room 702 because Mago Verde hadn't yet visited it.

He took out his cellphone and called the front desk. 'Detective Wisocky here. Can you tell me if Room Seven-Oh-Two is booked for tonight?'

'Please hold on a moment, sir.'

Walter sat and waited. As he did so, he felt a sudden draft, as if somebody had walked past him, yet the corridor was completely deserted. *Shit*, he thought. *I'm giving myself the heebie-jeebies. I don't seriously believe in any of this dream crap.*

The desk clerk came back to him. 'Yes, sir. Room Seven-Oh-Two is booked for tonight. One night only.'

'Under what name?'

'Wisocky, sir. Same as yours. Now, that's a coincidence, wouldn't you say?'

'It's been booked in the name of *Wisocky*?'

'Yes, sir. Cash in advance.'

'Shit. When was it booked?'

'This evening, sir. Six ten p.m.'

'Shit. Why the *fuck* didn't you tell me? I've just spent two hours knocking on every goddamned door on the sixth and seventh floors and I needn't have bothered.'

'I'm sorry, sir. You didn't ask.'

'What did the guy look like?'

'Excuse me?'

'The guy who made the booking. What did he look like? Thin, fat, short, tall? Black, white, Hispanic, Chinese, what?'

'White, sir. Thin. Not too tall, not too short. I can't say I got a really good look at him.'

'He made a booking right in front of you and you didn't get a really good look at him?'

'No, sir. I can't say that I did.'

'What about his address?'

'Give me a moment, sir. Oh, yes. Here it is. Five-one-oh-two, Pearl Road, Cleveland.'

'You know where that is?'

'Not exactly, sir. No.'

'It's the fucking Clown Museum.'

Walter snapped his cellphone shut. Again, he was tempted to call Charlie, but then he thought: *this is beginning to smell more and more like some kind of practical joke.* Maybe Charlie wasn't in on it, but that Henry Marriott could well have set it up. As elderly as he was, he was still a clown, wasn't he? And what did clowns do, except trip people up and make them look like suckers?

Stepping into other people's dreams, for Christ's sake. Henry had almost had him believing it, and Charlie had been taken in, hook, line and sinker.

He followed the sign to Room 702. He found it right at the end of the corridor, with a *Do Not Disturb* tag hanging on the knob. He knocked, and called out, 'Open up, sir! Police!'

He waited, but there was no response. He knocked again, 'Police! Can you hear me, sir? You need to open this door right now!'

Still no response. He took out the pass key that the hotel manager had given him, and unlocked the door. He eased it open an inch, and then he lifted his gun out of its holster.

'This is the CPD, sir! I want you standing in the center of the room with your hands where I can see them!'

He pushed the door wider. As far as he could see, there was nobody in the bedroom, although the bedcover was turned down and the bedside lamps were both lit. He edged his way past the closet, holding his gun up in front of him. He slid open both closet doors as he passed, and quickly glanced inside, but there was nobody hiding there and no clothes hanging up.

He checked the bathroom. There was nobody in there, either,

and none of the complimentary toiletries had been used. It looked as if 'Mr Wisocky' hadn't arrived yet. If this was a practical joke, he probably *wouldn't* arrive. But why spend nearly two hundred dollars to book a room, just for the sake of a practical joke?

He backed out of the bathroom, stowing his gun back into its holster. As he did so, a hoarse voice behind him said, 'Well, done, fatso! You worked it out!'

He turned around, yanking out his gun again, but two muscular hands gripped his wrist and twisted the gun away from him. He found himself confronted by a tall, angular man with wild white shoulder-length hair and a pale gray face. His eyes were surrounded by smudgy black make-up and his lips were painted into a glistening green grin. For some reason, Walter found it hard to focus on him, as if he were seeing him through a steamed-up window.

'Got you now, tin man, don't I? Thought you could stymie my sacrifice, did you? Well, now you can make amends! You'd like to make amends, wouldn't you?'

'Sorry, pal,' Walter retorted. 'I don't know what the hell you're talking about.' His gun had been thrown on to the bed and he glanced at it quickly, trying to work out his chances of diving across the quilt to reach it. Probably nil, for a man of his bulk.

'You and your friends caused the Grand Freak a whole lot of heartache last night,' the clown told him. 'Killing Doctor Friendly, and the Grand Freak's favorite fire-breather, and his harlequin, too. He never cared too much for Brown Jenkin, but then who did? But you still made the Grand Freak very angry by blowing Brown Jenkin's head off.'

'I told you,' said Walter. 'I don't know what the hell you're blabbering on about. However I do know that you're under arrest for assaulting a police officer.' He took out his cellphone and flipped it open, but when he tried to call Charlie, all he could hear was crackling. He hit the phone several times against the heel of his hand, but it still didn't work.

'OK,' he said, unclipping his handcuffs from his belt. 'Turn around and put your hands behind your back. You have the right to remain silent. Anything you say can and will be used against you in a court of law.'

'You *think*, tin man?' grinned the clown. He gave Walter a

low bow, and then he suddenly whirled around and he was brandishing a long serrated kitchen knife.

'Put the blade down!' Walter told him. 'You even *scratch* me with that, and you're going to do so much time you'll need a Zimmer frame when they let you out.'

'*Scratching* you? I wouldn't dream of *scratching* you,' said the clown. He prodded at Walter with the point of his knife. Walter lifted his left elbow to shield himself, and retreated across the room.

'You don't want to do anything stupid,' he warned the clown.

'Oh, yes I do! Clowns are stupid by nature! Stupidity is our bread and butter! Throwing buckets of water all over each other! Stupid! Tripping over each other's feet! Stupid! Cramming ten people into one car, so that the wheels fall off! Stupid!'

He kept on prodding at Walter, and Walter kept backing away. *For God's sake, where was Charlie? He must be missing him by now*. But then he backed into the coffee table, and stumbled sideways, and lost his balance, and fell heavily on to the floor, hitting his head on the arm of one of the chairs.

As he fell, the clown leapt forward, and seized his right leg. Walter kicked at him, but the clown dragged up the cuff of his pants, pulled down his sock, and sliced through the Achilles tendon at the back of his heel.

Walter shouted out in pain, but the clown took hold of his left leg, twisted off his shoe, and did the same. Walter managed to heave himself up into a sitting position, but now he was completely unable to stand. Blood was running quickly out of the cuts on his heels and spattering the light blue rug.

'You bastard!' he gasped. 'You bastard, what have you done to me?'

The clown leaned over him. Close up, Walter could see that he wasn't smiling at all.

'This is only the beginning, tin man. There's far worse to come – you'll see! But after what you did last night, you and your friends, what do you expect? Not *mercy*, surely!'

'I still don't know what the hell you're talking about,' Walter told him. He was breathing heavily and his face was ashen from shock.

'Of course you know what I'm talking about, Dom Magator the Night Warrior.'

'Who the what?'

'Don't deny it. You might have been wearing that helmet last night, but I'd know that fat gut anywhere! And who else would be looking for me, by day as well as by night?

He stood up straight. 'Anyhow, you've solved a problem for me. I needed to bring nine sacrifices to Brother Albrecht, as you know – nine souls who would happily commit themselves forever to the most terrible show on earth. Maria Fortales was number eight, and I'm happy to say that *you* can have the honor of being number nine.

'As soon as you take your place among your companion freaks, the papal sanction will be broken for ever. The circus will come rolling through to the world of reality! Drums beating! Trumpets blaring! *Tarantara*! *Tarantara*! And the world will collapse into wonderful, screaming chaos! Murder! Rape! Wanton vandalism! People set on fire for the fun of it! The human race is headed that way already, of course, but Brother Albrecht's circus will make sure you arrive in hell *so* much sooner!'

'I don't understand,' said Walter, weakly. 'What circus are you talking about? You're Mago Verde, aren't you?'

'Ah! You know who I am! A clever detective, as well as a formidable Night Warrior! Yes, tin man. I am Mago Verde, the Green Magician.'

'You're not Gordon Veitch, though, are you? You can't be. Gordon Veitch must have died a long time ago.'

'The *real* Gordon Veitch, yes. The human Gordon Veitch. The human Gordon Veitch was trapped when the cops set fire to Shantytown in nineteen thirty-eight. Smoke inhalation. But he was asleep when it happened, and dreaming, and his dreaming self survived, and his dreaming self is *me*. Get it?'

'So Henry Marriott wasn't shooting us a line after all.'

'Henry Marriott? Jesus! Is that punk still above ground? He used to be my gofer! What an idiot. Thought he was a clown? He couldn't make a hyena laugh.'

'But Henry Marriott told us you were trying to get Gilbert Griffin's dead wife back. He didn't say anything about a circus. What circus?'

'Oh . . . yes, that's how it started, with Emily Griffin. I was visiting other people's dreams, trying to find her. She was very elusive, to tell you the truth, young dead Emily Griffin. It was like trying to catch a shadow, or an echo, or the snatch of a song. I visited the dreams of most of her friends. I visited her parents' dreams. Never quite caught her.'

He turned back to Walter with a real grin underneath his painted grin. 'One night back in nineteen thirty-six I stepped into a dream that one of Gilbert Griffin's stockholders was having; and I was pleasantly surprised to find myself at Brother Albrecht's carnival and freak show. That was when I first realized what the power of true evil is all about. And, believe me, tin man, the power of true evil is the most intoxicating elixir that man ever drank!'

'I need you to call nine-one-one for me,' said Walter. 'This bleeding isn't going to stop.'

Mago Verde ignored him. 'I was looking for Emily Griffin at the time, yes, with the aim of reuniting her with her grieving husband. He was paying me enough, I can assure you! Three thousand dollars in just six months! But when I met Brother Albrecht, everything changed. My whole life was turned upside down. I forgot about Emily Griffin. Who cared about one dim-witted young woman who crossed the street without looking left and right? Brother Albrecht and his circus, *that* was the future for me!'

Walter rested his head against the seat of the armchair. 'Please. Call for a bus, would you?'

But Mago Verde came over and sat down cross-legged very close to him, so that Walter could smell vinegar and cigarettes and greasepaint. 'Let me explain to you all about Brother Albrecht's circus,' he said. 'You need to know this.' And he told Walter how Brother Albrecht had been mutilated in 1147 by his lover's vengeful husband; and how he had started his carnival; and how Pope Eugene III had sealed him in the world of dreams.

'I made a deal with Brother Albrecht. I would dedicate the rest of my sacrifices to *him*, and not to Gilbert Griffin, so that he could bring his circus back to the real world, where it belonged. In return, he would make me the head of all his clowns.

'He wanted freaks. He wanted women who had been sawn in half and men with six arms instead of legs. I'm sorry to say that quite a few of them went to meet their Maker while I was trying to oblige him. That's when the cops began to hunt me down for serious, and that's why I made myself anonymous and pretended to be a bum and hung out around Shantytown. Mistake, huh? I underestimated Eliot Ness, even worse than Al Capone did. But all's well that ends well, and here we are, you and me.

He stroked Walter's cheek, almost lovingly. 'I'm going to get you ready for your journey to the freak show, and then I'm going to sleep for a while, and dream what I did to you. When I do that, there won't be any evidence that you were ever here. No blood on the carpet, nothing. Nobody will ever know what happened to you, not your family, not your fellow detectives. Not unless they visit Brother Albrecht's circus when it arrives in the waking world. Ha! Ha! Then they'll see you! Dom Magator the Castrated Night Warrior!'

'*What*? You're making a big mistake here, pal. My name isn't Dom anything and I still don't know what the hell you're talking about!'

'Well, you *would* say that,' Mago Verde replied, pretending to be petulant.

He stood up. Out of one of the pockets of his shabby black coat he pulled a grubby gray scarf and a length of tarry cord.

'Very considerate of you, bringing your own handcuffs,' he said. 'Saves me tying your wrists together, and I was always crap at reef knots.'

He pushed Walter over on to his stomach. Walter thrashed and struggled, but Mago Verde was so bony and strong that he couldn't prevent him from wrenching his arms behind his back and hooking them together with his handcuffs.

Once he had done that, he rolled Walter over on to his back.

Walter yelled out, '*Help! Help! Somebody help me! Police! Help! Somebody help me, for Christ's sake!*'

'Nobody's going to hear you, tin man,' leered Mago Verde. 'Better off saving your breath!'

He forced the scarf into Walter's mouth and tied it tightly behind his head. It tasted foul, like dog grease. Walter bounced himself up and down and tried to scream, but he only managed to produce a muffled gargling sound.

Mago Verde unfastened the buckle of Walter's belt, and tugged down his zipper. Then – grunting with the effort – he dragged down his pants and his floral boxer shorts as far as his knees.

Walter lifted his head up as high as he could, his eyes bulging, staring at Mago Verde in a helpless appeal not to mutilate him. '*Mmmfff!*' he cried out. '*Mmmmmmfff!*'

Mago Verde looked down at him and gave the slightest shake of his head. 'Sorry, tin man. This has to be done. The Grand Freak wants a fat man who won't ever feel like messing with his women!'

He held up the serrated kitchen knife and ran his fingertip along the blade. Even though he did it only lightly, it still drew blood. He smiled and sucked his finger, and then he lifted up Walter's shirt.

'*Mmmmmffffff!*' shouted Walter, in desperation.

He felt almost nothing. A sharp coldness between his legs, and then a flood of warmth. In fact he couldn't believe that Mago Verde had really done what he had threatened to do. He tried to raise his head again, but he didn't need to, because Mago Verde was holding up something that looked like a bloody fledgling that had fallen from its nest.

'There!' he said. 'Extraordinary, isn't it, that the only difference between a man and a eunuch is one insignificant piece of gristle!'

Walter's head fell back on to the carpet. He felt darkness overwhelming him, as if he were sinking into a black swamp, and he did nothing to resist it.

Mago Verde stood over him for a while, and then he went through to the bathroom and dropped his bloody prize into the soap dish. He stared at his painted face in the mirror for a while, expressionless. Sometimes he was so cruel that he amazed even himself. Could this really be the same Gordon Veitch who had loved puppies when he was a small boy, and whose mother had sung him to sleep with *Golden Slumbers Kiss Your Eyes*?

Well, not really, he decided. The real Gordon Veitch had died a long time ago, without even waking up.

He went back into the bedroom and lay on the bed, with all of his clothes and his shoes on. Walter was still lying unconscious on the floor, his shirt-tails stained dark with blood. Mago Verde closed his eyes and thought about nothing at all. He could fall asleep at will. Within moments he was breathing steadily, and dreaming.

TWENTY-ONE
Hot Pursuit

It took Charlie over an hour and a half to check every room on the third, fourth and fifth floors. After he had visited the last of them, he called Walter to see if *he* had found anything suspicious. When he got through to Walter's cellphone service, however, an automated voice insisted that there was no such number.

He called Walter again and again, but each time he had the same response. *The number you have dialed is not in service. Please check the number and try again.* In the end he took the elevator up to the seventh floor and walked up and down every corridor. No Walter anywhere.

He knocked on the door of one room after another, asking the guests if they had been visited by a well-built detective in a red-and-green plaid coat. All of them said yes, they had. 'He told us he was looking for signs of disturbance. Whatever that meant.'

If a room was unoccupied, he used his pass key to open it up. In two of them, he came across people asleep, but there was no sign of Walter in any of them. When he looked into Room 702, however, he found that the bedside lamps were both lit, and that the bedcover was rucked up, as if somebody had been lying on top of it.

He circled slowly around the room. Apart from the bedside lamps and the rumpled bedcover, there was no other evidence that anybody had been here, yet Charlie felt distinctly unsettled. He tried calling Walter's cellphone again, but there was still no response.

He sat down on the end of the bed and called headquarters. 'I know this sounds crazy, but I've lost Wisocky. Yes. I know. But we were searching the Griffin House Hotel and he's vanished into thin air. His cellphone's out of service and I have absolutely no idea where he is. I'm going to need backup to look for him.'

He snapped his cellphone shut and sat still for a moment, trying to work out what was disturbing him. He sniffed, and then he realized what it was. The faintest smell of Walter's aftershave, Tom F Extreme. He sniffed again, but the smell had gone. Maybe he had imagined it. But he still had the feeling that something highly stressful had happened in this room; something so stressful that it had left a resonance, like the lingering resonance of a violin concerto, even after the very last screeching note has been played.

Kieran and Kiera came out of the elevator into the lobby. John gave them a wave with his rolled-up newspaper and called out, 'Man, am I pleased to see you two! I thought I was going to die of malnutrition.'

Kieran said, 'We looked pretty much everywhere. Nothing. I don't think Mago Verde's going to show.'

'Springer seems convinced that he will,' said Kiera.

John eased himself out of his armchair. 'I'm never too sure about Springer. Sometimes he seems to know everything and at other times he seems to know squat.'

'I can't really work out who he is,' said Kiera.

John sniffed. '*Who* he is? I'd like to know *what* he is. Once or twice he's showed up and he isn't even a he, he's a she. Anyhow – listen, you guys, I'm going to get myself some chow before the restaurant closes. Have a boring time, won't you? I sure did. Do you want to read my *Baton Rouge Advocate*?'

He turned around, and he was just about to make his way to the restaurant when the elevator doors opened and Kieran saw Mago Verde step out, wearing his shabby black suit and his greasy green grin.

'Shit!' he said. 'He's here! *Mago Verde*! Look!'

Kiera said, 'Oh my God, yes! But where's he going?'

John spun around and around. 'Where? Where is he? I don't see him!'

'He's crossing the lobby in front of the reception desk! He's just passing the portrait of that sour-faced old man!'

'I don't see him! Why don't I see him? I can usually see Dreads, but I don't see him at all!'

'But where's he *going*?' Kiera repeated. 'I thought he was supposed to be coming to the hotel to dream about his last victim. But he's leaving. There – he's walking out through the front door. There – he's gone.'

John thought for a moment, and then he said, 'I think I know why he's going. He's going because he's done the dirty deed already. He's caught his victim, and mutilated her, and he's dreamed her into the hotel walls. Now he's gone off to find somebody who's dreaming about Brother Albrecht's circus – anybody. Then he can do the same as we do, and step inside their dream, and he'll be back there – back at the freak show.'

'But what about his victim?' asked Kiera. 'If she's *here*, inside of the walls, how is going to take her to Brother Albrecht?'

'I don't know for sure,' John told her. 'But I guess that this hotel is like some kind of way through to the dream world – a gateway. A normal person wouldn't be able to step into somebody else's dream the way that we do, or the way that Dreads like Mago Verde can. Once Mago Verde is back in Brother Albrecht's dream, he must have a way of arranging for his victims to follow him there.'

'What the hell are we going to do now?' said Kieran. 'If he's taken his ninth sacrifice already, and he's on his way back to the circus—'

'You heard what Springer said. We'll have to go after him, and try to catch up with him before he manages to deliver his victim to Brother Albrecht. Otherwise, all hell is going to bust loose.'

They took the elevator back up to Rhodajane's room. Springer was still there, watching the fire escapes. He looked sicker and grayer and more hunched-up than ever.

Springer said, 'What's happened? Have you seen Mago Verde?'

Kieran nodded. 'He came out of the elevator and he left the hotel like he was in a hurry. Our guess is that he's found a ninth victim already.'

'But you didn't see him *enter* the hotel?'

'I don't know why,' said John. 'I can only think that his real self is dead. The twins here, they can see dead people, but I can't.'

'You need to get after him right now,' said Springer.

'You look like shit,' John told him. 'Why couldn't you choose somebody healthier than Deano to impersonate?'

'Deano was your closest friend, wasn't he?'

'Sure, but I had plenty of other friends who were much fitter than him. My old buddy from my restaurant-inspecting days, the late lamented Laurent Pannequin – he was fit as a flea. He could run a half marathon and then sing three verses of *Jolie Blonde* without even pausing for breath.'

'The late lamented Laurent Pannequin?' asked Kieran. 'What happened to him?'

'Choked on a fish bone at The Bonefish Grill. Tragic. Couldn't have happened to a nicer guy.'

'Listen, we don't have time for this,' said Springer. 'If you can all recite the invocation to Ashapola and get yourselves to sleep, I'll get in touch with Katie and Lincoln, and try to locate somebody who's dreaming about Brother Albrecht's circus.'

With that, he walked out of Rhodajane's room, leaving the door open behind him. Kieran and Kiera followed him, but when they stepped out into the corridor, they found that there was nobody there, and that Springer had disappeared.

'I think John was right,' said Kiera, as they jogged along the corridor to the elevators. 'Springer isn't a *who*, he's definitely a *what*.'

'If you ask me,' said Kieran, 'he's more of a *how*.'

Katie was almost asleep when she felt somebody shaking her shoulder. She turned over and opened her eyes. To her surprise, it was Davina, one of her old school friends from Beach High. Davina had long dark hair and dark wide-apart eyes and very pale skin.

'Davina?' she said. 'What on earth are *you* doing here?'

Davina put her finger to her lips. 'I'm not Davina. I'm Springer. But I didn't think it appropriate to come into your bedroom as Mr Flight, or any other mister for that matter.'

'What do you want, Springer? It's past ten thirty!'

'I know. But we believe that Mago Verde took his ninth victim this evening and we need to get after him. Now.'

'*Now*? You have to be kidding me! I'm tired enough from last night!'

'We don't have any choice, Katie. If Brother Albrecht gets his ninth sacrifice, that will be the end of everything as we know it.'

Katie sat up. 'OK. OK, I'll do it. Where's your dreamer?'

'Cleveland. He's a music promoter called Mickey Veralnik. He's been trying to get Kiera on his books for over a year, as a solo act. It could be that he has subliminally sensed her Night Warrior personality. That can happen sometimes, especially when somebody is in love with a Night Warrior, or obsessed by them. Night Warriors have a vibrancy about them which few ordinary people possess. Veralnik might be dreaming about Brother Albrecht's circus because he subconsciously expects to find her there.'

'All right,' said Katie. 'Just tell me where he is.'

'The Cleveland Marriott Downtown. Room one-oh-three-three. He has had a lot to drink this evening so there isn't much chance of him waking up any time soon.'

Katie lay back on the pillow. She could feel her heart beating hard. She knew that tonight was going to be critical, and that it would be much more dangerous than last night. Brother Albrecht and his freaks would suspect that the Night Warriors would be coming, and they would be prepared for them.

She recited the words of the invocation to Ashapola. '"*Now, when the face of the world is hidden in darkness, let us be conveyed to the place of our meeting, armed and armored; and let us be nourished by the power that is dedicated to the cleaving of darkness, the settling of all black matters, and the dissipation of all evil. So be it.*"'

She had barely reached the words 'so be it' when she was asleep; and within a few seconds, An-Gryferai arose from her somnolent body, and floated upward to the ceiling.

Lincoln was watching MTV when Springer came into his room at the Case Medical Center. Springer had taken on the appearance of Eulalie Passebon again, so Lincoln immediately knew who he was.

'How are doing?' Springer asked him, drawing up a chair and sitting beside his bed.

'Not so bad. Doctors say I should have my spine operation tomorrow. I like your cornrows, by the way, sweet cheeks.'

Springer remained serious. 'You have to go back to the circus tonight. In fact you have to go back right now.'

'Don't tell me. Mago Verde kidnapped victim number nine.'

'We're almost certain that he has, yes.'

'This is it, then? Armageddon come early?'

'It will be, unless you can stop Brother Albrecht from receiving this one last sacrifice.'

'OK, then. Let's lock and load.'

Springer reached out and held Lincoln's hand. He was even wearing all of those elaborate silver rings that Eulalie wore, with tigers' eyes and garnets and opals. 'I want you to know how much Ashapola will appreciate what you and your fellow Night Warriors are doing tonight. Whatever happens, your names will be celebrated for all eternity.'

'Hey, Ukulele, we ain't dead yet!'

Springer stood up. 'Your dreamer is a music promoter called Mickey Veralnik. He's asleep in Room one-oh-three-three at the Cleveland Marriott. The sooner you can join us there, the better.'

'Mickey Veralnik? I know that slimeball. He *would* have a dream about freaks. He's a frickin' freak himself.'

'I'll see you at his bedside,' said Springer. 'I'll tell the nurse that you're feeling tired and that you need a few hours' sleep. I'll tell her not to disturb you.'

'Thanks. I don't want her trying to wake me up in the middle of a firefight to give me a bed bath.'

Once they had recited their invocation to Ashapola, the Night Warriors fell asleep in less than twenty minutes. Their dream personalities rose from their beds and floated up into the night like ghostly kites. They sailed high above the sparkling streets of downtown Cleveland until they reached the Cleveland Marriott on Public Square, and then they descended through the ceiling of Room 1033. Dom Magator was first, followed by Jekkalon and Jemexxa, and then Xyrena and Zebenjo Y'xx. Shortly afterward, Springer appeared, looking like An-Gryferai's music teacher, Mr Flight.

The magnolia-painted bedroom was vast, with a bed wide enough for three people to sleep in, but tonight the only person sleeping in it was Mickey Veralnik. He was lying on his back with his mouth open, snoring. His dyed black comb-over had flapped to one side, like a crow's wing, and he was puffy-eyed and unshaven. He reeked of Jim Beam.

The Night Warriors looked at each other and none of them could hide their anxiety.

'This is crunch time,' said Dom Magator. 'If any of you want to back out, that will be perfectly understandable. We won't think any the worse of you.'

Springer added, 'There's a blessing that Ashapola bestows on those who are about to go into battle on the side of purity. "May your way be brightly lit by your devotion to duty, and may you be protected at all times by the shield of your honor."'

'And may we kick Brother Albrecht's ass into the middle of next week,' added Zebenjo'Yyx.

Mickey Veralnik snorted and mumbled and said, '*For Christ's sake, Vera, what have you done to your hair?*'

The Night Warriors all held their breath and stood absolutely motionless. Ten long seconds passed, but Mickey Veralnik didn't wake up. 'OK,' said Dom Magator, at last. 'Let's get going.'

He raised both hands and drew the brilliant blue octagon in the air. It opened up, but this time it seemed to shimmer and flicker more unsteadily than usual, like a faltering fluorescent tube before it pops out for ever.

'What the hell's wrong with the goddamned portal?' asked Dom Magator. 'Why is it jinking around like that?'

'Mickey Veralnik's dream is highly unstable,' Springer explained. 'Partly because he's drunk, and partly because he's dreaming that he's in Brother Albrecht's dream, and Brother Albrecht's dream is close to becoming reality. It's like a storm approaching. More than a storm – a major earth tremor. Go very carefully, all of you.'

Zebenjo'Yyx said, 'Come on. Let's do it, before it's too late.'

With that, he ducked his head down and disappeared through the portal. Jekkalon followed close behind him, and then An-Gryferai and Jemexxa and Xyrena. Dom Magator went last, but before he went through, Springer laid a hand on his arm and said, 'Ashapola be with you, Dom Magator. Ashapola be with *all* of you.'

'Yeah,' said Dom Magator. 'And you, too, Springer, whatever the hell you are.'

He stepped through the portal. The crackle of energy was much fiercer than it usually was, and showers of sparks bounced off his armor.

He found himself in Brother Albrecht's dream again, but this was a very different landscape from the dark and rainy hillside that they had visited last night. This was a sunbaked prairie, with fields of tawny wheat stretching all the way to the horizon, and not a single tree in sight. The sky was purple, with huge white cumulus clouds rolling slowly across it from west to east.

An-Gryferai turned around and said, 'There it is. Look.'

About a mile away, they could see a small township, with a church spire and a water tower and a single main street lined with stores. A few hundred yards to the south, Brother Albrecht's circus had been set up, with its black tents and its black caravans and its black pennants flapping in the summer breeze.

Very faintly, they could hear the discordant strains of *In The Good Old Summertime*. An-Gryferai shivered. For some reason, she found the sound of that music even more unsettling than that cluster of black tents. It was like all her childhood fears returning to visit her. And more than anything it reminded her of Daisy, her dead sister, and Daisy's persistent nightmares about circuses.

'How about an aerial reconnaissance?' Dom Magator asked her.

'Is that such a good idea?' said Zebenjo'Yyx. 'As soon as those clowns see An-Gryferai circlin' around, they'll know we're here, won't they?' .

'Yes, they probably will. But they'll soon spot us, right out here in the open, even if they haven't spotted us already. And don't tell me they haven't been expecting us.'

'In that case, I ain't takin' no chances,' said Zebenjo'Yyx. He cocked the quarrel-firing mechanisms on both of his forearms. 'One peep out of any of those freaks, and they're goin' to wind up seriously ventilated.'

An-Gryferai took a short run through the wheat field, flapping her wings. The air was warm and she rose quickly, until she was nearly a hundred feet up. She looked up at the clouds as she flew, and she saw that as they rolled their way from one horizon to the other, they continually changed their shape, from ghostly galleons with tattered sails to monstrous dogs with bulging eyes. For a brief moment, she thought that one of them looked like the face of her dead grandmother, watching her with sadness in her eyes.

As she approached the township, she could make out its name painted on the side of the water tower, Melancholy, IA. The main street was almost deserted except for three or four pick-up trucks and a few pedestrians. She could see a store with a sign saying Clavicle's General Supplies and a barber shop named for its proprietor, W. Severe.

Melancholy could have been a typical mid-West farming community except for the its purple sky and the fact that its perspective was all wrong and everything about it was out of proportion. An-Gryferai caught sight of a German Shepherd at the far end of the street that was almost twice the size of its owner, but as they came nearer, the German Shepherd shrank and its owner grew taller. At the other end of the street, the church was no bigger than a doll's house.

She circled around the township twice, and then she angled her wings and wheeled toward Brother Albrecht's circus. The big top and all of the other tents had been erected in the same pattern as last night's dream, with the animal cages in a line between the caravans. The site was teeming with circus hands and clowns and freaks, as well as scores of ordinary, bewildered-looking people who must have been dreamers. She was sure she glimpsed Mickey Veralnik amongst them, but she could have been mistaken.

'D.M? I don't think the show's started yet,' she told Dom Magator. 'Everybody's milling around outside. But there are ten times more dreamers here than there were last night. It looks like Brother Albrecht is really pulling them in.'

'No sign of Mago Verde?'

'Not so far. I'm going to go round one more time, lower this time. I don't think anybody's noticed me yet. Maybe they think I'm a turkey buzzard.'

She swooped around the big top once again. She could hear the organ music playing, and the braying of a distressed donkey. As she circled over the caravans, however, she heard a high voice screaming out, '*Lookit! Up there! Up in the sky! It's that bird-woman!*'

She twisted her head around and saw a midget clown in red suspenders jumping up and down and frantically pointing up at her. '*There! It's that bird-woman! The one who blew up Flammo!*'

Another clown tossed a tent peg up at her, which hit her on the left thigh. Then a circus hand threw a mallet, and another clown tossed up a bucket. A whole shower of tent pegs flew up, as well as throwing knives and more buckets. She urgently beat her wings to gain more height, so that none of the missiles could reach her. Then she tilted herself back toward the west, so that she could rejoin the rest of the Night Warriors.

As she flew over the main entrance to the big top, past the sign which read *Albrecht's Traveling Circus & Freak Show*, a man stepped out from underneath the archway. A man in a dusty black tuxedo, with ragged white hair and a pale gray face and a sharp green grin.

He looked up at her, his arms folded, but because of his make-up she couldn't tell if he was really grinning or not. She guessed that he was probably scowling.

'*He's here!*' she told Dom Magator. '*Mago Verde is already here! I just saw him standing outside the big top!*'

'In that case, we'll have to go in right now. You keep circling around, An-Gryferai. I need you to be ready to dive down and grab Mago Verde's victim, if she's here. The rest of us will have to try a full-frontal assault.'

An-Gryferai wheeled around again. Below her, the circus hands and the clowns and the freaks were already picking up pitchforks and tent pegs and machetes and beginning to pour between the tents toward the western side of the circus site, where the Night Warriors would be coming from. They were whooping and howling and calling out, '*No more nightmare! No more nightmare! Real! Real! Real!*'

Out in the wheat field, Dom Magator lifted a heavy chrome-plated carbine from the rack on his back. He unhooked a long magazine from his belt and clicked it into the carbine's rear handgrip.

'What's that?' asked Zebenjo'Yyx. 'Not another one of your pansy-assed Knock-'Em-Off-Balance-But-Don't-Hurt-'Em Guns?'

'Not this time,' Dom Magator told him. 'This time I've brought something seriously lethal. A Scythe Rifle.'

'A *what* do you say?'

'You'll see. And pretty soon, too. Here they come.'

Through the heat-distorted wheat field, trampling down the crops as they came, over a hundred clowns and circus hands and freaks came storming toward them.

'Oh my God,' said Xyrena. 'We don't stand a cat in hell's chance.'

'Yes, we do,' Dom Magator retorted. 'So long as we don't lose our nerve. What are they? *Clowns*, OK? Clowns and tent riggers and midgets. And what are we? Natural born highly-skilled warriors. Absolutely no contest. Now remember – don't fire until you see the reds of their noses.'

'We're about to get ourselves slaughtered to death and you're makin' a *joke* out of it?' Zebenjo'Yxx protested. 'You're really somethin', man!'

'What do you want me and Jemexxa to do?' Jekkalon asked.

'Hit as many of the clowns as you can. But don't use up all of your energy, Jemexxa. I want to see that circus razed to the ground before we leave this dream.'

'You got it, dude.'

By now the howling rabble of circus folk was almost on them. Dom Magator stood in the center, with Zebenjo'Yyx on his left-hand side and Jekkalon and Jemexxa on his right. Xyrena stood back behind them. She knew that her time would come, but it wasn't yet.

'*No more nightmare! No more nightmare!*' screamed the clowns and the freaks. '*Real! Real! Real!*'

Up above them, the huge white cumulus clouds boiled up, taking on the shapes of skulls and phantoms and human faces with their mouths dragged down in agony. The whole of Brother Albrecht's dream was thirsting for battle.

TWENTY-TWO

Full Circle

The circus folk were less than a hundred yards away. '*No more nightmare! No more nightmare! Real! Real! Real!*'

Dom Magator waited until the last possible moment, and then he said, very quietly, 'OK, everybody. Let 'em have it.'

Zebenjo'Yyx released a blizzard of arrows from both hands. They clattered and whistled as they flew from the release mechanisms on his forearms, and the clowns collapsed into the wheat by the score, their bodies bristling like porcupines.

Jemexxa kept her back to the circus folk, so that she could raise the palm of one hand and reflect a bolt of lightning into Jekkalon's hand. The lightning jumped from one twin to the other with an ear-splitting crack, and Jekkalon aimed it into the thickest part of the crowd. It exploded with such force that they could see a visible shock-wave ripple across the field, and fragments of clown and clothing were blasted high up into the purple sky.

Now Dom Magator hefted his Scythe Rifle up to his hip. He squeezed the trigger and it uttered a piercing, continuous scream. A stream of liquid lead poured out of the muzzle like water from a high-pressure hose, cutting the circus folk into pieces as he slowly swung the rifle from left to right. Soon the field in front of them was heaped with bodies and the wheat was stained rusty with blood.

Within minutes, fewer than a dozen clowns and circus hands were left standing, apart from three or four freaks – one of them a boy with six legs, like a huge spider.

'*You want some more, you bastards?*' Dom Magator yelled at them, and he shocked himself by the harshness of his own voice. '*There's plenty more where this came from!*'

The circus folk hesitated for a moment, and then they turned around and began to scamper and hobble back toward the black tents.

'Come on,' said Dom Magator. 'No time to waste. This is where we go for the Grand Freak himself.'

They stepped gingerly through the scattered bodies. Xyrena kept saying, 'My God, my God, what have we done?' but Dom Magator didn't answer her. He remembered the first time that *he* had fought a battle in a nightmare, and inflicted casualties, and he remembered how shocked he had been, even when he had woken up the following morning.

'We're on our way, An-Gryferai,' Dom Magator told her. 'See if you can pinpoint Mago Verde.'

'OK, but I'll have to dive down lower. They're all hiding themselves underneath their awnings now.'

'Be careful, that's all.'

He saw An-Gryferai circle over the big top, and then dive downward. But suddenly she appeared to jerk, and thrash, and her wings folded up. She disappeared from sight behind the tents, and he could hear a shout of triumph from the circus folk.

'An-Gryferai! An-Gryferai! What's happened? An-Gryferai, get back to me!'

Over his intercom, he picked up struggling noises, and static, and somebody saying, '*Got her, the bird-bitch! Got her!*'

He heard An-Gryferai grunting with effort, and then saying the single word, '*—net*!'

'Did you hear that?' he asked the other Night Warriors. 'Sounds like they've caught her in a snare!'

They began to jog more quickly toward the circus. The morning was even hotter now. Their boots crunched through the trampled wheat stalks and the black pennants on the big top made a lazy, slapping sound. As they approached the outlying tents, a single figure appeared, in a black tuxedo, with a bright green smile. He waited for them patiently as they came nearer.

'Well, well, what a surprise!' Mago Verde called out. 'It appears that I'm guilty of mistaking your identity, tin man! But then one lard butt looks *so* much like another!'

'Where's An-Gryferia, you creep?' Dom Magator demanded. 'If you've so much as touched her, I'm going to rip off your head off and piss down your neck!'

'An-Gryferia? Is that her name? The bird-bitch who blew up poor Flammo? She's OK for now, maybe a little bruised. But I warn you. If any of you try anything funny, she's going to suffer. And not just suffer for now, but for ever and ever, amen. She wants to be a bird-woman? We can make her into a bird-woman for real!'

Dom Magator lifted his Scythe Rifle. 'This is the end, you piece of shit. This circus is going out of business, permanent.'

'I don't think so,' grinned Mago Verde. 'You know why I came here tonight. That's why you followed me. I have a ninth sacrifice for Brother Albrecht, and once we've enhanced his appearance, so that he *begs* us to stay with the freak show for the rest of his life, it will be time to pack up the tents and hitch up the caravans and trundle our way through to the wonderful world of wakefulness!'

'Take me to An-Gryferai,' said Dom Magator, pulling back the bolt on his rifle. 'Take me to An-Gryferai or so help me I'll cut you in half.'

'I was going to anyhow,' said Mago Verde. 'Come on, tin man, follow me!'

He turned around and started to walk between the tents toward the big top, his thumbs in his lapels, strutting like Charlie Chaplin.

Zebenjo'Yyx looked at Dom Magator and said, 'What do we do now, man? He might have caught An-Gryferai, but we can't let him take this circus through to the real world, can we?'

'Let's play it as it comes,' said Dom Magator. 'I don't want any casualties if I can help it. Especially not An-Gryferai.'

Mago Verde led them through the archway that said *Albrecht's Traveling Circus & Freak Show* and into the big top. Inside, the noise was overwhelming. The Night Warriors stood in front of the stage and looked around, and every seat was taken – by a clown, or a freak, or a dreamer. This was going to be Brother Albrecht's big night – the night when he and his circus at least broke the sacred sanction that had kept them imprisoned in the world of dreams for over eight hundred years.

'Here's your precious An-Gryferai,' said Mago Verde. And there she was, on the far side of the stage, gagged with a red scarf and tightly bound to a wooden chair, her wings folded behind her. A tattooed strong man in a leotard stood next to her, grinning toothlessly, holding a long-bladed knife in his hand.

An-Gryferai stared at the Night Warriors with her eyes wide, shaking her head from side to side as if she were appealing to them not to surrender.

Zachary, the bald Freakmaster came strutting up to them, wearing his long black rustling raincoat. He smiled at Jekkalon and Jemexxa and he obviously recognized them, even with their helmets on. 'We meet again, then! Kieran and Kiera! Your mother the Demi-Goddess is *very* well, you'll no doubt be pleased to know! You will see her in a moment!

Then he turned to Dom Magator and said, between gritted teeth, 'Your weapons, please, all of them.'

'You're kidding me,' said Dom Magator.

Zachary, still smiling, shook his head. 'We can't allow you to jeopardize Brother Albrecht's greatest night, now can we?'

'Go screw yourself,' said Zebenjo'Yyx. 'You ain't havin' my arrow storm stuff.'

'Well, that's your choice,' Zachary told him. 'But if you don't hand over your weapons, your feathered friend here is going to be disemboweled before you can blink.'

Dom Magator looked across at An-Gryferai. He had seen other Night Warriors give their lives in the struggle against evil, and Brother Albrecht's circus was one of the greatest evils that the world had ever faced. Corrupt, cruel and merciless. But how could he allow An-Gryferai to be cut open, right in front of him?

He unbuckled the rack of rifles on his back, lifted it off, and lowered it on to the ground. Zebenjo'Yyx said, '*No*, man! *Shee*it! You can't do that! We're goin' to be defenseless!'

Even Jekkalon said, 'Yes, come on, D.M.! We're warriors, dude! We know what the risks are!'

But Dom Magator shook his head. 'I can't let them butcher An-Gryferai, not in cold blood. Not when I can stop them.'

'And how many other people are going to be butchered, because we didn't stop Brother Albrecht? Thousands, maybe! *Millions*! You know what Springer told us! The whole damn planet is going to go to hell!'

Dom Magator loosened his belt and let all of his knives and handguns and ammunition magazines drop with a clatter around his feet. Zachary snapped his fingers and one of the circus hands came over and collected them up.

'Now your friends,' he said. 'Come on, please. We're running out of time here.'

'*Shit*,' said Zebenjo'Yyx, and reluctantly unfastened the arrow-firing mechanisms on his forearms. Another circus hand lifted the curved quiver off his back.

Jemexxa took off her power pack and that was carried away, too.

Zachary approached Xyrena. She looked up at him with a challenging expression on her face.

'And what weaponry do *you* have, beautiful lady?' he asked her.

Xyrena shook her head. 'Only my irresistible looks, baldy.'

'She's Xyrena the Passion Warrior,' put in Dom Magator. 'That says it all. Don't tell me she isn't turning you on already. She can turn on a cigar-store Indian.'

'*OK* . . .' said Zachary, although he didn't look totally convinced. 'Now why don't you people take a seat beside the stage? I believe that Brother Albrecht is quite keen for you to watch his final sacrifice. He always savors the taste of revenge.'

A clown with a miserable blue face led them to a collection of chairs not far behind An-Gryferai. They sat down together, feeling defeated, not even talking to each other. An-Gryerai twisted her head around to look at them and her expression was filled with pain.

Almost immediately, there was a shrill fanfare of trumpets, and the curtains at the back of the stage were drawn back. The audience clapped and whistled and whooped with excitement as the ringmaster came striding out in his bottle-green tailcoat, cracking his whip.

'Ladies and gentlemen and those who cannot decide which they want to be! Welcome, welcome, welcome to Albrecht's Traveling Circus and Freak Show! Today is the most momentous day that this circus has ever known! Today is the day that we make our ninth and last sacrifice to Brother Albrecht, and return this circus at last to the world where it rightly belongs!

He spun around on the heel of his black polished jackboot and cracked his whip again. 'I give you! Albrecht's Traveling Circus and Freak Show!'

The audience rose to their feet, roaring with excitement, as the stage was flooded with scores of clowns and freaks. Dom Magator saw Jekkalon and Jemexxa's mother, the Demi-Goddess, being wheeled to one side. To his horror, he also saw Maria Fortales, Brother Albrecht's eighth sacrifice. Her face looked more like a Mayan death-mask than a human face, with empty eyes. The operation on her arms had been completed by another surgeon, and now she had two huge cross-bred pythons writhing from her shoulders. Their jaws had been wired together to prevent them from biting anybody while they were on stage.

Once the throng of clowns and freaks had filled the stage, a gurney was wheeled out, and brought right to the very edge of the stage. Pinned to the gurney with leather straps was Walter Wisocky, dressed in nothing but a filthy white T-shirt. His face was swollen and his hair was sticking up and he looked as if he were only half conscious. Between his thighs there was nothing but a blood-crusted surgical dressing.

'*Jesus*,' said Dom Magator. 'Do you know who that is? Rhodajane – can you see who it is? It's that detective who gave me a hard time when I first took you into the Griffin House Hotel. Windsock, or whatever his name was.'

'That's probably what Mago Verde meant when he said that he'd mistaken your identity,' said Xyrena. 'He must have caught *him* by mistake, thinking he was you. What did I call you two? Tweedleydum and Tweedleydee.'

'Jesus.'

But now the ringmaster cracked his whip yet again, and

shouted, 'Ladies and gentlemen! Furr-eaks and misfits! I give you . . . the Grand Freak himself, for the very last time in the world of dreams, Brother Albrecht!'

Accompanied by another fanfare of trumpets, Brother Albrecht's black-canopied contraption was pushed on to the stage by his naked, tattooed entourage. The ringmaster wound the handle, and the canopy gradually opened up, revealing Brother Albrecht. His hair was tangled with fresh yellow flowers from the wheat fields around the circus site, and he was smiling in triumph.

He nodded to acknowledge the clapping and the cheering of the crowd. 'And now,' he announced. 'The ninth sacrifice! *Opfer nummer neun*!'

Walter moaned and struggled against his restraints, but it looked to Dom Magator as if he were either sedated or in shock. He hoped for his sake that he was sedated, and heavily. God alone knew what Brother Albrecht and his assembly of freaks were planning to do to him next.

'Now we can say goodbye to eight centuries of enforced exile!' Brother Albrecht cried out. 'Now we can exact our recompense for being treated as outcasts and inferiors! *Es ist Zeit für unsere Rache*!'

From the rear of the stage, a man with spiky straw-colored hair appeared, wearing a long green surgeon's robe. He was carrying a wire cage, holding it up high so that everybody in the audience could see what was inside it.

'Oh my God,' said Xyrena.

Leaping and jumping inside the cage was a thin black river otter, with white markings on its face. The crowd roared again, and whistled, and applauded, and the otter went into a frenzy, hurling itself from one side of the cage to the other.

'What the hell they plannin' to use *that* for?' asked Zebenjo'Yyx. 'Dom Magator – we should never of given up our weapons – we gotta stop them!'

The ringmaster led the man in the surgeon's robe up to the front of the stage. 'Ladies and gentlemen! Nondescripts! You are about to witness the conversion of our ninth sacrifice to a *willing* sacrifice! A freak who will agree to stay with us for ever! I give you Doctor Norman Agnew, and in turn Doctor Norman Agnew will give you Detective Walter Wisocky, Otter Lover!'

Doctor Agnew gave a gap-toothed grin, and unfastened the wire latch on the cage. He reached inside and lifted out the struggling otter, raising it up over his head. The crowd went wild, drumming their feet on the floor and standing on their seats and waving their arms.

'Otter Lover—' said Xyrena. 'My God, I know what they're going to do! That poor man!' Without any hesitation, she stood up and walked around An-Gryferai's chair and across to the center of the stage.

Dom Magator said, '*Xyrena*—!' but she ignored him. She went right up close to Doctor Agnew and stood beside him, until he realized that she was there. Very slowly, he lowered the wriggling otter and stared at her.

'Yes, madam?' he asked her. 'And what do you want?'

Xyrena smiled at him. 'More to the point, doctor, what do *you* want?'

Doctor Agnew continued to stare at her. He didn't say anything, but it was obvious that he was breathing more deeply. He licked his lips, and then he looked toward the black contraption where Brother Albrecht was ensconced, as if he were guilty about feeling so aroused.

In his grip, even the otter began to rise up stiffly, as if it were a huge sleek member covered with shiny black fur.

Brother Albrecht called out, 'You again, Xyrena, you Lorelei! We didn't finish our conversation the last time, did we, when you and your friends caused such havoc?'

'So sorry about that,' said Xyrena. She reached out and stroked the otter all the way down its back and Doctor Agnew shuddered as if she had stroked his penis. Then she walked over to Brother Albrecht's contraption and said, 'Congratulations are in order, then, your Grand Freakiness? Your ninth sacrifice, all ready to be converted into a sideshow attraction? What's so special about a girl with snakes for arms, when you have a man with a living otter for a *membrum virile*?'

Brother Albrecht said, 'Come closer. How is it you make me feel like this, Xyrena?'

'Just my personality, I guess.'

'No . . . you have much more than that. You have a power which I recognize. You remind me so much of the woman for whom I lost everything. Your eyes. Your hair.'

Between his truncated, tattooed thighs, his brown leather

jerkin was swelling up. Xyrena reached her hand over the edge of his seat and almost touched him with her fingertips. Even though she didn't quite make contact, Brother Albrecht quivered, and closed his eyes, as if she had.

'*Who are you?*' he whispered. All around them, the circus folk on the stage were attentive and hushed, and even the assembled audience were much quieter, although they shuffled and coughed like any other audience.

'You know my name,' Xyrena told him.

He opened his eyes very wide. 'Yes. But you look so much like my Lisbeth. How can that be possible?'

'Coincidence,' said Xyrena. 'Fate. Or maybe you've forgotten what your Lisbeth really looks like. It's been eight hundred years, after all. A body can forget a whole lot in eight hundred years.'

'A body, yes,' Brother Albrecht, with an unexpectedly wry smile. 'A body without arms and legs.'

'You have everything that counts,' said Xyrena, her hand stroking up and down in the air, less than a half inch away from the contours of his bulging jerkin.

'What does that matter? You wouldn't willingly make love to me.'

'Who says?' she said, in a steady voice. And at the same time, she thought: *would I? Could I?* God, I sound like Barbra Streisand. But then she looked intently at his beautiful face and thought: I could, as a matter of fact. Plenty of women have lovers who are amputees or very special people. Even Prince Randian the Human Torso was married and had four children.

'You would try to kill me,' said Brother Albrecht.

'What?'

'You would try to make my blood boil, the same way you made my harlequin's blood boil. That's what you're here for, isn't it? You don't find me alluring at all. But you would be prepared to make love to me, just to slide those long fingernails of yours into my skin. *Aber Sie konnten mich nicht töten. Ich bin nicht der selbe wie Sie. Ich nicht sogar komme von der Welt von Träumen.*'

'What did you say? I don't understand Krautish.'

'I said that you cannot kill me, Xyrena. I am not the same as you. I am not even from the world of dreams. I was sent here by God as a punishment, but I ended up being punished far more harshly than I ever imagined possible. I can never forgive that.'

Xyrena said, 'I wasn't going to kill you, anyway. You're too beautiful to kill.

For the first time, she saw uncertainty in Brother Albrecht's eyes.

'We've tried all of our best weapons,' she said. 'Dom Magator even fired his Absence Gun at you, which is supposed to stop you having ever existed. But I thought, maybe you *do* have a heart, underneath all of that rage and all of that cruelty and all of those tattoos.

'And then I saw your face as close as this, and I thought, in spite of everything, maybe this man needs only one thing to change him back to what he once was. You were a man of God once. You were a lover once. You could be those again, if you could find somebody to love you for who you are.'

Brother Albrecht said, 'You're lying to me, Xyrena. You're trying to deceive me. You could never love me.'

She rested the palm of her hand between his legs, and squeezed him very gently, and looked intently into his eyes. 'I could – and if you want me to, I will. But I need to see the true Brother Albrecht. I need to see you for who you really are. I need to see what you've been denying for eight hundred years.'

'I can't. I've hurt and mutilated too many hundreds of people, all in the name of my own anger. Look at this circus! Look at these freaks! Look at these clowns! Nobody could forgive me for all this!'

'*Me*,' said Xyrena. 'I can. If you're not the same as me, and you don't come from the world of dreams, then show me who you really are.'

Brother Albrecht's nostrils flared with passion and lust. '*I can't! It's impossible! I can't!*'

'Then I'll go, shall I?' said Xyrena. 'I'll let you take your circus through to the waking world, and cause even more havoc, and even more pain, and even more killings. I just wonder what your Lisbeth would have said had she ever known what you would do.'

She turned away from him. All of the hundreds of people in the big top were standing silently, staring at her – even Mago Verde and the ringmaster.

'What have you done, you slut?' said Mago Verde, his voice quaking. 'What have you done?'

'I've tried the only weapon against Brother Albrecht that I thought might work.' said Xyrena. 'Now why don't you get on with your sacrifice, you ghoul?'

'*What have you done?*' he screamed. '*What have you fucking done?*'

Xyrena gradually became aware that the faces of the people who were staring at her were becoming more and more brightly illuminated. She could see reflections in the visors of the Night Warriors' helmets, and on Jekkalon and Jemexxa's black and silver suits. Within a few seconds, the whole interior of the big top was lit up so intensely that by comparison the chandeliers looked dim.

She turned around. Behind her, a tall figure of a man was standing, but a man so dazzling that she had to shield her eyes with her hand. Although she was almost blinded, she recognized his face. It was Brother Albrecht, as beautiful as ever, but now the wild flowers had blown from his hair and he was crowned instead with scintillating sparks, rather like the crown that she herself was wearing.

He was wearing a golden robe that matched her golden cloak, and his arms were spread wide. His arms were whole again, and his legs had been restored, and the demonic tattoos had all been bleached from his body. Now Xyrena was sure what he was.

The whole of the big top was filled with a high singing sound that was barely audible to human ears, and every chandelier was jangling with its resonance.

Dom Magator stepped forward and put his arm around Xyrena's waist. 'You did it,' he said. 'I don't know how you did it, but you did it.'

'I told him I could love him, that's all. Don't you understand? *He's an angel.* That's why the Absence Gun didn't work on him. He was never born in the same way that you and me were born. You can't reverse something that never happened. But give him love – that's something different. God didn't love him any more. He lost the woman he loved. That's why he was always so vengeful.'

Brother Albrecht reached out his hand. 'Are you prepared to come with me, Xyrena, and love me?'

'Where?' asked Xyrena, but she already knew the answer to that.

Dom Magator said, 'I can't ask you to do this, Rhodajane. You can't sacrifice yourself for the rest of us.'

Xyrena looked at him and smiled. 'Yes, I can. And how much of a sacrifice are we talking about? Heaven has to be better than Cleveland.'

Zebenjo'Yyx came up to her now and held her tight. 'You had the best weapon of all of us, all the time, didn't you, sweet cheeks, and Springer knew that. You was the only one among us who could bring this full circle.'

Jekkalon and Jemexxa hugged her, too. 'Thank you, Rhodajane. We're never going to forget you, ever.'

'*What about the circus?*' screamed Mago Verde. '*Albrecht, you treacherous bastard! What about the circus? What about me?*'

Brother Albrecht raised both arms. Shafts of bright light radiated from his outstretched hands like a brilliant sunrise. 'The circus is over,' he said. 'The tents are struck. The dreamer awakes.'

He took hold of Xyrena's hand and drew her toward him. He put his arms around her, and kissed her, and then they slowly streamed upward toward the roof of the tent, more like a shining golden fountain than two people embracing each other.

The roof of the tent opened up like the petals of a huge black flower. Brother Albrecht and Xyrena rose up into the purple sky, and with a last scintillating glitter they were gone.

There was a moment's silence. Then, with a soft thunderous sound, the big top started to collapse. The audience screamed and panicked and rushed for the exits, but even as they struggled to escape they began to disappear. Brother Albrecht's dream was over and they were waking up, too.

Tonnes of black canvas dropped on top of the stage, drowning the clowns and the freaks and the circus hands like a huge black tidal wave. Jekkalon tried to battle against it, shouting out, 'Mom! Mom! Mom – where are you? Mom!' Dom Magator grabbed his arm and shouted, 'It's too late, Jekkalon! It's all over! There's nothing you can do!'

'But that's our mom!'

'She *died*, Jekkalon. She died a long time ago. We need to get out of here before Mickey Veralnik wakes up.'

Zebenjo'Yyx was tugging loose the knots that had fastened An-Gryferai to her chair. He untied her gag, and helped her down from the stage. Her wings had shed some feathers, and her arms were badly bruised, but otherwise she was unhurt.

Together, the Night Warriors struggled their way out of the big top and jogged out between the marquees and into the wheat fields. When they were clear of the circus site, they turned around to see the last of the black tents collapsing and the last of the caravans falling apart. In only a few minutes, the entire traveling circus and freak show was blowing away in a boiling cloud of black dust, which rose hundreds of feet in the air. Clowns and freaks blew away with it as if they had never existed, which most of them never had. The last structure to teeter and fall was the archway carrying the sign which said *Albrecht's Traveling Circus & Freak Show.*

As it fell, though, An-Gryferai said, '*Look! Over there!*"

Running across the fields in the opposite direction was Mago Verde, his white hair flying behind him. His head was lowered in determination and his arms and legs were moving like a clockwork spider.

'He's escaped, the bastard,' said Zebenjo'Yyx. 'Why didn't he blow away like the rest of them?'

'He's a Dread, that's why,' Dom Magator told him. 'He belongs in his own dream, not this one. He's trying to get back there before this one collapses for good.'

'He's not getting away,' said An-Gryferai. 'Not after what he's done.'

She started to limp after him. Dom Magator said, 'Stop, An-Gryferai! You're hurt! He's not worth it! We'll get him some other time, in some other dream, I promise you!'

But An-Gryferai was determined. She ran faster and faster, and she began to beat her wings, harder and harder, and at last she took off and climbed up into the dark purple sky.

'*An-Gryferai*!' called Jekkalon and Jemexxa, but she ignored them and flew after Mago Verde like an eagle flying after a coyote. Stray feathers blew from her wings, and the crosswind made her angle and dip, but it took her only a few minutes before she had caught up with Mago Verde and was flying right over his head.

Panicking, he turned his head around and looked up at her,

but he kept on running. '*Go away, you bird-bitch! Get the fuck away from me!*'

But An-Gryferai was thinking of her grandmother Gryferai, and the way that Gryferai had finally destroyed the Black Shatterer. She knew now that it was a Night Warrior's duty to annihilate every kind of evil, regardless of the danger and regardless of the cost.

She opened up her talons and swooped down on Mago Verde, grasping his shoulders. Her claws pierced his black tailcoat and buried themselves an inch deep into his flesh. He screamed in pain and rage, but she beat her wings in a deep, steady rhythm, and she lifted him clear of the ground and up into the air. His legs pedaled wildly, but she took him higher and higher.

As she flew, she looked down and she could see her shadow flickering across the wheat fields, with Mago Verde dangling below her. She saw her fellow Night Warriors, the sun glinting off their armor. They waved up at her and she tried to smile back at them, although by now she was gasping with effort.

She turned in a semicircle and flew with Mago Verde back toward the township of Melancholy. Mago Verde was screeching and cursing, but he was helpless.

'*You will suffer for this, bird-bitch! You will suffer so much!*'

She reached Melancholy and flew along the main street. Strangely, nobody looked up at her. The dream was coming to an end and their existence was gradually fading away.

'*I am Mago Verde! I am the Green Magician! I am Mago Verde!*'

An-Gryferai lifted him up over the diminutive church. He was screaming and sobbing now, because had had guessed what she was going to do. She took him up a little higher, and hovered over the church spire, flapping her wings steadily to keep her position against the wind.

'Do you want mercy?' she shouted at him.

'*Mercy!*' he screamed. '*For Christ's sake, mercy!*'

'You should have thought of that, a long time ago,' she told him; and then she released the mechanism of her claws and he dropped from her grasp, his arms and legs windmilling wildly.

He fell directly on to the gilded cross on top of the spire. It pierced his belly and was driven right through him. He ended up face down, his arms and legs dangling, with blood slowly sliding down the spire.

An-Gryferai circled the church once, and then she flew back slowly to join the rest of the Night Warriors. When she skip-landed in the wheat field next to them, they all whistled and clapped her, and Jemexxa hugged her tight. 'You're so brave, An-Gryferai. You're amazing.'

Together they walked through the fields toward the flickering blue portal in the distance. Halfway there, they saw four faded figures standing in the wheat, their images blurred in the dust and the sunlight. When they came closer they saw Kieran and Kieran's mother Jenyfer, in a simple gray dress, her hair pinned up, smiling at them. Not far away stood Michael-Row-The-Boat-Ashore-Hallelujah, holding his puppy. A little further in the distance stood Detective Wisocky, one hand in his pocket, chewing a wheat stalk, and next to him, smiling, Maria Fortales.

Dom Magator raised his hand to Detective Wisocky and Detective Wisocky waved back. Then he turned around and started to walk away.

'*Mom!*' shouted Kieran and Kiera, and ran to put their arms around her. 'Mom, you came back!'

Jenyfer Kaiser kissed each of them. 'No, darlings, I haven't come back. I've just come to say goodbye, and thank you for saving me. I belong in dreamland now. But this is a *happy* dreamland, with good people, and you can always come visit me, any time you fall asleep.'

Dom Magator went up to Michael and hunkered down beside him. 'How are you, little fellow?'

'I'm happy, too,' smiled Michael. 'Jenyfer and me and Froggy, we're going to stay together and Jenyfer's going to bring me milk and cookies.'

Dom Magator took off his helmet, and tousled Michael's hair.

'Did I ever tell you that I love you?' he said.

Michael shook his head. 'You didn't have to, Mr Dauphin,' he said. 'I always knew.'

TWENTY-THREE
Awakenings

Kiera was woken by a persistent hammering on the door of Room 237. She lifted her head from the pillow and looked around, blinking. The clock beside the bed said seven fifty-three a.m. and the sun was shining between the drapes.

'Kiera! Kiera! It's Lois! You have to wake up!'

Kiera drew back the covers and climbed out of bed. She felt bruised all over, as if she had been riding on roller coasters all night. She shuffled across to the door and opened it. Lois was standing outside, already dressed in a black polo-neck sweater and a black beret, and huge dark glasses, so that she looked like a giant insect.

Several other people were hurrying along the corridor behind her, carrying suitcases and coats.

'Lois? What's wrong?'

'They're evacuating the hotel. You have to get dressed as quick as you can. Jessie will pack up your things for you.'

'They're evacuating the hotel? Why?'

'I don't know exactly. But there's cops swarming all over the place. I've arranged for rooms at the Renaissance downtown.'

'OK,' said Kiera, blearily. 'Just give me five minutes. I really need to take a shower.'

'Quick as you can, sweetheart. I'm going to wake up Kieran now.'

Kiera closed the door and went through to the bathroom. In the mirror she looked no different from usual, although her hair was tousled and her eyes were puffy. But she raised her right hand, palm outward, as if she were Jemexxa, about to fire thousands of volts of lightning to Jekkalon; and as if she were pledging her allegiance to Ashapola.

She knew that her life had changed for ever, and that standing in front of three thousand applauding fans would never match the feelings that she and Kieran had experienced when the fire breather had exploded over Brother Albrecht's circus, or Xyrena and Brother Albrecht had risen into the sky in a fountain of fire.

But she had achieved something even more important. She touched the mirror's surface with her fingertips, and said, 'Goodbye, Mom. We love you.'

John arrived at the Griffin House Hotel to find its driveway blocked by more than a dozen police cars, as well as ambulances and TV vans. He parked on the opposite of the road and walked across to the main entrance. As he mounted the steps an officer came to meet him with his hand raised.

'Nobody's allowed inside, sir. The whole hotel is being evacuated.'

'I'm a cabbie. I've come to meet up with a couple of guests.'

'OK, then. Who are they? I'll have them paged for you.'

John tried to see inside the hotel lobby. It was crowded with guests and luggage and police officers. 'What's going on here? Why is everybody having to leave?'

'Just tell me who you've come to collect, sir, and I'll have them fetched out.'

'OK. It's the Kaiser Twins, Kieran and Kiera.'

'The Kaiser Twins have their own limo, sir.'

'I know that. But I have to talk to them. It's important.'

'Sorry, friend. That's not going to be possible. We have a major situation here. Why don't you write them a fan letter or something?'

'Tell them that D.M. is here. That's all I'm asking.'

'I'll see what I can do. But wait here.'

The officer disappeared into the hotel lobby and John knew that he wasn't going to make any attempt to tell Kieran and Kiera that he was here. Guests were already starting to leave the hotel, and police were escorting them to a line of taxis waiting in the side street.

He was about to give up when Detective Hudson came down the steps, looking harassed.

'Hey!' he said. 'Remember me?'

Detective Hudson frowned at him and then nodded. 'Sure I remember you. The cab driver with attitude.'

'What's going down here? Why is everybody having to leave?'

'You'll see it on the news soon enough. They found dead bodies in nine of the rooms.'

'Jesus. Do they know who did it?'

'All of them killed differently. Including my partner.'

'You mean Detective Windsocky? The guy who looked like me?'

'Yes,' said Detective Hudson. 'The guy who looked like you.'

'I'm real sorry for your loss,' John told him.

'Well, I doubt if you are, but thanks.' Detective Hudson's lips tightened and John could see that he was close to tears.

'Listen,' said John. 'You're tired. You're in shock. But take it from me, your partner is in a real nice place now, with real friendly people. And he's a whole man again.'

Detective Hudson stared at him. 'What do you mean by that?'

John realized that apart from the police, and whoever had found his body, only the Night Warriors knew how Detective Wisocky had been mutilated.

'I mean he's at peace. I'm sure of it. That's all.'

At that moment, a woman TV reporter came pushing her way through the crowds calling out '*Detective! Detective!*' and Detective Hudson turned away. John walked back across the road and climbed into his cab.

He wasn't entirely surprised to find Dean Brunswick III already sitting in the passenger seat. Dean looked haggard and very sick now, and as John made himself comfortable behind the wheel, he started to cough.

'You're in a bad way, Dean,' John told him.

'Oh, I'll get over it. We all get over it, in the end.'

'Cheer me up, why don't you?' said John. He started the engine, and checked his rear-view mirror. 'So, where do you want to go?'

'Someplace happy. I always like a happy ending.'

'OK,' said John, 'Quizno's it is, for a triple meat sub, and onion rings. And try not to cough all over it.'